# DYNASTY

## IRIS QUINN

QUINLAN PRESS

Published June 2025

Identifiers:

ISBN 979-8-9925438-7-2 (hardcover) | ISBN 979-8-9925438-3-4 (paperback) | ISBN 979-8-9925438-2-7 (ebook)

Printed in the United States of America

www.irisquinnauthor.com

## House Galvan

**Sigil:** Gold two-headed dragon, black field

**Patron City:** Solera

**Head of House:** Cyrus Galvan, 45 years old - married to *Aurora Galvan*

**Ashton Galvan:** Heir of House Galvan, dragonrider to Heartfyre, 24 years old

**Luxana Galvan:** First-born daughter, 23 years old

**Sage Galvan:** Dragonrider to Halcyon, 22 years old

**Deon Galvan:** Brother to Cyrus Galvan, 42 years old, married to *Zaria Galvan*

**Rune Galvan:** Son to Deon and Zaria Galvan, dragonrider to Kallix, 24 years old

**Dahlia Galvan:** Twin sister to Rune Galvan, first-born daughter to Deon and Zaria Galvan, former rider of Khione *(deceased)*, 24 years old

**Natalya Ember:** Sister to Cyrus and Deon Galvan, 40 years old - married to *Bruno Ember*

**Jocelyn Ember:** First-born daughter to Natalya and Bruno Ember, dragonrider to Xantha, 22 years old

**Jasper Ember:** Son to Natalya and Bruno Ember, dragonrider to Tanith, 20 years old

**Heartfyre:** red dragon, gold eyes, dragon of *Ashton Galvan*

**Halcyon:** iridescent white dragon, emerald eyes, dragon of *Sage Galvan*

**Kallix:** silver scales, white fire, dragon to *Rune Galvan*

**Khione:** white dragon, purple eyes, lavender fire, *(**deceased**)* dragon of *Dahlia Galvan*

**Xantha:** gold scales, dragon to *Jocelyn Ember*

**Tanith:** green scales, dragon to *Jasper Ember*

5 dragons, formerly 6

## House Noctis

**Sigil:** Silver dragon, black field

**Patron City:** Esmeray

**Head of House:** Eren Noctis

**Vesper Noctis:** Former Head of House, Eren Noctis' father *(deceased)*

**Syrinthia Noctis:** Mother of Eren Noctis, widowed

**Eren Noctis:** Heir of Vesper and Syrinthia Noctis, dragonrider to Cantorix, 25 years old

**Kamari Noctis:** First-born daughter, dragonrider, 23 years old

**Blythe Noctis:** dragonrider, 22 years old

**Soraya Noctis:** dragonrider, 18 years old

**Neith Noctis:** dragonrider, 17 years old

**Elodie Noctis:** 10 years old

**Hadeon:** red and gold dragon of *Syrinthia Noctis*

**Cantorix:** white and red scaled dragon to *Eren Noctis*

**Nimue:** frost blue scales, dragon to *Kamari Noctis*

**Iskra:** orange scales, dragon to *Blythe Noctis*

**Drazhan:** silver scales, green flames, dragon to *Soraya Noctis*

**Nevian:** brown scales, orange flames, dragon to *Neith Noctis*

6 dragons

## House Dysis

**Sigil:** Sun with black dragon (sun on a jade field)

**Patron City:** Aruna

**Head of House:** Soren Dysis, dragonrider - married to *Delphine Dysis*

**Valen Dysis:** Heir to Soren and Delphine Dysis, dragonrider to Astaroth, 25 years old

**Chantelle Dysis:** First-born daughter, dragonrider, 23 years old

**Fintan Dysis:** Second-son, dragonrider, 22 years old

**Lore Dysis:** dragonrider, 19 years old

**Keres:** sand-colored scales, red eyes, dragon to *Soren Dysis*

**Astaroth:** gunmetal gray scales, dragon to *Valen Dysis*

**Varuna:** jade scales, dragon to *Chantelle Dysis*

**Deyanira:** blue scales, violet eyes, dragon to *Fintan Dysis*

**Anahi:** silver scales, dragon to *Lore Dysis*

5 dragons

## House Tesar

**Sigil:** Gold banner with three blue claw marks

**Patron City:** Narelle

**Head of House:** Kieran Tesar, dragonrider - married to *Lyra Tesar*

**Xavier Tesar:** Heir to Kieran and Lyra Tesar, dragonrider, 25 years old

**Ronan Tesar:** Second-son, dragonrider, 24 years old

**Leon Tesar:** Dragonrider, 22 years old

**Agni Tesar:** Dragonrider, 20 years old

5 dragons

## House Althea

**Sigil:** Silver shield with white phoenix

**Patron City:** Marici

**Head of House:** Idalia Althea, dragonrider - widowed by Jensen Althea *(deceased)*

**Davina Althea:** Heir to Idalia and Jensen Althea, dragonrider, 25 years old

**Nikita Althea:** dragonrider, 24 years old

**Nyra Althea:** dragonrider, 23 years old

**Sienna Althea:** dragonrider, 22 years old

**Hakan:** bronze scales, malachite eyes, dragon to *Idalia Althea*

5 dragons

# GODS

**Vulcan:** Dragon god of the sun

**Anvi**: Goddess of water and rainfall

**Linette**: Goddess of mercy, "Maiden of Mercy," child of Anvi and Vulcan

**Elion**: God of war, child of Anvi and Vulcan

**Oryn:** God of justice, husband to the goddess Linette

**Nyra**: Goddess of death, "Maiden of Death," wife to Elion

**Aeris**: God of crops, child of Oryn and Linette

**Seraphina:** Goddess of love, child of Elion and Nyra

# PRONUNCIATION GUIDE

## Houses

Galvan: Gal-van

Noctis: Knock-tis

Dysis: Die-sis

Tesar: Teh-zar

Althea: Al-thee-ah

## Names

Cyrus: Sigh-rus

Ashton: Ash-ton

Luxana: Lu-zan-nuh

Deon: Dee-on

Dahlia: Dal-lee-uh

Natalya: Nah-tall-ya

Jocelyn: Joce-lynn

Heartfyre: Heart-fire

Halcyon: Hall-see-un

Kallix: Cal-ix

Khione: Key-o-knee

Xantha: Zan-tha

Tanith: Tan-ith

Eren: Air-en

Kamari: Com-mar-e

Blythe: B-lie-th

Soraya: Sore-rye-ah

Neith: Neeth

Elodie: Elle-low-dee

Syrinthia: Suh-rin-thee-uh

Vesper: Ves-per

Hadeon: Hay-dee-on

Cantorix: Can-tor-ix

Nimue: Nim-way

Iskra: Isk-ruh

Drazhan: Dra-zon

Nevian: Neh-vee-un

Soren: Sore-n

Delphine: Dell-feen

Valen: Val-en

Chantelle: Shawn-tell

Fintan: Fin-tan

Keres: Care-res

Astaroth: Ah-stah-roth

Varuna: Var-roo-nah

Deyanira: Day-yah-nir-rah

Anahi: Ah-nah-he

Kieran: Kir-en

Lyra: Lie-ruh

Xavier: Zay-vier

Ronan: Ro-nin

Leon: Lee-on

Agni: Ag-nee

Idahlia: I-dall-lee-uh

Davina: Dah-vee-nuh

Nikita: Ni-key-tuh

Nyra: Nye-ra

Sienna: See-eh-nuh

Oddica: Odd-ica

Gannon: Gan-non

Draven: Dray-ven

Azara: Ah-zar-ruh

Melantha: Meh-lan-tha

Veronique: Ver-raa-neek

## Places

Solera: So-lair-uh

Esmeray: Es-mer-ray

Aruna: Ah-ru-na

Narelle: Nair-el

Marici: Mar-ree-see

## Gods

Vulcan: Vol-can

Anvi: Ahn-vee

Linette: Lin-net

Elion: El-ee-un

Oryn: Or-in

Nyra: Ni-ruh

Aeris: Air-iss

Seraphina: Ser-ruh-fi-na

HOUSE NOCTIS

SUMMER MANOR

ESMERAY

ISRA DUNES

THE WASTES

MARICI

HOUSE ALTHEA

THE CELOSIA DESERT

EMBER CANYONS

HOUSE GALVAN

SOLERA

THE RUINS

SAFEHOUSE

ARUNA

NARELLE

HOUSE TESAR

HOUSE DYSIS

*Dedicated to the cycle-breakers*
*This one's for you*

# PROLOGUE

*D*ragons are the most volatile at sunset, perhaps that is why we've chosen this time for executions.

Slashes of orange bleed across the horizon, fading to a bitter lavender as the light slithers behind the dunes. Four of the six dragons from House Galvan stir under the dying rays, jaws flexing, wings snapping. Piercing screeches of their dragonsong fill the air as if to mourn the loss of sunlight.

A woman in black and gold robes stands at the front of a wood pyre. Dragonscale armor encases her shoulders, chest, and waist. Her elaborate hair shines under the torches surrounding our sandstone stage, an array of precious jewels dangling from her head like a crown. Movement stirs behind her as the prisoners give a last-ditch effort to wring the rope binding them to the posts erected over the pyre. If she hears their struggle, she gives no indication as she glides forward.

*"There is a rot festering in our great city,"* her voice echoes, carrying on the sighs of restless dunes. "House Galvan will not tolerate *traitors* infecting the peace of Solera." Her stare sharpens, scanning over the crowd as if she'll incinerate the next person who moves.

Shadows creep over the sand as the sun sinks even lower. One of the dragons shifts, growling as their wings knock into another's, the insult returned by a snap of powerful jaws.

I switch my weight from one foot to the other, but the movement does nothing to calm my racing heart. A rock has lodged in the pit of my gut, and despite my better judgment, I dare a glance to my left.

A girl four years my senior stands as stiff as one of the posts, expression blank and without mercy. Dragon scales cover her shoulders and chest over the black and gold fabric beneath. Her outfit is the matching set to mine... and the woman leading the execution.

A muscle in her cheek twitches, the only sign she's aware of my lingering gaze.

To my right, a young man stands as tall and unapologetic as any dragonrider can be. Black dragon scales and steel make up his armor—no robes to be found or anything that could be misconstrued as holy. His face lacks any of the warmth I've been accustomed to all my life. Were it not for the presence of dragons, it would be easy to think he was the executioner.

Without warning, his eyes snap to mine like a serpent poised to strike. If I were any ordinary citizen in the crowd, I would think twice before running into him in the dark.

"We will burn out this infestation." The woman steps back, revealing an unobstructed view of the pyre and the dragons surrounding it. "May the fire purify their souls."

As the last dregs of sunlight slip beneath the horizon, a hush falls over the world. Each dragon's neck glows like embers, jaws parting to reveal a molten forge inside. The prisoners open their mouths to scream. I look away.

The screams don't come, but the fire does.

A blistering heat unfurls behind us. I squeeze my eyes shut as if it will block out the scene before me, but the sound of sizzling flesh paints an entire picture. My nose clogs with a sickening sweet scent polluting the air. Bile gathers in my mouth as the heat dissipates. I swallow it down, eyes watering.

Flames crackle into the night, reaching for the first stars of dusk. There are no bodies where the charred posts stand, only the faintest remnant of bones at the bottom of the pyre.

Claws dig into my arm as the crowd disperses, swinging me around to the woman whose face is so unlike my own. "The next time we hold an execution, you will *watch*. You do a disservice to this House each time you look away."

"Mother," the young male's voice prods from behind us.

Her attention flicks from my face to his. He gives her a flat look before his gaze falls to her grip around my wrist.

His jaw tenses. "Father sent word. Your presence is required at the Compound."

The woman releases my wrist. Whether or not she believes him, she whirls, striding toward the dragons. I let a shuddering breath loose, offering him a small smile.

His eyes do not leave the woman's back, but he starts to turn to the scarlet behemoth of teeth and scales towering over the other dragons. "Come, Sage."

The dragon's yellow eyes blink as we approach, our armored reflections glaring back at us.

"We have a rebellion to crush."

# CHAPTER 1

*T*here's nothing hotter than dragonfire, but the Celosia Desert comes as a close rival.

Condensation rolls off my glass in thick drops. I'm half-tempted to lick the running droplets. I grasp the cup instead, tilting my head. Water flows over my cotton tongue like silk, a sweet balm to soothe the insufferable itch at the back of my throat. My gaze sweeps the room, landing on Ash at the far end of the counter, sweet-talking the barkeep.

I roll my eyes. *Wrap it up, Ash.*

An abrupt scrape of a chair shatters the peace within the room before a single shot fires off in the back of the cantina.

I twist in my seat, lifting a brow. A patron stands on the other side of a table, arm outstretched to a smoking revolver. The person across from him bends over the back of his seat at an unnatural angle with a gaping hole in the center of his chest. Loose cards slip from his limp hand, fluttering to the floor.

I sigh, setting down my glass. *Three... two... one...*

A group of khaki-coated officers burst through the entrance, rifles trained on the man pointing the gun. Over their left breasts is the embroidered sigil of a gold, two-headed dragon, the crest of House Galvan, proudly stitched above their hearts.

"He cheated! He tried to steal my rations!" the man cries, dropping his weapon and falling to his knees as two officers flank him.

I find Ash's stare narrowed in on the commotion, his body taut and eyes sharper than the daggers on my hips. He's completely still, gauging–*calculating* the chaos. He doesn't even seem like he's breathing. It's so easy to forget how he can switch from a shameless flirt to a lethal predator. Gannon, the barkeep, hasn't noticed the shift, too busy gawking at the dead body in his bar.

Ash retracts his arm from the wall near Gannon's head, flashing a brilliant grin and uttering a few quiet words before peeling from the room and slipping out the back entrance.

I slide from the barstool and nod my thanks. Gannon half-nods, the damp curls around his head bouncing with the movement. His gaze flickers to me for less than a second before they're back on the officers arresting the man who was dumb enough to fire in public.

A few of the other patrons are like me: collecting their things, resuming card games, or continuing discussions. This isn't anything new to them. This is another day in Solera.

In the desert, the most precious resource is water. The ultimate price is death.

Street lights flicker above me as I make my way down the sidewalk. I tuck my hands into the pocket of my pants, grazing the revolvers on either side of my waist. It's not illegal to carry weapons, at least–not in House Galvan's territory. Still, I glance at the pair of officers posted on the corner across the street. At this moment, I'm no one special. Today I must follow the rules as anyone else does. Anyone sane, that is. Thirst has a habit of driving people mad.

Beads of sweat crawl below the nape of my neck and

dampen the hair at my temples. I make a swipe of my forehead, cringing when the skin between my armpits peels apart. A film of oil glares off the back of my hand and I grimace.

I turn into an alley between sun-bleached apartments. Rats scurry past my feet, but they're hardly the most dangerous thing lurking back here. A solid figure leans against a dumpster, arms crossed and wind goggles balanced on top of a mop of unruly black hair.

"Good work, Little Sister." Ash smirks, exhaling a turquoise smoke from his nostrils.

I squint at him, noting the thin rolled paper pinched between his fingers. *Dragon's Bane.* Practically the most popular plant in Solera. "We've visited three of the cantinas. All of our distributors are behaving as far as I can tell."

"Mmm, don't say *all* just yet." He kicks off from the dumpster, flicking the blunt on the ground and crushing it beneath his boot. He leads the path out of the alley with a little too much pep in his step. "We still need to fly out to the hospital in the lower district and make sure they're not using more rations than permitted."

A yawn slips out of me. "Let's be done with it then. I'm sick of this heat."

"*Come on,* Sage." Ash glances over his shoulder as he laughs. "What do you say we get a couple of drinks after recon is over?"

I scowl. "There's no time for detours, Ash. As soon as we're finished we need to go home. Father will be waiting for our report."

Ash heaves a sigh, running a hand through his hair. "You know," I can tell what's coming and I don't want to hear it. "You're allowed to live a little. It doesn't matter what the family thinks."

My hands ball into fists at my sides. Ash wouldn't understand. How could he? As the first-born son, he stands to gain everything. I exhale through my nose, fighting to steady my voice. "It's the *only* thing that matters."

*Pop!* A bullet flies past our heads, bouncing off the walls of the alley.

"Get down!" Ash roars, throwing me to the ground.

His pistol is out before I hit the floor. He fires back, dragging me behind a stack of wooden crates. I fumble for my weapons, sliding them from the holsters and peeking around the crates.

Three assassins take turns poking their heads out from behind the dumpster. Black fabric is wrapped around their heads, concealing their hair, mouths, and noses–leaving only their eyes exposed. They claim no crest, nothing that points to a rival House. My stomach sinks at a worse option.

*Rebels.*

"You were followed," Ash growls, but I know his anger isn't aimed at me. It's for whoever stands on the other end of the barrel.

I curse, returning fire, and duck behind the crate to reload. "How far is Heartfyre?"

The city patrol will be drawn to the gunfire soon enough, and then our cover will be blown.

A muscle ticks in Ash's jaw. "Too far. We're on our own."

We lunge at the same time. My bullet lands a hit, tearing through the flesh of an assassin's throat. Crimson splatters the alley walls, forcing the two others to take cover. Ash and I are in sync. One look is all it takes for us to flee down the back of the alley and onto the streets.

*Halcyon. Halcyon, if you can hear me–please. We need you!*

I don't hear a reply to my plea, or a tug on the bond that tells me my message was received. My heart twists. If Halcyon is as far as Heartfyre, we're screwed.

Ash pulls me by the arm, pointing above. "There! The fire escape!"

A metal ladder hangs off the side of an apartment building,

leading to a staircase that zig-zags up the windows to the rooftop. Ash kneels below the ladder, cupping his hands to give me a boost. I pull myself up, palms so slick that I nearly slip from the metal. Ash follows right below, pushing me on as shots fire beneath us. Bullets ping off the fire escape, shattering windows and cracking stone. Glass explodes beside us, shards scattering. Something wet slides down my temple, but there's no time to stop.

A shout echoes from the alley, met by several more gunshots in the opposite direction. I don't waste time looking. I clamber to the top where I stumble onto the roof. Harsh rays of light beat down from above, not a cloud in sight to conceal the sun's wrath. Ash stands over the ledge of the roof, whistling with two fingers.

For a moment, there's nothing.

I spin back to the stairs, pointing my gun and waiting for the inevitable. My hands shake, blood rushing in my ears. Sweat soaks my shirt, making it stick like a second skin as I count down the seconds.

Ash whistles again—a desperate call with no wind to carry it.

Nothing.

Nothing.

*Nothing.*

I lift my head at the roar that responds.

A smaller screech accompanies it as two winged shadows cut through the sky. A small tug reverberates in the back of my head, and then I see her. Halcyon's iridescent scales gleam against the sunlight. She's half the size of Heartfyre, barely fitting the perimeter of the roof. A lump forms in my throat at the sight of her—the instant relief almost too palpable to swallow, but I lock that whirlpool of emotion down and throw myself into the saddle, hand sliding affectionately over her white scales shimmering like moonstone.

Ash takes a running start and leaps from the roof as

Heartfyre sweeps the edge of the building, landing perfectly in his saddle. He flashes a cocky grin as he flies past. Halcyon flaps her wings, lifting off and joining her vermillion brother in the sky.

Solera passes below, a dusty city full of merchants and vagabonds. The glass dome of the Conservatoire sparkles near the center of Solera. A dazzling academy for mages to practice their magic. *'A school for gimmicks and charlatans,'* my mother's voice sneers.

I shake my head, banishing the thought and beaming at Halcyon instead.

*You came.* I send down the bond, tearing my gaze from the city. I'm met with a feather-light twinkle, something akin to a laugh that says, *'Of course I did! Somebody had to.'*

Dragons don't speak, but they do share an unbreakable bond with their riders. It's a mental link that binds us together, a trickling path leading to one another. It allows us to feel each other's presence and for Halcyon to understand my commands from a thought alone. It's a bond that can only be severed by death, either theirs or ours.

Ash and I don't speak over the ripple of the wind. I close my eyes, reveling in the silence and freedom of the breeze. As every other thought fades away, I listen to the flap of Halcyon's wings. Terror sheds off me like dead skin, forgotten. In the sky, there's a certain weightlessness that makes you feel invincible. Bullets from the ground would never hit us this high. No man or weapon can stand in the face of a dragon. It's a feeling unlike any other.

In the air, we are immortal.

We soar over the Isra Dunes, the city of Solera becoming a blimp in the distance. It's not long before we reach House Galvan and my temporary immortality wears off.

Halfway built into the Ember Canyons, the manor is cut from the same rock and styled more like a fortress than a home.

I find *'compound'* a more fitting description. Plants and trees native to the desert grow around the many wings of our oasis, providing shade for our patios and the open courtyard within the fence.

Heartfyre and Halcyon land near the left of the compound, far away from the main entrance. I clamber off Halcyon, dropping to my feet in the sand. She stretches tall, staring down at me with inquisitive emerald eyes. I smile, touching my hand to her nose. Sometimes I feel like a child under her massive form, but she doesn't look at me like I'm small. She looks at me as if I'm the only thing that matters. It's enough for the lump in my throat to return and I blink back the tears that come with it. I could have no one left in the world, but Halcyon would never abandon me.

"Gods, Sage." Ash appears at my side, turning me by the shoulders to face him. His face pinches. "Your brow."

*What about it?* I want to ask, but he raises his hand to my face before I can get the words out. A sharp tear bites at my eyebrow, ripping a hiss from my lips. Ash brings his hand between us as I cup my eye, reeling from the sting. A shard of bloody glass sits between his fingers.

Halcyon chitters nervously, tilting her head.

"I'm okay, girl." I pat the side of her face and let go of my brow.

Warm liquid oozes from the spot as I examine a bit of blood on my hand.

"Here." Ash holds out a cloth. "Let's get you inside."

We take the side entrance, a clever trick to keep us from being discovered. It's only let us down a handful of times. Sadly, this is one of them.

As we round the corner, boots echoing off the marble tiles, a girl in pink silks strolls into the hall. Her head turns at the sound of our footfalls, causing Ash and I to freeze midstep.

Her face blanches. *"Gods,* what's happened?"

Ash and I look at each other, the same plea for help reflected in our eyes.

"Lux, we were just–" Ash starts.

"Gah!" Lux holds up her hand, gold bangles around her wrists dangling. "I don't want to hear it! You guys are late, just hurry up."

Ash flashes her a million-watt smile and kisses her cheek as we pass her. "Thanks, Sis."

She scrunches her nose. "You reek of gunpowder." Her dark eyes land on me. "And you're bleeding."

I shrink, turning my wounded brow away. "It's nothing."

"Uh-huh." Lux rolls her eyes and whirls in the direction she came, hair swishing down her back. "Try telling that to Father."

Ash and I bound down the hall, retreating into our respective rooms. I lock my door behind me, letting out a breath. I exchange my boots for flat slippers, my riding clothes for green silks, and wash the blood from my face. For a final touch, I dab a bit of aloe gel on my cut, hoping for the best. It's already clotted, leaving my brow swollen with a noticeable red line slicing through the arch, but I've done all I can.

Either way, we'll have to answer for tonight.

The house staff are bringing out the first course by the time we arrive.

"Let me do the talking," Ash whispers, leaving my side.

Mother and Father take precedence at the head of the round table, our mother seated on Father's left and Ash slipping into the seat at his right. Lux is already sitting, taking her place as the second-born. My stomach knots as I take the third seat on her opposite side, separated from our brother.

Cousin Jocelyn sits to my left, offering a warm smile before her hazel gaze lands on my cut. Her brow lifts in question. I give a slight shake of my head and a look that says, *I'll tell you later.*

On Jocelyn's left, her younger brother, Jasper, is shoveling meat and potatoes into his mouth. Uncle Bruno sits beside his son, red in the face and guffawing at something clever Uncle Deon must have said if the smirk on his face is anything to go by. Bruno's wife, my Aunt Natalya, sips her wine, hiding her grin behind the glass.

In the next seat, Cousin Dahlia burns holes through my body with a heated glare. I don't linger on her, glancing at Rune, her brother, who scowls with equal intensity. Sweat beads at the nape of my neck, but I ignore it, staring at Uncle Deon, their father, instead. He's in an unusually good mood, but perhaps it's the whiskey. It's the only thing that ever brings about his personality. His wife, Aunt Zaria, lifts her glass of wine with a roll of her eyes, taking a long sip.

My mother watches on, distracted by Aunt Natalya's words across the table. She's as breath-taking as her sister-in-law, but with pin-straight onyx tresses, the same color Ash inherited, and an intense honeyed stare. To the untrained eye, there's a gentle beauty about Aurora Galvan. Her skin is as warm as the sunset and her white lace dress portrays a flair of innocence, such a stark contrast from the ceremonial robes worn for the execution weeks ago.

I drink in my mother quietly, surveying the precious gemstones hanging from her neck and wrists. Even Lux had inherited the same straight hair while I'd been left with a mass of lighter, thick waves that only grow worse if I dare take a comb to it. Most days, I keep it braided back, but I have to wonder if I'd been a little more like them, would that have saved me from her ire? Would she share the same fondness for me if I only reminded her a bit of herself?

As if she can sense the weight of my stare, her sharp eyes swing to me like an axe and the honey calcifies into steel.

I look away. *Guess I'll never know.*

Cyrus Galvan, our father, and Head of House Galvan, watches on as he eats his meal in unfettered peace. At forty years old, he's still in his prime, ruling one of the richest Houses in the Celosia Desert. Streaks of gray line each side of his head, but he wears it like a crown, unwilling to dye it like many other men in the noble Houses do. He looks more seasoned, I've heard him say. *'A dragon does not change his scales. Why should I?'*

I look on at my family, at the ones not actively plotting my demise, and the ones who do not notice me. This is a typical night for the thirteen members of our House. As long as I don't speak, don't move, eat silently, and not draw attention, there's no reason for this harmony to end.

I reach for the potatoes, unable to resist the mouth-watering scent of rosemary and butter when Dahlia pipes up. *"Sage,* what happened to your *face?"*

My stomach curls at the poison hidden beneath her feminine voice. I lift my gaze to find Rune smirking beside her, but Dahlia's head is titled in confusion and her face is the perfect picture of worry. The table has gone silent, and everyone's attention is zeroed in on *me.*

"It's nothing," I say, but my voice is tight and no one appears convinced.

"So your mission was successful then?" Rune swirls his glass nonchalantly.

*Bastard.* I open my mouth to respond, but Ash beats me to it. "Yes, it was. The cantinas in our assigned district were obeying the ordinances. All is well." He leans back in his chair, tipping his glass to Rune.

"And the hospital?" Our father inquires.

Ash hesitates.

Cyrus Galvan's face is an iron mask of indifference, but we know better.

Ash clears his throat. "Well, uh." I can see the hunch of his shoulders. "We didn't make it there."

Father sets down his knife and fork. No one in the room seems to be breathing, or maybe it's just me. "You didn't make it there?" He utters slowly.

Ash sucks in a breath. "There was a shootout, Sage was injured—"

Dahlia scoffs, tossing her fork on her plate. Rune doesn't bother hiding his grin as his eyes dance between us and our father.

Father's gaze slides to me and I want to shrivel up into nothing. His jade eyes—a distant mirror of my own—flick back to Ash. "How?"

"We were followed when we met up again."

"Who?"

Simple questions, direct and to the point. This is no longer a dinner, but an interrogation.

"We don't know. They weren't wearing a sigil—"

"No. Who was followed?"

Ash falters and I close my eyes. I'm suddenly four feet tall, hiding under my bed. '*A dragon does not hide!*' my mother's voice screams in my mind. When I open my eyes, I find her staring back across the table. "It was me. I was followed."

Rune laughs through his nose.

I wait with my eyes down, head bowed for the scolding that must be coming. Any second and I'll be a disappointment yet again—

"Are they dead?"

I lift my head only a fraction to see my father's face. There's no indication of anger, but none of us have ever been able to read him.

"Two of them."

"The city patrol showed up and kept the rest of them busy while we got away," Ash explains.

"Good." Father picks up his fork. "See to it that you visit the hospital tomorrow."

"*Yes, Father,*" Ash and I say in unison.

All is quiet. Faces around the table turn, eyes darting to whoever might question Father's verdict. Dahlia's lip is curled.

She opens her mouth to say something, but the retort comes from someone I don't expect.

"That's it?"

My father's gaze snaps to Uncle Deon who white-knuckles his glass.

Father cuts into his steak. "Is there something you wish to discuss, Deon?"

"Yes, Cyrus, *there is.*" He slams his glass on the wood surface, causing me to flinch. Jocelyn grabs my hand beneath the table and squeezes, but I can't bring myself to look at her. "How is it that my daughter loses a *dragon,* while your daughter walks *unpunished?* She can't complete one mission without jeopardizing your Heir!"

"Watch your tongue, *Brother,*" Father snarls, his grip tightening on his knife. "Before I cut it out."

For a moment there is no sound, just their barely-leashed rage suffocating the room. My father breaks the tension with a sigh, lowering his cutlery. "The way I choose to discipline my children is my business, not a family affair. I do not question the way you choose to raise yours. Do not think Sage hasn't suffered. Our entire *House* suffered for the loss of Khione, but this matter has been settled. Dahlia will receive a hatchling from the next clutch of eggs."

"Yes, a hatchling that will take *years* to train," Uncle Deon sneers. "It will take a decade for a hatchling to reach the size Khione was."

"Brother," Aunt Natalya cuts in. "We still have seven dragons. Losing one will not change the fact that we stand as the strongest House."

"This infighting should not be tolerated," my mother says at last, staring down each member of our family at the dinner table. "These are the squabbles of children. We are at *war.* We cannot expect to win without losses."

The doors to the dining room slam open and a messenger

boy pants, hands on his knees and soot covering his face. With wide eyes, he lifts his head and shouts. "The rebels! They're attacking a convoy!"

My mother's tawny skin pales.

A muscle in Father's jaw ticks. "Ashton," he says, low and sharp. "Take your squad. *Now.*"

"I pray to the Gods you're right, Aurora." Uncle Deon stands with his whiskey, placing a pointed look at my mother. His eyes shift to my Father. "Because if we lose another dragon to the incompetence of your children, I *will* demand satisfaction."

Father's knuckles tighten into a fist beside his plate. His gaze slices to Ash and I. "Take no survivors."

# CHAPTER 2

*D*ragons are utterly silent in the night—as if the sky holds its breath in their presence. The flap of their wings is little more than a gust of wind under the stars. To anyone unaware, we are passing shadows in the darkness. To anyone who looks up, we are winged Death.

Through a dirt path leading out of Solera, a convoy travels in the direction of the Isra Dunes. Five men on glowing metal boards with canvas sails—sandgliders—follow the convoy.

They do not belong to House Galvan.

Ash leads our formation. Rune and Jasper fly to his left, Jocelyn and I to his right. Ash gives me a nod, diving headfirst into the city lights. Heartfyre opens his mouth and wails a hideous screech of flame and fury.

Rune and Jasper descend. Kallix, Rune's dragon, a white-flamed devil with silver scales, unclamps his jaws. Fire rains down from Tanith, Jasper's viridescent dragon, trailing close behind Rune. Jocelyn flies behind me on Xantha, a dragon the same shade of gold as the Isra Dunes.

*Now.* I send through the bond.

Fire explodes over the sandgliders. A few of them are quick, sliding out of the way, darting between blasts, but not all are so lucky. There are no screams, only charred carcasses and metal pieces flying off the path. Trucks within the convoy swerve in panic, but they're in no danger of being burned. The water inside those tanks is more precious than any gold or jewels.

"Get ready!" Ash shouts over the wind as he descends further, pulling a gun from his holster.

Heartfyre and Kallix make a low sweep, allowing the boys to jump from their backs. Ash and Rune land on two separate trucks, sprinting across the tanks to the front where the drivers sit. My grip tightens on the saddle as I'm forced to watch this play out.

*You should be down there,* a voice says—the annoying part of me that wants to stand up and fight. I shove her down, fold her into a box, and hide that reckless part of me in the dark. A knot forms in my stomach as I recall the last time I took charge. Flashes of Khione appear in my mind, the furious beat of wings and fire as she plummets from the sky.

I blink, my knuckles white around the horn of the saddle.

Four pale lights of the sandgliders appear on each side of the convoy. My eyes widen as shadows jump from the gliders onto the sides of the trucks, climbing to the top. Ash and Rune spin in tandem as a bullet cracks from a rebel's outstretched arm.

"I'm going down!" I shout, not waiting for my cousins to stop me.

The driver of the first truck leans out the window, a silver object in his hand. I veer left, turning Halcyon's belly to the splash of bullets. They bounce off her scales, trickling down like rain. I turn her upright when the gunshots stop, getting her as close as I can to leap. Keeping a firm grip on the saddle, I lift my feet out of the stirrups and into a crouch. Right as I'm about to push off a loud *pop* whizzes past my head. I flinch, fingers slipping from the horn. I gasp, scrambling for purchase. Gravity yanks me back and I scream, sliding into freefall. My breath is lost to the torrent of wind whipping around me.

I hit the water tank with a *thud* and wheeze, gripping my shoulder. Lightning shoots up the side of my arm, deep in the muscle, but I can't think about the pain. Directly in my line of vision, I can make out the shapes of the rebels fighting hand-to-hand with Ash and Rune. I try to sit up, my eyes locked on their fight when a metallic *click* echoes from behind. I stiffen and slowly turn my head.

The barrel of a gun stares back at me. Gold dragons flank the barrel, leading to the hand of a masked rebel with gray-green eyes. Air catches in my throat. Only the bronze skin from the bridge of his nose, up to his eyes and forehead is exposed, but somehow, he is both equally beautiful and terrifying. He's dressed from head to toe in black like a harbinger of death with a black scarf hanging loose around his neck and over his dark hair. A few tousled strands slip through to frame his face around the eyes. He looms over me, his entire body packed with lean muscle accentuated by the leather of his uniform.

My heart stutters. This is only going to end one way.

*Which one of us is faster?*

A low chuckle stirs from his broad chest, a menacing sound that raises goosebumps on my skin. "Well, it's not every day a dragonrider falls from the sky."

"No," I say, holding his gaze to mine and willing him to look anywhere but the place I intend to move. "But it's another day a rebel *dies*." I kick out, narrowly missing his knee.

He moves to avoid my kick, giving me the chance to smack the gun out of my face. I throw my head back to dodge the swing of his fist, locking my ankles around his leg and pulling down on the arm that holds the gun. He loses his balance long enough for me to rise. I rip free the knives stashed at my waist and when he turns, I slash. With a quick dodge, he throws an elbow straight to my gut. I suck in a tight breath, moving out of the path of the gun as he fires again and again, each shot missing me by inches. I lunge, swiping a blade over the side of his arm. Blood gleams off the steel and I flash him a grin.

The truck swerves, throwing me off my feet. An iron grip locks on my arm, yanking me forward and twisting. I yell as my arm is pinned behind my back, a hand squeezing my wrist so tight I drop one of the daggers. Cold steel kisses the skin below my jaw.

"Easy, Killer," the rebel purrs, his voice dark as smoke and rich as honey. "Drop the blade."

The command is delivered with ease, meant for my ears alone. He knows he's in control and he's enjoying every minute of it. I struggle against his grip.

"You better kill me now," I seethe, letting my other knife clatter to the truck's surface. "Or you're going to wish you were dead!"

His chest rumbles with a laugh against my back. "Aren't you a brave little thing?"

The vehicle jostles.

Jocelyn sweeps down with Xantha, incinerating the path ahead and forcing the driver to swerve once more. I use the momentum to wriggle forward, snatching a knife from my boot. When he swings me back up, I plunge it down into his thigh. The rebel shouts, his grip loosening. He curses as I slip from his grasp. I spin and whip my leg around, kicking the gun from his hand. It skitters across the metal under our feet.

Our eyes lock.

With a growl, the rebel drags his leg, but I'm already halfway there. Shouting echoes from the fight ahead and I can't tell if it's Ash, Rune, or the rebels. A hand clamps down on my shoulder right as I reach the gun, jerking me around. Red-tipped silver winks in the light of the moon, flying toward my face. I catch his wrist with both hands, struggling under the weight of his force. Every muscle in his body pours into the hand that holds the blade—my own grip shaking, arms *burning* with resistance.

Then the weight is gone.

He slices at my arm and I suck in a gasp, barely enough time to breathe before he sweeps out my legs from under me. My head slams into metal. I blink, gasping. Pain throbs in my skull as the hazy silhouette of the rebel comes into focus. I scoot back, lifting my head in a desperate last glance to my brother.

Ash is on the ground. Rune is fighting his own battle, keeping the rebels busy in an attempt to defend Ash, but his fallen figure is noticed. A rebel creeps up, lifting a gun from their belt as they approach my brother.

I flip onto my stomach, reaching out for him when my hand bumps cool iron.

I whip back around, finger on the trigger. The rebel above me freezes. Maybe it's the adrenaline or the ache in my skull, but I swear he's paler, blood oozing from the wound I left in his thigh. He makes no move to surrender, staring at me with cold indifference.

'Go on, do it,' the challenge in his eyes seems to say.

But he's not the one I aim for when I pull the trigger.

The rebel looming above Ash clutches his heart, falling to his knees. My brother is up in seconds, putting down the last of them with Rune.

A shuddering breath escapes my lips.

Hands lock around my shoulders, slamming me on my back. I'm met with a pair of startling eyes and a tight grip pinning my wrist.

He presses the knife to my throat. "That was stupid."

I shoot him a hate-filled glare. "I'll always protect my family."

"Then you'll always suffer."

The truck swerves again, but a harrowing roar rips through the sky. The rebel's gaze glimmers as if we're sharing an inside joke, but I seem to miss the punchline. "Well, this has been fun, Killer, but my ride's here."

Blue fire ignites the sky, forcing Xantha and Tanith to pull back with furious shrieks. Before they can return the blast, the rebel pushes off me, sprinting to the end of the truck where he *jumps*.

A black-scaled dragon tears through the night, soaring into the clouds. If it weren't for the light of the moon, I never would have seen the dragon at all. I lay there, gaping at the stars for what seems like eternity. It's not until the truck stops that I sit up.

"Sage!"

I turn my head.

Jocelyn and Jasper come bounding toward me.

My cousin crouches, her brow pinched. "Are you hurt?"

Jasper remains on high alert, only half-listening as he keeps one hand on his gun, head swiveling for any threats lurking in the shadows of the city. The bodies of the rebels lay where Ash and Rune dispatched them, blood pooling over the top of the tank, but the boys are nowhere to be found.

"Sage?" Jocelyn's voice tightens.

"He had a dragon," I whisper, not quite seeing my cousin anymore.

The scene replays over and over in my mind, the way the rebel lept from the truck–identical to how Ash loves to land on Heartfyre. Only a dragonrider would make a move so reckless. Only a Rider would trust that *their dragon* was waiting to catch them.

"He had a dragon," I repeat, a wave of nausea rising to my throat.

*The rebels have a dragon.*

"Come on, let's get you up." Jocelyn helps me to my feet, and that's when I see the destruction left in our wake.

Several buildings are scorched around us, the road filled

with glass and debris. One truck is overturned, engulfed in flames, and leaking onto the pavement. I frown at the sight.

*What a waste.*

Movement causes me to snap my head to the side. City dwellers caked with ash or dust creep out between buildings. Their faces are drawn—devastated on a few. A hunched man stumbles from the crowd, withered and gray as he falls to his knees in the water wetting the pavement. He lowers his face, lapping at the water with his tongue. A child, a woman, and others join him.

"Enough!" An officer barks, smacking the elderly man with the butt of his gun.

*"Stop!"* I shout, but something has shifted in the wind.

An electric charge seems to crackle in the air as the faces of the people curl from devastation to what is unmistakable rage. They begin to crouch, rising with their fists locked back.

*"Death to House Galvan!"*

Rocks, wood, and debris fly at the officer and bounce off the side of the truck, unable to reach us where we stand. The city patrol closes in, forming a wall of bronze shields between us and the crowd.

"Sage!" Ash appears behind our cousins, placing both hands on the sides of my head. "Are you hurt?"

I shake my head, though a dull sting on my arm reminds me of the fight I just had. Ash's hands fall, and I twist back to the crowd inching closer to the barricade of officers. My brother guides me with a hand to my back, but I can't pry my eyes away from the hateful glares of our people.

"Ash, what are they doing? Why do they hate us?"

A muscle twitches in his jaw, but he doesn't answer. I climb on Halcyon, who waits with the other dragons. Ash mounts Heartfyre. Jocelyn, Jasper, and Rune return to their dragons as well, waiting for my brother's command.

It doesn't make sense to me. Our family, like every House,

protects the water supply from those who dare to take it. We protect our people from ruthless thieves like the rebels who only want it for their gain. They would sooner see the Celosia desert plunge into chaos than maintain this delicate order. Right as we're about to lift off, I watch the mob charge at the officers.

Heartfyre lunges forward, releasing a thundering roar. I clap my hands over my ears as the sound rips through Solera, shaking buildings and shattering windows. My gaze lands on Ash's face, stone cold and unyielding. Members of the mob shrink back, others run in the opposite direction, but there are those who stare Death in the face.

A shiver rolls down my spine.

Heartfyre springs into the air, our dragons following close behind him. It is a long, silent flight back to House Galvan. I can't help but glance through the clouds, over my shoulder, and into the night, searching for the beast that lit the sky with blue flames.

I can't squash the fear coursing through my blood. A cold settles in my veins and it has nothing to do with flying high enough to touch the stars. It ignites every nerve ending within me because the rebels have a dragon. And if the rebels have a dragon, that changes everything.

*The rebel is one of us.*

# CHAPTER 3

*I* pace the tiled hall outside of my father's office. I have to tell him what I saw—that the rebels have a *dragon*. Part of me wants to kick the wall in frustration, but my body aches from the events of the night. I rub a hand down my bandaged arm, holding the cut beneath.

*He could have killed me.* The rebel was faster. Stronger. By all means, I should be dead.

*No.* I'm simply smart and *lucky.* Lodging the knife in his thigh made a difference. If more time had passed, he would've died from blood loss. The rebel had to have known it. That must be why he picked his moment to flee.

I settle onto the bench across the carved double doors of the study. There's no use in trying to listen. The wood is thick enough to block out any sound I might hear. Instead, I take in the elegant dragon motifs etched into the wood as each agonizing minute ticks on.

The doors swing open, allowing the light of my father's study to flood into the hall. I'm met with Ash's taut face covered in a thick layer of sand, soot, and blood. Rune trails him out with a similar expression, but when his eyes land on me the strain shifts to something more intense.

"He'll see you now," Ash mumbles, turning down the hall.

I scowl at Rune, moving toward the study when his shoulder smacks into mine. The contact shoots lightning bolts up my bruised arm. I suck in a sharp breath and whirl, but Rune doesn't pay me a second glance. He merely tucks his hands in his pockets, drifting down the hall. I bite my retort.

Father sits behind an ebony desk, focused on the parchment in front of him. He scribbles for a moment as I hold my breath, unwilling to make a sound. His eyes flick up at me, the same peridot color as my own, and sets down his pen.

"Sage, sit." He gestures to the chairs in front of his desk.

I sink into one of them and fold my hands in my lap to hide their shaking.

My father leans back, drawing a hand down his face, and sighs. "I want to speak with you about what happened at dinner."

My heart stops. "What?"

He offers me a tired smile, though it doesn't reach his eyes. He refills a glass of amber liquid resting on the corner of his desk with a crystal decanter. My father sets the decanter back on the wood, turning his stare back to me. "Tell me the words of our House."

"Familia ante omnia."

"Which translates to?"

I fidget with one of the rough pieces of my cuticles. "Family over all."

He takes a long sip of his drink, placing the glass back on the wood. "That has been the sacred pledge of House Galvan for centuries, but our family is divided. Surely you can see that."

I don't say anything. I get the sense I'm not meant to answer, so I sit quietly and wait.

My father catches my gaze and leans forward. "Do not make

the mistake of trusting anyone who isn't us. I've held off my brother for the time being, but Deon will not be placated if we are to lose another dragon. I fear he will invoke the Ignis Mortem. Do you know what that means?"

My heart slams against my ribcage, the warmth draining from my face. The Ignis Mortem is a blood duel that only dragonriders can challenge each other to. If I weren't sitting, I'm sure my knees would've buckled. "He'll call for my blood."

Father nods. "He will have Dahlia challenge you. It will end when she has spilled enough of your blood to gain satisfaction, or one of you dies. I cannot allow such a thing to take place. Do you understand what that means?"

All I can do is gape. The words don't register in my mind. He cannot prevent an Ignis Mortem once it is invoked. What does he think can be done?

"I will have to intervene. The Ignis Mortem will not take place between yourself and Dahlia. It will be myself and Deon fighting to the death. If he wins, he'll take my place as Head of our House."

"No," I whisper, the horror evident in my voice.

"Be wary of your cousins. Keep your trust confined to Luxana and Ashton. Anyone who isn't us is a threat."

I bow my head, biting the inside of my cheek. I trust Jocelyn with my whole heart, but he won't want to hear that.

He starts again, softer this time. "I don't tell you this to scare you. I need you to know what's at stake and I cannot shield you for much longer. Someday, I will fall. Whether it be by age or by fire, Ash will ascend. You and your sister will be married to another House when the time is right. I can only hope to secure you both a match before I'm gone so that it is not Ashton's burden to bear."

I stiffen. This isn't the conversation I planned for. *I need to tell him about the rebel.* "Father–"

"We must protect the balance, Sage." He stands, moving

toward the open window behind his desk. "These rebels threaten to undo everything we stand for; peace, unity, *survival*. What do they think they'll gain from taking our water? Quench the thirst of a few and damn the others? What madness possesses them, I'll never know."

*"They have a dragon,"* I blurt.

Father stills. He turns, his eyes darkening. "What did you say?"

Every fiber of my being screams for me to run out the door and forget this conversation ever happened. *Dragons do not hide.* "They... they have a dragon. I saw it. Black as night with blue fire."

He returns from the window, placing both hands on the desk. I can hear my blood rushing through my ears. Did Ash and Rune not tell him? Did they not see the black-scaled dragon with their own eyes, or had they been too occupied?

"Tell me *precisely* what happened."

I force myself to start at the beginning. From the moment I dropped to the truck—not *fall*, because my father definitely doesn't need to know that—to the moment the rebel leapt off the truck onto the dragon's back. When I'm done, he stews in silence for a few heartbeats. It's quiet enough that I can hear the sand blowing outside, scraping against the walls of our fortress, each grain pelting the windows.

He swallows the last bit of liquid in his glass, knocking it back on the desk. "My child, you are lucky to be alive."

I'm not sure what I expected, but it's not that. "What do you mean? I've fought rebels before."

"The person you fought wasn't any rebel." Father's eyes meet mine. A cold rage simmers behind them. "You fought Damon Valour."

"I've never heard that name before."

"You fought the leader of the rebellion."

A stretch of silence spans between us.

"That's—that's insane," is all I can think to say.

Father leans back in his chair, seeming more aged than he had when I walked in. "What's insane is that you walked away *alive.*"

*Why?* The unspoken question lingers in the air. I don't know the answer any more than he does, but my shock veers into anger, hot as a molten ore. "Why wasn't I informed?"

He gives me a flat look. "You and the others are on a need-to-know basis. It's safer this way."

"Safer for who?" I retort.

"For everyone involved," he says with an authority that makes it clear this isn't up for debate.

I take a breath and stand.

"Sage."

I look over my shoulder.

"Be careful," he warns, folding his hands in thought.

I don't reply.

Out in the hall, shadows dance on the walls from the light of the sconces. *How does a rebel get a dragon? Where would he hide one?* The questions swirl in my head until I'm through the door of my bedroom.

I snatch a cluster of amethyst off the bookshelf above my bed and flop on the mattress with a sigh. Lux is gone, her bed lying empty across from mine. I turn the crystal in my hands, thinking. Alone in the dark, tendrils of dread wrap around my chest from a single thought.

*Damon Valour will be the ruin of us all.*

WHEN I OPEN MY EYES, I find that Lux has already left for the morning, her bed made as if she were never there. Pale sunlight filters through the curtains, bringing with it the heat of the day.

In the bathroom, I wash my face in the sink and pour myself a glass of water from the tap. I hold the glass to my flushed face for a moment, staring into the mirror. The swelling of my brow has eased, leaving behind a scabbed cut through the arch. How innocent the injury must look to any outsider, but to my family, it is a physical brand of shame.

I uncap a tin jar of white fluoride paste, imported from House Althea's mines, and scoop a white dollop on my finger. I scrub my teeth and tongue with it, thinking back to last night. *'I fear he will invoke the Ignis Mortem.'* My stomach twists. *'Anyone who isn't us is a threat.'* I spit out the paste and turn from the mirror.

In the dining hall, morning rays creep through the windows. It's a stark contrast from the previous night's dinner with the curtains pulled open, marble floors shining, and only my sister, mother, Jocelyn, and Aunt Natalya present around the table for breakfast.

Tarts, oatmeal, fruit, and pastries are spread across the surface with servants refilling water and orange juice to my family's glasses. My shoulders ease. I don't have to worry about a knife to my throat in the form of thinly-veiled threats at breakfast. Dinner, however, is a different game.

Jocelyn looks up at me and beams. Lux turns her head, giving me a slight nod of acknowledgment before turning back to her plate. My mother and Aunt Natalya are too engaged in conversation to notice me, my aunt's bracelets jangling with every hand gesture she makes. If my mother catches my movement, she pretends not to notice, keeping her attention focused on her sister-in-law.

I brush off the slight, bounding to the table and plucking a peach tart. "Anyone seen Ash?" I ask through a mouthful of flakey pastry, trying not to moan at the taste. If it weren't for the fruit groves on our land, I doubt we would eat half as good. House Althea may have struck it rich between water and fluoride, but House Galvan has far better perks.

"He's in the caverns tending to Heartfyre," Lux answers.

I swallow, weaving around Lux's chair to swipe her orange juice.

"*Hey!*" She cries, but I've already washed down the tart and abandoned the empty glass.

Laughing, I saunter out into the hall when a tall, lean figure rounds the corner, almost smacking into me.

"Hey!" I snap, digging my heels in as I meet Rune's scowling figure. He's geared up for the day, armed to the teeth with blades and twin pistols on his belt.

"I don't know what you're smiling about," he growls, onyx eyes filled with disdain. "Dishonor must not bother the likes of you."

"Bite me, Rune," I hiss, pushing past him.

He slams me back into the wall, smacking the tart right out of my hand. "You better start thinking about how you're going to repay my sister before your life gets *very* uncomfortable." Rune digs his fingers into my shoulder, rough enough to bruise, and releases me.

I wince, clutching my shoulder as he stalks off in the other direction. It isn't until he turns the corner that I smirk to myself, twirling his blade in my hand. House Galvan's two-headed dragon gleams from the polished steel, so light that he didn't feel me pluck it from the sheath.

*A fine blade, indeed.*

I shrug, tucking the dagger into a sheath on my belt and make myself scarce before Rune realizes his blade is missing

At the bottom of the Ember Canyons lies the gaping mouth of a cavern behind our home. A wash of heat lashes at my skin under the hot glare of the sun, but inside the cave, it's dark enough that the temperature drops. I touch a hand to the wall of the cavern, using it as a guide for the first few feet. Flecks of stars begin to appear overhead, illuminating the tunnel. I touch a finger to one of the tiny, glowing stones embedded into the wall. Sunstones are coveted across the Celosia desert for their phosphorescent properties, used as a luxury light source in the place of torches. When they grow in cave systems like this one, they're incredibly convenient.

A few more twists and turns between tunnels and light breaks through the stone. There's an opening within the cavern where trees and vegetation flourish near an underground stream.

I spot Heartfyre's crimson form before I see Ash rubbing a salve into the scales over his snout. Heartfyre huffs, steam twirling from his nostrils. He's the perfect picture of ease with his eyes shut, body limp, and teeth peeking out from his partly gaping mouth.

"Ash," I call.

My brother whips his head around. He gives a soft, close-lipped smile, but the corners of his eyes don't wrinkle like they usually do. There's something off.

I come to his side, careful not to knock over a bucket of turquoise powder. I glance at Heartfyre and spy traces of it near his nostrils. *Dragon's Bane.* Much like catnip to a cat, it can calm the most difficult or anxious of dragons. When ground up into a fine powder, Riders can use it for precise grooming their dragon may need help with. Or much like the better half of Solera—smoke it to take the edge off.

Ash continues with his work, rubbing the salve over the scales. I follow the trail of his hand, now spotting singed areas I didn't notice before.

"He was scorched by that black dragon," Ash murmurs. "Did you know blue fire burns the hottest?"

"I thought dragons were impervious to fire."

He takes a cloth from the handle of the bucket and wipes his hands. "Dragons are impervious to a lot of things, but not to each other."

I shift my weight between my feet, searching for something to say, and then it hits me. "Did you know the rebels had a Rider as their leader?"

Ash pauses, staring at the cloth in his hands. "I thought he was a myth."

I step closer. "Why didn't you tell me?"

"Look, I didn't want to keep it a secret, okay? Father made me swear not to tell anyone, not even Rune until it was confirmed. All we had was a name and a rumor."

I scoff, hardly believing my ears. "Well that rumor turned out to be true! I almost *died* fighting him, Ash. Thanks for the warning!"

Ash winces. Regret shines in his eyes, but it does nothing to soothe the jagged hurt piercing my heart. *How could he not trust me?*

"Sage, I'm sorry."

A hollow feeling nestles in my chest. Those words should make everything feel okay, but they don't. "It's fine," I mutter, but it's not fine. I swallow it, choke it down like bitter medicine. I make it my friend, an old one at that.

His hands rest on my shoulders, prompting me to lift my head. Ash's gold-flecked eyes pierce mine with an intensity I'm not prepared for. "I need you to listen to me. If you ever find yourself face to face with him again, *promise me* you'll run the other way."

I shrug out from his hands, pushing them away. "I held my own just fine."

"*Sage,*" he presses on. "That's not the point. He has a dragon. That means one of two things; he's either a no-name rebel who got his hands on an egg or he's one of *us.*"

My heart races at the implication. "There is no Damon Valour in the noble Houses."

Ash stares at me, waiting for me to tell him the other option I don't want to consider. I force myself to breathe. "You think it's someone using an alias?"

"I'm hoping I'm wrong, but if I'm not..."

A chill slithers down my spine. "Then one of the Houses betrayed us all."

"You see why Father didn't want anyone to know?"

"But surely the other Houses have noticed? This can't be his first attack with a dragon."

Ash shrugs. "How would we know? We don't share intel. We have no way of knowing if they've been attacked by anyone but us."

*We're all too busy fighting each other.*

My brother shakes his head. "It doesn't matter. If we're lucky, we'll end him soon enough, but I mean it, Sage. Stay away from him."

I roll my eyes, crossing my arms. "Are you ready to check out the hospital?"

Ash hesitates, turning his body from me to Heartfyre. "I already did."

My heart drops. "What?"

"You've been through a lot, okay? I didn't want you to get hurt again. Look at it this way, you and Lux have that visit at the Conservatoire. Now you'll have plenty of time to get ready."

There's nothing condescending in his voice, but my heart pounds, thrashing against my ribcage and rattling my bones. The words are genuine, and yet they make my blood boil. Heat rushes to my face and tears prick at my eyes. I blink them back, balling my shaking hands into fists behind my back in an attempt to hold myself together.

"So what then?" I snap. "You didn't think I could handle it?"

Ash stands straighter, but I don't miss the way his eyes widen at the venom in my words. "What? No, that's not–"

"And that's why you didn't tell me either, huh? About their

leader?" my voice cracks. "You're just like the rest of them, aren't you? You can't trust me not to fuck everything up."

"Sage, you know that's not true."

"Forget it." I turn on my heels.

"Sage!" He calls after me.

"Thanks for making things clear, *Brother*. I'm so sorry I wasn't worthy."

"Sage!"

My blood settles from a roiling boil to a dull simmer when I make my way back into the house. Maybe I should go back. I should apologize, but I can't bring myself to do it. Ash may have meant to look out for me, but it doesn't erase the sting of his words. Perhaps if my wounds weren't so fresh, I could believe his concern for my welfare. Right now, though?

I can't.

*Will anything ever wash the stain of my failure?*

My steps falter at the thought. Sage-colored eyes flash through my memory, a ghost fighting like a demon in the night. I'd been so painfully unaware of the threat in front of me. Despite that, despite being a man of legend, I still made him bleed. *I* sent him running back to his dragon. *I almost won.*

*What good did it do me?*

My anger wilts, drooping like Aunt Natalya's flowers in the garden. I sink onto my bed, hugging my knees to my chest when a knock taps at the door. Lux pushes in, a bronze pot with a paintbrush poking out from her hands.

"Hey."

"Hey," I mumble, tucking my mouth and chin behind my knees.

Lux rests beside me, close enough for me to see the thick, golden liquid in the bowl.

*Ichor.*

She plucks the brush from the bowl, letting a drop drip from the fine hairs. "I'll do yours if you do mine."

I sigh, glancing at the wardrobe in the far corner of the room. "Guess that means we should get dressed."

"I already am, but I can help you pick something."

I frown, taking in her gown for the first time. Red is my sister's finest color, the thin fabric hugging her hips and complimenting her rich skin. Her gold jewelry makes it pop, along with the combs and embellishments weaved into her dark hair. She sets the bowl on our shared desk and throws open the wardrobe doors, digging out a burnt orange dress with gold embroidery and jewels stitched in. My gaze snags on the scabbard hiding in the deepest corner behind the dresses, a long forgotten relic of our childhood.

"What about this one?" She beams, holding the dress high above her head.

"That'll do." I'm already stripping off my clothes when Lux shuts the doors.

"Try not to sulk. Ash has his reasons."

I suck in a breath, inhaling the words that are on the tip of my tongue, and shrug on the silks she hands me. "I don't care."

"But you do." She sets to work on my hair, pulling out the mess of my braid and retwisting it into some semblance of an updo. "And I think that's where you butt heads. Everyone in our family has reasons for what they do, but you're constantly in your head. You don't think about the big picture. Each choice affects us all."

I grind my teeth. Talking to my sister is a lot like talking to a wall. You can say how you feel, but you shouldn't expect to be understood.

"Your hair is so pretty," she says, an olive branch of words.

"I wish it were more tame," I mutter. "Like yours."

"Now where would be the fun in that?" Lux ties off my hair, letting a few curls loose around my face before she mixes the ichor and takes my hand.

She hums softly as she swirls the brush inside my palm,

painting over gnarled strands of scar tissue. The sensation soothes my jaw, easing the tension in my shoulders. Ichor, *'the blood of the Gods,'* is an old tradition in our House. Women in our family paint each other's skin with intricate designs used to honor the Gods. At least, that's how it started. Nowadays, it's mostly used for weddings or political visits, much like this trip to the High Mage's Conservatoire.

"What's she like? The High Mage," I ask as she draws up the skin of my inner arm.

"Melantha? Oh, I don't know. Rich. Beautiful. *Powerful.* I've never met her officially. This will be the first time for me too." She smiles, redipping the brush.

"I don't see why we have to go," I grumble, trying not to squirm when Lux decorates a sensitive spot near my elbow.

Lux moves to my other side, creating leaves and stars around my fingers and up my wrist. "We're older now. We can accompany her while Ash and Rune run a few missions for Father. Priorities, Little Sister."

I roll my eyes. Both arms done, Lux applies the finishing touches around my neck and over my jaw to my cheekbones. "There! Take a look."

"I trust you," I wave her off, taking the bowl and brush for myself. "Now come on, your turn."

Lux pouts, offering me her palm without complaint. I don't hum while I draw. I bite my lip instead, trying to hold the brush steady. Poor depictions of creosote blooms travel up Lux's fingers and form a bracelet around her wrist. I'm nowhere near the artist she is with ichor, but if she wanted perfect, she should have asked our mother.

Speaking of our mother, she waits in the corridor with a tight gaze. Her hands are folded, shoulders back, the very definition of poised. Her ichor is already done, probably by Lux if the sharp lines are anything to go by. Lux had to make a few minor adjustments to herself before we left our room, sliding the brush over the more noticeable lines near her face.

Place a sword in my hands and I can put it to good use. A paintbrush? Not so much.

A suffocating silence fills the drive to Solera.

It's true, dragonback is faster, but Lux and my mother aren't Riders and Halcyon isn't accustomed to passengers. I listen to the rumble of our armored vehicle as it bounces over the dunes, wringing my hands in my lap. Breathing is a conscious effort. Inhale. Expand. Release. A layer of sweat beads near my temples, dampening the hair there and more than likely ruining Lux's work. I draw in a sharp breath when our vehicle hits a hard bump in the road.

The action snags the frigid attention of my mother. She says nothing, only scrutinizes me from the seat across. Lux stares out the tinted glass of the window, content in her own little world. For me, it takes every cell in my body to focus my breath rather than hyperventilate under my mother's glare. I've never been one for tight spaces and these vehicles are no exception.

*Inhale. Expand. Release.*

I practically leap from the car when it stops in front of the Conservatoire. If our mother weren't here, I'd kiss the ground and weep. Except she is here, and I have to wait for a guard to open my door before I fling myself from our cramped space.

Out in the open, the Conservatoire shines bright, surrounded by pillars upholding the great glass dome sparkling under the sun. Acolytes in pale robes mill about the building, books in hand and walking in pairs. I rip my gaze from them, setting it forward on the path. Aurora Galvan struts in front of Lux and I, allowing the guards to guide us up the long set of stairs. Citizens and acolytes stop dead in their tracks, staring at our entourage. Although I don't meet their eyes, I can sense the weight of them. It's not often House Galvan makes official visits, especially without our dragons present.

I feel naked in an odd way, like a piece of me is missing. Within the walls of my mind, I reach out a hand, fingertips meeting the feather-light bond that links me to Halcyon. She reaches back in answer, a spark of curiosity beaming across miles of sand. I smile to myself, lowering that mental hand. Our bond fades to the back of my mind again, never fully forgotten, but tucked somewhere safe.

A regal figure waits at the top of the steps with two hooded acolytes in emerald robes. The woman in question clasps her hands, her garnet mouth splitting into a grin. "Lady Galvan, welcome to the Conservatoire." A lilt of an accent graces her words. "These must be your beautiful daughters."

I do not offer a smile when her dark eyes fall upon me and neither does Lux. We are here on business, not to make friends. Our mother rakes her eyes over the woman's dress—a slim, silk fabric hugging every curve.

Aurora's eyes cut back to the woman's. "Melantha. Do get us out of this heat."

"Yes, come!" The High Mage waves us in, the two mute acolytes following their master. "I was so pleased to hear of your annual inspection. I do hope the Conservatoire is to your liking."

Our mother scans the architecture within. From the polished statues of the Gods, golden archways, and marble floors, to the oil paintings on the walls, it seems more like the inner workings of a palace than a school. "Quite."

I share a look with Lux. My sister shrugs, tilting her head at one painting in particular. Melantha leads us up a grand wooden staircase to the second level where classes continue in full swing. Acolytes scratch tediously in their notebooks, hunched over short desks while teachers lecture within. We pass one arched opening in particular where massive bookcases tower above the students carrying tomes of their own. I stare a bit too long, catching Melantha's interest.

Her lips twist knowingly as her face shifts to my mother's. "Perhaps your daughters would like a tour?"

Our mother pauses, her gaze sweeping over Lux and I before giving a curt nod. "Very well."

"You two," the High Mage faces her acolytes. "Escort the sisters, yes?"

They nod in unison, remaining with us while our mother, Melantha, and the guards continue through the hall.

"Is there anything in particular you Ladies would like to see?" The taller acolyte asks.

I open my mouth, but Lux beats me to it. "I want to see the art."

I release a breath I shouldn't have bothered drawing. *Another waste of air.* But the shorter acolyte cocks their head. "Perhaps we shall split off. We can cover more of the Conservatoire that way."

I blink at the musical voice, glancing at Lux.

"Fine by me. Meet back here in an hour?" She doesn't stand around for my reply, following the taller acolyte down a hall of paintings.

Alone together, I try to discern the facial features of the young acolyte before me. Dark hair peeks out from the veil of her hood along with a button nose and full lips curving as if she knows exactly what I'm doing. "What shall we see first, my Lady?"

My gaze wanders to the room of books. "Is that your library?"

"Yes. One of the finest collections of all things magic."

An idea flares in the back of my mind. "Does that include dragons?"

"Why yes, my Lady."

"Show me."

A soft quiet fills the library. Footsteps, papers shuffling, and squeaking wheels of book carts fill the space. Elaborate windows stretch across the walls, exposing the room to natural sunlight. It bounces off crystal suncatchers hanging from the ceiling, showering the library with beams of rainbows. I can't help but sniff the air, inhaling the heady scent of leather and parchment.

"Is there anything specific you're looking for about dragons?"

I clear my throat, following her through towers of books. "Er, black dragons. I think they used to have a name, but they're all gone now."

I can't risk asking my family for details about a certain rebel's dragon. Lux isn't likely to know much and Ash would rather keep me locked at home than have me fight again. Finding answers about our new enemy in the Conservatoire's library is the best shot I have.

"Oh, is that so?" Her long fingers brush the spines of a few texts on the shelf, stopping on a leather-bound book and plucking it from the stack. She cracks open the cover, skimming the first page. "Ah, not just gone, my Lady. They're extinct."

She passes the book to me where I scan the first few sentences.

Scales the color of obsidian, flames bluer than the fiercest skies, Nightstalkers are capable of soundless flight. To their own detriment, they breed only once every fifty years, attributing to their eventual extinction three hundred years after the great Queen Solasta's conquest.

My gaze cuts to the acolyte, narrowing. "Queen Solasta is a myth."

A myth weaved into children's bedtime stories by mothers

and nannies alike. Queen Solasta is said to have led her people across the vast sands of the Celosia desert, making her court in this wasteland and forming the ruling Houses alive today.

The acolyte runs her fingers across the other books. "To some, but we mages keep meticulous records. It's for the reader to decide if they're fact or fiction."

She turns her veiled face to a gold-framed painting on the wall. An armored woman in leather and chainmail lifts a sword from the top of a Nightstalker, tresses of long hair whipping around her head.

Impractical, if you ask me.

My nose wrinkles as I envision choking on my hair in the wind, or worse, the tangled nest of knots that would be waiting after.

"Why don't you borrow it?" The acolyte clasps her hands behind her back.

I stare down at the pages in my hands that feel more valuable than gold.

"Okay." I snap the book closed, tucking it into one of the pockets under my skirt. "But I'd prefer if we kept this between us."

Her head cocks to the side. "Kept what?"

A conspirator's smile tugs at my mouth. "Nothing at all."

*"There you are,"* Lux's voice travels from the front of the aisle. Her red skirts swish about her legs as she makes a beeline toward me, her guard and acolyte following close. "Mother has summoned us."

I resist the urge to roll my eyes and fall back into our moving escort. The acolytes usher us up another flight of stairs and through a set of frosted glass doors to an office, though it could easily be more of a lounge with cushioned chairs, colorful rugs, and an empty fireplace near them. My eyes fall upon our mother and Melantha seated at a mahogany desk.

"Girls, sit." Aurora Galvan waves a manicured hand to the

chairs beside her. "There is one last thing I must inquire of you, Melantha."

I lock in on the High Mage's face. Her expression is unflinching, not a pinch of worry on her smooth skin. If anything, her head tilts with intrigue as she spreads her hands. "Of course. How may I assist the great House Galvan?"

"Perhaps you can pull a trick from your box of gimmicks that will help us locate a certain thorn in our side."

Melantha flashes a dazzling white smile. "Ah, I see. It's a tracking spell you seek."

My heart thumps, eyes dancing between the two women and Lux who remains unruffled. I, on the other hand, sit up straighter at the possibility of witnessing their magic up close.

"This is not a request," our mother snaps, lip curling. "Do I need to remind you it is your Blood Sworn duty to serve our House?"

"I need no reminder of the Blood Oath," Melantha hisses back, her control shattering.

Both women stare, holding each other in contempt. I squirm in my seat, nails digging into my palms as the tension thickens. A Blood Oath is not taken lightly. It's an unbreakable vow of fealty sworn by a High Mage to the Dragon Lord of their respective territory. It started as a way for Dragon Lords to ensure the mages could never rise against them, taking away the choice for them to cause harm to their House and ensure their loyalty in all things magical. To question that blood-bound loyalty is to question a High Mage's character, but my mother holds no love for them. I shouldn't be surprised.

Melantha's shoulders ease, her breath loosening from her lungs. She leans back in her chair, folding her hands. "Do you have any belongings from this... thorn in your side?"

"No," my mother answers begrudgingly.

"Then I'm afraid there is nothing I can do for you. A tracking spell requires a personal item from the one you desire to locate.

The energy within the item is used to track it back to the owner."

My mother's jaw twitches. "I see."

"My apologies, Lady Galvan," Melantha says, rising. "Do call upon us again if your situation changes."

Lux and I stand in tandem with our mother. "Cyrus will be in touch."

We pass the shorter acolyte as we file from the room, and the weight of the book within my skirt grows that much heavier.

# CHAPTER 4

*I* fall into step beside Jocelyn, skirt gone and the book in my hand.

She sketches a brow at me. "This better be good. I'm already late to meet Jas and Rune for drills."

"Forget about that." I tug her by the wrist, dragging us both into our family's library and slam the door shut. Our collection sits at the center of the compound, full of looming shelves and winding iron staircases for each level. No one ever comes here except for a few servants to dust, but it contains the history of Celosia, the founding families, desert herbology, and most importantly–dragons. It's where I intend to spend the next few hours, maybe with Jocelyn's help if this goes well.

"You remember how I told you there was a black dragon the other night?"

"Yeah, from the rebels, right?"

"Yes. They had a dragon and it didn't belong to just anyone. It belongs to the leader of their movement. Damon Valour."

A hint of shock flashes through Jocelyn's eyes. "You're joking."

"I wish I was, but I need you to look at this." I shove the book in her hands, biting my lip as she flips to the first page.

She mouths the words to herself, eyes widening when she looks at me. "A Nightstalker? Aren't they extinct?"

"They should be. It makes no sense, but if I can figure out where it came from then maybe we can find out who this guy is and put him down for good."

"Wait." Jocelyn snaps the book shut. "You're not thinking about going after him, are you?"

I chew the inside of my mouth, crossing my arms with a shrug. "Why not? I stabbed him once. I can do it again."

"Sage, you're going to get yourself killed."

"Why does everyone think that?" I swipe the book from her grasp. "I can take care of myself! If I hurt him once then maybe... maybe–" *Maybe I can kill him.*

I dare to hope. This one risk might be big enough to change everything. All I need to do is reach out and take it. What better way to prove myself to my family than to eliminate our greatest threat? No one would ever doubt me again. My failure would be forgotten.

"Maybe what?" My cousin leans in, brow furrowed with confusion. "Why would you be so reckless? Even if we went after him together there's no telling where they are, their numbers, or where to start."

"But we have to start *somewhere*," I insist, pleading with my eyes and hoping she'll see the desperation in them. I don't want to do this by myself, but if I have to...

Jocelyn leans back, her face softening. "Is this about Khione?"

It's like a blow to my sternum, knocking the breath out of me. "If I can offer something big, something that would make up for the loss... maybe I'll redeem myself. I don't expect Dahlia or Uncle Deon to ever forgive me, but at least I'll have our family's respect. Right now I have nothing."

She reaches for my hand, squeezing. "That's not true."

Someone clears their throat.

We whirl, spotting Ash mere feet away with an open book in his hands. His face is harder than granite, cutting between Jocelyn and I. "If you'll excuse us, Cousin, I need a moment alone with my sister."

Jocelyn visibly pales at his tone, clearing her throat. "Of course." She glances at me, silently passing on the promise that we'll talk another time. The door shuts, her footsteps fading in the corridor.

Ash sighs, heavy and resigned. "What are you doing?"

"That depends. How much did you hear?"

"Everything," he growls, shutting the book in his hands and starting towards me. "What did I tell you? I told you to stay away from Valour and here you are making plans to go after him!"

"So what if I am? Can't you even try to understand? This could be my shot at proving I'm not this waste of a Rider!"

He shakes his head. "You have a death wish. Let me save you some trouble–your idea is a dead end."

"What do you mean?"

Ash passes the book, tapping his finger on the cover. "This one states the last known Nightstalkers were possessed by House Noctis, House Althea, and House Tesar. Any of them could be a traitor or lost an egg decades ago. None of it matters now. They won't be eager to swap intel on the battlefield."

"No," I whisper, more to myself and the hope fleeing from my chest.

Ash pivots, running a hand through his hair before facing me once more. Lines of stress crease his face. "I don't say this to hurt you, but let this madness end. As Heir, it's my job to protect everyone in this House. Hear me when I say it doesn't matter who Valour is or where his dragon came from. We'll find him, kill him, and the rebellion will die with him. You need to focus on your future, Sage. I want you to start thinking about what's next."

I pause, my brows furrowing. "What does that mean?"

Ash runs a hand down his face. "You and Lux should have been married off a long time ago, but Father wasn't eager to lose another dragon after Khione."

I shake my head as if it will clear the words from existence.

He reaches out his hand, but lowers it when I lean away from his grasp. "Lux will be matched first, securing a deal that will mate our dragons with another House. When a clutch of eggs is produced, I suspect it will be your turn."

"No." I retreat a step. It's too soon. I should have more time. "Tell me it's not true."

"I've been in his office. I've seen the letters."

The words hit me like the ground after freefall. I don't know why I thought I would be spared from an arranged marriage. The truth is, I've been lucky so far. Now my luck has run out, and my freedom with it.

My chest tightens. "How am I supposed to marry someone I don't know?"

"We all have our duty. Not even I am immune."

"Surely you don't want this."

Ash looks away, his gaze miles from where we are. "What I want is irrelevant."

I can't bring myself to look at him.

"Rest assured, I will help Father secure a pleasant match for you. He will be kind and share your love of the skies."

*That's not enough*, I think, but the words are lodged in my throat.

Ash places a soft kiss on my cheek and ruffles the hair on top of my head. "Put away these books. Linette will guide us. Have faith."

But I don't believe him or any of the Gods I cannot see.

My lungs contract, hoping to fill with precious oxygen, but the air is thinner above the clouds. Halcyon turns her body and dives headfirst. My braid whips back, eyes protected by the goggles Ash always nags me to wear. Cloud mist splashes over my body, dampening my clothes as Halcyon tucks her wings in, aiming for the ground. I grip the saddle until my knuckles turn white. If I didn't know any better, I'd think my stomach shriveled up and died above the cloudbank, but it's the drop that always gets me. Our home is little more than a spec in the dunes, the city of Solera a mere twinkle in the distance.

Halcyon twists as part of our drill. With one more barrel roll, we can be done, but a strangled gasp escapes me. I'm no longer looking at empty land surrounding the compound, but the charred canyons near the city of Esmeray. I squeeze my eyes shut, shaking my head, but the echo of dragons shriek around me. A tug pulls on the bond, Halcyon, sending her concern into me, but I can't snap out of it. I open my eyes and find a white dragon plummeting below us.

Falling, falling, falling *again.*

Halcyon straightens, sweeping out of the barrel roll. She glides into a soft landing, allowing me to slide off her back and stumble onto the ground. I collapse to my knees in the sand and heave the contents of my stomach. A massive wing shields me from the sun. I rise on wobbling legs, bracing a hand on Halcyon's body for support. Pressing my forehead into her side, I breathe in.

"I can't let it go," I whisper, knowing Halcyon is the only one who would understand. "I can't let Khione's death haunt me forever. When am I going to get another chance like this?"

But where would I even start trying to locate a rebel? The resistance would be well-hidden and their supporters uneager to betray them. Bribes may not work. I might draw unwanted attention by asking just anyone. I turn back the wheel of my restless thoughts, combing through each detail I once deemed unimportant. A cantina sparks in my mind, the one particularly owned by a curly-haired bartender.

I mount Halcyon, sending the image of Solera through the bond. A bar is the perfect place for people to spill their secrets. Alcohol loosens one's tongue and Gannon would be privy to many confessions.

But will he be willing to share them?

I touch a hand to the pistol at my waist as the city comes into view. It's like Ash said, what he wants is irrelevant. I will not leave Solera without answers.

# CHAPTER 5

*I* don't take Gannon for a fool, but I do think he's kind at heart.

Pale blue smoke fills the air of the cantina, twirling against the lazy spin of ceiling fans. A second-hand high muddies my brain as I watch Gannon, creating a dull buzz behind my eyes. He's no older than Ash, but as perceptive as any Rider assessing a potential threat. He examines his patrons, gauging which ones might cause trouble, who may not pay their tab, and who's here to drink away their sorrows.

He makes his rounds, adding drops of amber liquid to the water rations of those willing to pay a few extra coppers. *Barrel Juice,* the fond name for the liquid within a barrel-shaped cactus scattering the desert. It's said to contain euphoric properties similar to alcohol, and is highly coveted in cantinas like this one. Half of the patrons come for the water, and the others to lounge in smoke and drown in barrel juice.

Gannon takes pity on a few of them, passing out crackers or bread in a feeble attempt to sober them up before sending them on their way. It's that same kindness I'm betting on as I wait in his office, feet up on the desk as I scan over his weekly shipments.

There's nothing useful for me between the pages, but it serves as more of a prop to aid my performance, because that's all this really is. An act. I don't have my brother to sweet-talk the answers from Gannon. I'll have to rely on myself.

I will my fingers to stop shaking when I hear steps approaching the other side of the door. The entrance groans open and I move a dust-covered boot to find Gannon's scowling face in the threshold. The contempt instantly switches to fear, then respect as he dips his chin.

"Lady Galvan."

*That's right. There's fear in a name. House Galvan is the sharpest weapon at your disposal. Act like it.* I slide on a mask of frigid disdain modeled after my mother's.

"Close the door." I set aside the papers. "Take a seat."

Throat bobbing, Gannon follows my command and sits in the chair across from me. I rise, taking a slow walk about the room, examining his shelves along the way. This is another part of the act I've learned from my father. Let his anxiety build as he wonders why I'm here. Cast the illusion of who's really in control.

"I wasn't expecting you again so soon," Gannon starts, his voice careful like any misplaced word might upset me. "Is your brother here?"

My attention settles on a piece of art in his office, a painting of a small body of water surrounded by wildflowers. A tree grows above the little pool, ripe with leaves of various shades.

"Gannon, you're a man of the people. Are you not?"

"I'm not quite sure what you mean."

"Something's been nagging at me." Snapping the cover of a book closed, I push it back into the empty spot on the shelf. "I hoped you might be kind enough to fill in the blanks."

He rubs his palms on his thighs. "I don't understand."

I've made a full circle around the room now, stopping at the desk. I slide on top, half-sitting to face him. It's enough to seem at ease while looking him in the eyes–a move I've seen my father make, and I've copied it to perfection. "What do you know about Damon Valour?"

Gannon's eyes widen. For a few heartbeats, neither of us blink. I'm not sure he's going to say anything at all until he breaks the silence. "Do you think I'm a traitor?"

I shrug. "That depends on your answer, which you still haven't given."

A muscle feathers in his jaw. "There are rumors he's the leader of the rebels. That's all I know."

I click my tongue. "Come on, Gannon. You own a bar. Surely you must hear people talk about him."

He straightens in his chair, face tight. "I don't know what to tell you, My Lady."

With a feigned sigh, I place a heavy leather pouch on the desk. Metal clinks inside. If he reaches for it, pulling aside the strings, he'll see a pile of gold coins. I can only hope it's enough to win him over, because I don't know what else to do if he doesn't help me. "I'm willing to make a generous contribution for any information that might lead to his whereabouts."

Gannon's eyes flick from the pouch to my face. "He's a whisper in the night, My Lady. You'd have better luck finding your own shadow in the dark than Damon Valour."

I guard my face from any emotion. *Fine, he won't talk? If he's not going to be honest, maybe I shouldn't be either.* "Would it make a difference if I say I'm not here on family business?"

A half-truth.

"Oh?" He lifts a brow.

"I want to talk to him, but it's difficult to speak to a man you can't find. Wouldn't you agree?"

Gannon leans back, tilting his head, his gaze narrowing.

"What business could a Lady of a powerful House have with a rebel?"

I ignore the skip of my heart, keeping my voice level. "*Peace, if he'd be so inclined.*"

"Peace?"

"There's no reason for us to keep killing each other. My family might not be known for negotiating, but I believe I can get them to come around. Valour doesn't have to meet with me, but he should know I'm looking for him. Can you at least spread the word to discreet ears?"

"I'm curious why you would think I know of such ears."

I muster an arrogant grin, hopping off the desk. "Call it intuition. I don't think you're a traitor, Gannon, but I do think you know more than you're telling me. I understand. You're afraid of retaliation. Treason is not taken lightly by any House, but I give you my word that no harm will come to you."

He glances at the pouch and I jerk my chin toward it. "Go on, have a look. Consider it a preview of what's to come."

Gannon reaches for it, loosening the strings and peering inside. He shakes the pouch, gold coins clinking in his grasp. His dubious eyes return to me. "You sure know how to drive a bargain."

I smile. "Is that a yes?"

He nods, tucking the bag into the pocket of his ale-stained smock. "I'll see what I can do."

As I rise, another memory flashes in my head of the people throwing stones. '*Death to House Galvan!*' I face Gannon, wondering if he might answer another question. "I'm paying you for your assistance and discretion, but... I'd like to include your honesty in our bargain."

"Honesty?"

"Yes, I have questions and I want you to speak freely."

Gannon quiets. "Very well."

"Why do people wish death upon my family?"

For a split second, he stares. I fight the urge to touch my hair or look down at my clothes. *Is something out of place?* Then he shifts in his chair, the strange look wiped from his face as his brow furrows. "You truly don't know?"

Crossing my arms, I lift my chin a fraction more. "I'm asking, aren't I?"

Gannon shakes his head, folding his arms. "You won't like what you hear."

"If I liked everything I heard, I wouldn't be standing before you now."

He sighs and hunches over, wringing his hands between his legs before he lifts his head. Darkness passes over his features. "From the view of the people, the Houses grow richer every day hoarding water for themselves, leaving us with little to go around. People of your station enjoy showers, baths, and a glass of water brought to you at your beck and call. These are luxuries many of us dream of. The rest of us will only experience a shower perhaps a handful of times in our life, maybe less."

I step back, as if the words are a blow to escape. "You're lying."

His eyes flick down to his hands. "I wish I were. People die of dehydration every day, My Lady. It's a struggle living off water rations, unless you're like me, someone who owns their own business. Then you can afford more water. But for most, the rations are barely enough to keep us from the brink of death. Maybe you can see now why they chant for the fall of your House. Maybe you can see how this rebellion took root."

I shove the chair away, pacing the room. "The Houses maintain *order*. Without us, everyone would die if we didn't ration! The springs would be sucked dry! There would be no regulation. It would be chaos!"

"With respect, My Lady, people *are* dying. While your family wants for nothing, mothers cry themselves to sleep and feed their tears to their desiccated children."

I stare at him. The images appear in my mind as I try to grasp what he's told me, and then they crack, at war with the knowledge of my House. We are their *protectors*, the only ones standing between order and chaos. If the rebels have it their way, there'd be nothing left for the rest of us. "It can't be true. We're trying to *save* people from the rebels. If they take control we'll all suffer!"

Gannon smiles weakly. "We are already suffering. Have you ever stepped foot in our hospitals? Or the morgues? Seen the mummified bodies yourself?"

I wince.

He chuckles, though there is no humor in it. It is a bitter, lifeless sound. "No, of course you haven't. Why would a Lady of your station see fit to bother with the likes of us?"

A fire burns within me, my blood molten as his words ring in my head. My hands curl into fists at my sides. Perhaps he's right, but I don't plan on letting him watch as I crumble.

"We're done here." I bite through clenched teeth and slam the office door behind me.

I don't go home right away.

I sit with Halcyon, overlooking the tangerine splash and lavender haze creeping behind the dunes. She's curled up behind me, snoozing while I contemplate life from the top of the canyon. Sand clings to my skin, itching inside of my clothes. A droplet of sweat rolls down my neck, though I can't be bothered to fly home and wash it away. It seems wrong now. What did Gannon say? That our people would experience less than a handful of showers throughout their life?

I can't wrap my head around it. Part of me wants to dismiss it. I haven't seen anything to support his claims, but to speak of such atrocities... I think back to the shadows in his eyes. *'Have you ever stepped foot in our hospitals? Or the morgues? Seen the mummified bodies yourself?'*

No. I haven't, because the thought has never crossed my mind. My stomach churns at the realization. Ash and I had planned to go to a hospital after the cantina, but... after the attack on the convoy, he'd gone by himself the next morning.

I push to my feet, waking Halcyon with the sudden movement. She shakes off a bit of sand that's collected on her scales and rises. I need more answers. There's only one person I can think to ask, someone who's holding back every time we speak.

Ash knows something I don't.

# CHAPTER 6

*S*unbreaker, the weaving dragon of the north guides us home. Halcyon would know the way should my memory ever fail me, but it's an excuse to look up at the stars, a challenge to navigate using one of my first lessons as a child. Following constellations reminds me of a simpler time, like when my brother didn't lie to me.

I suck in my cheek, wondering how I'm going to approach Ash. Yelling and shouting won't do, not if I want to wake the whole compound. I'll have to keep a clear head, stick to the facts, and keep Gannon far from the equation.

An explosion pounds through the horizon like a thunderclap. Flames unfurl in the distance, lighting the ground in an amber glow where House Galvan resides. I spot the compound immediately, heart in my throat, and trace the distance back to the fire. Several columns of black smoke rage from our water tank reserves, hidden in the hills near the mines.

House Galvan is under attack.

The question of *who* rings in my mind, ensnared by the paralyzing fear surging through my body, gluing my hands to the reins and locking my muscles in place. As if sensing my terror, Halcyon surges forward with a powerful snap of her wings. Despite the fear, I know she senses the commands I cannot speak–the urgency to race home to our land, burning on the horizon.

The lurch of Halcyon's body against the wind reignites my senses, shaking me from the shock. My hands tighten on the reins as I lean toward the destruction, my heart pounding as we fly into a storm of cinders and ash. This battle will be different. It has to be.

*I have to be.*

We nearly collide into a wall of green scales. Jasper shoots into the air on Tanith, Jocelyn and Xantha close behind him. Halcyon reels back, screeching. Smoke smothers the air around us as her wings flap in place. Xantha turns, hovering close enough for Jocelyn's wild eyes to meet mine.

"It's House Dysis!" She shouts across the wind, soot smearing her face.

My breath catches. House Dysis is here to settle the score.

A flash of dragonfire searing their fields resurfaces in my memory, an arid summer full of blood and scorched earth. Sure enough, I spy a jade dragon sweeping through the destruction below. A crest with a yellow sun behind the silhouette of a dragon clings to the armor of one of the enemy dragons, proclaiming to everyone that House Dysis has come to repay the debt.

"Where's Ash?" My eyes dart through the plumes of smoke, though no dragons zipping past are the fierce crimson of Heartfyre.

Jocelyn opens her mouth when Jasper yells from above. *"Incoming!"*

A torrent of fire severs the air between us. Halcyon flings us back with a roar, whipping around to return the blast. Scales the color of gunmetal fly toward us, enormous wings shooting out to avoid Halcyon's flames. Valen Dysis, heir to his House, glares from the back of his dragon, burn scars crawling from his neck to the side of his jaw. My stomach plummets. Ash is the one who gave him those scars, but Valen Dysis has his sights locked on me.

With half a thought, Halcyon dives through smoke and ash, serpentining between other dragons locked in battle while explosions continue on the ground. I catch a glimpse of Rune on Kallix, firing shots at the two riders chasing him.

A flash of crimson barrels down.

Heartfyre catches one of the dragons with his claws, dragging an ear-splitting shriek from the smaller dragon. Ash clutches the saddle, teeth gritted and covered in soot, but otherwise unharmed. I choke on a sob, about to shout to him when Halcyon banks a hard left.

Flames sear the air above, narrowingly missing my head. I dare a glance behind me, spying the gray dragon that's three times the size of Halcyon. Valen's dragon tails us, refusing to back down even when its rider's golden eyes spot Ash. A slow, cruel grin slides across Valen's mouth as his dragon reels its neck back, a fiery light shining behind its scales as the flames gather in the back of its throat.

Valen is going to roast me alive, in front of Ash.

I fumble for the gun at my waist, never taking my eyes off Valen. The flames scatter around the dragon's mouth—until a set of black jaws snap around its throat.

A larger obsidian dragon, rivaling the size of Heartfyre, tackles Valen's dragon. With a powerful swing, the black dragon launches the other into the abyss of flame and smoke below. The dragon—a *Nightstalker*—turns, a reflection of moonlight and flames gleaming off its scales. Its midnight blue eyes settle on Halcyon and I. It twists its body, revealing the masked rider on its back.

Damon Valour, in the flesh.

"I hear you're looking for me, Killer," he calls out and I can

hear the smirk in his voice. "I'm all yours... if you can catch me."
He winks.

In a single flap, the Nightstalker shoots into the stars above.

Eyes wide, I glance behind me. Everyone else is locked in battle. Ash and Rune are now fighting the same jade dragon, Jocelyn and Jasper are leading two others away from the water reserves. I'm on my own and the only one who knows Damon Valour is here.

*Why?* The question screams in my head, but my body is already turning with Halcyon as she pushes through the air. The why becomes less important, fading with the wind blowing through my singed hair. Fire and smoke become a distant blur on the ground below as we fly into a realm of stars.

Damon waits patiently, watching as I keep a fair distance between us. Halcyon is half the size of Heartfyre, but beside the Nightstalker, she's little more than a hatchling in comparison. If there's anything I've learned, it's that smaller is faster. Halcyon will grow in time, but until then, I must always be on my guard with larger dragons. Tonight is no exception.

"Well, Killer," he purrs, leaning forward in his saddle. "You found me."

"You're their leader," I breathe. It's all I can think to say in this madness.

His mouth curves, eyes sparking. "Someone's learning."

*More than I ever thought.*

"I want to make a deal." My heart pounds as the lie rolls past my lips. I resist the urge to pull the dagger strapped to my thigh or the gun at my waist. I only get one shot at this. I need to get as close as possible.

"So my sources say," he drawls, looking none too convinced as he drinks me in like a man savoring every last drop.

I fight the urge to shiver. "You don't believe me?"

He crosses his arms, leaning back. "I find it hard to believe that a *Rider* is willing to negotiate."

I can't contain my scowl. "You say Rider like an insult, as you sit from the top of a *Nightstalker*."

His eyebrows rise suggestively. "Is there another place you'd rather see me on top, Killer?"

"Don't call me that," I growl, temper flaring, but I leash it in. I can't afford to lose my cool, not when my House is at stake. Every moment I sit here with Damon is another moment my family is down one dragon. "You came here for a reason."

The amusement in his eyes dwindles, his features hardening to stone. "Out with it then. Let's hear that deal before your House burns."

I swallow, but my tongue is drier than the dunes. "House Galvan will increase water rations for your people. In exchange, you end the attacks on our supply routes."

A moment passes where neither of us speaks. I hold my breath under the weight of his stare until a low, dead chuckle emerges from his mouth. "More rations, huh?"

I say nothing, my heart thumping too loud to string together a coherent word.

With a shake of Damon's head, the Nightstalker shifts as if to leave. "You're out of your depth."

"Wait!" I blurt, grasping for anything that might make him stay. "What about your own supply?"

The dragon and rider stop. His eyes fall upon me once more. "I'm listening."

My heart beats wildly in my chest as I attempt to piece together the lies. "There's a spring in the canyons–too small to bother harvesting, so we use it as a getaway. Your people can have it. You can fight the other Houses, but leave mine out of your war."

"You must be desperate to save your family."

In a single snap of black wings, the Nightstalker hovers beside me, spooking Halcyon enough for her to let out a sudden shriek.

Damon sits mere feet from me now, offering his hand. "You have a deal."

I slip my hand into his, my other palm flat over the blade on my thigh. He grasps my hand tight, jerking me closer as I wrap my fingers around the hilt of my weapon.

His voice slithers in my ear like a caress, warming my face. "I think this is the start of a beautiful alliance."

I pull back, shoving the blade forward into his gut. Damon sucks in a breath, eyes wide as I glare back at him. "I will *never*, *ever* betray my family."

His hand clamps over mine, squeezing my wrist until I cry out, losing my grip.

"Oh, Killer," voice thick as he rips out the dagger himself. "You shouldn't have done that."

The Nightstalker screeches at the top of its lungs and flaps its wings, creating a wide berth. It folds its wings into a dive, seeking the cover of the clouds.

*No!* Damon's blood is still warm on my hand, my gloved fingers slick as I tighten my grip on the saddle. *He can't get away.* Halcyon dives after them. Through smoke and cinders, we give chase past the clouds and into the fray.

House Dysis' riders flee toward the Isra Dunes, retreating, but no matter where I look I can't see my family or their dragons through the thick veil of smoke. We're barely keeping up with the Nightstalker, whose form is becoming smaller in the distance.

*Higher, Halcyon!*

She soars, her pale wings flapping harder as she rides the current of the wind. I palm another dagger as we loom over the Nightstalker, struggling to keep pace.

*Steady.* I command, keeping one hand on the horn of the saddle as I push up to the balls of my feet. I've seen Ash jump a hundred times. Each time he landed with precision–the only difference is that the dragon waiting to catch him was *his*. I gulp, the knife shaking in my grasp as my whole body trembles. Redemption is close enough that I can almost taste it. It's the one thing that convinces me to loosen my grip and jump.

Wind lashes at my face, ripping my hair from my braid and drawing tears as I plummet. I reach out, flailing for the saddle as Damon's head lifts. Air breaks from my lungs as I plunge the dagger into the dragon's hide, lodging it between scales. Damon turns, the muzzle of his gun pointed straight at my head. I swing my leg over and duck as the shot fires. A shrill ring reverberates through my right eardrum. Gritting my teeth, I slam my hand on Damon's arm and use it to level myself onto the dragon.

He rips his arm from my hold, striking my temple with the butt of his gun. I shout, palming for my own when the Nightstalker roars, winding against the wind to shake me off. Damon rises from the saddle, mimicking my crouch on the back of the dragon. He's far paler, the blood from his stomach now soaking the front of his clothes. I don't have to be a better fighter. I just have to outlast him.

Sweat beads from his brow as he takes me in. "You're going to get yourself killed."

I unsheath a pair of twin blades and rise as the Nightstalker levels out. "I won't be the one dying today."

His eyes narrow as he sheaths his gun, swapping it for two curved daggers of his own. I lunge. Our weapons clash, steel flashing. A hot sting pulses through the skin on my bicep, but I don't dare take my eyes off the man in front of me. For the first few hits, he meets every strike, forcing me to dodge and deflect each swipe at my body. Blood seeps into my clothes, sticking to my skin. I kick with my leg in a desperate attempt to force him back. As he deflects my kick, I twirl, slicing across his chest. I retreat a step, dodging a blow from his fist. Movement stirs behind Damon's head, snagging my attention—a dragon the color of gunmetal.

Before the warning can leave my lips, he uses the distraction to swing his dagger at my head. I drop low, only to be met with his knee pounding into my stomach. I gasp, legs crumbling out from under me as a blast of fire sprays from above. Damon's dragon twists, flinging us both. By some cruel miracle, Damon catches the saddle in time, while I slide off the dragon's scales and into the air.

Stars and smoke spin around me until I'm staring at the belly of the Nightstalker, fading from existence as I fall further and further away. A familiar shriek pierces the night as I struggle against the wind, turning to face the pale dragon racing to catch me. I reach out my hand, tears pricking my eyes as I feel her terror shoot through the bond. Halcyon screeches, each flap harder than the last.

A blanket of calm settles over me as gentle as a hand on my shoulder. Halcyon won't make it. I'm going to die. I let the tears fall and offer her one last smile. One more moment of love and gratitude.

*Thank you.*

A jade dragon slams into Halcyon, sending them both hurtling to the earth.

*"NO!"* I scream.

But where Halcyon had once been, a winged shadow dives with all four legs tucked close to its body–a singular bullet aimed at an impossible target. I see the speck of my reflection in the tundra of those glacier eyes until its jaws open, revealing rows of obsidian teeth that close around me.

# CHAPTER 7

*M*y eyes crack open to a sandstone ceiling. A dull thrum pounds in my ears, pulling me back from oblivion. Sweat rolls from the side of my temple and I reach to wipe it, only for my arm to come to a shrill halt. My head snaps to the right. I blink the sleep from my eyes, just to be sure that what I'm seeing is real and not a horrible nightmare. An iron shackle encircles my wrist, connecting to a chain that wraps over my chest and around the metal chair I'm slumped in.

I jolt, whipping my head around to peer through a hazy cloud of dim light, searching for any clue that might tell me where I am. I try to swallow, but my tongue is drier than sandpaper. A thick, impenetrable fog drapes over my mind like a curtain blocking the sun. No matter how hard I scour through the mess, I can't drag anything to the surface. I can't place this room or how I got here. My gaze lands on the leather of my pants and jacket, and I realize I'm dressed for flight. A nagging sensation prods at the back of my scalp, an incessant feeling of needing to be *somewhere*. Somehow, I know that place isn't here.

"Hello, Killer."

A shockwave of recognition rips my stare to the far wall

covered in shadows. A tall figure strolls forward, dressed in black with a mask covering everything below the bridge of his nose. His smokey green eyes beam with amusement, like this is a game and I'm a player who doesn't know the rules.

"Where am I?" The words come out hoarse. My throat is raw and I can't recall a reason why, but I know those eyes. I'd know them anywhere.

*Damon Valour.*

"Home sweet home," he sings, removing a blade from his belt. I suck in a breath, pulling at my chains as he slides a finger over the edge. "Well, my home. Not yours."

As quick as a sandstorm, it all comes rushing back. Our fight in the sky, Valen's dragon, and Halcyon racing to catch me as I fell. I lurch forward with a growl, tears pricking my eyes as the chains dig into my ribs, preventing me from ending the one person whose death was supposed to fix everything. I've failed so astronomically that I don't know how I'll ever find my way back from this.

*"Where is she?"* She can't be dead. Halcyon isn't dead. I would feel it.

He pauses, as though taken aback by my question. Damon fixes his posture, cool indifference filtering his gaze. "Your dragon lives."

The relief is instant, a broken dam that forces my chest to shudder as it rips through me, stealing my breath with it. *She's alive.* But now I'm forced to question why I am.

Damon watches me, waiting for the moment my eyes lock with his. He brings the knife to my throat, tilting my chin up. "You're going to answer a few questions."

I gulp, feeling the sharp bite of steel at my pulse. "And if I don't?"

He chuckles, kneeling to face-level with me. He scrapes the knife along my neck, pausing at the base of my throat. "Then you'll find my hospitality at an end." He draws the knife from my neck, allowing me to fill my lungs with air. "First question. What's the real reason you came after me last night?"

I send him my most scathing glare. "Was I not clear enough when I lodged a knife in your gut?" I glance at his stomach. "How are you even alive?"

"I have a talented Healer, and don't lie." He places the knife back at my throat. "I don't believe you're that stupid. You set up a meeting with Gannon hoping to get my attention with talk of peace, but that isn't a Rider's way. Each House would want to claim victory for themselves in the glory of battle, not send their youngest daughter as an assassin. What were you hoping to accomplish?"

I squeeze my eyes shut. *Just tell him what he wants. What does it matter now?* When I open them he's staring back, waiting. "I... am not the strongest Rider in my House," my voice wavers, body trembling, but I hold my ground. If I'm to die, I will do it with dignity. "I hoped if I could kill you, I'd prove myself to my family. I was supposed to gain my honor back."

Instead, I've landed in a hole deeper than I can ever crawl out of.

The knife disappears. I meet his gaze and find no pity there, only intrigue. He huffs a dry laugh. "I suppose I should be honored that you went through all this trouble for me."

"Please," I say, the fight draining from my bones. "Just let me go home. I won't breathe a word of this."

"You wanna go home, Killer?" He tilts his head. "Then bleed."

I gasp as a sharp sting slices my palm. The exit door scrapes open, hinges whining as a robed figure strides in with a bronze bowl in a pair of dainty hands.

I stiffen at the sight of those emerald robes. *"You."*

Her mouth pulls into a sly grin as she sets the bowl down on a table near the shadows and pulls back her hood. A sinisterly sweet oval face shines under the light, her thick lashes fluttering as she takes me in.

"I hope you enjoyed the book, My Lady." She eyes Damon for a moment, particularly the bloodstained knife in his hand. "Though perhaps a bit too much."

Her dark hair is piled high on her head, messy and yet elegant with gold embellishments and charms weaved in. She's almost the spitting image of Melantha, though a decade younger and a lot less pale.

Before I can think of a response, Damon drags the blade across his palm, unflinching as he makes a fist. The acolyte strides over, holding the bowl beneath his hand. Blood seeps from his clenched palm, splattering into the bowl in thick droplets. When a small pool of it collects in the base of the bowl she moves toward me.

I strain against the chains, leaning back as far as possible. "What are you doing? Get away from me!"

"Behave," Damon's voice rumbles from behind.

The edge of his blade presses back to my neck. One wrong move and it'll pierce through the skin. I'm helpless to watch as the acolyte kneels at my side, holding the bowl below my bleeding hand. A sick, heavy ball settles in my stomach as my blood mixes with Damon's. He removes the knife when the acolyte stands, carrying the bowl and its contents back to the table.

"What are you doing with that?"

"Damon here is generous enough to let you return home." She mixes the blood together, taking a pinch of white substance from other supplies laid out on the table and adding it to the bowl. "On one condition."

"Which is?"

Damon crosses the room, settling into a chair that faces me.

Her dark eyes slide back to mine as she works. "I provide him with reassurance."

"Reassurance?" My gaze flicks between them. "Reassurance of what?"

But my question goes unanswered. The acolyte begins to chant, a lyrical incantation that sets our blood ablaze. White fire crackles from the bowl, casting an eerie glow upon the room. Damon rolls up his sleeve. I fight against the chains, struggling to no avail. The flames wither and die, but the acolyte does not stop chanting. She comes to me first.

My arm locks into place against the arm of the chair, bound by a magic I can't see. "Stop. What are you doing? Stop!"

The acolyte doesn't. She dips her first two fingers into the blood and brings them to my inner forearm. She draws a winding symbol along my skin, chanting faster. When her fingers come away, an incessant burn sears my arm in the shape of the mark. I shout, thrashing in the chair. She moves on to Damon. As she traces the same symbol on his skin, he locks his stare to mine. I send him the most hate-filled glare I have within me.

The symbols on our arms glow with the same spectral light as the flames. Damon's jaw locks, fist curling as both our arms tremble. I cry out as the blood sears the soft flesh of my arm. A thousand needles seem to pierce my skin in the shape of the symbol, stabbing over and over.

And then it's done.

The light fades, leaving behind a detailed black mark of a Nightstalker in mid-flight. A shuddering breath escapes my lungs at the sight of it. My shoulders sag forward, a mix of relief and horror. *What did they do?* I pry my gaze from my arm to find the same mark on Damon's.

"What did you do to me?"

Damon rises from his chair, pulling down his sleeve as he stalks toward me. "You and me, Killer? We're blood-bound. Thanks to Oddica, I'll always know where to find you."

The acolyte—Oddica—offers a soft smile on her way out.

As the door groans shut, Damon circles me. "You're not

going to tell anyone what you saw here, because if you do, it will only end badly for you."

The chains rattle. With a small *click,* they fall loose in a pile around me. A fist curls in my hair, yanking me up from the chair. I shout, fighting the shackles still locked around my wrists.

"We're going to take a little walk."

Damon pries open the door, moving swiftly through stone corridors. A handful of guards peel off the walls, masked in black from head to toe. Damon pushes me forward, cupping a hand around my elbow. My heart pounds in my chest, blood rushing in my ears. I'm only halfway certain that I'm not being led to my execution, but somehow, the possibility of death isn't the thing that bothers me. It's the dry, stifling heat of the corridor and the thought of never feeling the desert wind on my skin again. I would have liked to experience it, just one last time.

*Will Halcyon miss me? What does the echo of a dragon's grief sound like?*

I'm not sure if I'd prefer the other option. If he keeps me prisoner, a hostage, then who knows how long it'll take for me to go home? I might spend the rest of my days rotting down here. If I die, Halcyon will most likely be given to Dahlia, the blood debt paid, and my name a distant memory to my family. The idea sits like lead in the pit of my stomach. I've done nothing with my life except disappoint the people around me. I haven't done anything worthwhile, not a single thing to be remembered.

We move out from the winding halls into a chamber teeming with life. At first glance, they look to be nomads by their well-worn clothes, many not native to the neutral colors of Solera. Shades of green, blue, yellow, and white from the other cities fill the chamber, but this is no market, no convention to draw in travelers. Their dull, lifeless eyes appear only half-aware of my presence as they amble past. Those who are more than half-alive part for us, eyes narrowing in on what they must perceive as a strange girl in a strange place, led by the leader of their movement.

On the other side of the room, Damon veers left, guiding us into a smaller chamber where the cries of children and wounded pierce the air. Not just people, I realize as their presence comes into focus. *Refugees* sit bleeding in chairs, stone slabs, or makeshift examination tables. Mothers hold their wailing babies close, tears streaming down their faces as they weep with them. Others stand against the walls in a daze, eyes not quite seeing what's in front of them. Some wait in scorched clothes, their skin bleeding, and the sight accompanied by the putrid scent of burnt flesh lingering in the room.

"What is this?" I can't have managed more than a whisper, but Damon hears it.

"Our infirmary."

Their cries of pain pierce my ears.

This isn't right. Why would rebels be hiding refugees? Mending the sick and injured in their base? Damon is a murderer. A thief. A threat to my family who's branded me with a mark I don't fully understand. I spy another mother and her child clinging to her breast, but her eyes are vacant, face gaunt as she crouches near an empty wall.

*'While your family wants for nothing, mothers cry themselves to sleep and feed their tears to their desiccated children.'* The dryness of my mouth is little more than a quiet nuisance in the face of their suffering.

"Why are these people here?"

"While your family burns House Dysis in retaliation for last night's attack, their people were caught in the crossfire."

The world tilts on its axis. *No... it can't be.* Why would House Galvan harm innocents? Why would these people seek shelter with the rebels unless...

*We're the thing they need protection from.*

I pull from the catalog of my memories, struggling to recall every attack I've been a part of. How many times did we raze villages to the ground? Burn fields and topple buildings in the name of defeating a rival House? A horrific realization creeps into my head, stealing the breath from my lungs. We never stopped to consider their people–the innocents running below us as we descended from their skies. We never looked back.

*I never looked back.*

It's too much, too fast. My stomach twists. An acidic taste rises in my mouth as I picture the bodies burned in our wake. I always did as told. I never had a reason to question what my brother or father thought was right, what they deemed was necessary in the sky.

*I never looked down.*

Numbness settles, hollow and cold, as we leave the infirmary and come to a stop in an empty cavern. *If he kills me now I deserve it.* The thought is fleeting, but it doesn't change as the seconds pass. The faces don't disappear with distance. *I did this. I helped do this to them.* It's just as Damon calls me–*Killer.* My teeth gnaw at the soft skin of my inner cheek, knees wobbling as he prowls closer. It's all I can do to keep a straight face.

*Does he see it? Does he see my whole world collapsing around me?*

He stops, reaching behind his back for what I assume is the knife he'll plunge into my gut. My spine straightens and although my body quakes, I glare back at him, throwing every ounce of fury I have into it.

In that same breath, his hands are around my wrists, a silver key twisting in the lock that binds each shackle. They collapse to the ground, kicking up dust between our boots. I lift my head, not quite believing the new weightlessness.

"You're not going to kill me?"

Damon takes a step back, about to turn. "No. You're free to go. I'll take you back to Solera."

He makes it a few feet as I stare.

No. This has to be a game. I run after him. The guards keep a steady pace behind us, but make no move to intercept me.

"I don't understand!"

He replies without stopping. "You don't understand that you're free?"

"I don't understand *why*," I huff, drawing his attention long enough to make him pause. "I tried to kill you *twice*."

His brow lifts. "Are you trying to convince me not to let you go?"

"I–" I struggle for the words.

I wouldn't do the same, plain and simple. But he's right. If this is my shot at freedom, at going home, why am I sabotaging it? I sense the weight of the mark on my arm, pulsing like a living, breathing thing. If it truly tells him where I am at all times, what's his real motive for letting me leave? Whatever the purpose is, I know it can't be good.

"Aren't you afraid I'll tell my family about your base?"

"I don't think I need to worry about that." He smirks and keeps moving through the cavern. "Besides," he calls over his shoulder. "Something tells me you won't send hundreds of innocent people to their deaths."

I open my mouth to retort, but the words die on my tongue like smoke lost to the wind. Maybe I wouldn't hesitate to kill him, but innocents? He's right. I can't cross that line.

"Why do it? Why bring me here?"

"You fell off the back of a dragon." I can practically hear his eyes rolling as he states the obvious. "I couldn't drop you on the ground without risking being caught by your family."

"Then why not let me die?" I challenge. "One less Rider to fight against your movement."

"Do you think your life is worth so little?"

A heavy silence stretches between us. When I try to swallow, it's as if my mouth is full of sand.

*Yes.*

Rather than leave me to my embarrassing lack of an answer, Damon continues. "I've seen riders fall. It's not a death I'd wish on anyone."

"You talk as though you aren't one of us."

Whatever softness remained in his features has evaporated, flayed from his skin to be replaced with an unforgiving coldness. "I will *never* be one of you."

I scoff. "You have a dragon, and not just any dragon–a dragon that hasn't been seen in a hundred years. I'd say that's more than sufficient to call yourself a Rider."

His jaw flexes as though he's debating his next words. Damon's voice sharpens. "Keep walking. Before I change my mind."

I clamp my mouth shut, following him along when he turns.

*He has a dragon, but doesn't consider himself a Rider. Duly noted.*

We move deeper into the cavern where stalactite bursts from the ceilings, shimmering in the torchlight from the guards. A deep, guttural growl echoes from the darkness where the claws of the flames don't reach. My breath quickens, heels digging in place. Even the guards appear to tense, postures stiff and a sheen of sweat gleaming on their brows. I don't watch them for long, my gaze darting to the movement dancing in the shadows. Scales flash under the light of the fire like black tourmaline under the sun. The dragon's mouth curls to reveal two rows of black teeth longer than the length of my body. A crown of horns protrude from either side of its skull, twisting up to the sky. Perfect for killing a man... or another dragon.

Neither of the guards move, though I spot their grip on the rifles quivering. Damon, however, waits patiently. Bored even. I force myself to breathe one lungful of air to the next. The Nightstalker's ancient stare lands on me. It takes every ounce of will I have not to bolt when it takes a step towards us, shaking the ground as it closes in.

*I was already in those jaws.* I remind myself as the cavern quakes.

Air lodges in my throat when its snout appears inches from my face. I school my features, ignoring the beads of sweat collecting behind my neck as the creature inhales. *I've lived with dragons my entire life. I will not cower now.* Out of the side of my vision, I spy Damon watching the interaction with vague interest. The Nightstalker exhales a hot breath, whipping my hair from my face and retracts its long neck, its frame expanding as it inhales from above. I know what's coming before I can blink.

The dragon snaps forward, unclenching its jaws to release a hideous wail that shakes the cave so hard that stalactite crashes from the ceiling. I clamp my hands over my ears, shrinking under the dragon's roar. It's over in a matter of seconds, but my knees buckle in that same breath. A warm liquid coats my trembling hands, but I don't remove my palms until the dragon slinks back into the void of the cave. When I bring my hands away, blood shines in the center of them.

"I think she likes you."

I lift my head, swaying with the effort. Damon offers his hand and what I think might be a smile under his mask. He pulls me up, steadying me when I stumble. The weight of his hands burn where they grip my waist, keeping my body inches from his. I find myself staring into his eyes, so at odds against the shadows around us. As his other hand cups my jaw, shifting my head to check the bleeding from my ears, I think there's no way he could ever venture into a crowd with them. He would stop anyone with the way they burn. There's no mistaking the intensity when he watches me, as if he's stripping me bare, and that's exactly how I feel at this moment. Naked. With his fingers digging into my skin. Damon's hand drops, the other unwrapping from my waist as he takes a step back.

He reaches out an open hand. "I'll take you home."

I hold my nerve as Damon helps me into his dragon's saddle, even more so when his chest is pressed to my back, allowing me to feel each breath he takes. The contact keeps my spine tense as I try to focus on anything other than a rebel being close enough to cut my throat, should he feel so inclined.

The Nightstalker roars, crawling through the tunnels at a break-neck speed. Rocks and stalactite tumble loose as it climbs, finally reaching the end when sunlight blooms from the opening. In a few short leaps, we're airborne, bursting from the ground through a pile of sand. Golden light bleeds to orange, sinking low to the horizon.

The Nightstalker plunges forward, leaving my stomach in the clouds as we descend. Damon's arm snakes around my waist, holding me tight as the drop presses me into his chest. A warm flush heats my face and for the moment, I'm grateful neither of us can see each other. His dragon levels out, its wings beating a few times until all four legs touch the ground.

Damon's arm vanishes from my waist.

Buildings rise in the distance, the city of Solera surging from the hills. I glance toward the sun as it skates across the dunes. At least it isn't high noon. I'll never make it home if I have a heat stroke.

I shift from the saddle, sliding down the side of the dragon's back and praying to the Gods I don't do something to offend as I dismount. In a few quick movements, I make it to the ground without becoming a charbroiled lunch.

"This is where I leave you."

I shield my vision from the sun with my hand, staring Damon in the face at the top of his dragon. "So this is it then? You're really letting me go?"

"Don't sound so disappointed," he chuckles. "You get to go home to your mansion and pretend this was a bad dream. The rest of us live on to fight another day in the dunes, wondering if it'll be thirst or dragonfire that ends us."

I scowl. "That's exactly my point. What kind of rebel wouldn't use a noble's daughter as a hostage?"

A spark ignites in his eyes and I don't need to see through his mask to know he's grinning. "Oh, believe me. I know how valuable you are, but I'm going to let you in on a little secret." His dragon lowers its head, bringing Damon closer. "I don't need you to win."

Dread pools in my gut, curling so tight around my insides that I don't know what to say back.

"I'm sure I'll see you around, Killer." He winks.

With a single, powerful flap his dragon shoots into the sky, becoming a mere speck as the seconds pass on. I'm not sure how long I stand there staring, but when I turn toward the city, the sun yields to the cool embrace of twilight.

*Halcyon.* I tug on the bond with my mind, chewing my lip as I wait for the reply.

Sand swallows my ankles as I trudge forward. Thick grains of it sneak through the leather of my boots, sliding around between my socks and soles. Solera sits a hundred yards away, but it feels like an eternity.

A familiar presence tickles the back of my head, tugging over and over like a tolling bell. Two screeches pierce the night, accompanied by a deeper roar. I twist as the rhythmic sound of dragon wings beats closer. A sob breaks past my lips as I wave my arms at the iridescent dragon, a winding viridian serpent, and the crimson beast gliding behind them.

Jocelyn and Ash slide into the sand behind Halcyon, who wastes no time pouncing toward me. She nudges her enormous snout into my chest, throwing me off my feet and inhaling. Undiluted joy rings throughout the bond, flooding my senses until tears are rolling down my cheeks. I throw my head back and laugh.

"Sage!" Ash reaches me first, Jocelyn hot on his heels. His wide eyes take me in, scanning over me like he can't believe

I'm real. I flash him a grin as I run my hands over Halcyon's scales.

"I'm okay," I tell them both.

Jocelyn is the first to help me up, her expression wrought with worry and relief. "I thought we lost you."

"What happened?" Ash presses, taking me by the shoulders. "We've been looking everywhere for you." He studies me from top to bottom, moving my chin to take a better look.

"I'm fine!" I bat his hands away. "I was ta–" A searing hot pain engulfs my throat. I wheeze, doubling over in a fit of coughs. I suck in a mouthful of air, trying to get the words out. "I was ta–" Lightning shoots through my esophagus. I can't control the coughing, spit flying from my mouth as Ash reaches out to steady me.

"Sage?"

*I was taken!* I want to say, but even thinking it makes me nauseous. I drag in a ragged breath, the mark flaring with heat under my sleeve.

A cold horror spreads within me. *'You're not going to tell anyone what you saw here, because if you do, it will end badly for you.'*

I can't tell them about Damon.

It's the mark. Through whatever *evil* blood magic that mage performed, the mark won't let me say a word.

Jocelyn twists off the cap to her flask, handing it to me. "Here, drink some water."

I bring the flask to my lips and take several long gulps, trying to stitch together a lie for the moment, just until I can figure out what to do. I gather a few deep breaths, staying quiet while they watch me, concern etched deep into their faces.

"I chased after one of the dragons last night and fell near the ground. When I spotted rebels in the distance, I hid."

Ash's brow pinches. "Halcyon couldn't find you. We followed her all night searching."

I resist the urge to bite my lip. "I hid in some caves and slept most of today. I didn't want to die in the dunes, so I waited to leave until sundown."

Jocelyn nods, buying my explanation. "I'm glad you're not dead. Dinner would be so dull."

I roll my eyes, but my mouth betrays me with a smile. "Well, what's a family dinner without a grand entrance? If we head back now we'll make it back before dessert."

Ash is the least amused. He watches me carefully, but doesn't blink when I move to mount Halcyon. I can sense the weight of his stare the entire ride back home, beckoning me to turn, to spill my guts about where I really was. I lock away the guilt, wondering how I'll ever be able to convince my family of my whereabouts when I can't even convince Ash.

Half-eaten plates cover the length of the table when we arrive.

Jasper sports a wide grin with a day-old gash on the side of his head. Rune wears his infamous scowl, identical to Dahlia if it weren't for his split lip. Other than those tell-tale signs, you'd never guess our family was the center of a skirmish. Everyone sits prim and polished in their best clothes for dinner. The only things out of place are the three empty chairs waiting for us.

My father sets his cutlery down at our entrance, prompting the family to twist their necks and follow his line of vision. The dinner conversation crashes to a halt as Jocelyn, Ash, and I sink into our designated seats.

Someone clears their throat.

"We've gone through considerable effort to locate you, dear Niece," Uncle Deon sneers with a whiskey in hand.

"Now, Brother," my Father cuts in before I can deliver a dry retort, "is that any way to welcome my daughter home?" He signals to one of the servants holding a flagon of wine.

As his glass fills, his eyes flicker to me with little to no emotion. Uncle Deon, on the other hand, perceives me with the same derision one would offer a cockroach that just won't die.

"Welcome home, Dear." My father lifts his glass to me and takes a long drink. As his glass hits the wood with a soft *clink*, he scans the table in quiet calculation. "Now that our family is fully present, I have an announcement I'd like to make."

Everyone visibly straightens. Brief glances are exchanged with the same question in their eyes. *What announcement?*

Our father folds his hands. "I've sent word to all four Houses that we will be hosting a Conclave."

Chaos breaks out across the table. Cyrus Galvan does not flinch at the shouts of protest and pale faces seated around him.

"You can't be serious!" Uncle Deon slams his whiskey down, liquor splashing on the polished wood. "House Galvan does not surrender! You will make us look *weak!*"

"Not surrender, Brother, a temporary ceasefire." Father levels the table with a General's stare. "If the recent attack has shown us anything, it's that the rebels are becoming smarter. They're using our in-fighting to their advantage."

I sit up straighter, casting a sidelong glance at Ash in question. *Did you know about this?* But he avoids my gaze, keeping it firmly planted on his dinner plate.

"If our family cannot fight a war on two fronts," Father goes on, "neither can the others. Should the rebels manage to topple one House, it will send ripples across the Celosia desert. The rebellion will grow, we will see a rise in revolts, and if the people believe the rebellion stands a chance it will result in a sickening amount of charred flesh. If the noble Houses do not band together we risk the end of Dragonriders as we know it."

His words sink in during the silence, a terrible foreboding of his vision to come.

A dark chuckle rumbles from Uncle Deon as he picks up his glass. "My dear brother, always playing the long game."

Father picks up his knife and fork, slicing into his steak

without a word. As we sit, digesting the consequence of the potential threat he's laid at our feet, he takes it as his moment to go on. "This Conclave will serve as an opportunity to forge alliances long after the ceasefire. My children are of age to be matched with another House. I shall expect the same from the rest of my family." He gives Deon a pointed look.

Dahlia's face blanches and even Rune seems to have lost a hint of his color. Ash's shoulders tense and Lux hides her hands in her lap. Jocelyn peers down at her empty plate, refusing to make eye contact with anyone. Jasper slumps back in his chair, head pivoting to his parents as if they'll contradict his uncle's decree. Nobody does.

Cyrus Galvan's word is law.

*'Rest assured,'* Ash's voice echoes in my mind. *'I will help Father secure a pleasant match for you. He will be kind and share your love of the skies.'*

My body does not feel like mine. This life doesn't feel like my own. As I study each of the faces of my family I cannot fathom the incredible odds of being born into this House. *If I were the slightest bit unlucky, I would have been like everyone else... I may have grown to be a rebel too.* I jerk in my chair, ripping myself from the thought. The sudden movement catches my father's eye, but he does not comment.

I cannot restrain myself from staring at the full glasses of water beside my family's plates. Most of them did not bother with the water, preferring the wine in its stead. The water sits there, waiting to be drunk or discarded altogether. Faces of the patients in the rebel's infirmary flash to the forefront of my mind, how they might just kill each other for a chance to finish my family's glasses. My stomach churns at the idea. A sharp ache pulses behind my eyes as my thoughts spin.

"This paltry excuse for peace will be seen as weakness," Deon utters, white-knuckling his glass. "You will bring the downfall of our House, Brother, if your children do not manage it first."

"If you have anything to offer, Deon, please make your ideas known."

The silence alone could burn the manor to cinders.

"No?" Father lifts a brow, then smirks. "Then perhaps it is a good thing I oversee the survival of our House. I quiver to think where we would be if you had been born first, *Brother.*" His chair scrapes the tile as he stands, tossing his tablecloth on his plate. "Aurora will oversee training for the girls to procure an advantageous match. Tomorrow, the boys will attend a meeting in my office with their fathers present. Any potential alliances will require my final approval. With that, I take my leave." Father turns on his heel, his footfalls echoing out of the dining room.

My mother rises, dabbing at her mouth before she too discards her tablecloth. "Girls are to be present in the temple at dawn." Her gold gown twirls around her ankles as she departs, following our father's trail.

I'm going to be sick.

# CHAPTER 8

*a* s the sun ruptures across the morning sky, my skin is almost bleeding with it.

I scrub it raw over the sink as rushing water bursts from the spout. I've tried hot and cold water, soap and no soap, but no matter how much I scrub, the ink on my skin is permanent. I throw the sponge at the wall with a growl.

"This can't be happening." I knot my hands in my hair, tugging at the roots.

During my sleepless night, I realized two things. One: I'm screwed if anyone in my family sees this mark. Without being able to explain its origin, I'll be labeled as a traitor. Executed. *Dahlia would love that.* Two: if I'm going to keep this a secret, I'm going to need to get a hell of a lot better at lying.

I sniffle, turning off the tap and gripping the edges of the sink. I can barely look at myself in the mirror. Purple bags bruise beneath my eyes, my loose hair twisting and knotted around my face. I force myself to breathe, gathering my mess of hair and tying it back.

*Think.* I will my reflection to find an answer. *Think.*

I could go to the High Mage. But the thought crumbles to

dust the moment it's born. The acolyte–Oddica–did this to me. She might be related to Melantha if her looks are anything to go by. I could always find another mage, but that would take time, and I have no way of guaranteeing their loyalty.

*I'm so screwed.*

Walking across the courtyard to the temple, I try to keep the darker thoughts at bay. Will my family burn me at the stake just like any other traitor? Will they drive a knife through my heart? Would Ash defend me? Jocelyn?

*I can't even defend myself.*

Dahlia, Lux, and Jocelyn stand before a statue of Vulcan, the dragon god of the sun. Stained-glass windows flank each side of the temple, conjuring a mosaic of color as dawn cracks over the compound. Each window features a different god. There's Anvi, Goddess of water and Vulcan's wife. Their children: Linette, Maiden of Mercy, and Elion, the God of war. There's also Oryn, the God of justice, Nyra, the Goddess of Death, and their children. I peel my gaze from Vulcan when the doors behind us creak. My mother strolls in wearing slim black robes with gold embroidery and her hair pulled into a sleek bun at the nape of her neck. Guards close the doors behind her.

She climbs the dais in front of Vulcan, scrutinizing the four of us. "Each House offers their own merits, some more valuable than others. We will need a clear strategy to strengthen ties between each House. Dahlia," my mother faces her niece. "I've spoken with your mother. House Tesar should be your focus at the Conclave, particularly the heir, Xavier. He is the first son, a rider who's about your age. Twenty-four, yes?"

"Twenty-three," Dahlia mutters.

"Excellent. He's one year older. Jocelyn." My cousin jumps, snapping to attention. "Your focus will be the heir of House Dysis. Valen holds no love for our family, but you should try to appeal to his interest at the Conclave."

Jocelyn pales, mouth gaping. "Aunt Aurora, forgive me, but

I've fought him myself. Ash scorched him in a raid last summer. He is ruthless and vengeful and–"

"And that will be a thing of the past when you are wed," my mother says, unmoved. "With any luck, you'll have his respect for being such an adept rider. Securing a marriage with the Dysis family will bring any vendettas to a halt. Raising a hand against us after the marriage would label them as kin-slayers. Every House would turn against them for their betrayal and they will be found untrustworthy for decades to come."

My hands tighten into fists behind my back. Fear of scandal isn't enough to hold someone like Valen at bay. *They're going to sacrifice her and hope for the best.* It's enough to make my stomach roil.

"Luxana, I know we've prepared you for some time." Mother folds her hands, stepping in front of Lux. "This assignment is crucial. I want you to approach Eren Noctis."

My muscles lock. I'm no longer in the temple, but above the dunes near the city of Esmeray. *Khione screeches, wings shredded, her coppery blood splattering my wind goggles as she falls... falls... falls–*

"What do I need to know?" Lux asks without fail.

"He's twenty-five, head of his House with six dragons strong. Each of his siblings are riders except for the youngest."

Lux gives a curt nod. "I will not fail you."

Dahlia snorts. Jocelyn's face is tinged green. I'm five seconds away from screaming.

Aurora Galvan turns to me next. Her face may as well be cut from the same stone as Vulcan. "You are also assigned to House Tesar. Target the second son, Ronan, but more importantly," she steps closer, glaring down her nose at me. "It is critical that we create ties to House Noctis. Do not do anything that will jeopardize your sister's chances with the Heir."

A laugh bubbles to the surface, slipping past my lips, and I can't bring myself to care. My mother's shocked face only exacerbates my laughter until tears prick at my eyes. "Oh, that's rich, Mother. I didn't realize our only value lies in whoring ourselves to the richest House."

A hard *smack* reverberates through the temple. Lux gasps beside me. My cheek stings, stunning me into silence. My mother grips my chin, jerking my face to meet hers. Fury lashes behind her eyes as her nails dig into my jaw. "You have failed this House in every way imaginable. Your only value left is your dragon and the alliance you may secure. Do not fail your family in this task."

She releases my chin, but tears something with it. My fear.

Indignation crackles to the surface, wrath and ruin along with it. I have bled for this family from the moment I learned to fly.

"I have *always* fought for our House." My words are slow. Deliberate. I can't believe what I'm saying even though the words are mine. "I barely survived the last two days. Do you remember? You never asked, but it's a *miracle* that I'm home and all you can do is tell me how I've failed?" My voice sharpens, hitching as the next sentences tumble out. "What did *you* do while the rest of us fought? Hide? I am a warrior of a great House and you're a *coward!*"

Her mouth sits in a thin line. A couple of seconds tick past, letting the words hang heavy in the air. Full body tremors rattle down my spine, but I refuse to cower. I look my mother in the eyes and show her I mean every word. Then she sighs through her nose. No one speaks as she glides to the podium to the left of the statue and reaches down, procuring a leather whip.

Lux, three shades paler, steps in front of me. Her voice shakes. "Mom, no–"

"Step aside, Luxana. That's an order."

"It's fine, Lux." I squeeze my trembling hands tighter. "I can take it."

Her lip quivers as she looks at me in horror, but she steps aside.

Our mother's heels click as she approaches, stroking the end of the whip with her fingertips. She stands face to face with me on the dais. "Step forward, Sage."

I join her, holding her stare with contempt.

"Turn to your family."

I'm forced to face Lux, Jocelyn, and Dahlia. Jocelyn's head is down, hands balled into fists at her sides like it's the best she can do to restrain herself. Silent tears trickle from Lux's eyes. Dahlia smirks. I bite down on my inner cheek, unable to watch as she relishes every minute of this.

"Hold out your hands."

I lift my palms face up. Familiar scars slash across the skin. I haven't added to the collection in five years. I suppose this was inevitable. Exhaling, I pick a stained glass window to watch. It's a portrait of the goddess Linette, Maiden of Mercy.

When the first lash cracks, adrenaline sucks the air from my lungs, numbing all sensations radiating from my hands. With the second snap, I'm not as lucky. I flinch, sucking a sharp breath when the skin breaks. I press my lips tight, blinking away tears as the pain shoots up my wrists. *I won't let them see me cry.* On the third whip, my knees wobble. A metallic taste fills my mouth, and I'm not sure if it's my lip or my tongue that's bleeding.

*Crack!*

The fourth lash extracts a whimper from me. Skin rips open over my fingertips.

*Breathe.* Stars twirl in my vision, warping the Maiden as she observes in silence. *Don't look. Don't look. Don't look.* If I look now, I'll see my palms in ribbons and I'll never make it to the fifth.

The fifth lash collides with my palms and I sob, dropping to my knees. My hands shake so hard I can't lower them. They curl on their own accord, pulsing with fiery pain.

My mother lowers her face to my ear. "You are no warrior. You are a soldier and a daughter of House Galvan *first*." Her presence leaves my ear as she straightens, addressing the room. "That will be all for today."

I hear my mother's steps leave the temple as my blood hits the marble in a steady *drip... drip... drip...*

Lux and Jocelyn sprint up the dias, crouching on either side of me.

"Sage," Lux squeaks, tears rushing down her face. "Sage, I'm so sorry. I shouldn't have let her."

I can't find my voice, but Jocelyn answers as she pulls me up. "She would have done the same to you, Cousin."

It's true. I knew the consequences.

My vision slides in and out of focus. I can't recall the majority of the walk back to my room. Lux sets to work washing my hands when I hiss, flinching each time she dabs the blood away.

"I know, I know. I'm sorry," she murmurs.

Jocelyn brings aloe and bandages, watching as Lux wraps my hands.

"I should have stopped her." Lux's hands shake with what might be rage or fear, I'm not certain.

"It's fine." The words are hollow. "I had it coming."

Jocelyn's head snaps up. "No, you didn't."

"I did," I repeat, watching the bandages wrap over severed flesh. "I spoke out of turn. I insulted our mother."

"You had a good reason to," Jocelyn mutters, tucking her knees to her chest.

Lux finishes, but continues to hold my hands. "No one deserves this, Sage. You're the youngest of us. She can't expect this to be easy for you."

I pull my hands from her soft grasp. "It's not about age, Lux. Don't you get that?"

Her lips purse as she lowers her head. "No, I know, but... they've been so hard on you–"

"And I deserve it. I failed everyone when we lost Khione. The death of a dragon is a stain I'll carry with me for the rest of my life." My voice cracks. "Just leave me alone."

Her face crumbles as she rises. I turn away as the door shuts behind her. The bed dips where Jocelyn joins me. She doesn't offer words of comfort, but sits beside me quietly.

And that is enough.

IN THE DAYS THAT FOLLOW, we return to the temple two hours a day for debriefing. We're given a rigorous crash course on the four other ruling families, reading over a list of our personal targets. We learn their physical descriptions, their dragons, their family's strengths with potential weaknesses, and their dating history.

Ronan Tesar seems like he's no more than a boy content to play with his family's fortune. According to our intelligence, he often frequents bars, gambles in pleasure houses, and refuses to be brought to heel despite his family's best efforts. I huff, reading over the information with bandaged fingers. Pain shoots through my hands where the skin folds, but I bite my tongue and ignore it.

Lux appears content from where I'm sitting, pouring over the file on Eren Noctis. I don't need to read the report to know he's rich, powerful, and head of our rival House. I disassociate from the page I'm reading, thinking back to our last battle with his family. Khione never would have died if it weren't for Eren, and remembering puts a bitter taste in my mouth. I shove that battle to the back of my head, into the vault with other painful, useless memories as Jocelyn slips into the chair next to me.

"We could kill him," I say after a beat, Jocelyn's face scrunching as she studies her target.

She sighs, checking behind her before she leans in and lowers her voice. "We'd have a better chance at killing Damon Valour than Valen. How's that going by the way?

I'd rather reopen my wounds than talk about it.

I sink further into my seat. "Terrible."

Jocelyn doesn't push, but her eyes flick from the paper in her grasp to Dahlia on the other side of the room. "Why does she get the Tesar heir and you the second son?"

I shrug. "I'm the third heir in the Galvan line and the second daughter. It makes sense."

"None of it makes sense. Why not throw her at Valen? Their tempers would match well."

"A little too well," I whisper with a shake of my head. "It's bad enough Uncle Deon is always undermining my father. The last thing he needs is to pair Deon's kids with a powerful ally. Better to reel in Valen using ties to someone loyal, like your mom. Aunt Natalya would never turn against him, so he probably feels safe using you to broker that alliance."

Jocelyn stares for a minute. "Sometimes I forget how much you see."

"Like it does me any good."

She squeezes my shoulder. "Hey, if they don't value you here maybe House Tesar will."

"Doubtful." I turn the page a bit too sharply, causing a new sting in my palm. "If Dahlia succeeds she'll become my sister-in-law and tell them all about me killing her dragon."

"That's not how it happened," Jocelyn insists.

I don't say anything more. People tend to believe the worst before they hear the truth.

When our meeting breaks, Ash is waiting in the hall. It's one of the few times he seeks me out instead of the opposite, and my stomach twists at the sight of his tall frame. For once, he's not dressed for flight, which signals to me that this isn't for a mission. Neither one of us is geared up, but the apprehension collecting in my gut makes it feel like I should be.

He jerks his chin, his tousled hair scraping over his forehead. "Walk with me."

I decide I won't be the first one to speak, better to let him tell me what this is about, although I have my suspicions. *He's going to ask about the night I disappeared. Get your story straight.* In those next few precious seconds, I've chosen the position of the sun, the stars I followed home, and the number of rebels I came across. I feel the imaginary weight of the mark beneath my sleeve as though summoned by my anxiety.

Ash brings me to an alcove far from where the others departed. My chest contracts as he wets his lips, preparing a question that might damn me. "Who did you get?"

My heart skips a beat. "What?"

"Who did you get for your assignment?"

"Oh. Ronan Tesar."

Ash releases a breath. "Thank the Gods. I worried they'd use you to tame Valen."

I can't help but let my shoulders slump as relief washes through me. "Yeah, I think everyone saw him try to kill me. Jocelyn got him."

He scowls. "I have the pleasure of seducing Kamari Noctis."

It's like a punch to the gut. "You and Lux then?"

Ash offers a smile that doesn't reach his eyes. "It seems we're both destined to marry into the Noctis family."

I cradle my hands together, stepping around Ash to the open

balcony overlooking our courtyard. Clusters of yellow flowers bloom on the creosote bushes below. A stone fountain rises from a pool in the center, promising a reprieve from the scorching heat of the day. Wind chimes sing to the empty space, echoing off the walls. I rub my thumb over the top of the bandages as I look out. The news tastes like bitter wine.

"I know it's not what you want to hear." Ash joins me, leaning over the rail.

I'm lost as I try to find the words and fail.

My brother sighs, hanging his head, then lifts his face to peer at me. His eyes are softer in this light, safe and warm. "When you disappeared and House Dysis retreated, we realized the rebels swept in. They took what was left in our tanks and almost got away with it. A few of them did get away," he amends. "Father's right. We can't fight a war on two fronts. He's trying to make contingency plans for us. If he can lock in alliances now, then we'll survive what's to come."

"An alliance with every House? Don't you think that's too many hands in one pot?"

He gives me a wry smile. "No. He's playing it very strategically. Why do you think as the third born you were given to a second son? The higher our rank, the more valuable we are. By choosing me and Lux for House Noctis, they'll become our closest allies—the right hand to House Galvan. Dividing the rest of us up, he establishes goodwill with the others and profits from trade, dragon eggs, dowries, and whatever else he deems fit to name in the contracts."

I exhale. "The strategy isn't lost on me. I just wish..."

"That it wasn't Eren?"

"Yeah."

We don't speak, content to listen to the windchimes for a moment.

"I'd kill him if I could."

Shaking my head, I twist to face Ash as he turns to me. "And what would that do? It won't bring Khione back."

Ash takes my hands, turning over my palms to reveal the blood seeping through the bandages. "It's my job to protect you. I keep failing."

I pull my hands away. "You can't protect me from our family. But maybe there's something we can do about Jocelyn and Valen. I don't think she'll be safe."

He runs a hand through his hair. "It's better not to interfere, Sage. Our father hand-picked these alliances. To go against it is to go against *him*."

Which would be treason.

"If it were you and Valen, I'd fight like hell to break that assignment, but Jocelyn can handle her own. My only concern is you and Lux."

I snort. "Like Noctis will be any better."

"Look, I'm telling you this because I love you. Don't let your feelings about Khione's death cloud your judgment. Don't let *him* drive a wedge between you and Lux. She doesn't have a choice. None of us do."

I nod a bit stiffly, retreating a step. "I'll keep that in mind."

There's no response when I turn, no movement to hold me in place. He lets me go. My feet carry me to the one source of comfort I know I can rely on. The one constant in my life when everything else is uncertain.

I lay eyes on Halcyon in the caverns through the tunnels beneath our manor. Her wings are folded close to her body, but her eyes snap open and her head perks up when I walk in. Halcyon chitters her greeting, neck stretching to nuzzle my frame. I pat her on top of her head, soft enough not to irritate the lashes on my hands any further. Halcyon notices immediately. She sniffs at my hands, careful not to graze them with her scales. A nervous chirp leaves her mouth.

Tears pool in my eyes, blurring my vision. *I can't fly with you for a while. Please don't hate me.*

"I thought I'd find you here."

I whirl.

In the back of the cave near the entrance, Lux moves into the light. She comes to my left, gazing at Halcyon with a half-hearted smile.

"Did Ash send you?" Part of me doesn't want to know.

"No. I wanted to talk to you."

"About?"

She breathes, long lashes fluttering as she pries her stare from Halcyon. "I don't–" she bites her lip. "If I'm successful, I don't want it to come between us."

"You don't have to worry about that."

"Really? Because it feels like I do."

I throw my head back and exhale, staring at the sunstone embedded in the rocks above. Leave it to Lux to always be the sincere one. The rational one. The one who refuses to let things lie where they may. *A sincere pain in my ass.*

"I'm not mad I'm just... having trouble picturing them as family."

"You heard about Ash's target?"

I nod. "The oldest sister."

"It's all hypothetical," Lux tries to lessen the blow, but it's long since landed. "He might not even like me."

"He'll like our money," I answer, giving Halcyon my full attention. "Besides, how could he not love you?"

"It won't change anything." She takes hold of my wrist. "I promise."

I can't bring myself to look at her as I ease away from her touch. "It'll change everything."

Lux drops her hand, chin low and eyes down. She takes a final glance at Halcyon. "You know, I envy you sometimes."

My brows furrow. "Me?"

A small, resigned smile crosses her lips. "I always wanted to be a Rider, but I was never chosen."

Streams of questions open in my mind.

Lux shrugs, looking over her shoulder at Halcyon and then me. "You were."

She leaves me in the darkness of the caverns, wondering what might have been and what never will be.

# CHAPTER 9

*S*cabs cover my palms, itching and threatening to crack with too much exertion. It takes a whole lot of aloe to prevent me from scratching, but I apply a thick layer to soothe them before I rewrap.

Daring a glance at the mirror, I skim over the gold and black fabric tight around my body. Black, just like our House banner–*or a funeral*–and a gold two-headed dragon with rubies for eyes pinned above my heart. The dress itself dips into a low neckline, approved by my mother if only to capture a certain son's interest. Two gold combs crafted in the shape of dragon wings flare on either side of my lifted curls for the final touch.

I look over my skin one last time, inspecting the ichor I attempted on myself tonight. It swirls my arms, blooming up my neck and flaring in tendrils near my jaw. It took more than two pain-staking hours to get the lines sharp enough not to look sloppy, but taking a bit more time beats Lux discovering the new mark on my arm.

*I look like a small tiger.* My eyes fall to the bandages around my hands. *Declawed.*

Movement stirs in the corner of the mirror, taking the lithe shape of Aunt Natalya as she slinks into my dressing room with a flute of champagne in her hand. Her ichor shines as bright as the bubbles in her glass while she drinks me in, maroon lips pursing.

"I see my sister-in-law has been doling out punishments."

I slip on two silk gloves over my hands, tensing as I slide one over the mark concealed by a fresh bandage. "It's nothing. I spoke out of turn."

"So I heard," she replies dryly, leaning against the wall. "I'm surprised it wasn't your tongue."

"Did you need something, Aunt Nat?" I ask, searching for my daggers in the mess of cosmetics on the vanity table.

"I can't visit my favorite niece?" She beckons me over to the balcony.

Holding in a sigh, I join her as she bathes in the golden rays of the sun's descent. "You see me every day."

"Not recently." She knocks back her flute, humming in delight. "There hasn't been a Conclave in over fifty years."

"So?"

"*So,*" her eyes hold a mischievous glint. "A lot can change in one night."

"What are you getting at?"

Her eyes lock on my hands. "If I were you, I'd find a way to make myself indispensable."

I lift a brow.

She shrugs. "Ah, don't listen to me. I'm old now, but I must admit it'd be a shame to watch you go quietly. You've always had your father's fire. It's a shame he doesn't see it."

"Aunt Nat, you're only forty, and whatever you're getting at– I don't want any part of it. I have my assignment for tonight. I imagine you have yours too."

"Ah, yes." She shudders. "Play the enchanting, accommodating sister. The buffer between my brothers. You're right, Little Firedrake, we all have our roles to play." Aunt Nat takes a step, then pauses at my shoulder. "But if you want them to stop clipping your wings, you're going to have to pick a different role." She glances again at my hands and strolls back out of the room, her heels clicking on the tile.

Dragonsong echoes from the clouds.

I peek out over the ledge. A trail of dragons stretches over the eventide sky, sporadic shadows screeching high above the sands. Down below, our family gathers at the top of the stairs leading up to the stone veranda wrapping around the manor.

Unlike the harsh lines of the fortress we call home, the summer manor's architecture flows with pure luxury. Thin pillars hold up the second floor's open terraces, perfect for midnight walks in the moonlight. Torches burn on the perimeter of the veranda, illuminating the path up the steps, the balconies overhead, and a circular pool in the gardens. Sunstone string lights wrap around palm trees on the property, dangling from the arches of each story to add an extra sense of extravagance to the evening. It'd be hard to miss the manor, shining like a beacon to whatever lurks within the dunes.

The first to land is House Althea, an all-female House with five dragonriders. Idalia, Matriarch of her family, slides off a bronze behemoth of horns and teeth. Its slitted malachite eyes scan over the property, squinting with what can only be described as utter disdain. Idalia's dragon is old, nearly the same size as the manor, and capable of leveling the building if it wished. The dragon hisses its warning as the rider steps forth from its shadow. A silver, gossamer dress hugs the curves of Idahlia, cutting into a sharp V at her neckline to show off her ample cleavage. The sigil of her House hangs in the center of her chest, a silver shield with a phoenix at its center.

Four daughters flank their mother as they dismount from their dragons. They move in synced steps, drifting as silent as wraiths behind their mother. Each one is almost identical with pitch-black hair hanging in tight braids and four sets of neutral expressions. With a sharp snap of wings, Idalia's dragon takes to the sky with the smaller dragons following after it.

"House Galvan welcomes you to our Conclave," my father greets, using his warmest political smile.

Idalia cracks a wrinkled smirk as they shake hands. "Cyrus, it's been too long." She leans in to kiss Father's cheek.

Our mother stiffens.

"Your father nearly wed Idalia," Aunt Nat whispers from my right, "and left quite an impression on Deon. Alas, she married someone else for love and now she's a widow."

On my other side, Lux casts a wary glance in our direction.

Father proceeds to introduce our family while I survey Idalia's children. Thanks to Jocelyn, I know Jasper and Rune are destined to marry the two oldest Althea sisters, but it's difficult to tell them apart. Only their noses and perhaps the fullness of their lips separate one from the other if you look long enough. They even stand at similar heights, but upon closer inspection, their eyes range from gold to ice, to peridot, and carnelian.

"These are my daughters." Idalia gestures to each one. "Davina, Nikita, Nyra, and Sienna."

I try to commit their faces to memory as they file inside, but the next House lands, ripping my attention away. Five dragonriders in the finest silks of blue and gold dismount from their saddles.

House Tesar.

Kieran and Lyra Tesar stride forth hand-in-hand, their scowling children following behind them. Similar introductions are exchanged and I discover that Ronan Tesar isn't unpleasant to look at. His dark hair is slicked back with a few loose strands curling around his face. Dimples flash on either side of the not-so-discreet grin he passes between his brothers. I wish I knew what was so funny because my stomach churns at the thought of having to seduce anyone.

*Why would a rake like Ronan find interest in you?*

"Wipe that scowl off your face," my mother snaps under her breath as the Tesars enter the manor.

"Sixteen Hells, Aurora, haven't you maimed your child enough?" Aunt Natalya drawls, glaring at my mother.

My mother's cheeks flush red under her ichor, but she only glowers back. My father pretends not to notice the tiff, lifting a gold pocket watch from his coat and inspecting the time.

"If you'll excuse me," my mother growls. "We have guests to entertain." She spins on her heels, storming inside.

House Dysis and House Noctis have yet to arrive. If they don't, it will signal their preference for war.

"Your mother is right." Father snaps his watch closed, prying his gaze from the empty, star-speckled skies. "We have guests."

Servants flee to and fro, balancing trays of petite appetizers, fruit, cheese, wine, and champagne flutes. Our families mingle, polite conversation floating about the room over the violins.

A soft hand clasps the middle of my back and I'm brought face to face with Jocelyn. Golden floral patterns and vines race up her wrists to her shoulders, petals curling in near her collarbones. She worries her bottom lip between her teeth, glancing at the main entrance. "You ready for this?"

I snatch a glass of champagne off a server's tray and bring it to my lips with a shake of my head. "Not even a little."

Ronan leans against the bar to the left of the room with one of his brothers, drinking in the sight of other noble girls in attendance. I roll my eyes, but then my gaze catches on the condensation rolling off my flute and I frown. *How much water goes into making this?*

Jocelyn bites her lip, checking the open archway of the front entrance every few seconds. At least I know my target is already here. The dread of meeting Valen must feel unbearable.

"Are you okay?"

"No, I'm going to throw up."

"Aim for his shoes," I snicker. "He'll never agree to marriage then."

"Ugh." She shudders, taking another sip like her life depends on it.

I hear wingbeats before the roars.

Tremors rock through the floor of the summer house as dragons land outside. Like sandwraiths in the night, House Dysis prowls straight into the gathering. At the front of the show, Soren and Delphine stand bedecked in jade and gold with their children at their sides. Valen catches my gaze and smirks, the movement tugging on the burn scar climbing up his jaw. Conversation hushes as they enter, though they pay it no mind as they stroll toward my parents.

As our family moves from all angles of the room to join Mother and Father, I catch Jocelyn freezing in place. I've never viewed Jocelyn as meek, but at this moment, it appears as if the room could swallow her whole and she would welcome it with tears. With a shake of her head, she downs the last of her drink and abandons the glass on a passing servant's tray. I follow as we take our rightful places.

"Soren," my father addresses the Dysis Head of House. "I welcome your family to our Conclave."

Soren's eyes scan the faces of our family one by one, examining his hosts. He's graying at the sides of his head, much like my father, but the similarities end there. Where my Father commands order and respect like a warlord entering a room, Soren exudes a bored arrogance, like a cat waiting to be entertained. The corner of his lips curves in a feline smile as he offers my father his hand.

I release a breath as their hands shake and it seems I'm not the only one relieved. Conversation begins to flutter about the room once more, the tension momentarily forgotten. Although the feeling is not mutual to my family. Each person around me wears a set of rigid shoulders, their mouths clamped shut as my father carries pleasantries with the House that attacked us a mere week ago.

An incessant weight prickles from the corner of my eye while each of us is formally introduced. I look up to find Valen watching me, ignoring the fact that everyone can see him leering.

Ash steps in front of me, cutting off Valen's stare as he moves forward to shake hands with Soren.

"You fight well," Soren states, seeming to measure the sight of my brother. "Were it not for your dragon, Astaroth might have been in better condition to fly today."

"A pity," Ash replies without the slightest hint of remorse.

A shriek echoes from outside as new dragons land. Even the Dysis family twists their heads, glowering at the last guests of the evening. Footfalls echo up the steps from the veranda as we wait in painful anticipation.

Warmth flares from the mark.

Electricity races up my arm, shooting through my blood. I suck in a breath, my heart racing as I jerk my head to the door. I clamp a hand over the glove hiding the mark, attempting to crush the surge of energy radiating through me. My eyes dart around the room, searching the faces of our guests. I don't know how I know it, but every cell within me screams that we're no longer safe. I didn't understand it before, but I do now. There's a living chain of magic stretching between spaces and binding us to each other. Somehow... I can sense *his* presence.

Damon Valour is here.

I open my mouth, only to be met with a shock of pain burning up my throat. I clutch a hand to my neck, choking on my words, but no one in my family even notices. They're too busy staring at the guests stepping into the light.

I've never seen Eren Noctis up close, only from afar in the midst of battle, but when his towering figure darkens our threshold, voices fall silent. The men in the room stand straighter, jaws locked and shoulders back as if bracing for impact. Every woman seems to preen for his attention, mothers quickly moving to present their eligible daughters as he steps into the torchlight.

But he doesn't so much as look at them, doesn't so much as glance in their direction. He runs a hand through his obsidian hair as an older woman, who I assume is his widowed mother, flanks his right and his infamous sisters at his left. I can still hear their cackling laughter as their dragons scorched the skies. Now his family stands in our doorway in black and silver brocade, commanding the full attention of the Conclave. It isn't until he raises the sharp cut of his jaw that I freeze in place.

Eyes the color of desert sage sweep the room and land on me. Eren Noctis stares, soaking me in like the last bit of sunlight left in the world. He flashes a devilish smile as my world shatters around me.

And winks.

# CHAPTER 10

*S*oren Dysis offers a sharp smile. "If you'll excuse us."

Father's eyes flicker briefly to Soren, giving him a curt nod before they're locked on the new predators of the room. My hand twitches to the small gun strapped to the thigh holster under my dress. Damon Valour has infiltrated our Conclave, and no one knows it but me.

The energy from the tattoo pulses in waves, stronger now more than ever. It tugs me from within like a living magnet, pulling me to Damon as he approaches. Adrenaline locks me in place, squeezing like a vice. I'm torn between shooting him where he stands or yelling for everyone to run, but even as I think about it the burning in my throat remerges. A living reminder that I can do nothing–*say* nothing to expose him. If I shoot him now, everyone will think I've shot a Dragon Lord. They'll think I killed Eren Noctis, not the leader of the rebellion we've gathered here to fight. I will bring war upon my House and my own head on a pike.

Eren joins hands with my father.

"Welcome to our Conclave," my father's voice is nothing more than a dull echo in my ears.

Each breath I take is more difficult than the last, my lungs seizing with the rapid beat of my heart. *Do something!*

Eren's four sisters stand behind him, chins high and heads tilted as they devour the exchange between their brother and my father. Kamari is the tallest sister, her eyes a few shades darker than Eren's. A sparkling black dress shimmers like stardust on her body, hugging her hips tight and wrapping up her waist to criss-cross over her breasts. A belt of silver scales clatters together over the waistline, dropping delicate chains of teardrop diamonds.

Her cruel laughter bounces off the walls of my memory.

Blythe, Soraya, and Neith are the other sisters, but I can't stop myself from planning their brother's imminent demise to give them much thought.

My father flags over a servant carrying a tray of drinks. Each member of the Noctis family accepts the offer, breaking off to mingle in the crowd. I don't lose sight of Eren as he departs without so much as acknowledging me, tracking him as he engages with Soren and his wife. A chill shudders down my spine.

*A dangerous combination.* I can't help but wonder if it's intentional. My gaze bounces between the two families. Who else knows his secret? *Is Soren in on it? An ally, perhaps?* And then there's the matter of his own blood. *Do they know? Are the whole lot of them traitors?*

"Hey, are you alright?" Jocelyn appears at my side. "You look like you've seen a wraith."

I swallow hard. "I think I have."

Jocelyn must follow my field of vision. "Oh… right. I'm sorry, Sage. It must bring back a lot of memories."

"Something like that."

Lux cuts into my line of sight, a glass of wine in her hand. Adorned in the signature colors of House Galvan, my sister is stunning in her gown. The bodice shines with black scales sewn in a pattern to create whorls of fire. Below her hips, the fabric fades to a cascade of red and gold licking up the length of her dress.

"What are you guys doing?" She hisses. "Go find your assignments. Fathers' watching."

She's not lying.

Over her shoulder in the far center of the room, Father glances in our direction.

Jocelyn swipes Lux's wine. "Fine, but don't expect me to do it sober." She downs the last of the drink and shoves it back into Lux's stiff hand. With a flick of her hair, Jocelyn strides toward Valen. I suck in a deep breath, ignoring Lux's shocked face as I make my way to the bar, each step further from the pull I feel in the opposite direction.

*Focus. You have a job to do. Get him alone later and maybe...*

Ronan is right where I last saw him, resuming conversation like the rest of the room has deigned. Holding my nerve, I slip into the open stool on the other side of him.

"I'll take a gin," I say to the barkeep.

Ronan turns, a spark of curiosity lighting up his face.

"Sage Galvan." I offer my hand.

He flashes a dimple, grasping my hand in his and bringing it to his lips. "Ronan Tesar. A pleasure to meet you."

"Seems manners aren't lost on you," I smirk, taking hold of the glass the barkeep sets on the counter.

He laughs. "What makes you say that? Have you read my file?"

*Not as dumb as he looks.* I give him a conspiratorial wink as I take a long sip.

His brows raise. "You have, haven't you?"

"I'll tell you my secrets if you share a few of yours."

Ronan's boyish grin stretches the length of his face. He checks over his shoulder for any sets of watchful eyes and faces me. "I'm supposed to charm one of the Dysis sisters."

"Ooh, ambitious." Warmth flutters through me as the gin settles, easing the thrum of the tattoo. "Why aren't you over there wooing her then?"

He takes a drink, his tongue lapping the excess on his lips as he watches me. "I found better company."

A laugh bubbles to the surface, convincing enough that I almost believe it.

Ronan leans forward, bringing with him a rush of creosote and charcoal. "How about we ditch this party?"

I finish my drink, about to conjure a flirtatious response when someone slips into the space behind me, radiating a familiar heat into my back.

Ronan's face drops.

"Leave." Sharp as a blade, the command slices through the shock of his presence.

I see Ronan's eyes widen, helpless as he chokes on the breath in his throat and stumbles off his seat. For a second, I don't breathe, but the energy of the mark flares stronger than ever, encouraging me to turn. I come face to face with Eren Noctis and the ruthless delight shining in his eyes.

"Two snapdragons for me and the Lady."

Heat rushes to my cheeks and my fists ball, the ache of my wounds long forgotten. Our drinks knock against the polished wood of the bar, flames guttering around the rim of the two whiskies.

"Hello, Killer."

It's jarring to have a face to put to his voice. A rich tan covers the expanse of his skin and the wisps of dark locks I'd seen peeking through the cover of his mask now slink over his ears to curl near his face. With leather armor swapped for a suit, I can make out the hardness of his body. Every curve is cut sharp and each muscle is honed like a weapon. His full lips pull into a smirk when he notices what I'm doing. Unencumbered confidence oozes from him as he leans against the bar like he doesn't have a care in the world.

I don't know whether to hit him or vomit.

"Drink with me." He nudges one of the glasses closer with scarred knuckles, a signet ring for House Noctis glaring in the light.

I pry my gaze from the silver dragon on the black shield of the ring. "Are you out of your mind?"

"Quite the opposite. To anyone watching I'm the ruler of a powerful House who's just ordered my enemy's daughter a drink. Nothing surprising for a Conclave."

My voice falls to a whisper. "And when they're not watching?"

"Our little secret."

I want to scream, but my options are severely limited. I breathe, taking a moment to think. I might not be able to warn anyone, but I can play along with this little ruse of his. Maybe I can get some answers while I'm at it, like what the hell he plans to do tonight.

"What are you doing here?"

"I was invited."

I glance at the barkeep who's attending guests on the other end of the bar. No one is within earshot. If I'm smart, I can talk my way into leading him somewhere quiet.

*But what then?*

"I'll tell you what, Killer. I'll answer a question for every sip." He taps his finger on the rim of my glass. "Finish your drink and we'll talk somewhere private."

The flames around the rim disappear, leaving behind a simple whiskey that sits there mocking me. Perhaps it's the false courage of the gin pooling in my gut, flushing my chest, but I don't spare a second thought as I grab the glass and throw my head back. I slam it on the bar as I choke down the amber liquid. The sting of it clogs my nose, sears my throat, and forces me to cough twice before it clears enough for me to get control of myself. I stare back at Eren, daring him to challenge me.

He takes his time, raking over me with an appreciative gaze. "Good girl."

Eren tosses his drink back and leans straight into my personal space. An intoxicating haze of cypress and crisp amber stuns my senses.

I'm dizzy with his scent as he whispers in my ear. "You're going to take a walk around the room and check in with your family. When you've done your rounds, meet me on the third-level balcony."

No sooner than the words leave his mouth, he's gone. His back becomes a retreating shadow fading into the gathering. I rise from the stool, tripping over my feet in the process, and grip the edge of the bar like a lifeline. I take a stroll about the room, trying my best not to teeter in the heels I'm wearing.

Jocelyn flirts with Valen, who's leaning with his back against the wall. If his pinched expression is anything to go by, I don't think either of them will have much to remember in the morning. In the back of the room, I spot Ash dancing with Kamari, his most brilliant smile on display for her as they sway. A few other potential couples join in as the musicians strain their violins, but I don't care to watch. My sight lands on Lux, her back to me while she speaks to Eren near the far left wall. He tilts his head, the twitch of a smile on his lips.

A twinge of anger flares in my chest. My sister has no idea what she's getting herself into and Eren's smug, self-assured face appears so very punchable from this distance. But as I peel back my stare to scan the figures next to them, I find someone much more interesting. Syrinthia Noctis, Eren's mother, observes the couple with serpentine eyes.

Champagne rests in her hand, half-full, and more than likely a prop than a crutch to get through the evening. No, this woman doesn't need the added courage. Shoulders back and head held high, she saunters through the room like she owns it, casting a dazzling smile on all who approach her. Gray streaks through her ebony tresses, a testament to any seasoned dragonrider. Only the strong survive long enough to grow gray in their hair. Riders, unfortunately, tend to live a very short lifespan in times of war.

Without warning, her eyes flick up to meet mine. My bones stiffen. Syrinthia's mouth curves, a grin almost identical to her son's. She turns her back, content to meld into the array of guests. When I look at the spot Eren and Lux last occupied, Eren is gone and Lux is delivering a progress report to our mother.

I survey the guests, debating whether to leave now or wait. If I can waste a few more minutes talking to someone, then I can sneak away without anyone noticing.

"You have friends in high places."

I spin, finding Ronan behind me. He holds a half-empty glass, looking me over with suspicion.

"I barely know him."

He shrugs, bringing his glass to his lips. "He knew you."

I purse my lips, unsure of what to say. One thing is clear though, I can't have Ronan watch me leave the Conclave. The last thing I need is a tail when I meet with a certain rebel.

"If you'll excuse me," I dismiss myself, striding toward Aunt Natalya. My dear aunt has taken up residence near the buffet table, snacking on a quail leg.

"Ah, there's my sweet niece!" She sucks her index finger clean. "Make a big catch this evening?" She wriggles her eyebrows.

I note the flush in her cheeks and spot her husband, my Uncle Bruno, in deep discussion with my father, Uncle Deon, and Kieran Tesar near the bar. This could work in my favor.

"I don't know what you're up to, Aunt, but maybe you can be of assistance."

"Oh?" Aunt Nat lifts a brow, tossing the quail bone on an empty platter.

"Cover for me."

A slow grin spreads across the sensual curve of her mouth. "Anything for you, Little Firedrake."

I nod and pivot in the opposite direction. When I'm certain I'm not followed, I bound up the stairs to the second level of the manor. I take a few winding turns in the corridor, then climb the next set of steps that lead to the third story. Eren's looming silhouette leans against the wall near the balcony, watching a set of dragons fly overhead.

With the dizzying warmth of the alcohol fading to dim a flush, I'm able to move much faster. I reach under my skirts and rip the gun from my thigh, using my other arm to swing his shoulder and slam his back into the wall. He chuckles as I shove the gun into the flesh beneath his jaw.

"Give me one good reason why I shouldn't blow your fucking head off."

His eyes spark like a devious god. Swift as a ghost, he throws up his arm, swiping it down over mine to break my hold. Before I can react, his foot hooks my ankle, throwing my balance as he swings us around, pushing me into the same wall. Rough stone bites into my cheek as his hard body presses against my back, one hand locking my arm behind me and the other pinning my neck at an awkward angle with my own gun.

"For starters," his breath sends shivers down my spine. "You're outmatched."

His weight disappears. I whirl in time to see him emptying the bullets of the revolver. They spill to the tile, clattering like wind chimes.

"Second," he slides the cylinder closed, chucking it across the floor where it scrapes to a stop near my feet. "You can't prove who I am. If anyone here discovers you've killed a noble at a

Conclave, your family can kiss any allies they had goodbye. All four Houses will declare war for the betrayal."

"You have the nerve to talk to *me* about betrayal? You've betrayed all of us!"

He smirks, tucking his hands in his pockets as he takes a step toward me. He stalks forward until his proximity forces me back into the wall of my own volition. Cypress and amber invade my senses once more.

He lowers his voice, audible only for me to hear it. "Third, you owe me a life debt. Consider this me coming to collect."

My last thread of self-control snaps as I tug the dagger free from the opposite thigh.

Eren has my wrist pinned in a second flat, a hand around my throat, and not a perfect hair out of place. Amusement glitters in his eyes as he tsks. "What is it with you and sharp objects?"

"*I hate you*," I seethe, trying to wrench my hand free even though we both understand there's no use. "This is all your fault! All of it!"

His amusement gutters out like the stars. I see him trade the Dragon Lord for the rebel. One mask for another.

"How can you do it?" I growl. "You're not just a Rider. You're one of *us*. You're a Dragon Lord trading power for anarchy."

*If I had half the power he has, I'd never be weak again.*

Eren's gaze darkens. "This power tastes like ashes." He takes my dagger as he releases me, quick to part as if my skin's burned him. "Did you learn nothing? Have you already forgotten everything you saw?"

I think of the broken faces of refugees still haunting me. "I can never forget."

"Neither can I."

I glower at him, willing fire to spring at his feet, or another blade to materialize and let me finish what I started.

He shakes his head, adjusting the cufflinks at his wrist. "You're all so wasteful. Nearly a thousand years after the

Conquest and Riders are still the same. Each House wants more power and they don't care what it takes to get it. It's why this Conclave is nothing more than a farce. The Houses may join together to eliminate the threat I pose, but make no mistake. You'll turn on each other the moment it's convenient to do so." He takes another step, shadows falling over the harsh lines of his face. "I will never be one of you, because I despise everything you stand for."

"We stand for *order*," my voice trembles, fighting against the faces of our casualties, but the words taste bitter as I dig my heels in. "Without us, there's no control–"

"Control of what, exactly? The fields burning beneath your dragons? The villages swallowed by ash as the sky turns black? The water your family hoards while people die of thirst in the streets? That's what you call *order?*"

I clamp my mouth shut, biting so hard that a metallic taste blooms over my tongue.

He huffs a humorless sound. A hollow victory. "I didn't think so."

"Like you're so perfect," I snarl. "It must be nice to judge the rest of us while you sit from Esmeray's throne."

Eren closes the distance, backing me into the wall. I clench my jaw, glaring into his eyes. He smirks at my rage, lifting my chin. He brushes his knuckles over my jaw and down my shoulder, sending a shockwave of goosebumps along my skin. "I wouldn't point fingers, Killer." The tip of his finger traces over the patterns of ichor on my inner arm and I shiver. He pauses at the top of my glove concealing the tattoo. "Not if you want this mark off your skin."

My heart skips a beat, eyes widening. "What?"

"You heard me." He pushes off the wall, walking back to the edge of the balcony. "I'd like to offer you a deal."

Blood rushes in my ears. *It's a trick.* "A deal?"

"I'll have Oddica remove the mark on one condition."

"Which is?"

He turns around with a half-mad grin. "Help me help *you.*"

My eyes narrow. "I don't know what you mean."

"I think you were moved by what you saw," he says, inching toward me. "I think you're lost in your world, questioning things you never thought about. But who do you ask? Your family? No, of course not. They'd think you're a sympathizer. The truth is they've hidden the real world from you. They want you to be a pawn in their game, another piece to move for their own benefit. How long do you intend to let it happen? Don't you want… more?"

*Yes.*

I crush the thought like an insect. "Just tell me what you want."

His hand comes to brush a loose curl behind my ear. I force myself to keep breathing, not to shudder in disgust. "I want you to use that pretty little mind of yours to find me information."

Time slows to a crawl.

The realization stabs me like a knife. "That's why you let me go. You want a spy."

He grins. "Guilty as charged."

"Screw you." I lunge to my left, desperate to leave when his arm cuts off my path, locking me in place.

He uses the leverage of the wall to lean closer. "I'm not asking you to help me destroy your family. Tell me what they know about the other Houses. Trade routes, meetings, business deals, battle reports. Anything House Galvan knows, I want to know. I'll even show you all of the things your family doesn't want you to see."

For a moment I stand there, considering it, teetering on the precipice of change. *'It'd be a shame to watch you go quietly.'* Aunt Natalya's voice echoes. I think about the times I've felt helpless—each time I've submitted without question, playing the dutiful daughter. Flashes of my bloody, broken hands rise to the surface.

*Where has that ever gotten you?*

"Think about the leverage you'll gain, Killer," Eren purrs, smooth as silk. "Each House has secrets and secrets are power. It's up to you to decide what to do with it."

*'If I were you, I'd find a way to make myself indispensable.'*

"What do you say?" He offers his hand.

I don't know if it's Fate or something greater beckoning me, something I dare not reach for in my twenty-two years of living.

Ambition.

"Nothing about my family?"

"Only the others," he confirms.

I grasp his hand and squeeze. "Then you have a deal."

He doesn't bother to hide his smug face as he detaches from my hand and turns.

"Eren," I say, halting his retreating figure.

He's halfway across the balcony when he looks.

"You came here on a different dragon"

He considers for a moment. "Cantorix. He was my father's."

"And the Nightstalker?"

A smile flickers on his mouth. He lifts a finger to his lips. "Our little secret."

I stare, trying not to stand there gaping. It's not unheard of for a Rider to bond with two dragons, especially during war. There are times when a dragon will survive a battle, but their Rider will not. If the dragon is left unclaimed, a Rider might attempt to bond a second one to ride if their own falls injured, but it's a strategy that walks the line of madness.

It's reckless. Double the opportunity to get yourself killed, but Riders can never leave well enough alone. Anyone bold enough to bond two dragons is either desperate or dangerous.

Eren doesn't strike me as desperate.

I watch him descend the staircase until I'm alone on the balcony, left with a storm of memories sweeping me away.

*"DAHLIA! THEY HAVE JASPER!" I yell over the windcurrent as Kamari Noctis soars on her frost-scaled dragon, Jas unconscious in her lap. The three other Noctis sisters cackle above the clouds, their dragonfire severing the path between us and Kamari.*

*"Jas!" Jocelyn screams, Xantha twirling into a barrel roll to slice through the fiery blockade. She makes it past the fire, but one of the sisters gives chase.*

*Dahlia and I are left with the remaining sibling whose dragon makes a lunge for us. We break apart, narrowly missing a snap of jaws that could swallow both of our bodies whole.*

*Heartfyre roars from above, locked in a struggle with a white and red-scaled monstrosity that's a horrifying match for size. The dragon is far older than Heartfyre, thick-bodied with sharp horns and claws larger than Halcyon's head. It belongs to none other than the Heir of House Noctis, Kamari's brother—Eren.*

*I can't bring myself to look up and search for my brother. One false move—one second of hesitation might mean the difference of leaving the sky alive or hurtling toward my fiery death. I set my jaw, clamping my teeth fierce enough that I taste blood. The metallic tang pierces through the dread, reminding me I'm still alive and if my heart continues to beat, I can make a difference in how this ends.*

*"Come on, we have to help Jocelyn!" I shout, sending the command in a series of images to Halcyon. Planning with my girl is second nature. There's not a move I make that she doesn't see coming. Our bond means our minds are one. Always together. Never apart.*

*"We'll never catch up!" Dahlia races beside me. "If Tanith is lost then so are we. We can't afford to lose another dragon!"*

"Tanith's alive!" I insist. I never saw Jasper's dragon fall. Until I see a body, no one in our House is dead–cold-blooded or otherwise. "But Jocelyn won't be if we don't help!"

Dahlia's face twists, but she doesn't argue. Through a mist of clouds we swoop into the throes of battle, dodging spouts of dragonfire between our House and theirs. Rune zips above on Kallix, disappearing through whorls of smoke in the air. Beneath us, dragon scales glare like golden daggers off the sun. Jocelyn's dragon looms above Kamari, hidden by a thin layer of cloudmist. My cousin rises in her saddle, gun in hand and dives into the air below.

A screech from the left steals our attention, leaving us with only seconds to spot the incoming collision with an orange dragon. Halcyon snarls, spewing a torrent of fire. Khione joins her, unleashing a blast of her own lavender flames.

"Distract her!" I bank a hard right, flying to assist Jocelyn.

Dahlia remains behind, unsheathing her gun when Khione's flames die. I hear three shots pierce the air, but keep my gaze forward. Dahlia can hold her own out here.

Jocelyn throws a sweeping kick from the top of Kamari's dragon. Xantha follows close, sinking lower, but unable to help her rider. Jasper lays on his side, out cold on the saddle. If House Noctis takes him hostage, we'll never get him back. If Kamari's dragon banks, then both of my cousins will be dead. I glance over my shoulder.

Khione and the orange dragon have locked claws, battling for dominance. Jaws snap, furious shrieks fill the air, but when I find Jocelyn again, she lies crumpled on her back with Kamari's hands around her throat. Xantha roars.

Halcyon surges forward, reading the thoughts in my head before I have enough sense to question them. I'm already rising, flinging myself off the saddle once I'm close enough to jump.

I tackle Kamari from the side, sending us tumbling until I manage to straddle her. She gasps, but I don't give her enough time to recover. I reel my fist back, throwing a punch that meets its mark. She quickly dodges the next one, kicking me in the gut as Jocelyn sucks in lungfuls *of air behind me, clutching her neck and wheezing. Red hand prints encircle the base of her throat.*

*Kamari dives for Jasper, but I grab a fistful of her hair and swing her around, using my free hand to smack the butt of my gun against her temple. Kamari flops back on the saddle, limp and out cold.*

*Jocelyn reaches for her brother, pulling him up from under his arms. She looks back, eyes wide as she drags Jasper over the edge of the saddle. I give her a nod, grinning in the chaos around us. A broken laugh escapes her lips before she jumps with Jasper in her arms. I sprint to the edge of the saddle, right on time to witness Xantha catch the two. I exhale, laughing quietly to myself as I turn back around.*

*Dahlia doesn't see the red and white beast.*

*Eren's dragon locks its jaws around Khione's throat, tearing her off of his sister's. Khione unleashes an ear-splitting wail. The dragon jerks its neck back, ripping a chuck of flesh from Khione's neck. Dahlia screams echo with Khione's.*

*I dive off Kamari's dragon, landing clean on Halcyon's saddle. Halcyon beats her wings forward, wailing with Khione as we're forced to bear witness to teeth and claws shredding her wings like paper. The dragon's teeth stab into Khione's neck, over and over, shaking it back and forth until Khione goes limp. Only then does he release her, allowing the body to plummet.*

*Dahlia flies off the back of Khione, helpless as her dragon hurtles from the clouds. Halcyon tucks in her wings and dives. In a stroke of pure luck, her claws manage to lock around a screaming Dahlia. We jerk back, putting distance between ourselves and the ground as Khione screeches, wings eviscerated, her coppery blood flying up, splattering my wind-goggles as she falls... falls... falls–*

I BLINK. Laughter and music ring out as I resurface from the haze of bitter truths I thought I locked in the deepest vault of my mind. I don't remember returning to the Conclave or venturing into the mass of people around me. I turn, placing both hands on the buffet table as I focus on short, measured breaths. Temples pounding, I peer through the moving bodies.

Eren stands next to my father, too far for me to hear their conversation. I steal a glass of champagne from the table and press it to the side of my cheek as I make my way over. A couple of girls giggle near a pillar by Eren, stealing glances at him. I stop at a reasonable distance, sipping my drink as I blend in and listen.

"I think your father would have been proud," Cyrus tells him.

"Thank you. I believe he would too."

"You've done excellent work following in his footsteps. Which brings me to a topic I've considered for some time."

Eren cocks his head.

"I would like you to consider unifying our Houses." My father points with a whiskey in hand. "My eldest daughter, Luxana, is of marrying age. She would make a fine wife. My son, Ashton, seems to have gotten on well with your sister."

"Ah," Eren muses, spying Kamari arching a brow at Ash where they sit. "So it would seem."

"We are the two most powerful Houses. Why should we continue to battle each other when we can stand united and be stronger for it?"

Eren smirks. "I'm afraid that's where you're wrong."

I swear my blood freezes as my father stills.

Eren's gaze hardens. "House Noctis is the most powerful House. I made sure of that when I killed your dragon."

My father's face darkens. "You'd best watch your words, *boy*, or your next breath may be your last."

Eren chuckles to himself. "My apologies. I don't mean to

insult your House. Your daughter is quite lovely, but she's no Rider." His voice drops to a menacing growl. "Now call your son before I wrench him by the neck away from my sister."

I choke on my champagne.

"Ashton," Father barks, locked in a vicious staring contest with Eren.

Ash leaps from his seat, a shade paler from our father's tone. He joins the two of them, standing at Father's side.

Eren's smile is positively feline. "That's better. I don't take kindly to suitors I didn't approve of. Surely as Head of your House, you can understand? I'll tell you what, Cyrus. I'm not unreasonable. I will sanction a marriage between my sister and your son. On one condition."

"Which is?" Comes my father's terse reply.

Eren's eyes snap to me. "I want *her*."

Ash and Father follow Eren's gaze to where I'm standing as the glass slips from my hand, shattering on the floor. The music cuts as the five noble families of the Celosia desert turn to gawk at the commotion.

*Oh, fuck.*

# CHAPTER 11

$\mathcal{E}$very member of the nobility watches on in morbid fascination. My Father's face has gone blank. Ash is speechless, gaze bouncing from the two men. If I dare to take my eyes off them I'm more than certain I'll find equal expressions of shock and horror amongst my family. The only person who appears pleased is Eren, who tilts his glass to me in acknowledgment.

"Perhaps we should discuss–"

"There's nothing more to discuss," Eren shuts down my father. "I'll have *her* or no one. And you'll have none of my sisters. House Noctis can stand on its own. I hope House Galvan can do the same."

Under the scrutiny of the nobility, bound by the rules of the Conclave, my Father cannot strike a killing blow for the insolence, nor can he withdraw his proposal without appearing weak.

"I shall take your terms under consideration," he responds, his tone clipped.

Eren extends a predator's smile. "Don't consider it too long."

*"Clean this up,"* I hear my mother hiss.

A servant scrambles to gather the broken glass. Another one runs forth with a broom, sweeping the mess. Glass scrapes along the tile as my father calls for music. The musicians resume their song and quiet murmurs fill the space. As eyes begin to fall away, heels march in my direction. Unbridled wrath fills my mother's stare, although, on the planes of her face, she presents the essence of calm.

"Drawing room. *Now,*" she spits as she advances past me.

Father leans in, whispering something to Ash that causes my brother to follow. He hooks his arm with Lux's, pulling her with him as they trail the path our Mother has set for us. She slides the thick wooden doors shut when the four of us are inside and spins. She doesn't get a word out before Lux is in front of me.

"*What have you done?*"

I gape at her. "Nothing!"

"You did something, Sage," Ash accuses, his arms crossed. "When the hell did Noctis decide he wanted you as his wife?"

"How should I know?" I snap with the same intensity, a feat that makes them blink. "You know that I hate him!"

"Then why would he choose *you?*" Lux demands, a sharp edge lingering in her voice.

The words don't sit right with me. They agitate my nerves, lacerating old wounds, and dredging up feelings I thought I locked away.

"What do you mean, Lux?" I utter. "Am I not good enough for the Head of a powerful House?"

Lux flinches. "That's not what I meant."

"Then what did you mean?" I insist, stepping closer, daring her to shrink back. "He said it himself, you're no Rider. Is it such a surprise I did what you could not?"

Lux's hand flies out, colliding with my cheek. She inhales a sharp breath, the same hand covering her mouth in horror. My cheek vibrates with the string. A numbness spreads over me, decaying the last shreds of doubt in my mind.

I laugh through my nose. "Funny. I expected that from *her*." I glance pointedly at our mother, then back to my sister. "Guess you're not so different."

Tears well in Lux's eyes. She shakes her head. "No, Sage," she sobs. "I'm not a *dragonrider*. Securing a good match is the only thing I've been trained for. A good match is the best hope I have for my future. Your engagement with Eren jeopardizes that."

"It jeopardizes our whole family," our mother clips. "You're to refuse his proposal. *Immediately*."

"And if I don't?" I challenge, blood hot in my veins—a fire I've never encountered. It's a flame possessing me, urging me to burn the whole damn world.

She pauses, looking me up and down in a fruitless attempt to find what's changed.

"You're right, Lux." I nod, ignoring our mother's scrutiny. "You're not a Rider. You're the first-born daughter. I get it." I stop at her shoulder, folding my arms behind my back, and lean in to whisper without an ounce of sympathy. *"Pick a different role."*

I throw open the doors of the drawing room.

In the hall, Aunt Natalya leans near the threshold with a smile. "Well done. I was wondering when you'd show your teeth."

I shake my head, blowing past her to the Conclave. Eren is the first to notice me, his jaw clenching when his eyes catch the side of my face that still stings.

A glass clinks three times from above.

On the balcony overlooking the first floor, my father stands with his hand on the rail. His signet ring for House Galvan gleams off his knuckles, the two-headed dragon glowing under the light of the chandelier.

My father lifts his drink. "I'd like to make a toast to each of the noble families for attending this Conclave, a feat that has not been seen for nearly fifty years. With all five Houses in attendance, we have unanimously chosen *peace*."

Begrudging words flutter between guests, but my father moves on. The cadence of his voice drops to an unforgiving echo. It bounces off the walls and tiles, reverberating through the manor and into the night where words and vows are carried on the wind amongst the sands.

"The time has come for us to unite against a common foe. An enemy who *threatens* our very way of life. Survival depends on our unification not as *people*, not as *Riders*, but as *Sovereigns*. We will protect our dynasties for centuries more to come, but only if we band together. This rebellion must be crushed by any means necessary and it starts here."

Cheers and whistles break out with the applause that follows. I watch Eren's face as he claps beside his family. With the slight smirk he wears, he seems like any other noble stirred by my father's speech.

But I know better, and so does he.

"As our evening draws to a close, I hope we will stand united at tomorrow's conference where we will vote on our next course of action." Father raises his glass. "May Vulcan guide us in the dark."

The guests murmur the same sentiment, breaking off with their families to flood the stairs to the upper levels where their accommodations wait. Cyrus Galvan observes the departing families, taking stock one last time. I don't move from the spot I stand in, watching my father until his gaze flickers to me. He regards me with a look I have not seen before. It disappears in a matter of seconds, a flame stomped out before it catches fire to the world around it.

It looks a little like... apprehension.

My father turns his back, leaving the balcony behind. A smile creeps onto my lips as I blend into the throng of guests walking up the stairs. I will not pay a price for the events of this evening.

But my family will.

THE TRUE CONCLAVE begins in the morning.

At the crack of dawn, the Houses gather in the conference room in the left wing of the manor. Like a grand theater, rows of seats wind around the front of a stage, rising higher with each level. On the stage, a table stretches out, the dark wood polished and warped by time. Elaborate, cushioned chairs are set out for the Heads of House, along with bejeweled flagons of water and wine.

Eren lays claim to the chair on one end of the table, my father on the other. Two opposing forces locked in a collision course. Ash is given a seat to Father's right, a parchment and pen in hand. Any brotherly love is wiped clean from his face, replaced with an emotionless mask that mimics our father more than ever.

Lux hasn't looked at me once, but I don't miss the way her shoulders tense when I'm near. I don't know if she's doing it out of shame or anger, but I'm not sure I care. I know I'm done apologizing. Done playing the role I've been given. I'm going to forge a new path for myself, even if I have to carve it out with my teeth. It starts here, at the Conclave, as the last stragglers find their seats.

My father clears his throat, surveying the final tally of guests present. "Let us begin."

No grand introductions are exchanged and no preamble is offered. The time for pleasantries has ended.

"We must acknowledge the figurehead of this rebellion—a

Rider by the name of Damon Valour," his voice booms like a thunderclap.

A chorus of unease gushes in the crowd of the gathered Houses. Eren's face is the first one I look at. He waits for more information, his expression neutral. Unshaken. I don't think he's alone in concealing his true agenda. At least two other Dragon Lords watch my father with the same dead eyes.

"What breed is the dragon?" Soren inquires, fingers folded together under his chin.

Father's eyes sweep the room. "A Nightstalker."

Sharp whispers erupt through the Houses. Whether or not their families knew this detail, it becomes clear that a few did not.

"That's impossible," Eren utters, his gaze darkening. "They've been extinct for three hundred years."

His feigned disbelief is executed so perfectly that my father levels him with a glare. "Do you take my children for liars?"

Eren's lips twitch.

"Our intelligence has gathered the same," Kieran Tesar admits. "The claim is true."

"The last known Nightstalker perished without progeny. How is it possible?" Soren sneers.

Idalia shakes her head. "I think the more important question is what we intend to do about it."

Eren leans back with a flippant wave of his hand. "House Noctis will implement a bounty in Esmeray. I suggest the rest of you do the same for your territories. That ought to weed him out."

A few of the Dragon Lords grunt their approval.

I can't help but marvel at how pure his intentions seem, how none of the other Houses suspect that anything is amiss. Eren is nothing if not clever, a viper lying in wait.

"We should focus on weeding out the *traitor*," Soren argues. "The Nightstalker came from somewhere–hatched by *someone*."

Yes, Ash's original suspicion is correct, and the other Houses have connected the dots too.

"Cut off the head and the body will follow," my Father's voice rumbles. "We can sit here pointing fingers for hours and it will be to our own folly. We know full well what one another is capable of. What we don't know are the lengths Valour is willing to go *armed* with a dragon."

A distinct murmur passes along the lips of those seated at the table.

"If and when a traitor is found, we will deal with them accordingly," my father proclaims. "Until then, we should give our full focus to hunting this renegade down. Mobilize our ground forces, impose curfews, and post bounties. I propose monthly Conclaves to maintain our progress."

There's a reason House Galvan stands as one of the strongest Houses. It isn't from riches or dragons alone. Uncle Deon's words reverberate in my skull. *'My dear brother, always playing the long game.'* It makes my stomach churn.

I play back Eren's insolence with my father and the barely-leashed rage in his eyes. Control and patience are my father's specialty, but to what end? Do we truly need House Noctis that badly? Or does Father know something I don't?

The Heads of House begin to name strategies, put forward ideas, and debate their faults. I watch Eren soaking in their plans, contributing thoughts and proposals of his own with the same ease he used to order me a drink from the bar.

It's infuriating to witness.

Ash scribbles the key points of their tentative alliance, jotting down ordinances they agree on. When the Conclave breaks, a peace treaty is signed by the five Heads, declaring their commitment to squash the rebellion.

I don't waste time sneaking off in the throng of withdrawing guests.

Eren's long, deliberate strides carry him out to the foyer

with his family, forcing me to walk faster if I have any hope of keeping up. His mother takes his arm, bringing them to a stop near the center of the room. I hold back, tempted to hide, but Eren turns his head, spotting me near the pillar by the conference hall exit. He whispers in his mother's ear, glancing at me as he makes a subtle jerk of his chin.

Syrinthia's four daughters frown in my direction, gazes filled with warning. Their mother studies me, tilting her head like I'm a puzzle she hasn't quite solved. With a shrug, she pivots on her heels, her daughters following her to the door.

I shoot after Eren, racing up the stairs to the third-floor balcony. He waits near the wall he pressed me into last night. The bite of the stones against my cheek rings fresh in my memory. It's honestly a miracle there isn't a bruise after the beating it's taken.

I charge over to him. "What the hell do you think you're doing? Rejecting my sister and asking for my hand?"

He chuckles and I hate the way the sound makes my heart race. "I figured it'd be much easier for us to meet if there's a reason for it. Sneaking around only gets you so far. Being engaged allows us to hide in plain sight. Believe me, I'm an expert in that."

"I didn't ask for this! You have no idea what you've done!"

He tilts his head, his eyes tracking the right side of my face. The same side that my family seems to favor slapping. I summon every last nerve not to cover my cheek. I have nothing to hide. I will not cower. I will face him with every last scrape and bruise and fractured pieces until one of us is dead. Because that's what this is, isn't it? A means to an end? I have no intention of marrying Eren, even for the sake of our deal, because at some point we will outlive our usefulness to each other. I will be forced to pick a side and it will always be my family, for better or worse.

'Family over all.'

"My father will never agree to the engagement," I say at last.

Eren slides his hands into his pockets, unfazed by my words. "He will. He's more desperate than you think."

"Desperate?" I laugh, folding my arms. "My father isn't desperate. He's playing you. I just haven't figured out what his game is."

Eren flashes me a smile as he walks back to the staircase. "I figured as much. Until we have an answer, I'll enjoy testing him."

"You shouldn't underestimate my father. Even Cyrus Galvan has limits."

His lips curve as he saunters past me. "I appreciate the concern, but he'd do well not to underestimate *me*."

Eren makes his exit while I remain on the balcony, peeking over the edge to watch him mount his father's dragon. Sunlight gilds every inch of his body, washing his obsidian locks in a heavenly glow. His eyes find mine when he's seated, holding my stare. Cantorix roars, breaking the spell. A shudder rolls through me as the dragons of House Noctis shoot into the clouds, fading, but I'm still trapped on the ground, haunted by the price this alliance might cost.

House Galvan makes our inevitable return home.

I'm not five feet through the front doors when my father's voice thunders to the rafters. "Sage. Office. Now."

My pulse quickens, heart in my throat as I fight the urge to flee on dragonback. He shuts the door of his study once we're there, circling the chair of his desk. My father rests his hands on it, fingers digging into the leather as he sighs.

"Sit."

I'm weightless as I lower myself into the chair on the other side, the scene familiar and no less terrifying. He slides into his seat, leather creaking, and interlaces his fingers. "Sage," he says slowly. No emotion. Leveled and firm. "Did you have anything to do with Eren's decision?"

I muster all my courage. "No. He ordered me a drink at the bar. That's it."

I hope he can see it in my eyes as he burns holes through them. Eren surprised both of us, that part isn't a lie. The alliance was planned. The engagement wasn't.

Father sighs, rubbing a hand over his forehead. "It was never my intention to place such a burden on your shoulders. Luxana was raised to handle a high-level alliance, but the Noctis heir has forced us to change our strategy." He pops open the decanter on his desk, sliding a crystal glass closer. "I will approve of this engagement if you give your consent, Sage. I will not force this upon you, but you should know…" the whiskey splashes into the glass as his eyes flicker to mine. "Our family needs this."

"Why?"

He stops short, pausing right when the glass should be hitting his lips. Cyrus Galvan is not often surprised, but I don't waver. This is the first time in my life that he's needed something from me—something I can refuse. For once, I'm the one holding the cards. Hell, I can't remember a time I've ever had cards to hold.

He sets down his drink altogether. "What I tell you does not leave this room. Is that understood?"

I nod.

"I intended to betroth my heir and a daughter to House Noctis as a means of survival. If we cannot fight an enemy, we must create ties with them. Or has the Conclave taught you nothing?"

I force myself not to shrink. "They really are stronger… aren't they?"

"That depends on one's interpretation," my father drawls, swirling the whiskey. "I see you watching things, Sage. Always watching. You're a lot like me in that regard. It's how I know you understand that the balance of this House is hanging by a thread. Heirs can be overthrown. I must do everything in my power to ensure that does not happen."

I'm not sure I buy his reasoning. It sounds awfully familiar to the last conversation we had in this room, but for the moment... I'll let him think it's enough. "I consent."

Relief washes over his face as he finally tilts his glass, drinking the contents. "Be wary of Eren. I suspect he has no interest in losing a dragon with Kamari's hand. By requesting you, it became an even trade."

I don't intend to correct him.

He waves a hand. "Go get ready for dinner. I'll make the announcement."

As soon as the words leave his mouth, I'm out of the chair, but dinner proves to be a whole different battlefield.

I don't see Lux when I stop by our room to shower and change, nor do I run into anyone else in the halls. It's as if the Conclave sucked the energy from our family. Even Aunt Nat appears drained, sporting lavender bags beneath her eyes and sipping on water for a change.

Mother and Father are the last ones to arrive. When they join the table, the chefs set about bringing our appetizers. I barely touch the soup laid in front of me. Lux pretends there's no one next to her, spooning her meal like it's any other day.

Ash hasn't tried to talk to me. His nod of greeting proves I'm not invisible to him, but the fight with Lux seems to have created a rift between us three. I try not to let it bother me.

Father leans back as we wait for the main course. Uncle Deon side-eyes his brother, sensing the shift. Dahlia and Ash seem to have keyed into the change too, pausing to watch Father. A part of me wants to bask in the smugness of knowing something the others don't.

*Is this how everyone else usually feels?*

"Sage will be wed to Eren Noctis," my Father decrees. "We

will be hosting him for dinner tomorrow to discuss matters further."

It's quiet enough to hear the rustle of sand against the windows.

Lux's jaw tenses.

I take the wine beside my plate and meet the stare I sense first–Dahlia's. She's red in the face, gaping like she can't get enough air. *"Is that a joke?"*

"Dahlia," Aunt Zaria snaps, grabbing her daughter's outraged attention. I seldom hear Aunt Zaria speak and this is one of the times I'm shocked.

It does nothing to tame her. "No! *No*, she-she gets everything! The dragon, forgiveness, and a *Dragon Lord?* He killed Khione! They both did! She killed my dragon and I have to watch her get *everything!*"

"Dahlia, that's enough!" Aunt Zaria shouts.

Dahlia's fist squeezes the knife in her hand so tight her knuckles whiten. Her molten rage shines back at me through hate-filled eyes.

I don't know what possesses me to do it, but I wink.

Dahlia roars, lunging over the table with her knife raised. Dishes crash, glasses shatter, and I scramble for my dagger–a second too late for the blow that's coming.

A hand slaps around Dahlia's wrist.

Her blade is caught mid-stab, both of us staring wide-eyed at each other before turning to the owner of the hand.

Aunt Natalya stands with a mother's wrath on her face. Venom drips from her mouth in the warning she snarls. "Unless you invoke the Ignis Mortem, you will not harm your kin."

Dahlia's head swivels to her father. Uncle Deon gives a shake of his head. Dahlia spins back to me, tears welling. She sobs and drops the blade. It clatters to the table with a *thud.* Aunt Natalya releases her hand, raising her chin to stare down her nose at my mother, sitting unruffled.

Aunt Zaria helps Dahlia off the table as she cries into her mother's chest. "She gets everything! *Everything!*"

"This infighting must cease," my mother hisses, ignoring Aunt Natalya's glare. "The future of our House depends on this alliance. We *need* dragon eggs if Dahlia is to ride again. With any luck, Luxana will too."

We stew in an uncomfortable silence, save for Dahlia's sniffling. I rise from my seat, chair scraping, drawing the gazes of our family. I lift my glass, wine sloshing within as I raise it over the shards of broken porcelain.

"I'd like to make a toast to my imminent engagement. May this union bless our House." I take a long sip and place the glass back on the table.

"Now," I fold my hands and smile. "What's for dessert?"

# CHAPTER 12

*M*ost deals in the desert begin at sundown. Tonight's dinner is no exception.

Dragon wings beat like my racing heart, pounding to a crescendo as they draw near. I dare to peek out the curtains of my bedroom and find the menacing face of Cantorix in the lead of two other dragons, landing in perfect sync. Kamari, Eren's eldest sister, slides off her frost-scaled dragon. Syrinthia dismounts from a red and gold one, neither approaching the size of Eren's.

Mother and Father, along with Ash, wait in the front of the compound to greet them. I'm to remain in my room, hidden away until the ink is dry. My healed fist balls the gauzy fabric of my gown. I suck in a deep breath and exhale, willing myself to release the dress. My thumb and index finger pinch the fabric in between, rubbing it over the pad of each finger. It tethers me to the present, keeping the bitter thoughts at bay.

Lux has taken another room, leaving me with an empty space I haven't decided what to do with. In the time she's been gone, I've grown used to added silence. Strangely, it brings more comfort than her presence ever did.

Conversation falls silent as I approach the dining hall, more than a dozen sets of eyes on me. Jealousy, rage, calculation, and vengeance all glare back in the form of my family gathered around the room. Our usual seating arrangement is gone, vanished in favor of a long, rectangular table to accommodate our guests. Eren sits on the opposite end of one side, his mother seated at his right hand and Kamari at his left. His eyes rove over my face, down to the A-line of my dress where silver embroidered dragons decorate the edges dipping between my breasts.

"There's our girl of the hour," my Father beams with unfamiliar enthusiasm. He's one of the few people standing, opening his arm to present me.

I pause beside my father as Eren rises from his chair, buttoning his coat. "It will be a while before dinner, yes?"

My father nods.

"Then I believe it's time Sage and I were properly acquainted. A stroll in the gardens, perhaps? Kamari," he glances at his sister. "You are free to do the same with your betrothed."

She gives a subtle nod, rising in tandem with Ash.

Eren saunters around the table, his cat-like eyes never leaving mine as he stands before us, offering his hand. "Shall we?"

I look at my father who dips his chin in answer. My palm slips into Eren's. An unexpected heat nearly causes me to jolt. His skin is feverish to the touch and yet there's not a single drop of sweat on his brow. As I fall into step beside him, his warmth radiates against my exposed arm. In the coolness of the night, a slight breeze billowing off the canyons, he almost feels like the steam of a hot bath. I fight the urge to lean in, to bask in the seductive heat rolling off him in waves.

When we make it to the courtyard, I can't bear the silence any longer. "What happens when we're done with each other? They expect us to marry."

Eren hums in thought, taking in the soft clamor of wind chimes over the pool. "Is that so? I hadn't noticed my signature on the contract."

I move to rip my arm from his elbow, but he holds fast. "*Easy*, wouldn't want to ruin the appearance of our happy engagement."

He chuckles when I growl, reluctantly keeping my hold around his bicep. A hot flush sinks into my cheeks when I notice just how hard the muscle is, barely contained and masterfully hidden by his black clothing.

"I considered breaking the engagement," he muses, "but that would leave you disgraced in the eyes of the nobility. If you have issues with your family now, I can't imagine what the loss of your marriage prospects would do for your reputation here."

I make a choking sound, the words dying in my throat. He's right. Breaking the engagement would be the final log in my funeral pyre. I'm not sure there's enough leverage in the world to save me from my family's wrath.

"We'll prolong it as long as we can, but if they force our hands, we could live separate lives. You'll have to move to Esmeray, but you'll want for nothing. We simply won't consummate the marriage and remain free to take lovers of our own. It will be another secret of ours."

My heart takes a jilted beat at the words. *Can I do that?* Can I enter a loveless marriage to the man plotting the destruction of Riders? I think of the stricken faces of refugees. Eren isn't wrong in wanting to ease their suffering, but we both know Riders will never relent. No matter what he says, he won't be able to stop until all of us are dead, and then we'll never have a chance to change.

*I just need to figure out a better way and convince my family of it.*

Until then, marrying Eren might allow me to get close enough to kill him. What is marriage but a contract sealed by a few soft words and empty vows?

"Is it a secret your family can keep?"

His eyes shine with amusement. "Let me worry about my family. You focus on getting closer to yours. The next time we meet I expect new secrets I can use."

"And you'll show me a few of yours?" I counter.

"It would be my pleasure."

My hand slips from around his arm, only to be caught by his own. His fingers graze the bottom of my palm where they squeeze. I'm about to protest, to wrench my fingers free when Eren stills. The sudden shift in his body silences me. His face is a frozen mask as he turns over my palm to expose the scars layered through my skin, the fresher ones still red and pink.

"Who did this to you?" The words are low, teetering on the edge of a knife.

I tug my hand again and this time he lets me go.

"*Sage*," it's the first time he says my name, and there's nothing soft about the way he says it. "What happened?"

I squeeze my hands tight and lift my chin, fighting to keep my voice steady. "There are consequences for stepping out of line in this House."

"They hurt you."

I suck in a breath like he's stabbed me. I'm not bleeding, but it's as if every piece of me lies on the pavement of the courtyard, torn and strewn to places I can't follow.

"*I'm fine.*"

The murderous glint in his eyes dulls to a simmer, but Eren appears no more convinced by the lie than I am. "We should get back."

I take the arm he offers, my pulse still racing. Why should he care? We are two forces on opposing sides. Eren said it himself. *'I despise everything you stand for.'*

A malignant quiet slithers off him as we walk. His mask is back in place, leaving no telltale signs for me to read. I don't know how he does it, turning his emotions off like a switch. I try to do the same, unclenching my jaw and willing my shoulders back as if there'd been no exchange at all. Just a pleasant conversation. A new courtship between two people.

Eren accompanies me to my seat, sliding my chair in for me as I sit before he rounds the table to the spot beside his mother and the empty chair of his sister. Jocelyn's gaze is trained on me, her brow pinched. I offer her a kind, reassuring smile and follow a heavy weight in my peripheral. It leads me to a heated glare from Rune. Dahlia, however, looks anywhere but my direction, finding her wine much more interesting.

Ash and Kamari return a few minutes later, prompting the servants to deliver the first course. While the plates are set down, a chair scrapes back. Each head in our family drags to the owner of the sound.

Eren stands, his glass of whiskey in hand. "I'd like to propose a toast to my fiancée." He gives me a lopsided grin, but there's a sharpness to his stare as he levels it over each face seated before us. "Allow me to make one thing clear... Sage is *mine* now. Going forward, if any harm comes to her–if she is returned to me harmed in any way–you will feel the full wrath of my House."

I'm paralyzed, eyes wide as Eren gives a self-satisfied smirk to my family. My gaze flies to my mother, maintaining a poisonous stare with Eren. Aunt Natalya hides her grin behind her wine. Jocelyn's mouth hangs open.

Father's jaw flexes, but he reaches for his glass and lifts it. "To a happy engagement."

Our family reluctantly follows suit. Eren's mother arches a brow at her son before taking a sip. He sits, cutting into his dinner like he hasn't dropped a bomb on my family who exchanges glances around the table.

"*Well then,*" Uncle Deon breaks the silence, drumming his fingers. "When can we expect the wedding?"

"Oh, Deon," Syrinthia finally speaks, setting down her drink. "Always straight to the point. Never one to mince words."

"Is it not prudent," Deon sputters, "to solidify alliances in a time of war?"

A sharp smile twists on her mouth as her head tilts. "Come to think of it now, you never were one for poetry."

My father clears his throat, shooting a glare at his brother. "Perhaps the couples should spend some time getting acquainted."

Eren's eyes cut to my father. "I agree. Sage is welcome to visit our home each weekend. I give Kamari my blessing to visit yours if that is what she desires."

His sister's eyes slide to Ash, considering.

"Excellent." Father smiles, addressing Kamari directly. "Our home is yours."

Kamari returns the smile, murmuring her thanks.

"A toast to two beautiful couples." Aunt Natalya raises her drink, meeting my eyes with a knowing look.

Aunt Nat picks Syrinthia's brain for the rest of the evening, from her sense of style to her thoughts on other Houses' future marriage prospects. Deon, Bruno, and my father discuss recent trade negotiations while Ash tries to nudge Lux into their own conversation. My sister is more stoic than ever in Eren's presence, hardly giving Ash more than a soft smile to appease him. I've never seen her this quiet, poking at her food. Even Jocelyn notices the change in our dynamic, raising her brows at me in question. I lower my gaze, unable to answer.

She doesn't know that Lux hit me or how I became Eren's fiancé. She's probably heard the gossip of our family–how Eren innocently bought me a drink and chose me instead. I haven't even told her how Lux moved out of our room. They're all fine details I wouldn't have hesitated to share a week ago. The mark on my arm flares beneath its bandage, reminding me that everything has changed.

By some miracle, our dinner draws to a close.

I watch from the gates of the compound as Eren and his family fade into the dark. My family returns inside, and for a while I gaze at the stars alone. Soft footsteps pad through the sand. It takes longer than I expect to look away from the sky, but when I do, I find Jocelyn a few feet behind me.

She's not smiling. Her lively eyes are guarded with a distrust I know I've put there. I don't know how to tell her that everything is different, but I'm going to have to think quickly.

"Are you..." she starts, biting her lip, fidgeting with her thumbs. "Mad at me?"

My eyes grow wide. "*No.* Not at all."

"Then why haven't we talked?"

"I..." I hesitate. What do I tell her? That I've agreed to spy on our family? That I've aligned myself with a rebel? That I found Damon Valour and will soon *marry him?* It's a laughable thought with the tattoo binding me to silence. I never imagined I'd keep secrets from Jocelyn, but here we are.

"It's just-" she winces. "We haven't talked since the Conclave. I've barely seen you leave your room and I'm worried. You're set to marry Eren of all people, Lux won't speak to you, Dahlia tried to *kill* you, and suddenly my mom's your biggest fan and it feels like so much has happened, but we haven't-" She sucks in a breath and exhales, pleading with her eyes. "We haven't talked."

"I'm sorry," I say, because at least that's the truth. "It's just been a lot to process. I don't... I don't know what I'm doing."

Her stare softens. "You know I'm here for you. Always."

I nod, fighting not to cry, but I can feel the sting in my eyes. "I know."

Jocelyn's lips twist in a half-smile. "So... what's he like?"

I laugh, blinking away tears as I look up at the stars. "Annoying."

She giggles, and damn if it isn't a healing sound.

"Brave," I admit, quieter this time.

"He protected you at dinner tonight."

I lift one of my palms, staring at the scars Eren didn't ignore. "Yeah. He did."

Jocelyn crushes me in a fierce hug. "Get as far away as you can."

I close my eyes, squeezing her back, and it oddly feels like I'm saying goodbye.

# CHAPTER 13

*H*ouse Dysis will be moving a water shipment from their treatment facility to their patron city of Aruna. My eyes scan the parchment, reading the report for the fifth time to be sure. When the location, date, and time are burned into my memory, I set the paper back in the drawer of my father's desk.

I pry the doors open as gently as possible, peeking into the hall. There's no sign of any servants, guards, or wandering family. Stepping out, I draw the doors closed and make a swift exit with a harmless bit of information I can pass along to Eren.

All I have to do is hold my nerve.

My stomach churns when I throw open the door to my room. A single duffle bag sits on my bed, ready for departure. As I make my way through the manor with the bag in tow, my jaw clenches at the thought of a weekend with Eren's family and what it might entail.

*I'll be surrounded, alone with no allies.*

The only thing guaranteeing my safety, apart from the marriage contract, is the exchange. Ash and Rune will escort me to Esmeray and return to Solera with Kamari. When the weekend ends, they'll bring her back and I'll be free to go. This process will repeat until wedding dates are agreed upon or... Eren meets his untimely demise as Damon Valour.

A twilight city sparkles to life below us as we cut across the sky. Esmeray gleams like moonstone in the evening. Dome buildings held by pillars rise above the sands, stacking on top of one another, linked by stairs providing shade to those who dwell beneath them. Palm trees grow higher than some of the structures, stretching to meet the last rays of dusk. They trail either side of long city streets, encircling parks and buildings. I can't help but find it both beautiful and efficient.

Far on the outskirts of Esmeray, cut into the wavering cliffs of metamorphic rock, an estate filled with lush desert plants looms over the city. We pick an open expanse near the cliffside to land.

No sooner than my feet hit the ground, Ash is there, crushing me into his chest. "If you need anything—if you need to come home early, just send word. I'll be here as soon as I can."

I shut my eyes, forgetting the harsh words and old wounds that have been exchanged over what feels like such a short time.

He lets me go, but as I start to turn he speaks again. "Sage."

I raise a brow.

"I love you."

I stare, trying to recall the last time I heard those words. We use them sparingly in our family, if at all, but it warms a fragile part of me that has always longed to hear them.

"I love you too."

Movement snags my attention as two figures descend from the steps leading to the manor. Eren and Kamari move with such grace I could mistake them for lost spirits the desert has swallowed. Kamari is half-dressed for war with her hair braided back, daggers at her waist, and a pistol on her belt. Eren, on the other hand, appears more at ease than I've ever seen him. The first three buttons are popped loose from the top of his white shirt, his hair windswept and eyes bright. Perhaps it's the languid posture, an illusion of unshakable confidence, but his shoulders are back and his face relaxed as he waits for us to draw near.

Kamari's dragon wails from above before touching down near our dragons, hissing a warning as Halcyon and Heartfyre snap one of their own.

"Take care of my sister," Ash warns, shaking Eren's hand with more force than necessary.

Eren's lips curve. "Likewise."

Ash turns and squeezes my shoulder, his eyes conveying the things he can't say in front of our tentative allies. I offer what I hope is a convincing smile, that I'll be okay entering this den of rattlesnakes. Eren and I may have our agreement, but his family holds no love for me. I don't know what awaits when I cross the threshold, but I can't let Ash see me waver.

"Don't wish me luck, Brother. I'm not the one who needs it." Kamari winks at Ash before stepping forward, only to linger at my shoulder where she smirks. "If you fuck as good as you fight,, you'll win my brother's heart in no time."

I stiffen, my face flushing as she saunters past Ash and Rune to mount her dragon. The boys follow her, Ash reluctantly peeling his eyes from me. I'm left with Eren who's still watching his sister as they take to the sky. As though he deems her safe enough, he rips his gaze from the clouds to capture mine, pinning me with those startling eyes.

"Here, allow me." He steps forward, taking hold of the strap to my duffle bag and sliding it off my shoulder onto his.

"Thanks," I mutter, following him up the steps to the estate.

It's a grim walk up to the manor until the stones give way to the stunning landscape of House Noctis. Drought-resistant plants grow on either side of the path leading to a pair of intricate glass doors beneath the archway. Pomegranate trees flank the front of the manor, providing shade to the veranda in front of the entrance.

Eren opens the door, allowing me to take my first step within. White marble floors shine in the last glare of sunlight, coating the surface in a fierce tangerine glow. Gold accents cover the chandeliers, windows, and banisters of the staircases. Potted plants flourish in each corner, breathing life into the interior. I'm wonderstruck by the pure beauty of it, craning my neck as my gaze travels up, snagging on the true show-stopper of the dome-shaped ceiling. Around the base of the dome, gilded dragons dance in mid-flight. Further above, a mural of a midnight oasis steals my breath. Plants and trees I don't recognize grow within the painting. Mountains of gray rock and waterfalls spilling from them are depicted in the idyllic scene. Embers glow over a body of water, drifting up to the trees. At the center of it, a Nightstalker stretches its wings as it glides toward the moon.

"My great, great, grandmother painted it herself." Eren takes a moment to stand beside me, staring up at the mural. "They say she worked thirty days and thirty nights, only stopping from exhaustion or to tend to her most basic needs."

"She was a talented artist," I say, wondering what it must be like to be so passionate about something you couldn't pull away from.

"She was," he agrees with a wistful sigh. "I'll show you to your room."

We ascend the grand staircase to the next level. A few turns within the corridor bring us to a stop in front of a door with wildflowers etched into the wood. Eren twists the knob and holds it open. Apricot walls surround a gracious space filled with a round bed, a stone table, and an array of succulents. Crystal suncatchers shine near the opening to a balcony where a couch and a firepit wait to be used. On the left, I spy an archway leading to a tiled bathroom with marble countertops and a quartz crystal sink.

Eren strides to the bed, placing the duffle bag on top while I stare. This room is far more generous than anything I could have asked for. It's not that my family can't afford these same luxuries, but the best rooms in the compound are reserved for the older members of our House, those who rank higher than me in particular. I never even had my own room until Lux moved out and the quiet made my ears ring.

"What's wrong?" Eren asks, gauging my stillness.

I force myself to swallow. "Nothing. You have a lovely home."

He nods, giving the room a brief once-over. "I'll leave you to it. Dinner is in two hours. I'll send for you then."

I watch him twist to the door, about to leave when a thought occurs to me. "I have something."

Eren comes to a halt, turning.

"House Dysis is moving a water shipment tonight."

His eyes flare. "What time?"

"Midnight."

He gives me a terse nod, shoulders tensing. "We'll have to move quickly. Dress in your flight clothes after dinner. Wear nothing that identifies your House."

My heart hammers through my ribcage. "Why?"

A slow curve of his lips reveals a devious grin. "Because we're going to intercept that shipment." He disappears out the door, leaving me in silence.

I chew my bottom lip. Dragonsong echoes from outside, leading me out to the balcony. Halcyon twirls in the air with a brown-speckled dragon of a similar size. A smile stretches across my face as I watch them glide back and forth in a game of tag. As if sensing my delight, a child-like presence fills my mind, tugging at the bond. I send Halcyon my reassurance, spotting how she twists her head in my direction until the brown dragon nudges her. Halcyon chitters and gives chase, shooting up into the clouds.

I take a deep breath, allowing my worries to drift on the wind with my girl in the air. If I can survive Dahlia trying to stab me at dinner, I can get through a meal with our rival House. Besides, our enemies are much less likely to kill me than my family. I sigh, turning back around when my eyes land on the firepit. A slow, destructive thought crosses my mind. It's so obvious, I don't know how I never thought of it.

I dart to the bedroom, rifling through the drawers at the bedside. A box of matches sits at the bottom. I snatch it from the drawer, storming back to the pit. I shake out one of the matches, scraping it across the rough side of the box. The head of the match bursts with a single flame flickering in the shadows. My hand shakes. Am I really about to do this?

*I have to try before I'm too far in this mess.*

I drop the match.

Flames scatter over one end of a log, lapping at the wood until the rest of the logs catch fire. They burn together, crackling to life until the pit is consumed by flames. I reach for my arm, unraveling the bandage. The Nightstalker's wings spread below the hollow of my elbow, its tail slithering down a few inches above my inner wrist.

*You don't know if it'll work.* A part of me doubts. *But I'll never know if I don't try.*

I curl my trembling hand into a fist and stretch my arm over the fire. Heat licks the base of my arm and I lower it further, directly above the flames. A strangled cry rips from my throat as my skin sears.

A force yanks me back, throwing me into the wall. I blink stars from my vision and find Eren standing there, his hand wrapped around my throat. His eyes are darker than ever, his jaw clenched.

"What do you think you're doing?" His voice has fallen to a dangerous octave, sending cold ripples down my spine.

I stiffen under his grip. "How did you know?"

"We're bonded," he growls. "I could feel your pain like it was my own."

*Oh.*

I grimace, hands flying to his wrist in an attempt to rip his arm off me. Eren doesn't budge. He grabs me by my scorched wrist and lifts it to the light. An angry red burn covers the skin beneath the tattoo. Right before my very eyes, it starts to dissipate. The burn shrinks in on itself until the red fades completely, like it was never there.

"No," I whisper in horror.

Eren releases my wrist, but keeps me pinned. "Let me make one thing clear. The mark is indestructible. It can only be removed by the mage who cast it. Until then, I'd get comfortable with it." He leans in close enough that I can feel his breath fanning my lips. "The mark guarantees your silence, but if you find any means to betray me, I *will* kill you."

He lets me go.

I gasp for breath, coughing as I clutch my throat.

Eren takes a couple of steps to the center of the room before facing me, his jaw set. "This isn't going to work if we don't trust each other."

"How can I trust you when you put this mark on me?"

"How can I trust the girl who planned to kill me just to prove a point to her family?" He shakes his head. "For all I know, Killer, you might still slit my throat in my sleep."

"I thought about it," I admit, staring defiantly as he closes the distance.

He chuckles, low and dark. I have to crane my neck to keep eye contact, but it's almost painful to look at him when he towers over me like this. I can see every inch of his infuriating, heart-breaking face. A girlish part of me wonders what it would be like to run my hands through the dark wisps of his hair or trace the sharp lines of his jaw. If I didn't hate him so much, I might be as smitten as the girls at the Conclave.

He raises his hand, brushing his knuckles over my cheek. "For now, let's keep those filthy thoughts inside your head. I'd hate to explain your untimely demise to your family."

I glower. "How convenient that would be for you."

Eren smirks and offers me his arm. "Shall we?"

Squaring my shoulders, I take his arm and let him lead me to the dining hall. Five members of House Noctis are seated at the table.

"Eren!" A little girl, no older than ten, bolts from her chair.

I stiffen. Eren kneels as she crashes into him, throwing her arms around his neck as he lifts her up and squeezes her with a laugh. He leans back. "Elodie, I want you to meet the future Lady of our House. Sage, this is Elodie."

The girl beams, dimples pinching her cheeks. She's the spitting image of Eren with the same dark hair as her brother and light eyes. "Hi, Sage."

I offer a small smile. "Hi, Elodie."

Eren sets her down, his mother watching with a fond smile as her youngest daughter races back to the table. I slide into the open chair on Eren's right and can't help but notice another empty seat beside Syrinthia, right about where Kamari should be. I meet the inquisitive eyes of the other girls at the table, their faces ranging between teens and young women who might be close to my age.

"Neith Noctis," a grinning teenage girl with luscious cropped curls and a heart-shaped face hovers close with her hand extended. "At your service, my Lady."

I shake her delicate hand as another sister pipes up. "Quit sucking up and give her some space, Neith." This girl, slightly older with pin-straight black hair, rests her face in one hand.

Neith sticks out her tongue. The other sister rolls her eyes, shaking her head.

"Well, you've officially met Neith," Eren drawls, giving Neith a pointed look before he jerks his chin to the other one. "That's Soraya."

"Your favorite sister." She flutters her lashes.

"Nonsense. Elodie's my favorite."

Soraya's jaw drops as Elodie giggles, sticking out her tongue while Neith laughs.

"Moving on," Eren chuckles, looking at the last girl on the other side of Kamari's chair. "That's Blythe."

Her dark hair is elegantly braided in two sections, leaving her sharp angular features on full display. She picks at the skin of her cuticles, not paying me a glance. "The only sensible one in this family."

"And lastly," Eren ignores her. "Our dear Mother."

Syrinthia peers at me from the other side of the table with a smile on her lips. "A pleasure to have you in our home, Sage. I hope you'll consider us family soon."

I reflect the smile back at her, not trusting the warmth in her voice for one second. She might very well be her son's accomplice. She may even be the one guiding him.

I think of a few kind words. "It will truly be an honor to join our Houses."

Syrinthia reaches for her wine. "Now that introductions are out of the way, tell us something about yourself. Any interests outside of politics?"

I sense the eyes of Eren's sisters. Even Blythe has looked up from her nails.

"Well, uh," I rack my brain for an answer, but I haven't thought about anything except politics for the better part of a year. Ever since Khione's death, I've dedicated myself to training, to becoming a better fighter and strategist. What can I offer my future mother-in-law that doesn't have to do with war? "I like to fly, mostly."

"As does every Rider," Blythe mutters.

"Tell us about your hobbies," Neith suggests, eagerness glittering in her eyes. "Maybe we have something in common."

My stomach twists. I'm not artistic like Jocelyn. Most of the books I used to read sit on a dusty shelf in my room, but I recall the stones on that same shelf, the one's I collected as a kid before my life became flying drills and training. "I used to collect stones as a child. Crystals. Fossils. And I used to read."

"Used to?" Syrinthia quirks a brow.

"War has a way of keeping one occupied," I say with a half-hearted smile.

"What kind of books?" Soraya chimes in.

"Adventure. Romance." My face heats. It seems so silly now, reading about imaginary worlds and a love that sweeps you off your feet. This is the world I live in, one that allows no time for imagination. Losing one's focus is more likely to get you killed or backstabbed.

*Love is the only luxury we can't afford.*

I risk a glance at Eren who takes a long drink of his water. He seems more settled in this setting, at ease amongst his family. I envy it.

"Ah, I love a good romance. Do you fancy yourself in love, Brother?" Soraya teases.

*Oh, Gods.* I bring my glass of water to my face, if only to give my hands something to do. The servants shift around the table, bringing out the first course and giving me a few more seconds to collect myself for the lie Eren must spin.

He cocks a brow at his sister. "Come now, Raya. A gentleman doesn't kiss and tell."

Blythe snorts. "That's a hard *no*."

I choke on my water, earning a snicker from Soraya and a worried glance from Neith.

"On the contrary," Eren answers, cutting into his food.

"What is love but a handful of sand slipping past our fingers? I crave something far more permanent." He turns his head, eyes boring into mine. "Loyalty. Devotion. An alliance forged with mutually assured destruction is far more valuable than love. Sage and I have found something in one another that the other Houses should be so lucky to find."

I stop breathing. I know I should look away, but doing it feels the same as admitting defeat, so I hold his stare, losing myself in the tide of it. I hope he sees the storm brewing within me. I'll fight him for the rest of this "alliance" if I have to.

Syrinthia clears her throat. "Well, I think that answers the question."

Eren smirks, winking. My shoulders slump, the stress evaporating from my body. No one else pokes fun at our supposed relationship for the rest of the dinner. While I eat and listen, I find this scene so at odds with my own family dinners. There's no residual tension between siblings. No invisible ax hanging over anyone's head. There aren't any vipers waiting to strike at the first mention of mistakes. And there is far more joy in one evening than I've been accustomed to in a lifetime.

I watch Eren laugh at one point, study the dazzling grin I've never seen him wear before. It's then, at that moment, I realize his family doesn't sit at this table out of obligation. They sit here because they love each other.

It twists in my chest like a shard of glass.

Eren walks me back to my room after dinner. We pass through a corridor of portraits and my gaze snags on a man identical to him. He slows to a stop when he catches me staring.

The man in the painting is older, with streaks of gray peppering his black hair. His skin is worn, wrinkled by time, and a hardness rests in his eyes.

"That's my father," he says quietly.

"How did he die?"

"He fell."

Eren doesn't spare any details. He starts walking again, leaving me at a loss for words when we come to a halt in front of my door.

"Meet me in the corridor when you change."

"Eren." I pause in the doorway. "I'm sorry."

He takes me in, his eyes peeling apart layers I'm not sure I want him to see. I wonder if he'll speak at all when he finally nods and pivots in the other direction. He disappears into the shadows of the hall and I shut the door, resting my forehead on the wood. There's no one here to tell me if I'm doing this right, and the thought unnerves me.

I strip off the gown and don my flight gear, ripping off the patch of House Galvan's sigil from my right bicep. The two-headed dragon sits in my hands, waiting to be worn by the proud daughter I once was. I toss the patch on the bed and turn my back on the room.

# CHAPTER 14

*esper Noctis* gleams in gold script across the bottom of the portrait's frame.

*What could make a rider fall from their dragon?*

It's a horrible thought, one that lurks in the back of every Rider's mind. We meet our end in one of two ways: by fire or the fall.

I can't remember which House took part in the battle that claimed Vesper's life. It was inconsequential to me back then. Five years ago, my family considered it a victory. One less enemy to battle. So why does it feel hollow now?

My mind drifts. *Is this why Eren became a rebel?*

Footsteps approach from the hall. When I turn, Eren isn't looking at me, but at his father.

*What would Vesper think seeing his son in the black uniform of the rebellion?*

Eren's eyes flick to my face as if sensing the thought. He jerks his chin. "This way."

I follow him deeper into the manor until we reach a staircase leading down to an open library far more stunning than House Galvan's. Rich brown shelves line the walls with books, stacking high to meet the ceiling. A rolling ladder rests in the corner, waiting to assist with the tallest shelves. On one side, a fireplace crackles, soaking the room in an amber haze. Oil paintings decorate the available wall space, landscapes from Esmeray or the native plant life.

"You're welcome to our collection any time," Eren says, strolling to a shelf near the fire. "But that's not why we're here."

He pulls down the spine of one of the books, causing the wall to shudder. The bookshelf to his left scrapes open to reveal a tunnel entrance. My jaw drops. I creep toward the opening, gawking down the dark trail into Gods know where. Eren grabs an ore of sunstone from the mantle and comes to my side, the rock glowing in the presence of darkness.

"Stay close, Killer," Eren teases, brushing past me. He glances over his shoulder. "Wouldn't want you to get lost down here."

I shoot him a glare, half-tempted to steal the stone from his hand and bash him over the head with it. I fall into step beside Eren, our footfalls echoing through the darkness.

"Where does this lead?"

"Beneath the manor into the canyons," he answers. "It's where our dragons nest."

"Oh. Ours nest underground too." I pause, lips clamping shut before I can say more. *Is that saying too much? Don't all dragons do that? Gods, why am I so stupid!*

Eren must note the panic in my face. "Most dragons do. It's safer, keeps their eggs hidden as opposed to being out in the open."

I do my best to nod and search for a different topic. I think about the dinner and everything I learned. "Elodie wasn't at the Conclave..."

"No, she wasn't," his voice softens. "Elodie has a gentle heart. I don't want to teach her how to be ruthless and cunning or all the reasons why she has to be. I just want her to be a kid as long as she can."

The Gods must have a sense of humor, because what are the odds that my enemy—my *ally*—is a brother trying to protect his sister? "As someone who was shielded all their life until recently, I can tell you that you're doing her a great disservice."

"I know, and I hate myself every day for it. It's selfish, but part of me believes I can change things before that time comes."

"You're hoping she'll never have to know our world for what it is now."

He laughs bitterly. "I'm a fool."

I chew at my lip, weighing the words. He seems so human now, not the person who threatened to kill me hours ago. He's someone who wants to protect his family.

*Isn't that what I want too?*

"No. I think you're someone who loves their family, and I think... I think she'll forgive you, even if you can't change the world."

Eren doesn't say anything for a while. Until he does.

"We'll see."

A gap opens up at the end of the tunnel. Sunstone and stalactites hang from the cave ceilings, illuminating the extent of the caverns. Steam twirls from pools of water throughout the cave, radiating heat. Nestled at the center of it, Eren's Nightstalker curls inward, snoozing the night away. She cracks open an eye, the pupil dilating as she zeros in on us.

"Sage, you remember Noxainia." Eren strolls toward the dragon, placing a hand on her snout.

She unfurls her wings, neck uncoiling to peer down at us. I maintain eye contact with her, even as her eyes form into slits. You can never let a dragon take you for a coward, not unless you want to be their lunch. Noxainia huffs, steam billowing from her nostrils as she allows Eren to climb into the saddle on her back. He leans down, extending a hand to help me up.

I cross my arms. "Why can't I ride Halcyon?"

"Your dragon is tied to House Galvan. Other Houses will

recognize her from battle and anyone who isn't a friend to the rebellion will sell you out as a traitor. You want to protect your family, don't you?"

I bite my lip. "Yes."

"Then get on."

With a deep breath, I move closer, ignoring his hand and hopping into the saddle myself.

Noxainia rises, stalking to the closest side of the cave where she sinks her talons in, scaling the wall. Loose rocks crumble, crashing to the ground as she climbs. Eren wraps an arm around my waist, holding me closer to his back. I should think of the gesture as an insult to my skill as a Rider, but the pounding of my heart has nothing to do with irritation. I try to ignore the nervous sweat rolling off me and will myself not to think about his chest pressing into me, or his thighs straddling me from behind. For a second, my mind drifts, imaging those arms locking me down in a much different position.

I jolt, shaking my head as Noxainia crawls through the opening of another tunnel, breaking into the sky with a beat of her wings.

"You can let me go now," I snap, hands digging into the leather of the saddle.

Eren's arm slips off, but there's a lingering smugness in his voice. "My apologies."

Noxainia soars as high as she can take us, Esmeray fading into a shining speck under the cloudbank. The Isra Dunes blend into a haze of shadows under the moonlight. I'm not sure I could make out any sort of rebel base from above, but I track the constellations, searching for the dragon of the north, Sunbreaker, to pinpoint our location.

Noxainia sweeps left, circling the sands below as she glides to stop near an inconspicuous pile of sedimentary rocks. Eren jumps off first, boots sinking into the sand. Scanning the empty dunes, I fail to see how a base could be hidden here, but Eren keeps moving toward the rocks. He stops in front of the cluster, pressing a palm to the flattest portion of the stone.

The rock glows beneath his touch, a section of stone wavering like water until it disappears. I suck in a breath, skidding to a stop. Steps lead down into the earth, another tunnel to another cave, and I gulp.

"Don't tell me you're afraid of the dark."

"I'm not." I shoot Eren a glare. "I just don't like dark, cramped spaces."

"Uh-huh," he says, gesturing to the entrance. "Ladies first."

Glowering between him and the opening, I make no attempt to move.

"That's what I thought." Eren pulls the sunstone from his pocket, shining it over the stairs and tugging up a mask that shields his face from the eyes down.

I glance over my shoulder as the opening disappears, once again concealed by the illusion of rock. "An enchantment?"

He nods.

My stomach wrenches. Perhaps it's only Oddica at his disposal, but a handful of mages could change the game entirely. What hope do Riders have of finding an enemy we can't see? Any rock could be a hidden door. Spies could be listening anywhere. A shudder rolls through me. With mages on their side, the odds of them winning feel that much greater.

Torchlight flickers from the bottom of the stairs where music and voices stir. We step into the light of a gaping cavern. Refugees gather over fires, roasting meat or playing card games. I immediately spot the rebels amongst them, dressed in black with knives shining at their waists and guns on their hips.

"Oddica." Eren strides to a girl with dark hair kneeling by a child and her mother.

She turns. Her cloak is gone, replaced with khaki pants and a cropped black shirt. She spots Eren in an instant, moving toward us.

"Damon," she uses his alias. Her brow lifts when she sees me trailing beside him. "I see our guest has returned."

I glare, crossing my arms. I haven't forgotten the pain of the tattoo. If she's the only one who can remove it, maybe it's time she and I have a little chat.

"I need you to gather the team," Eren tells her. "We need to be topside before midnight."

She blinks. "What's happening at midnight?"

"I'll explain later. Gather the others. We'll meet in the armory." Eren retreats, heading to the far left side of the cave.

I follow behind him, sneaking a glance at the mage. *This isn't over.*

Eren leads me through the cave system full of tunnels and soldiers on patrol. Each person we come across refers to Eren as *Damon*, and it leads me to the terrible suspicion that I might be the only one who knows his true identity. My head spins with the idea, rotating it over from every angle, but I can't fathom how he could start a movement based on a lie and expect it to succeed. How long until his army finds out? Would the lie be enough to make his people desert him?

We halt outside of a bolted metal door with two guards posted. The guard to the right nods his greeting and pries open the door for us. We slip into a room where racks of pistols, rifles, knives, daggers, swords, and crossbows hang from the walls. As the door clicks shut, Eren glides to the steel island in the center of the armory, leaning down to pull open a drawer.

He begins to stack boxes of bullets on the table. "Get what you need. It's going to be a long night."

I round the island as I watch him, stopping at the side of it. "Your people... do they know who you are?"

Eren pauses. "Some do–the important ones, but no one says my true name here. It's too much of a risk. If any of us are captured, they'd torture every bit of information they could carve out."

"That's why you wear a mask, isn't it? Not just to hide from the other Houses but... your people too."

He mulls over the words. Right when I think he's going to reply, the door scrapes open. Four heads walk in, four sets of eyes landing on my figure. Oddica is the first one I see. The young man behind her towers high, a wall of cut muscle with dark skin and bright eyes. A girl with short hair steps around him, her gaze narrowing in on me. The third one through the door is familiar, lean with a head of curls that scratch the back of my mind. Our eyes meet, his face paling, and I realize I know him.

*"Gannon?"*

His eyes widen. "Lady Galvan?"

A furious scream tears through the armory. The girl with short hair flies at me, fist raised. I barely manage to block her punch before she sends another one into my sternum. I wheeze, grabbing her head with both hands and slamming her skull into the island. She locks her foot behind my leg, dragging it out from under me and sending us crashing onto the floor. Shouting echoes behind us. Her nails dig into my face as she's ripped off of me. Eren hauls me up. I pant, touching my fingertips to my cheek. They come away red.

"That's enough!" Eren roars as the girl attempts to lunge from the arms of Gannon and the tallest rebel. "Sage Galvan is under *my* protection! She's our ally now, risking discovery to aid our cause. The penalty for harming her will be your execution. Do I make myself clear?"

"She torched my family!" The girl shouts. "She should be the one executed!"

"I've torched plenty of families," he growls, taking a menacing step closer. "I've listened to their screams while covered in the ashes of their kin. Would you say the same about me?"

She stills. "You're different."

"No. I'm not." He casts a hardened stare on the rest of them, the promise of death lurking in those cold eyes. "Each one of us is here not for the things we've done, but for what we intend to do for our future."

The girl stops struggling, glowering back at Eren as she jerks free. The boys let her go, keeping wary gazes trained on her.

"Here." Oddica appears beside me, her fingertips pausing near my face. Soft, white light glows from her hand. A tingling sensation blooms along my cheek until she lowers her fingers. When I touch the skin, I can't find a trace of the wound.

"Now that that's over with." Eren plucks a gun from the rack on the wall and places it on the island to load. "Let's get to know each other. You've met Gannon, our personal spy."

Gannon's color still hasn't returned as he stares, taking me in with a skeptical face.

Eren jerks his chin to the taller rebel who offers a mischievous grin. "That's Draven, our weapon's master and my appointed General." He glances at the girl who looks like she might grab a dagger from the wall and lunge. *Her and Dahlia would be fast friends.* "I believe you and Azara are already acquainted."

The girl spits blood in my direction, hitting the stone a couple of feet from my boots. "Great, let's tell the enemy everything."

Oddica passes me a rueful smile. "And you've already met me, Healer of the Rebellion."

"The mage who marked me," I correct her, not about to gloss over that fact.

Her lips press into a thin line.

"None of you have to like each other," Eren continues, subjecting each person to the heat of his glare. "But you do have to work together for our cause to succeed. I hand-picked each one of you for a reason. If you trusted my judgment then, it shouldn't change anything now. If it does, then get out. *Leave.* I don't have room for doubt in my circle."

Nobody dares to speak. Even I find myself waiting with bated breath for the next sign of discord. When it fails to manifest, Eren clicks the chamber of his gun shut. "Good. Sage has brought us valuable information. House Dysis is moving a water shipment from their treatment plant into Aruna at midnight. Pick your weapons and let's move. We can intercept them if we head out now."

That seems to get them moving. Their group breaks apart, each person snatching weapons from the wall and attaching them to their body. I step back, already armed with my own from home. The group gathers up their choices, filing out of the room like they've done this a hundred times.

Eren jerks his chin to me, shouldering a rifle and a duffle bag. I hurry to follow him, somehow ending up in the back of the line, straining to catch sight of the back of Eren's head. I try to decipher the direction he's taking us, but huff with defeat. Every tunnel looks the same and each guard is masked. Until these tunnels are explained to me, I'd have better luck tracking a firedrake in the dunes.

Eren leads us through a wide cavern where the ground is flat and torchlight gleams off spears of stalactite hanging from the ceiling. A convoy of armored vehicles waits in the center of the room. Their trucks are lifted, prepped with sand tires half the size of my body. Iron bars guard the front grill of the vehicles, acting as a cage for the engine inside. Sunstone bars of light shine from the front windshields, casting a white glow across the cave.

Off to the right, a dozen sandgliders stand with their canvas sails extended, their brass boards ready for someone to step on. Oddica, Draven, and Azara approach a board of their choosing, placing one foot on the brass and twisting their heels. It triggers the gears within. A whirring sound emerges from the boards as the sails retract, folding into a small square that disappears into a hidden section in the middle of the board where a metal plate slides over to conceal it.

Eren joins me while I observe them. "You're going to be with Draven and Oddica."

My head whips around. "We're splitting up?"

A smile plays at the corner of his mouth. "Don't worry. I'll be in the sky with Nox."

I cross my arms, glancing at the vehicles. "I don't know about this. It's one thing to pass you information, but if I'm caught robbing a water shipment..."

Treason. Death. A path I'll never come back from.

Eren tilts his head, reading the doubt on my face. "Help us take this shipment and we'll talk more about the mark."

At that, I look up.

He smirks, knowing he's once again caught me in his snare. "Besides," he continues. "A little groundwork will be good for you. Just pretend the truck is a dragon."

"There's a big difference between a hunk of metal and a *dragon.*"

He shrugs. "A bullet is still a bullet. Where you fire from doesn't change how deadly it is." Before I can say anything else Eren reaches into his pocket, pulling forth a black scarf-like fabric. "Here, you never know who might be on the ground."

I clutch the fabric in my hands, rubbing it between my fingertips. It's light, breathable, and identical to the wrap Eren wears to mask his own face. I meet his eyes then, my lips about to mouth the syllables that lead to *thank you* when two slaps over metal echo through the cave.

"Let's go!" Draven hollers from the driver's seat of the truck.

I square my jaw, thinking better of it, and turn from him.

Dry leather wafts through the backseat, filling my nose with the scent. With a lurch, the truck starts moving, carrying us through an endless passage. I make quick work wrapping the scarf over my head and around my neck, covering my chin and nose until only my eyes are visible. By the time I'm done fastening the scarf, the faintest hint of moonlight glows from a circular opening at the end of the tunnel.

Our vehicle passes through the mouth of the cave, Gannon and Azara following close. Sand kicks up from the tires as we speed over the dunes, bouncing over every dip. I peer out the window, searching the stars for some hint of Eren. I sit back, disappointment flaring when I find nothing in the sky.

*Why are you surprised? Nightstalkers earned their name for a reason.*

"Don't worry, he'll be close," Oddica assures from the passenger seat. I notice she wears a similar covering over her nose and mouth, though instead of black it's an off-white like the rest of her clothing.

"I'm not worried."

"It's your first raid on the ground. Plenty of reason to be."

"Is that supposed to make me feel better?" I snap.

I have no interest in small talk. She's every bit the enemy that Eren is and I'm not about to let her forget it. She's the reason I'm a part of this raid in the first place.

Oddica shrugs. "No, but we've done this before. Shoot straight and you should be fine."

I wipe the sweat from my palms on my pants. *A Rider on the ground... yeah, everything will be great.*

"We got movement," Draven warns, pushing his foot on the accelerator.

Leaning forward, I'm able to count several lights moving across the sands. It's three water tankers with four sets of guards escorting the shipment, but there's no way for us to count their numbers inside the vehicles. We'll be attacking blindly in a five-person unit until Eren intervenes.

Draven cuts our sunstone lights. On my right, I find Gannon

and Azara doing the same. Darkness swallows us, serving as our cover as we converge on the transport team.

They never see us coming.

Oddicia shoots first, firing at the tires of the last truck in their convoy. I throw open my window, aiming at the driver who flings his weapon out to return the shot. My bullet grazes his head, delivering a crimson blast from the remnants of his ear. Their truck swerves, forcing the two trailing it to veer in opposite directions to avoid collision.

"O, you're up!" Draven reaches behind his seat, lifting the board of his glider. He flings open the driver's door. Air and fine grains of sand whip through the truck as Oddica slips into his seat. Draven hangs out the side of the vehicle, lifting the wrap around his neck over his nose, and winks. He leaps off the truck, the sandglider's sail unfurling beneath him as he lands on the board, zipping through the dunes.

Oddica yanks the door shut. "Sage, get up here!"

I spring forward, climbing into the other seat as bullets ping off the truck. I roll down my window, aiming for the guards poking their heads out from the passenger sides. As bullets crack from the barrel of my gun, my mind races with the things I can't do. If I were on dragonback, I'd drop from the sky onto the tankers, disarm the driver, and steal the truck for ourselves. But my plan is moot, as useless as I feel while I watch Draven overtake the driver, firing two bullets into the tires.

A hard *slam* rumbles through the desert.

Gannon's vehicle ricochets off the last truck Azara dangles from, caught in a struggle for her gun with the driver. The driver flies back with the impact, their truck spinning out of control and allowing Azara to break free. She laughs over the wind, hollering a joyous cry before zipping through a flurry of sand.

I poke my head out the window, prepared to fire the next round when a thundering roar shreds the night to pieces. My head snaps up. Air rips from my lungs, stopping my heart and chilling me to the core.

A long, menacing shadow peels from the sky. It's not the onyx silhouette of a Nightstalker flapping its wings, but labradorite scales shining in the light of the moon. Its jaws unlock, a swirl of citrine flames unfurling from its neck. Winged Death swoops down from the stars, unleashing a torrent of fire upon us.

Oddica jerks the wheel left, sending me tumbling to the opposite end of the backseat. My head smashes against the door, the impact rattling my teeth. I blink black dots from my vision, groaning as I haul myself up. The dragon makes another sweep, flying low enough that its body blocks out the moon, encasing us in darkness.

Oddica flips the truck's lights on, her eyes widening at what she sees in the rear-view mirror. "Sage, jump!"

I twist my head, scanning the back window. Slitted eyes the color of violet lock onto our vehicle. A white-hot glow rises from the dragon's neck, an inferno barely contained by its scales. Oddica unbuckles her seatbelt, flinging open the door. I scramble to pull the latch, not giving myself time to rethink it when the molten light grows brighter. I throw myself to the dunes, crashing through the sand.

I gasp, coughing up straight dirt. I turn my head and spit, teeth crunching fine grains of it. Head spinning, I push myself up to my elbows right as a familiar shriek pierces the air.

Noxainia tears through the night, slamming into the dragon taking another sweep at us. I rise on wobbling knees, searching for Oddicia in the chaos around us. Another truck is overturned, the other on fire, leaving the two water tankers defenseless. Azara and Draven are off their gliders, exchanging rounds with the surviving guards.

I reach for my gun, patting an empty holster. My own eyes widen, searching the sands. Nothing silver sticks out, the weapon swallowed by the desert. A volley of bullets whizzes past my ear, forcing me to break into a sprint. Blue flames clash with orange fire, a twisted light show flickering against the stars. A gust of orange flames torches the sand between me and the trucks, severing my path to an overturned vehicle. I dig in my heels, shouting as the heat lances my skin. It's gone in an instant, the dragons soaring back into the air. Sand sucks my boots to the ankles as I spin around, desperately seeking any form of cover.

Bullets fly toward me. I dive, hands sinking straight into the sparkling sand. Pain sparks in my palms and I yelp, bringing my hands to my face. Fine shards of coarse glass bite into the flesh of my palms, adding to the scars that have barely healed. I bite my tongue hard enough to draw blood, quickly plucking the glass from my skin.

My vision blurs as I watch the blood ooze from my palms, my heart thumping in my ears. They bleed, just like the lashes. I hear the hard *crack* of leather. Over and over. I draw in a shaking breath, but it doesn't seem to be enough. I can't fill my lungs. I inhale again, chest tight–growing tighter by the second. I gasp for breath, my throat constricting. My body trembles from my arms to my legs. I look up, paralyzed as the others dodge the next assault of flames.

Never in my life have I run from fire. I am the one who *burns.*

*Get up.* I squeeze my eyes closed, gasping. *Get up. Get up. Get. Up.* But I can't move. *I'm on the ground. I'm on the ground and I'm going to die down here.* I remain on my knees, watching the hazy trails of blood drip from my hands.

Screeching echoes through the dunes as dragons crash into each other, a cacophony of claws and teeth. I clap my hands over my ears, shutting my eyes. Fire crackles in the air like lightning. Gunfire rings out. Voices are shouting–no–*screaming.* It paints an all too familiar picture in my mind, the scenes of slaughter I've flown away from, the ghosts of my victims claiming their vengeance at last.

*'She torched my family!'*

A sob breaks from my lips. Faces of refugees flash behind my eyelids. Another sob. Then another.

*"Sage!"*

I suck in ragged breaths, my fingers digging into my hair as I will back the faces. I know my death is coming, and I can't find one reason why I shouldn't pay the ultimate price.

*I'm going to die. I'm going to die. I'm going to die.*

*"Sage!"* Someone jerks my shoulder.

My eyes snap open. Gannon's face is inches from mine, eyes wild and covered in soot. "Sage, get up! We have to go!"

I shake my head, throat tight, unable to fight the tremors rolling through my body. Numbness settles over me, chaining me where I kneel. Everything is both far away and too close for comfort.

"Come on!" He lifts my arm and I break.

I crumble into a fit of sobs, tears spilling over my cheeks, shaking my head. I can't breathe. Can't he see? My body won't listen. With every ragged breath, I realize I am nothing and I should not be saved.

*I deserve this.*

A bullet cracks.

Gannon drops, collapsing into the sand. I scream and scramble back. Gannon lays on his back far too still.

"Gannon?" I crawl to him, flinching with each pop of gunfire.

A spot darker than the rest of his uniform blooms over his shoulder. Gannon groans, arm lifting to touch the spot. His fingers pull back, revealing thick red liquid.

I throw my whole weight forward, pressing both hands over the wound. Wounds are familiar. Wounds are fixable.

*If there's time.*

"Gannon? Gannon, tell me what to do!"

I can't save him. I can't call Halcyon. I can't fly him to safety. There's nowhere to hide in the desert. We're stranded on the ground, exposed to every threat imaginable. My breathing hitches, threatening to throw me back into a fit.

"Oddica," he rasps. "Find Oddica."

I scan our surroundings, catching no sight of the mage. But the guards are down, the dragons gone, and the night has fallen eerily silent.

"*Oddica!*" I scream across the dunes.

Gannon's skin has faded to a startling pallor, a thin sheen of sweat coating his face.

"*Oddica!*" I howl, straining my vocal cords to the max.

He'll die if I don't get help. He'll die if I leave him. My sight blurs, arms trembling.

*My fault. My fault. My fault.*

"I'm here!" The mage appears in a flash of light, her musical voice like rain in a drought. "Let me see him." She drops to her knees with me, gently guiding my hands out of the way.

She covers the wound with her palms, whispering an invocation to herself. Light bursts from her hands, showering Gannon's entire chest with it.

I collapse on my side, sand sticking to my sweat-drenched clothes, and heave into the dirt. I heave again. I'm still dry-heaving when Draven and Azara find us.

"D, help me," Oddica calls, lifting Gannon into a sitting position.

The wound appears to have stopped bleeding, but I can still feel his blood on my skin, wet and slick with a coppery sting. Bile floods my mouth again.

Azara watches, expressionless like the scene doesn't phase her. Her stare flicks to me, hardening. "What the hell is wrong with you?"

"Azara!" Oddica snaps, trying to stabilize Gannon when he

sways. Draven hooks Gannon's uninjured arm over his neck, taking the brunt of his weight and guiding him to a surviving vehicle.

"What's wrong? Were you *scared?*" Azara sneers, snatching my chin when I drop my head. "Let me tell you something, *Lady Galvan.* The way you felt tonight is how innocent people feel every day. While your family burns this world to ashes, the rest of us are left to outrun the flames. What do you think happens to those who can't run fast enough? They *burn!*" She drops my chin in disgust.

"Zara!" Oddica shoves her. "That's enough!" Fury rolls off her in waves, her eyes blazing.

Azara scoffs, but she eventually turns, joining Draven and Gannon in the truck.

Oddica kneels, straightening me by the shoulders. "Are you hurt?"

I shake my head, but Oddica finds the cuts on my hands, her brows furrowing. "Yes, you are."

Her fingers pluck a few splinters of fine glass, and then a white glow emerges from them. I watch numbly, unable to feel a thing and the walk from the ground to the truck passes in a blur. I hear words exchanged, doors shut, and two more engines sputtering to life. Gannon remains slumped in the front seat with blood-drenched clothes, looking more dead than alive. I press my forehead against the door, forcing myself to focus on the dunes slipping by.

"*What happened?*"

I blink.

I don't remember closing my eyes, but the world around me is different. We're back in the caverns, sheltered from the world outside. A dull thrum beats along the base of my skull. How haven't I dropped from exhaustion?

Bodies part, making way for Eren who charges in with wind-blown hair. He tenses when his eyes land on me.

"Everyone get out."

"But Damon–" Azara starts.

"Out! Now!" He shouts, crossing the distance between us.

Oddica squeezes my shoulder before she joins the others. As the last footfalls fade, I sense the fury radiating from him. I wait, bracing myself for the yelling.

"What happened?" He asks, gentler this time.

His voice stuns me. There's no harshness to it. No verbal lashing. It's an honest question.

I pull my mask down to my neck, catching sight of the dried blood on my knuckles, and swallow. "You... left me."

"What?" He steps closer like he can't hear me.

My knuckles tighten into a fist. "You *left* me." But the words do not come out strong. My voice does not shake, it cracks. "You left me! You *left me* and I *froze!* That's what happened!"

Eren recoils as if I've struck him, but his eyes are wide, unsettled in a way I've never seen them. "I–"

"No, you listen!" I bite through the tears. "I don't know what game you're playing, but if you want me dead just kill me now!"

"Sage–"

"My life isn't a game! I made this deal to get the mark off. You were supposed to give me secrets I can use and you haven't delivered! I didn't make this deal to become a pile of ash. If you can't hold up your end then the deal's off!"

His mouth snaps shut, twisting into a snarl. "My end? *My end?* I ask you for intel and you give us a water shipment. Do you think that's special? You think I don't raid a dozen of those every month to keep my people hydrated? *No.* I went along with it to teach you what it means to be one of us–so that you might understand a fraction of what we're fighting for. Putting you on the ground was a risk, but it was meant to show you what your people face every day! Instead, you've learned *nothing.* You choose to remain blind and it makes me *sick.*"

There it is.

I shove him back, jabbing my finger into his chest. "You don't get to judge me! I'm not blind! I see clearer now more than ever and you're *exactly* who I thought you were! A traitorous snake with no sense of honor!"

He takes another furious step, his face darkening. "And you're a coward. Tell me, have you found the courage to ask Azara what you've done? Or are you still hiding from it?"

I don't back down, glaring into his face. "I hide from nothing. I owe you *nothing*. The next time you want to teach me a lesson, I'll gut you in your fucking sleep."

Eren's jaw clenches. He takes a step back, his voice lowering to a dangerous octave. "Threaten me again, and I'll show you what it means to be a pile of ash."

He stalks from the cavern, leaving me under the stalactite and sunstone, the only witnesses to the tears that escape.

# CHAPTER 15

*a* soft hand runs a cloth over my palm, wiping the red crust from my skin.

"You're in a shock," Oddica says after a minute, dipping the cloth into a bucket of water. Excess drips from the rag, plunking back into the bucket as she squeezes.

She'd been waiting outside the cavern, prattling on about cleaning me up. I barely heard her. Now, here we are, in a washroom lit by sunstones and surrounded by silence.

Her gaze searches my face. "People freeze sometimes. It's okay."

I bite the inside of my mouth, loosening a shaky breath. "I almost got Gannon killed."

"He's fine. He's recovering."

"It's still my fault," I insist, pulling my hand away. "I've never been on the ground like that before. Not with… not with…"

"Not with a dragon trying to roast you?"

I nod.

Oddica sets the cloth aside, facing her body to me. "For the people on the ground, dragons were wonderful, enormous creatures of beauty. Many of us grew up racing after them, searching the skies in the hope of a dragon flying overhead." She sighs, her face drawn heavy with sorrow. "But that was before the war. Now, children hide in their houses, covering their ears when they hear their roars. Their beauty has become synonymous with destruction. To see a dragon is now considered an omen of death."

Tears well in my eyes, but I have no right to shed them. I recall the days when people cheered for my family, the days where children chased, peering skyward with wonder. The terror I felt tonight sinks its talons deeper into my chest, squeezing my heart in its fist. Our people hate us, and they have every right to.

*I never looked down.* The thought reappears in my mind. *We never restricted our wrath.*

"Oddica," my voice cracks. I take both of her hands, squeezing as tears blur her face. "Please. I need you to take this mark off. I can't be here. If I'm caught, my family will kill me. They won't have a choice. I swear, I'm not a bad person. I never meant for any of this. I didn't… I didn't *know*."

Oddica pulls her hands from mine, a sadness straining her features. "I don't think you're a bad person, but I do think you've been fighting for the wrong side. It's not your fault. It's just the station you were born into, but I can't remove the mark until Damon orders it. It's the only thing protecting us from discovery."

"*I won't tell,*" I plead, wiping at my tears. "What does he want me to do? Betray my family even more? Send them to their deaths?"

She shakes her head. "No one would ask that of you. It's natural to want to protect your family, but they're not the ones who need your protection." Oddica stands, wringing her hands. "Trust Damon. He never breaks his word, but he has a lot of people to look out for."

I turn my hand over, tracing one of the scars with my thumb. "I guess I don't have a choice, do I?"

She gives me a pitiful look. "There's always a choice."

Oddica guides me back to the caverns where Noxainia slumbers. Eren's back is turned to us while he tends to the scorched buckles of her saddle. I square my shoulders, willing myself to look ahead rather than at him. As far as I'm concerned, there's nothing more to say. Whether or not he agrees is another matter.

"Take care, Sage," Oddica murmurs, excusing herself.

It's a long, silent flight back to the manor in Esmeray. I hate myself for noticing the weight of his arm missing around my waist, how my stomach sits cold without the warmth of it. I envision a cold shower, silk sheets, anything but the burning of my back where I sense him breathing against me. It's too close. I wish I could say it makes my skin crawl, but it doesn't.

We make a swift landing, slithering into the caves beyond the manor. I leap from the saddle first, eager to separate. I take no notice of where I'm walking. I don't care what tunnel it is as long as it takes me far away from Eren.

"Stop," his voice echoes.

I halt, fists tightening.

"You're going the wrong way."

"I don't care."

"You might if you wander into Cantorix's nest. He doesn't take kindly to strangers."

I huff, facing him with a pointed glare. "I want to go home."

"That wasn't part of our arrangement."

"I don't care."

Eren's jaw ticks, and then he shrugs. "Fine, suit yourself. I thought you might be interested in what your uncle does during the day."

My neck snaps at that. "My uncle?"

He picks at a scorched spot in his jacket, leaning a shoulder against Noxainia. "I planned to show you tomorrow, but if you want to go home…"

He knows exactly what he's doing, dangling that tidbit in front of me. If I go home now, I might as well admit I'm a coward.

I grit my teeth. "Fine."

A triumphant grin graces his features. He takes his time brushing past me. "This way, Killer."

I burn holes in his back as I follow.

We return to the manor through the library, using the same passage we left from. Embers dwindle in the fireplace, casting a dim, red glow on the books and furniture. Eren escorts me back to my room while I fight the urge to snap at him. I don't need his guidance, but my limbs wobble like jelly, my mind slow to pick apart the differences in the halls. I might wander the whole night, never finding my door.

My fingertips graze the brass handle, ready to lock myself in when Eren's hand catches the crook of my elbow. He studies me with an otherworldly awareness. Each breath I take seems measured, each blink noted, any shift of my expression weighed and filed to be studied later.

"I will never leave you again," he vows, and it is nothing short of an oath as he swears it. "From this point forward, I won't leave your side so long as our alliance lasts. We're bound. I intend to honor that."

My face heats and I blink, struggling to break this connection, searching for a way to challenge this promise. "And what about now?"

He cocks his head.

"Do you intend to leave my side now, or should I expect you to join my bed?"

A slow, wolfish grin slides across his lips. He adjusts his hold, his hand slipping from my arm to my neck where he pushes, ever so gently, backing me into the door. He runs his knuckles over my jaw, leaning down to whisper in my ear. "If you want me in your bed, Killer, all you have to do is ask."

My breathing hitches, voice locked under the thumb caressing my pulse.

Eren pulls back, smirking as his hand drops. "Goodnight, Sage."

I slip inside, close the door, and shiver. I bite my lip, staring at the handle. With a shaking hand, I lock the door.

SUNLIGHT SHINES high in the midday sky, blinding and miserably hot. Sweat drips into the creases of my skin, soaking my back as we move through the streets of Solera. I want to rip my face covering off and feel the dry air on my face, but the mask is my only protection in my home city. Solera guards stand at each street corner, some patrolling the markets. I don't remember many faces of my family's guards, but I can't say they won't remember mine.

Eren and Oddica walk on either side of me, masks up as we move through the teeming crowd of travelers. Spices and mouth-watering scents of meat waft past my nose, beckoning me to wander, but I stick to our route, searching for the sparkling dome of the Conservatoire.

At the turn of a corner, the dome gleams brilliantly upon the entire block. The Conservatoire rises in its full glory, stretching higher than the buildings that flank it. We climb the steps, passing acolytes entering and leaving the academy.

Inside, Oddica removes her mask, cheeks flushed red and hair sticking to her temples. "Ugh, bless Anvi! I thought I was going to pass out."

A dull ache pounds in my skull. Solera heat is no joke, but unlike Oddica, I can't remove my mask.

Eren doesn't seem too bothered by the heat, his eyes scanning the interior of the Conservatoire. "Is she expecting us?"

"I sent word last night," Oddica answers, leading us up the staircase Lux and I once climbed with our mother. My heart twists at the memory. *Was it so long ago I was here for different reasons?*

She takes us past a corridor, right up another flight of stairs where familiar glass doors lay. Oddica waves her hand, causing the handles to twist and pull open on their own free will. They close behind us as we step into the High Mage's office.

Melantha grins, rising from her desk. "If it isn't my dearest niece!"

My heart stutters. I watch as Oddica comes around the desk to hug her aunt.

*How can it be? She is bloodsworn to my family!*

Melantha settles back in her chair, her eyes falling upon Eren and I. "I see you've brought friends. Please, sit."

"That won't be necessary." Eren steps forward. "We're here for information."

"Oh, Damon, such a *bore*." She drums her polished nails on the desk.

Anger flares hot in my veins. *All this time, Solera's High Mage has been in league with the rebellion!*

Melantha's gaze cuts to me, her head tilting in interest. "My apologies, Lady Galvan. Could I offer you some refreshments?"

I tug my mask down, seething. *"You traitor."*

Melantha gives Eren a deadpanned look. "I hope you didn't bring a spy into my home."

"On the contrary." Eren yanks my arm forward, shoving up the sleeve to reveal the mark. "She's my spy."

Her lips form a small 'o,' her stare flicking to Oddica. "Your work, I presume?"

Oddica crosses her arms, a slight frown on her face. "Yes, though she isn't too thrilled about it."

"I can imagine."

I rip my arm from Eren, starting forward. "How can it be? You are Bloodsworn to protect my family!"

Melantha folds her hands together, leaning back in her chair. "You see, that's the funny thing with Blood Oaths. They must be painfully specific. In my oath, the terms your father laid out were very clear. *I* can do nothing to harm his line... but others can."

"You don't think partnering with rebels is harming his line?"

The High Mage shrugs. "The terms depend on one's interpretation. I define harm as picking up this blade," she lifts a letter opener from the desk, meeting my stare. "And slitting your throat with it." She sets the letter opener down. "Trading information is hardly the same."

"Enough of this," Eren says. "Why did Deon Galvan schedule a meeting with you?"

A knock taps at the door.

Melantha smirks. "Why don't you ask him yourself?"

Oddica curses, snatching a green cloak draped over a chair. "You two need to hide."

"What?" My heart pounds.

Oddica moves to the wall behind Melantha's desk, tugging on a sconce. It pulls down, popping open a hidden door to a room without light.

"If you want to know what your uncle's up to," Eren passes me, slipping halfway into darkness. "Then get inside."

My pulse rushes in my ears. Another knock, more incessant, rattles through the room, deciding for me. I swallow the budding fear in my chest and force my feet to move, stumbling as the door shuts. Eren's hands seize me by the shoulders, holding me steady. I step back, attempting to pull away when my heel brushes the door.

*Oh, Gods.*

This isn't a room at all. It's a damn coffin.

I draw a ragged breath, trying to turn. My shoulders scrape the wall, stuck between the stone and Eren. *It's fine. This is a closet. It's just a closet.*

He grunts when my elbow pushes against his chest. *"Watch it."*

I can't begin to muster an apology. A cold sweat breaks out on my neck, beading over my chest. It's all I can do to place my hands on the wall and breathe.

"Are you okay?" Eren whispers.

I shake my head. I can feel the rise and fall of his chest on my spine, but unlike dragonback, there's no comfort of air or sunlight. There's only darkness–blinding, deafening shadows of it.

"You don't like dark, cramped spaces," he remembers.

Panic crawls through my veins, tendrils tightening around my heart and squeezing my rib cage. *Get it together! Come on, just breathe.*

*"Took you long enough,"* Uncle Deon's voice trails from the office.

I suck in a sharp breath, jolting back from the wall. It brings me flush with Eren's chest, eliciting a soft groan from his throat.

"I'm sorry," I swallow, trying to see over my shoulder. "Did I hurt you?"

"No," comes his strained reply. "Just stay still or you're going to get us caught."

I nod, though my heart still pounds.

*"What brings you to my humble academy, My Lord?"* Melantha purrs.

A chair scrapes back. *"I'm in the market for a protection spell."*

*"Protection? Whatever for?"*

"None of your business, Mage," Uncle Deon sneers. "Can it be done or not?"

"Perhaps if I knew what the bearer needed protection from."

A pause.

"Death."

I stop breathing. Eren stills behind me. What in Gods' names could Deon need a spell to cheat death for? He never does anything dangerous except–my eyes grow wide.

The Ignis Mortem.

"You speak of necromancy." Amusement vanishes from Melantha's tone. "I do not deal in such things."

Of course. It makes perfect sense. What better strategy for a guaranteed win? My father would never see it coming... and neither would I. If Dahlia's indestructible, I don't stand a chance at winning. She would win at the cost of my life because no amount of blood would be enough to satisfy her loss. A ragged breath escapes my lips, one after another. I palm the wall, searching blindly.

Get out. Get out. Get out. Get out!

"No, not necromancy. I'm not asking to be brought back from death. I'm asking you to prevent it. Surely you must have some sort of shielding spell?"

"What is it? What's wrong?"

"I have to warn them." I fight for air, but pure panic crushes my lungs. "I have to warn them."

I push on the wall, but it does nothing. I step back, craning my neck for some other way out when my back slams into Eren. He groans, and this time, a hard length meets the curve of my ass. I freeze.

"Turn around," he says, voice thick.

Slowly, I twist until I'm face to face with him.

"Let me see your hand."

I raise it, fingers trembling.

Eren takes my wrist, placing my palm under the opening of

his shirt, right above his heart. His skin is warm under my touch, heating my numb fingers.

"I want you to breathe with me."

He sucks in the first breath. I draw a ragged breath with him, holding it until he exhales. His heart beats beneath my hand, steady and strong, and I let it ground me.

Melantha laughs, low and bitter. *"Unfortunately for you, I serve the Dragon Lord of House Galvan, not his little brother."*

I can't see his face, but I sense Eren watching me. With each breath our chests brush. Every second that passes, I feel the heat of his bare skin travel through my fingers, spreading from my face to my body, pooling low in my center. No part of me is shaking anymore. Instead, my fingers move with a mind of their own. They slide from his heart down to the hard planes of his torso. A low noise rumbles in the back of his throat, but he doesn't stop me.

I squeeze my eyes shut, willing myself to let my hand fall away. *Gods, it's not fair.* All the thoughts I've been suppressing rush to the surface, breaking through carefully crafted chains I've spent hours forging. It isn't fair how soft his lips look, even in the heat of the sun, or how effortlessly disheveled his hair is, and it's downright despicable how bad I want to arch into him, to feel his body against mine.

*Has anyone ever touched me the way he does?* I think of all the stolen caresses, how inconsequential they'd seemed at the time, simply another way for him to get under my skin. Now we're pressed so close together, I can't think of anything else but the feel of him.

His hand threads into the back of my hair, tugging my head back. "Careful," he breathes against my lips. "I might start to think you like me."

Something possesses me in that moment, a part of me that rallies at the challenge. I press closer, grinding my hips against his. That hard length drags over my core, igniting a kindling flame into a roaring fire.

"You're one to talk," I whisper.

He chuckles, sending goosebumps down my spine. "Don't start something you can't finish."

I grab the hilt of the knife on his belt. His hand clamps over mine, preventing me from pulling it from the sheath. "I've finished men with far less effort."

"Oh, Sweetheart, anyone who fell against you wasn't worth your effort to begin with."

"I'll be sure to tell that to the dead."

"By all means. They might still be alive if they'd been worth the steel in your blade."

The door swings open, throwing off my balance. I flail my arms, reaching for the door frame when Eren catches me by the elbow.

Oddica claps a hand over her mouth, a sorry attempt to hide her laughter. "Did I interrupt something?"

"No." My face heats.

Eren steps past the threshold into the light, sliding a hand through his hair. "We need a minute with Melantha. Sage, would you mind waiting outside?"

I roll my eyes, storming from the office and yanking the door shut. I wait a moment, pressing my ear to the glass. Nothing.

*Soundproof?*

Intricate runes swirl up the length of the door frame and over the arching entrance. Sighing, I wander around the corridor and back into the library. Queen Solasta's portrait still hangs where I last left it, but I find no clues in the paint of whether she'd been real at all.

"Some still pray for the old ways."

I whirl, finding a green-cloaked acolyte paused a few feet

from me. Her hood is drawn, revealing only plump berry lips and dark skin.

"The old ways?"

She smirks, coming closer. "When monarchs ruled, keeping the Dragon Lords in line."

I snort.

"You don't believe it?"

"Legend says they killed her, didn't they? It's hard to imagine anyone keeping the Houses in line."

"Yes. Times have changed, it seems."

I watch her, trying to place her low, honey-rich drawl. Most acolytes are young mages eager to practice their magic, but this woman sounds much older. "Who are you?"

She smiles. "A friend."

"Friends don't hide their faces."

Her hand flies out, locking around my wrist and pulling the bandage loose. Eren's mark flares in the light, glowing an iridescent blue. I gasp, wrenching my arm free.

"A Nightstalker. Interesting."

I rip the dagger from my side, pointing it at her. "What the hell do you want?"

"You're Bloodbound, aren't you? I could break the bond—rid you of that mark in the process."

I pause, lowering the blade. "Only the mage who cast it can remove it."

"Is that what you were told?"

My eyes narrow. "What do you want in return?"

"Smart girl. It's true, nothing comes free." She glides to my shoulder where she pauses, staring forward. "Do you see that there, around Solasta's neck?"

"Around her–" I turn, facing the painting, the words dying on my tongue. Sure enough, beneath the hair and armor, the faintest hint of gold drapes the Queen's neck. I squint my eyes, moving closer. A tiny shape of the sun rests below the valley where the Queen's collar bones meet. An indistinguishable stone glares in the center as though reflecting off the sun.

"I want what is owed. I believe your family has it."

"You want me to find a thousand-year-old necklace?" I gape. "I assure you, if it exists it's not with us. I would have heard my family speak of it."

She shrugs. "If it is in your family's possession, then it will not be something your Lord Father would share willingly." She makes for the exit. "You're a clever girl, give it some thought. Without my help, you'll be bound until death."

"What is it to you? This necklace."

She pauses, pivoting ever so slightly on her heels. "We all have secrets, Sage. Wouldn't you agree?"

Words I gathered in my throat deflate as I cover the mark, holding my arms to my chest.

The acolyte's steps echo off the floorboards.

# CHAPTER 16

*Impossible.* The word bounces off the walls of my mind as I rack my memories for the faintest hint of that necklace.

*Insane*, is what it is. Of course the first mage I meet who's not tied to my family or loyal to Eren would turn out to be utterly mad! If a piece of jewelry survived the last thousand years, why would my family have it in their possession?

*And that's if I accept Queen Solasta existed to begin with.*

I sigh, resting my face in my hands. The door to Melantha's office remains shut, locked from the other side, and more than likely protected by a silencing spell.

*But the mages seem so certain, and if I don't find this necklace, who knows how long I'll be shackled to the rebellion?*

I lean back on the bench in the hall, shaking my leg. *There has to be another way.*

Melantha's door swings open. Eren passes through the doorway, his eyes finding mine.

I stand, squaring my shoulders. "I need to leave. I have to warn my family."

"First, tell me why your uncle would need a spell to cheat death."

My jaw ticks. The last thing I want him to know is the political state of my House. Should word get out that House Galvan is nowhere near the united front we pose to be, it will make us appear weak. Eren doesn't budge at my silence. He merely tilts his head, seeming content to wait as long as it takes to wring the answers from me.

"I think he wants it for his daughter." Not a lie. Deon might very well have Dahlia challenge me, if only to bait my father into taking my place.

"And why would his daughter need it?"

I bite the walls of my inner cheek. "To challenge me to an Ignis Mortem."

Surprise flickers in his gaze. "Your own blood?"

"I don't need your pity," I snap, crossing my arms. "Just take me home."

"Can't do that, Sweetheart. Your weekend with me isn't over." He brushes past me, heading for the stairs. "Oddica's staying. We'll head back to Esmeray and I'll bring you home tomorrow as planned."

"But—"

"Let's say for a moment that you go home now." He lingers by the stairs, leaning a shoulder against the wall. "How do you intend to explain yourself? What lie will you spin to cover the fact that you caught your uncle here when you should have been in Esmeray with your betrothed?"

My response crumbles into dust. He's right. I can't explain what I'm doing here, not without my father digging deeper.

He smirks at my lack of an answer, pushing off the wall. "Like I said, I'll bring you home tomorrow."

"It'll take *hours* to drive back to Esmeray," I grumble, trudging from the corridor.

"We'll drive as long as we can," he dismisses me, guiding us back into the foyer of the Conservatoire.

Acolytes stream in through the open archways, filing in and out between classes. We keep our masks up, blending back in with commoners on the streets.

For the life of me, I can't decide what to do next.

I stare out the window, not quite seeing the rolling dunes as Eren drives. I can't keep my uncle's scheming to myself, not if it's liable to get someone hurt, but warning my family comes with a risk of its own. *If Deon won't fight fair, I need my own bit of magic.* I glance at my bandaged arm. *Or less of it.*

I almost don't register when the car stops.

An adobe inn glows in a sea of sand, lit by torches and surrounded by palm trees. Multiple levels rise upon one another with wide windows gazing out across the desert. I step out of the car with Eren, spying other vehicles parked on one side of the inn and sandgliders near the stables. Horses whinny from their stalls, watching us as we walk.

"I'm surprised you're not making us camp in the sand."

"It's too dangerous," he answers, holding the door open for me. "Sand isn't the only thing you'll find out there in the dark."

I lift a brow, but he doesn't elaborate. With a huff, I cross the entrance into the inn and find what looks like more of a tavern. A cloying smoke fills the air, along with the sour smell of barrel juice. Barmaids flit between tables, setting pints filled to the brim in front of travel-weary patrons. Nobody looks up when we enter, too occupied with card games or digging into stew.

Eren strolls toward the front desk, to the graying wrinkled man on the other side of the counter. "A room for two and fuel for the vehicle near the palm tree."

I vaguely hear the exchange of coins over the clamor of musicians. Eren returns with two bed rolls and a key. He passes me one, leading the way up the stairs. On the third level, he turns the key in the furthest door on the left.

A glass ceiling allows the moon and starlight to filter in, casting a silvery glow on the room. There isn't much within, a small bathroom to the right and a low table with a chaise on the left. Eren unrolls his bedroll in the center of the floor, leaving space for mine beside it. I set my own on the table, shaking my head. *This is stupid.*

I stride for the bathroom, locking myself within. Sunstone lights flash on in the presence of darkness, showing my dingy reflection in the mirror. Bags hang beneath my eyes and when I lower my mask, I find my own sour expression reflected back at me.

*You shouldn't be here.* My face seems to say. *You're wasting time.*

As I undo the two braids on either side of my head, letting thick waves loose, I consider how hard it would be to escape. *Take the vehicle. Go back to Solera. Tell them everything—as much as you can—and beg for mercy.*

Eren's voice rings in my memories. *'I'll always know where to find you.'*

I unravel the bandage, running my fingers over the Nightstalker. As long as I have this mark, there's no escaping him. My eyes flick back to my reflection and find an odd truth hidden there. *I don't feel like a prisoner. I'm not shackled, and without him—I wouldn't have known what my uncle was up to. I'm getting something in return for this. It was part of our deal.*

But isn't the deal an illusion? I might not wear chains, but I *am* shackled by this mark. If there were no spell binding me to him, would I have taken Eren's offer all the same? *'I'll even show you all the things your family doesn't want you to see.'* I unlock the bathroom door, spying Eren on his back, gazing at the stars. *'Each House has secrets and secrets are power.'*

As I place my bedroll beside him, I have to wonder... what is the cost of power?

"What made you like this?" I ask him after a beat. Staring at the stars doesn't make me tired. It makes me feel restless. Lonely.

Eren opens his eyes, turning his head to look at me. "You really want to know?"

I shrug, feigning indifference. "Why not? I'm a great listener."

He laughs quietly. "Yeah, but who listens to you?"

It's my turn to grow quiet, the sad truth sinking in.

He doesn't say anything at first, and I almost wonder if he'll leave us trapped in this vast silence. "I was angry when my father died. What was the point of everything? What was I fighting for? How could I ever fill his shoes? I drank a lot. I stayed as far as I could from home. I had no interest in leading my House and I wasn't ready for what that would mean. One night, I went out with two of my closest friends." He quiets.

His eyes are distant on the stars, lost to that other world. Another life. "We drank so much I blacked out. When I woke, I was in a hospital triage. We wore commoner clothes, you see, so we wouldn't be recognized. No one could tell I was their new Dragon Lord, so I was cast aside like the other lost souls waiting to die. When I could summon the strength to stand, I wandered. I could barely see straight. My head felt like it was about to split. Then I came upon the children's ward."

It takes a moment. Part of me thinks he won't continue, but with the bob of his throat, he does.

"There was a little girl there. Lips cracked. Skin pale. Covered in sweat and barely alive. I thought she was dead at first, but I heard her rasped breath. I came over to her, this little bony body laid out on a bed with nobody around. My sister, Elodie... she must have been around the same age as her, and Ellie was all I could see.

I yelled out for help, tried to get anyone to listen, but the staff was overwhelmed. No one could be spared. No water could be rationed. They already wrote her off so... I held her," he whispers, jaw clenched. "I held her in my arms and I told her I was sorry, like that would make it better. I said it over and over, telling her I didn't know. I never thought to look. I never wondered. The only thing I cared about was myself. And when that little girl died in my arms, I didn't even know her name. I sat there and I swore to myself I would do something–anything to fix it. To make it right."

"So you became a rebel," I whisper.

He glances at me. "I decided to make a difference. If it weren't for our station, it could have been Elodie in that bed. When you realize you were born lucky, it makes you see things in a different light."

"Couldn't you do more as a Dragon Lord? You rule over a whole territory."

He shakes his head. "It's not that simple. I can make it better for my people, but where does that leave everyone else? The other Lords will never bend. It took a rebellion with a Nightstalker for them to come together, and that was only to preserve their ways."

I swallow the lump in my throat. "You'll kill them... won't you?"

Our eyes meet.

"If I have to."

We fall into silence then, and neither of us seems eager to break it. Hours must pass, but I'm lying here awake, trying to make sense of what I've learned. Perhaps Eren and I are more similar than I thought, and yet... we walk such different paths.

I steal a glance, finding his eyes closed with a steady rise and fall of his chest. Asleep. I chew my lip, debating my options. Do I run? Do I stay? *If we're bonded until death then...*

My thoughts screech to a halt.

Could the answer be so obvious?

As quietly as I can manage, I lift my leg, reaching into my boot. My fingers curl around the handle of the blade I keep hidden there and lift it from the sheath, carefully sitting up. Eren doesn't stir, not even when I crawl forward. I straddle him, resting the blade on his throat.

Eren's eyes flash open, but he doesn't seem the least bit surprised. His eyes darken under the curtains of my hair, studying my face before they fall to my lips.

"I have a theory," I whisper, dragging the knife over his pulse. "What if this mark disappears with your death?"

"That's quite a gamble," his voice rumbles. "You might wear the mark forever. Is that a risk you're willing to take?"

"I've wanted to kill you from the start. Seems like we're coming full circle."

He lifts his arm to the side of my face, grabbing a fistful of hair and gathering it in the back of my head where he gives it a hard yank. I gasp, blade pressed further to his neck with the movement. A small slice oozes red against the steel. I hardly notice it as his eyes pierce mine.

"You can kill me, but it won't save you. If your uncle is snooping around for spells, imagine what the rest of your family is doing. End me here and another will take my place. Then you'll never know."

My hand begins to shake.

"Face it, Killer. You need me."

I blink back the sting of angry tears. "I don't need *anyone*."

He swings me around, slamming me on my back and pinning my wrist. The blade is gone, now in his hand. He hovers over me, body flush against mine as he presses the steel to my throat. It shouldn't set my blood on fire like this, but it does.

"You defy me at every turn. Why is it so hard for you to trust me?"

"You're my enemy!"

"No," he tsks, pressing the tip of the knife to my bottom lip. "It's not that. It's something else. What aren't you telling me?"

He removes the blade. I weigh the benefits of telling him

where to shove it, but the fight dies in me. My muscles slacken, eyes blinking rapidly to hold back the tears. I turn my head, but he uses the knife to turn my face back to his.

"Tell me." His voice is my undoing.

I lick my lips, his gaze tracking the movement. "I'm afraid."

Admitting it should feel like the greatest shame, but a weight lifts from my shoulders. Saying it aloud makes it real. A tangible thing I can conquer, even if I don't know how.

Eren sits up, untangling himself from me.

I rise from the floor, hugging my knees to my chest. "My cousin is going to kill me and I can't do anything to stop it."

"Melantha assured me that her mages are banned from helping your uncle."

I shake my head. "He'll find someone eventually."

Eren thinks for a moment. "If I were you, I'd use your uncle's scheming to your advantage."

"How? I can't warn anyone."

"Play the game. You've been watching from the sidelines your whole life. Like it or not, you're a player now. Make a move."

I turn the idea around in my head.

"Now, if you don't mind," he raises the dagger, letting it shine off the moonlight. "I'll be keeping this."

He settles back on the bedroll, closing his eyes. It takes a moment for me to calm, but I lay down and fall into a restless sleep.

HOUSE NOCTIS IS quiet in the early hours of the morning.

Halcyon shrieks in delight at my presence, her dragonsong bouncing off the canyons. Sparkling joy fills the bond, pushing back the weariness in my bones. Eren and I go our separate ways, off to opposite wings of the manor. I push open the bedroom door, only to stop dead in my tracks. A tiny gasp trails from the bed where one of my bags is open to the weapons hidden within.

Elodie lowers the dagger in her hands, eyes wide with fear. "I'm sorry! Blythe doesn't let me play with hers."

It's like looking into a mirror. Suddenly, I'm eight years old again, watching Ash spar with Rune from one of the balconies. I would slip into his room while he practiced, fiddling with blades I wasn't allowed to touch.

I blink.

"Well," I take a hesitant step toward her, then another. "That's because a blade isn't something to be played with."

I remember cutting my hand when Ash found me. He had to wrap the wound himself and find a Healer, rather than have our mother discover it.

I sit on the edge of the bed, pushing back the memories. "You shouldn't pick up a blade unless you're prepared to use it." My hands come around hers, but I don't take it from her grasp. I adjust her hold, using her wrist to guide her movement. "The blade is an extension of yourself. Think of it as part of you."

Elodie continues the movement when my hand falls away. Then she lowers the dagger, peering at me. "You ride the white dragon, don't you?"

"Halcyon," I say with a smile.

"What's it like to bond?"

I loosen a breath, thinking the words over. "It's like having a best friend who always knows where you are and if you're in trouble. It's like having a soulmate who knows you better than you know yourself."

"Blythe says it's better if I don't bond." Elodie frowns, staring at the dagger. "She says if I have a dragon, I'll have to fight."

My heart twists. "What do *you* want?"

"I want a friend."

I'm about to answer when another voice beats me to it.

"Ellie." Eren leans in the doorway, arms crossed. "Sage needs to pack."

"Sorry," Elodie mumbles, passing me the dagger as she slides off the bed. She bounds to the door, pausing at Eren's side to shoot me one last glance. "I hope I'm like you someday."

I stiffen.

She disappears into the hall, leaving just the two of us. Eren's gaze catches mine. For a moment, I am filled with regret. I was prepared to kill him last night. I would have taken him away from Elodie, right after his family welcomed me into their home.

*You don't want to be like me, Elodie.* I tuck the dagger into my bag. *I'm a mouthful of sharp teeth and a heart forged with jagged edges and I bite without meaning to. I'm the worst thing you could possibly be.*

"Thank you," Eren says, crossing the room.

"For what?"

"Being kind to her." He offers me the hilt of the dagger he confiscated last night. I go to take it, but he keeps a firm grip on the blade. "I won't forget that kindness."

I scowl. "I'm not always bloodthirsty, you know."

He grins, releasing my blade. "Could have fooled me." Eren turns. "I'll wait for you outside."

Halcyon prods through the bond, like a child tugging their mother's hand.

"I'm coming," I mumble, gathering my things.

Her wings flutter when I get out there, her saddle buckled and ready for me in the front yard. I run a hand over her scales, sending my affection back to her. Her prodding continues, like she knows something is wrong.

*Not now, please.*

She can't fix what's wrong with me any more than she can change her scales.

When we touch down on my family's land, I'm all too eager to slide off Halcyon. Eren leaps from Cantorix, coming to my side. As orange bleeds across the sky, I stare at the compound, trying to summon the strength to go inside.

"I'm very fortunate to have the family I do." He watches the sunrise with me. "You might think I can't understand, but I see the strain this bargain has brought you."

"Then you know what this will cost me."

"I won't let it come to that," he insists. "The next time we meet, I'll train you for the Ignis Mortem. I swear it."

"I know how to fight," I mutter, unable to bring myself to look at him.

"I'm not teaching you to fight. I'm teaching you how to win." He lifts my chin, capturing my eyes with his own. "Trust me."

My skin turns molten. A distant warning bell rings in my head. This is wrong. I shouldn't like his touch. I shouldn't crave more of it.

I swallow, trying my hardest to think straight and not let stupid words tumble past my lips. "If you knew me at all, you'd understand that's a lot to ask for."

"What if I want to know you?" He murmurs low and soft. His thumb brushes the side of my chin in soothing sweeps, beckoning me to give in. "Give me your darkest secrets and I'll give you mine."

It's an effort to give a feeble shake of my head. "I can't."

"Can't?" He raises a brow. "Or won't?"

My eyelids flutter, the sensation of his thumb creating a fog in my mind. I shouldn't let him touch me like this. It's far too intimate, but is there any other word to describe what's happening between us? I see his own eyes darken, his thumb pausing.

Eren drops his hand, prying his gaze from me. He reaches

into his pocket, producing a rough stone in his palm. Holding it between his hands, he lifts it in half, bearing a rose gold ring in the dazzling center of a geode. A lavender tanzanite stone shaped like a dragon's egg sits in the middle of the ring. A dragon curls around it, stretching each wing to the opposite ends of the filigree band. My eyes widen, meeting Eren's when he grasps my hand, slipping the ring onto my left finger.

"You should have a proper ring." He holds up his left hand, showing that he is now the owner of a black steel ring. "For the engagement."

"Oh… Thank you." *Smooth, Sage. Really smooth.*

"What are fiancés for?" He winks, releasing my hand.

I splay my fingers, lifting my hand to the fiery glow of the sunrise. The tanzanite sparkles brighter than any diamond. It's breathtaking—more than I could have ever dreamed, even if it is another means to an end.

*All in the name of the rebellion.*

I lower my hand, the thought grounding me. This bond between us is blurring the lines. Yes, that must be it. It's the spell at play, messing with my mind. Eren is a traitor, even if his intentions are noble. I'm just a pawn in his game.

*He's no different than my family.*

"Now, where should we meet to train?" He muses, staring out to the dunes. "The safe houses are too far. Is there anywhere close you can think of?"

An idea comes to mind. "Our summer manor."

Eren cocks his head to the side.

"We only used it out of season for the Conclave. Nobody ever goes there. If we're caught it'd be easy to say we wanted somewhere to be alone."

A devious smirk slides over his mouth. "A quiet place to defile my future bride."

I scoff, but my heart skips a beat. Somehow, it's too easy to forget who he is, what he's done. I can feel my defenses lowering. I want to laugh, but I force myself to hold back. I don't want to trust Eren. I don't want to be surprised when he inevitably betrays me, because deep down, at one point or another—one of us is going to have to choose. The rebellion... or my family.

*You're nothing to him, just a spy.*

The smile on his face drops, his gaze zeroing in on the manor. "Your family's watching."

I turn my head, about to look when his hand catches my chin. I suck in a breath, freezing as he reads my face. Whatever he finds there, it seems to be enough.

Eren lowers his head, his mouth crashing onto mine. My eyes fly shut as I suck in a breath, lips desperately moving with his. His kiss is slow and soft, a languid feel of my lips against his. But my hands fist the fabric of his shirt, tugging him closer, and it shatters into something greedy, nearly starved. His mouth lays claim to mine and I can't stop the fire burning within me or the damning need to be *closer*. He tilts my head back, making a swipe of his tongue over my bottom lip. I gasp, and he takes that opening to deepen the kiss.

A small noise escapes from the back of my throat.

Eren pulls back, just as breathless as I am. Lust flashes in his gaze, so unmistakable I wonder if he'll take me back to Esmeray and finish what he started. For a fraction of a moment, he seems to struggle between focusing on my lips or my eyes.

Then he nods, releasing me.

*'Goodnight, Sage.'* His voice rumbles in my mind.

I reel back, gasping.

He smirks as he withdraws, tapping the side of his temple. *'If you ever need me, I'm only a thought away.'*

I'm left gaping as he mounts Cantorix. Kamari's dragon screeches behind me in the distance, shooting into the air to follow her brother back to Esmeray. I wait until they're two specks in the distant sky. Only then do I turn and spot two figures at the gates.

Jocelyn and Ash remain where they stand while I approach. Ash takes my bag from me without saying a word, bringing it inside.

Jocelyn grins, nodding to my brother. "I think he went a little green there for a second."

Heat rushes to my face. "You guys saw?"

"Yes!" She squeaks. "You didn't tell me the engagement was going that well! Last time we talked, I thought you might kill him in his sleep."

"Yeah well," I shrug, my voice souring with the words. "That's still a possibility."

I curse myself for being so stupid. Not only can he locate me with the mark, he's inside my head!

"Ah!" She walks with me into the compound, lowering her voice so as to not disturb the others. "I bet he's incredible in bed. Do you think it'd be a hate-fuck situation or–"

"*Jocelyn!*" I cry, utterly mortified.

"Sorry!" She offers a sheepish grin. "Can't blame a girl for asking."

I pinch the bridge of my nose and rub my eyes. "I appreciate the support, but I'm really tired."

"Oh." Her face falls and I wince at the shift. "Of course. You've had a long flight. We'll talk tomorrow?"

I nod, hoping my smile is convincing.

Jocelyn crosses into the opposite wing. I sigh, continuing through the hall. I touch my fingers to my lips, the ghost of Eren's kiss still lingering. An act or not, I've never... been kissed like that before.

Another set of quiet footsteps wrestles me from my thoughts. I lift my head, finding Uncle Deon walking with a book open in his hand, his stare glued to the pages.

"Uncle Deon?"

He jerks his head to me. "Sage... You're up late."

"I just got home from Esmeray."

"Ah," he nods to himself. "That's right. Your engagement."

How odd it is to speak to him outside of the dining hall, knowing what I know. This must be the most we've spoken to each other in years, at least without a sneer or a hateful glare. I glance at the tome in his hand. *The Behavior of Dragons* gleams across the spine in gold script.

"Doing some late-night reading?" I joke innocently enough, tilting my head. A muscle in his jaw flexes. "On the *Behavior of Dragons?*"

Uncle Deon laughs dryly, snapping the book shut. "Why, yes. Dragons are curious creatures, you see. Don't you ever wonder what drives them? Why did they pick us as opposed to any other commoner? Or the mages, who are much better suited to magic than we are? Is it because the Gods blessed us?"

"No. Our family was one of the first people brave enough to approach them. We did what no others dared to do."

"And yet," Uncle Deon steps forward. "Dragons are fickle creatures with minds of their own, picking and choosing riders at their whim."

I narrow my eyes at him, a sneaking suspicion of where this is going. The last time a dragon refused to bond was with Halcyon, until she chose me instead of Lux. If my uncle thinks he can serve me an insult disguised as a history lesson, then he has another thing coming.

"What are you getting at, Uncle?"

He shrugs, taking another mindless step. "I'm simply an old man with far too much time on his hands. With your father running things, I must busy myself somehow. Please, don't let me distract you from your wedding plans."

With that, he makes his exit, skulking down the hall with the book clasped to his chest. I shake my head. The encounter haunts me all the way to my room, right up until I throw my bag down and collapse on the mattress. I hold my hand up to the light, admiring the ring.

A soft knock beats at the door.

I sit up. When they knock a second time I stand, moving to unlock the deadbolt.

Lux waits in my doorway, hands folded in front of her. "Hey."

"Hey." I glance over her shoulder, not finding anyone else in the hall.

"I'm alone," she offers as if trying to ease my suspicion. "I just wanted to ask if we could talk."

I bite the inside of my mouth, debating. The memory of her slap is as vivid as Eren's kiss, and yet I open the door wider. "Okay. Come in."

I shut the door after her, observing as she surveys the changes of the room. "What do you want, Lux?"

She wets her lips and takes a breath. "I want to apologize for how I treated you. It was wrong and I'm sorry."

I cross my arms. "Which part are you referring to? Slapping me like Mom or pretending I don't exist?"

"Both." Her eyes seem to plead with me to understand. "I'm sorry for all of it."

"What brought this on?"

She sighs. "Can't I just apologize to my sister? Does there always have to be an ulterior motive?"

"There's always an ulterior motive. That's how this family works," I snap, fed up with the lies. "What do you really want?"

"I want my sister back!" Her voice cracks. She takes a shuddering breath, collecting herself. "I let my emotions get the better of me. I felt like a failure and I took it out on you. I know we haven't been speaking, but I still watch everything you do. You're doing great things now. You'll be the Lady to the second most powerful House and that power means something. You can do incredible things with it. I want to be there with you when you do."

"Ah." I pick apart her words, reading between the lines and finding what she doesn't want to say. "So it's about politics. Business as usual."

She scoffs. "Don't be ridiculous. It's about family. Ash will take over someday. With you living in Esmeray soon, it's likely Ash will keep me close. I'll be like Aunt Natalya, remaining here with the husband he chooses." Her shoulders start to sink, her mouth pursed. "I'm not prepared to be Ash's right hand like you were, and I know you're not prepared to be the Lady of a House. I want things to go back to how they were so we can help each other, like family should. We need to keep our bonds strong or we won't survive."

I whistle, low and appalled. "Wow. You really took Mom's lessons to heart."

Lux raises a defiant chin. "She wasn't wrong about certain things."

In the quiet moment my sister and I scrutinize each other, I realize things can never go back to the way they were. Lux may not know it, but I've seen too much, *know* too much to roll over in the name of peace. I'll protect my family until my last breath, but I can't let them abuse that loyalty.

"You're wrong, Lux," I say, taking a cruel pleasure in the shock on her face. "I don't need your help. I'm doing just fine on my own, and I think you know that too." I hold open the door for her.

Lux swallows, squaring her shoulders. She pauses on the threshold, twisting her head to me, her hazel eyes filled with sadness. "No matter what happens, I'll always love you. I hope you know that."

"Get out," I whisper.

Lux enters the hall and doesn't look back.

I lock the door, staring at the rock on my finger. The tanzanite winks back at me, like it knows all my secrets. With a groan, I flop back onto the bed and dream.

# CHAPTER 17

Family dinners have always been mandatory. Breakfast is not.

Water flows over my tongue, cool and refreshing. I set the empty glass on the table and cut into the sausage sizzling on my plate. I'm the only one at the breakfast table who's deigned to finish their water, aside from Ash, who appears to understand its importance. Jocelyn's glass is halfway empty. Rune's glass is a bit lower than that. Jasper has only bothered with a few sips, a behavior that will cost him if he isn't careful.

For once, our entire family is joined for breakfast, and it's not a sight I welcome. I'm not sure if those suddenly in attendance have been called upon, and if they have... for what reason?

My eyes flick to Ash, shoveling food into his mouth and appearing none the wiser to the tension of the room. I look to Rune, practically my brother's right hand, and find my gaze narrowing. Could *Rune* be aware of our uncle's plan to usurp Ash as heir? My cousin, who would sooner slit my throat on behalf of his sister than hold a pleasant conversation with me? I grip my fork a little tighter, weighing the benefits of stabbing it into his jugular. Rune pauses mid-slice, quirking a brow at me. I scoff under my breath and shake my head.

No. Rune isn't clever, but his father is.

My father is the last to join us. He unfolds the cloth napkin wrapped around his utensils and drapes it over his lap. With one hand grasping a fork and a knife in the other, he greets his family with a placid smile that scatters chills across my arms.

"Good morning. Now that we're all here, I'd like to discuss a few plans for our House. With Sage and Ashton's engagements settled, it's time we move our focus to furthering our other alliances."

I meet Jocelyn's curious gaze across the table, but I have no answers for her. Her eyes trail down, bulging when they land on my ring finger.

'Later,' I mouth.

My father continues, slicing apart the meat on his plate. "Tomorrow, Jocelyn will be accompanied by Sage and Dahlia to Aruna. She will spend the day acquainting herself with her fiancé, Valen, with you girls as her chaperones and the Dysis family as your gracious hosts."

Utensils clank against a porcelain plate. I trail the noise to Dahlia, simmering with her fists on the table. Her lips are clamped shut, holding in whatever outburst is threatening to bubble to the surface. Jocelyn stares at her food in silence, her usually tanned skin now a sickly pale color.

Dahlia clears her throat, gritting through half-clenched teeth. "With all due respect, Uncle, I don't think Sage and I would–"

"I won't hear any excuses," he cuts her off, fixing her with an adamant look. "Take it as an opportunity to leave the past behind and work as a team again. This is a new chapter in your lives. Treat it as such."

Uncle Deon flexes his jaw, but voices no objections. Rune pierces me with a warning glare. Should anything happen to his sister, he'll no doubt hold me responsible. I don't cower from his warning though, chewing on my breakfast while maintaining eye contact. His lip curls in a near snarl.

Dahlia meets my stare, her grip tightening on her knife. I continue to chew, wondering how I'm supposed to juggle the hornet nest of House Dysis, Valen, and Dahlia at once. Jocelyn doesn't look up from her plate, pushing around pieces of her meal like it will delay the inevitable. It makes my insides churn. I had no idea her engagement with Valen was official, no longer a plot but a reality.

She sets her utensils down, rising from the table. "Thank you for your consideration, Uncle." I hear the tremble in her voice. "If you'll excuse me."

My chair scrapes as I move to follow, not caring to be dismissed.

"*Hey,*" I call out when it's the two of us in the hall.

She turns, her mouth twisted like she's going to cry. "What?"

"You didn't tell me your engagement to Valen was official."

"Yeah well," she wipes a tear from her eye. "You don't tell me much either these days." She twists, not sparing me another glance before she darts down the hall.

I watch her fleeting figure, helpless to patch the gaping hole between us.

"Let her go." Dahlia leans against the wall, her arms crossed and a scowl on her face.

I bite my tongue. *Don't snap. You have enough to worry about.*

"Don't expect me to fly with you," she warns, gaze hardening. "I might have to be civil in front of your Father, but don't think this changes anything." She pushes off the wall, passing me by.

"I'm sorry." The admission surprises me more than it does her, but I swallow my pride, damning it all to hell. We can't keep going on like this. Even if the words mean nothing, there's a part of me that has to try. "I never should have left you behind. The choice I made cost you your dragon."

Dahlia turns, her hands balled into fists and a murderous glint in her eyes. "You know, Cousin, I learned something that day. When the fog of grief passed I began to see our family so clearly." She takes a step. "I learned that each of us is one bad day away from ending each other. I learned that family is just a word, because the people you think will have your back won't pay you a second glance when it comes down to it."

"I had to make a call," I whisper, but the words taste bitter on my tongue.

Dahlia nods, fists trembling like it's all she can do to keep herself from hitting me. "Then you'll understand when I make one too."

She pivots, leaving me with the threat hanging in the air.

*A HARROWING WAIL shakes the earth with sorrow.*

*Dahlia kneels in her dragon's blood, Khione's body a steaming pile on the battlefield. I can hear the roars above us, the battle raging in the sky. We don't have time.*

*"Dahlia." I reach for her shoulder.*

*"No!" She shakes me off, doubling over with another cry of agony.*

*Tears prick at my eyes. Halcyon stands guard above us, staring at the clouds overhead and growling each time there's a close shriek. Khione's body formed a crater on impact, but it won't be long before the sands claim her.*

*Sobs rack through Dahlia's body.*

*"Dahlia," I try again, my voice trembling.*

*I want to cry with her, to shriek and mourn for a dragon that just as easily could have been my own, but we're too exposed. If we're discovered, we'll share Khione's fate.*

*Dahlia growls and shoves me. I trip over Khione's limp tail, landing on my back. Dahlia leers over me, a blade in her hand. A veil of bloodlust shrouds her face.*

*"This is all your fault! Why didn't you listen to me?"*

*"Dahlia—" I hold my hand up.*

*Before I can get a word out, she charges. I snatch the wrist holding the knife, shaking with the entire weight of her as it gleams inches from my nose.*

*Dahlia takes her hand, wiping Khione's blood down my face. "This is your fault!" She screams. "Your fault!"*

*A smack echoes behind us. Dahlia's eyes roll back to her head, her body slumping to the side. Jocelyn stands over us, her revolver in one hand as she stares at Dahlia with a grim frown.*

I SHAKE MY HEAD, clearing my thoughts as I turn down the corridor. With everyone taking breakfast, the halls are empty. I'm half-tempted to turn down Jocelyn's wing when the crossroad of halls brings me to a halt. My gaze snags on my parents' hall and I sneak a glance over my shoulder. They'll be occupied for at least another thirty minutes. *If I were going to hide an old necklace...*

My feet are already moving before I finish the thought.

At first, it isn't the prospect of removing the mark that lures me. It's the opposite. I want to prove the acolyte wrong, that my family has no need for a near-ancient piece of jewelry that's probably tarnished beyond belief.

Lucky for me, my mother leaves her door unlocked.

Her room is separate from my father's, full of woven

tapestries and polished furniture. Perfumes line her vanity table, each glass bottle placed in a perfect row. Her books are shelved alphabetically. Nothing lies on the floor or is left scattered on an open surface. There's not a thing out of place and little room for error.

I sneak over to the drawers near her closet, pulling one open to reveal a collection of jewels. Rings, bangles, bracelets, and earrings fill the drawer with stones the size of grapes and diamonds like liquid teardrops. I slip it closed, tugging forth the next one. In the second drawer, necklaces lay on velvet cushions—gold and silver along with simple chains and pendants. None of which match the one I'd see in Solasta's portrait.

Heels echo along the tile outside of the room.

I curse, shutting the drawer and backing away to the bed. I plop down right as the door opens, plastering on a smile for my mother.

She pauses, blinking at my presence. "Sage." She gives the room a quick scan, finding us alone. "What are you doing in here?"

My heart pounds within, nearly rattling my teeth with the force. I've never dropped in on my mother. We keep as much distance from each other as possible, and I'm quite content with that unspoken rule.

My scarred fist tightens, nails carving crescent moons inside my palms. "I have a question for you, Mother."

"Be quick with it then." She folds her arms, waiting.

"I was wondering…" I trail off, wracking my brain for a clever lie. "Perhaps for my wedding, you might be kind enough to let me borrow an heirloom of some sort. I promise I'll bring it back after the honeymoon."

She slices into me with an unwavering stare. "There is no date set."

I chew my inner cheek. "Yes, but it's tradition, after all. A girl only gets married once."

"This is what you've wasted my time with?"

None of my intentions are real, and yet her tone still manages to wrap around my insides–twisting. Without a word, she moves to the dresser. She faces me again with a matching set of gold earrings shining in her hand. Two dragon wings flare around a cuff that curls around the shell of the ear. Below it, a shower of small diamonds dangles from the piece meant to pierce through the earlobe.

"They belonged to your father's mother. Consider it your wedding gift." She slaps them into my hands, pausing.

I'm too busy admiring the jewelry to notice where her eyes land.

"What's that on your arm?"

My eyes dart to the fresh bandage. "Oh, um," I swallow, rising to my feet. "I was cut while training."

She tilts her head, scrutinizing me from head to toe. As if I pass her examination, she turns her back, striding for the vanity. "How sloppy of you. See a Healer before infection takes. We need each Rider ready to fly at a moment's notice."

"Yes, Mother." I dip my chin, making my escape.

Relief washes over me in the safety of the corridor. *That was close.*

*'What was close?'*

I practically fly out of my skin. The ghost of Eren's voice rings in my ears, clear enough for me to whirl and search the halls for him. Then I remember–he's in my *mind.*

*Get the hell out of my head!*

*'Easy, Killer,'* he purrs. *'Think you can slip away for a while?'*

I slow to a stop. *For training?*

*'I promised, didn't I?'*

I bite my lip, glancing between the earrings and the hall leading to Jocelyn's room. *Okay... I'll fly out in a minute.*

I drop off the earrings in my room and wander outside. No one's around to witness when I mount Halcyon, disappearing into the clouds.

Cantorix snoozes outside of the summer manor, a giant heap of ivory and rust scales curled in the sand. His enormous eye cracks open at my landing, one huge pupil dilating. Halcyon chitters low, cocking her head at his massive form. As I slip from the saddle, I swear I see his eye roll before it closes.

Eren waits inside, leaning back against a table in the vacant ballroom. Behind him rests a duffle bag half-concealed by his towering form.

"I was starting to think you wouldn't show."

"You caught me in the middle of something."

"My apologies." He smirks, not meaning it at all.

"I want answers. How long have you been reading my mind?" My face heats at the idea. How many times has he known the filthy things running through my head?

"Not long." His expression falls to something much more serious. "Only when you're thinking loudly. There have been times when you've sent them unintentionally, like earlier. I can reach your mind at any moment, but consider it a half-built bridge. You have to be willing to respond for the connection to hold."

"So…" I fold my arms. "It's not constant then, right?"

"No."

"Is there anything else I should know about this… bond?"

"I've shared what Oddica's told me. As far as I know, that's the last side effect." He reaches into the bag, producing two wooden longswords. He hands one to me as he passes, stopping in the center of the room. "Now, show me what you can do with a sword."

I grip the hilt, adjusting to the weight of it. "Why a sword? If I have to duel I'd prefer a dagger."

"Swords are traditionally used in an Ignis Mortem. If your

family honors the old ways, I doubt they'll leave you with options."

I huff, falling into position across from him. The sword isn't entirely foreign in my hand, but it's a great leap from the smaller blades I've learned to love.

Eren strikes first, hard and fast. I flick my wrist and counter, side-stepping his attack. He grins, a stunning sight under the sunstone chandelier. Blood rushes through my veins, my muscles tensing in anticipation for the next blow. He swings, causing an echoing *smack* that fills the ballroom when our swords meet. I whirl, aiming for his neck. Eren dodges it, surging forward to counter my blow. I'm forced to retreat, defending my side when he charges to my left. Right as I bring my sword up, Eren feints, using the distraction to swing his sword around and strike the back of my knees. To add insult to injury, he locks the sword over the base of my neck when I crash to the ground.

"*Dead.*"

I growl, shoving the prop blade off my neck. "You're showing off."

"No, you're out of practice. I see you know how to hold a sword. Your stance and balance are correct, but you lack technique."

"Technique?" I scoff.

"Swordplay is like a waltz." He points the tip of the blade to the ground, resting a hand over the pommel. "You have to get a feel for your opponent without letting them overwhelm you. Then you outsmart them when you've learned their weaknesses."

I pick myself up, blowing stray hairs out of my face.

Eren watches me as I lift my sword again. "How far did you get in your training?"

I hesitate. "We all trained for a time. Every Rider in my family learns a sword after we bond, but it was brief. We started to train with more effective weapons on dragonback... I suppose we only learned swords for tradition."

"They did you a great disservice."

The words make my heart twist and I don't like the feeling one bit.

"Enough talking." I take another swing.

Hours pass, but time has lost its meaning. My hands are raw, blisters sprouting between scar tissue. Bruises ache along my body in the first yellowing stages of bloom. Sweat slicks my palms, coating my heaving chest in a drenched layer. Eren's barely broken a sweat, eager to drain every last murderous impulse in me, it seems. My wrist trembles when I lift the weapon, arm screaming in protest when Eren finally straightens.

"I've seen enough."

I drop the sword, letting the wood clatter against the ground as I fight to steady my breathing. He makes his way back to the table, reaching into the bag. I can't even muster the strength for a witty comeback. A weariness settles in my bones, begging for me to sit down and rest. I glance at the light filtering in through the windows. It's long past golden hour, dripping into twilight. We've spent the entire day here.

I give into the weight of my body, sitting on the cool tile floors and not paying Eren any attention when he settles beside me. At least, not until he offers his canteen. I pop the cork, throwing my head back and gulping down the precious water within, not caring if it drips down my neck.

"It wasn't your fault."

I lift a brow mid-sip.

"Khione. I remember the battle."

The name sends a cold chill through me. I lower the canteen, burning a hole in the floor. "You know her name."

"I shredded her dragon. Not you. Why isn't your cousin angry with me?"

"Because." I squeeze my eyes shut, blocking out the memories. "You're... untouchable."

And now it's in the open, my old wounds resplit and stinging. A part of me hoped he'd never speak of it, never recall, but now it hangs in the air–the battle that sewed an invisible thread between us.

My family fought House Noctis the day Khione died.

And they won.

"I should have gone back for her." I swallow hard. "But Jocelyn needed help. Kamari took her brother and we gave chase, but we were separated. I told Dahlia to stay behind, to cover us, and when we got Jasper back... it was too late. She was fighting one of your sisters when you came to save her."

His gaze is distant as he listens, probably reliving that day with me.

"I'm sorry for the pain I've caused you."

It's the surprise of those words that makes me turn my head. He's already watching, holding my stare when our eyes meet. It's too intense for me to maintain and my thoughts sputter for anything to break the connection.

"What do you know of Queen Solasta?"

He quiets, seeming to consider his answer. "Many Houses have discarded her as a legend, but I think they prefer not to believe a woman once ruled them. Many texts were said to have been burned after her murder, an attempt to erase her from history. Now she only lives in the stories we remember."

"Do you think it's true?" I flit through the fantastical tales Lux once told me. "She led our people from a war-torn land into this one?"

"It's possible. No one ventures past the Wastes anymore so it's difficult to be certain."

"I think I'd like to one day," I murmur. *I'd like to find somewhere no one knows who I am, or what I've done.*

"No one comes back from the Wastes."

Eren's demeanor changes. His muscles tense as he stands up, offering me his hand. Once I'm on my feet he lifts a bunched grip of black fabric in his fist. A dangerous tilt of his lips tells me I won't like whatever he's holding and he knows it too.

"You're in your head too much. You question what choice to make when your opponent already knows their next move."

"And you think a blindfold will help?"

"Do you trust me?"

"No further than I can throw you."

His lips twitch, eyes sparking with an irritating delight. "Pick up your sword."

I do as he says, holding still when he steps around me, fastening the blindfold over my eyes. My breath hitches as he yanks the knot tight behind my head, blocking out my vision. I can't see a thing through the woven layers and it leaves me with a severe disadvantage.

"I fail to see how this helps."

I jolt when his voice comes from the front of me. "Don't think. React."

I'm not ready when the blow meets my bicep.

*"Ow!"* I clutch my arm, shrinking back.

Another *smack* hits my thigh, leaving a trail of burning pain.

*"Bastard!"*

*"Listen."* His footfalls are suddenly audible, leather stepping over the tile on my right. "Don't get lost playing defense. Learn to anticipate your opponent's next move. React before they can."

This time, I hear a slight woosh of air.

I dive in the opposite direction, feeling the near-hit of the sword scrape the fabric of my pants.

"Better." His footsteps travel around me, circling. "This time I want you to fight back."

I move with him, keeping Eren from getting the drop on me. I hear the pound of his step when he lunges, swinging my sword to strike against his. Our weapons clash, but when he swings again I'm not prepared. It's a direct hit to my wrist, sending the sword flying from my grip and a shooting pain that slices up to my shoulder. I gasp, unable to react quick enough before he's locked me between his chest and sword.

We both pant and although my hands come to grip his arm clamped over my chest, I can't get any words out. I shudder at the muscle pressed to my back, his heady amber scent invading my senses. His breath ghosts the crook of my neck and I squeeze my eyes shut under the blindfold, like it'll banish the need to tilt my head back and meet his lips.

The memory of them is scorched into my mind, at how skillful they moved against my own. I find my face turning like a moth to the flame, a pull from deep within me that craves the taste of him. I should fight it, but there's a treasonous part of me that wants to explore the tug, even if it leads me down the path of ruin.

I dip my head back, mouth parting, searching for his. Instead, his lips brush over my pulse, gliding over my skin and sending a shiver down my spine. His sword clatters to the ground. I turn in his arms, his hand now on my hip, dragging me closer. I lick my bottom lip, heart pounding so fast I fear it might burst. I brace my palms on his chest, feeling one of his hands cup my jaw to lift my face.

*Kiss me.*

I hear the breath leave his lips before we collide. His kiss consumes me, taking everything I have to give. His mouth moves against mine, punishing, claiming, nothing like our first kiss. His tongue slides over my bottom lip, begging me to open. My lips part with a moan, a liquid fire pulsing through every inch of me, softening my bones and molding us together. His tongue glides over mine, prodding my own to move with him.

It ignites a new hunger in me.

I wrap my arms around his neck, sucking his lip between my teeth and biting. He groans, leaning down to cup the back of my thighs and lift me without breaking the kiss. He walks us forward, shoving the duffle bag aside and setting me on the table. His hands explore my body, squeezing the swell of my ass. My fingers find the hem of his shirt, reaching beneath to slide across the ripples of muscle lying there.

He breaks our kiss, using a fistful of my hair to drag my head back and bare my throat. He kisses a trail down my jaw to the base of my neck where his teeth nip my pulse, tearing a whimper from me.

'Mine.'

The possession in his words makes my eyes snap open. I push him back, ripping off the blindfold and leaping from the table. Shock mirrors our features as we stare at each other.

"No," I whisper. "I'm not."

I see a flicker of understanding. He exhales. "That's not what—"

"I shouldn't be here." I stride past him, out into the moonlit night where Halcyon perks her head up from the gray sand.

I sprint to her, climbing into the saddle and grabbing hold of the horn. The ring on my left finger gleams in the moonlight, winking like a small star as we flee to the sky. I feel the bridge between our minds slam shut as the manor fades.

The compound is dark and silent when I return. I creep through dimly lit halls, careful not to wake the ghosts within. In the safety of my room, an empty bed beckons me to collapse. I'm halfway to the promise of sleep when my gaze snags on the closet. I find myself turning, reaching for the door and pushing aside clothes for a distant memory still propped in the corner.

A brown leather scabbard hides behind a heap of fabric, stamped with the insignia of my House. I lift it from the confines of the closet, examining the leather and the single strap hanging from it. The blade sings when it's pulled from the sheath, glaring back at me as if to demand my reason for abandoning it. I hold it steady, taking a few practice swings to help my wrist adjust to the heavy weight of steel.

There's no protest from my aching muscles, just a feeling of rightness as I point the blade at my reflection in the mirror. I watch my eyes widen when Heartfyre roars outside. I slip the blade back into the scabbard, throwing the strap over my shoulder and flinging the bedroom door open. I hear the clamor of guards shouting outside and race down the hall to meet them.

Jocelyn and Jasper run past me, hair wild and flight clothes halfway buttoned.

"Joce!" I shout, running after them. "What's going on?"

"There's a riot in Solera," she snaps, charging through the foyer and out into the front yard where our dragons have gathered.

Xantha, Tanith, Kallix, and Halcyon sit in a row with Heartfyre. Ash waits atop his dragon, jaw tight as he stares across the dunes to the distant city beyond them.

"Your Head of House has spoken," Ash announces when we're mounted, his eyes burning like two dark coals in a funeral pyre. "Crush the riot and *burn* those responsible."

In a snap of wings, Heartfyre shoots into the air, leading the vanguard of our formation. I hardly register the flight, heart in my throat as we descend upon the smoking chaos of the city. Shops are on fire, glass litters the sidewalks, and people fight in the street. I watch as Heartfyre opens his mouth, unleashing a warning blast of flames.

Rioters leap out of the way, but the fighting turns to panic. Civilians run screaming, ducking into alleys, and tripping over their own two feet. Looters continue to pillage, piling goods into brown sacks or shooting at our dragons as we sweep low. Kallix blasts a group of looters to our left, showering them in a stream of white fire. Xantha unclenches her jaws beside me, snatching a handful of rioters between her jaws and grinding their bones between her teeth. Jocelyn's face reveals nothing as her dragon chews. She only urges her to move faster.

We dive through the city, flying to the heart of the capitol where the largest crowd gathers outside the gates of our water treatment plant. The rioters shake the chain-link gates, scaling up to the barbed wire as our soldiers shoot them down from the other side. Heartfyre unleashes a guttural wail that thunders through Solera. Screaming echoes next, the people scattering in all directions like ants fleeing a flood.

But there are those who stand and fight.

Kallix touches the ground first, shrieking in fury as bullets bounce off his scales. Jasper and Jocelyn break off in opposing directions, flying after the rioters who flee. Ash circles in the sky, creating a blockade of fire around the facility. I'm about to order Halcyon to follow him when something on the ground catches my eye. I spy a woman on her hands and knees, clutching her round stomach and a man desperately trying to help her up. Kallix wreaks destruction with Rune, tearing apart the rioters in front of the gates mere feet from the man and woman.

*Take me down!*

Halcyon circles in a low glide, tiling her wing for me to slide off onto the ground. I dash to the couple, taking the woman's other arm and hoisting it over my shoulder to help her stand.

"Than–" The man cuts off, eyes widening when he registers my face.

"Go!" I shout, waving them on as dragons screech above.

*"Please!"* Another woman cries, falling to her knees in front of the wall of fire that shields the gates. *"We're so thirsty!"*

My lungs tighten, the air knocked out of me like a blow to my ribcage. Faces of refugees burst to the forefront of my mind–their suffering, their loss, their *will* to go on.

*Gods... we're doing it again.* I draw a shuddering breath, looking out at the chaos around me. Blood and charred bodies fill the streets, buildings burn, and our people run for cover at the sweep of dragon wings. I turn back to the gates where the woman sobs into her hands, a few others now kneeling with her, calling out for mercy from the Gods.

The image becomes crystal clear to me, a newfound understanding cracking fissures in my world. Of course these people were at the gates. Of course they risked annihilation for a slim chance of quenching their thirst.

*And we're killing them. We're killing them over a drop to drink.*

The horror turns my blood cold.

Kallix lands with a roar, slinking toward the kneeling figures.

*No.*

*No. No. No.*

"*No!*" I hurtle for the gates, ripping the sword from my back and skidding to a stop as Kallix lumbers over them, scales glowing hot in the center of his throat.

Rune's eyes narrow as his dragon pauses, head tilting in recognition. I stare my cousin down, shielding the others with my body. I keep my sword lifted over my shoulder, both hands locked around the pommel and ready to strike.

Gears seem to turn behind Rune's stare, weighing the benefits of killing me now. After all, he'll never get another chance like this. He could say I burned in the crossfire and not a single soul would be alive to know the difference. But I hold my ground, staring death in the face and it's in that moment, I realize I'm not afraid to die. What more could I ask than to meet my fate protecting those who needed it the most? After all the bloodshed I've caused, the least I can do is give my life in return.

"*Rune!*"

Our heads snap to the crimson beast landing. Ash's eyes rage with fire, burning holes into our cousin. The glow in Kallix's throat disappears as Rune bows his head, jaw clenching as our eyes meet one last time. Kallix flaps his wings, launching into the air.

I don't lower my sword when I meet my brother's gaze, or when it lands on the people cowering behind me. Ash's eyes cut to mine, hardened with disappointment. He shakes his head, commanding Heartfyre to turn. I watch as he leaps into the air, loosening an earth-shattering roar to signal our retreat. Tanith and Xantha appear in the sky along with Kallix.

I shudder, a long breath escaping my lungs that almost breaks into a sob as I lower my sword. Halcyon lands near me, screaming her displeasure. I take a weary step toward her, one after another when someone shouts.

"*Reina!*"

I freeze with my hand on the saddle and turn.

"*Reina! Reina! Reina!'* They shout in Solera's native tongue—a forgotten dialect composed of fragments not even noble families care to speak anymore.

A crowd assembles despite the warning shots fired from soldiers within the gates. I shake my head, hands trembling as I fling myself into the saddle and command Halcyon to launch. Their chanting haunts me, carrying on the wind and beating off the walls of my skull.

*Reina! Reina! Reina!*

But the words they claim—they shout without understanding. That time of history is long forgotten. I am Sage Galvan, third-born heir, second daughter of my House, engaged to Eren Noctis, and Bloodbound to Damon Valour.

I am a traitor. A killer. A girl of no consequence.

I am no Queen.

# CHAPTER 18

*I* slam to the tile, holding my cheek as my face throbs.
My father stands over me, expression unreadable as our family gathers around us. Ash has the decency to step forward, but one look from our father brings him to a halt.

Father crouches, gripping the back of my head and pulling my face back. "Were it not for your betrothed, I'd take a hand as tribute for your insolence. Consider yourself lucky."

He lets me crumble back to the floor as he rises, adjusting the cuffs of his sleeves. "I want you gone at first light. Should you fail to guard your cousin in Aruna, there will be consequences."

He departs with our mother. Our aunts and uncles withdraw, leaving the rest of us amongst ourselves. Ash kneels at my side, helping me up.

"What were you thinking?" Lux starts, eyes wide with disbelief.

"It was wrong," I croak, spitting blood on the floor.

"They were rebels, Sage," Ash whispers, hardly able to look at me.

"No, they weren't! They were *innocents*."

Rune crosses his arms. "How can you be sure?"

As the thought rises to answer, a burning in my throat muzzles me–compelling me to swallow the words.

He scoffs. "Exactly. You can't."

I open my mouth to retort, but Ash turns me by my shoulders. "Look at me. You were *this* close to being accused of treason."

My eyes well with tears. *If you only knew.*

"You can't do things like this, Sage. When we stand together we must stand as one. What we do out there sends a message. It's *them* against *us*."

"Maybe it shouldn't be!" I shove his arms off. "What I saw out there... what almost happened to those people was wrong! They're not rebels, they were just thirsty! They just wanted a little bit of water and we burned them for it."

"We held the line," Jocelyn cuts in. "We protected our city from anarchy. If they're fools with their rations, Cousin, it can't be helped."

"She's right," Ash says. "It's not our place to decide what's best. It's Father's. When we have orders we are expected to follow them."

"If you have such a weak stomach then you have no business being a Rider," Dahlia sneers.

I back away from them, shaking my head.

"Sage?" Ash sees me take another step.

I ball my fists, staring through tears. "The only fools I see are in this room."

No one calls after me when I leave them.

I'M HALF a ghost watching Jocelyn help Dahlia onto Xantha's saddle. Touching a hand to Halcyon's scales, I press my forehead to the side of her face and bask in the warmth fluttering through the bond. No matter what I've done, or the mistakes I've made, Halcyon will never see me any different. I can't fathom losing her the way Dahlia lost Khione and I dread the day I ever have to draw breath without her.

If a Rider doesn't die in battle with their dragon, they'll wish they were dead.

Aruna is the neighbor to Solera, with miles of sand being the fragile wall between our territories. The flight to Aruna stirs a frigid apprehension in my chest, the ghost of last summer's battle haunting me with each mile that passes. I can't trust House Dysis to receive us kindly, despite our alliance. I have to assume Valen hasn't changed his mind about killing me.

Jocelyn should have been my ally going into this, but unbreakable silence stretches between us since last night's events. She's barely looked at me, and it hurts far more than losing Lux. I glance at Dahlia sharing Jocelyn's saddle as we descend. Whatever happens within these walls, I can't trust Dahlia to help me. My gaze falls to my left hand where the tanzanite ring seems to sparkle in reminder of a different ally.

*If I can call him that.*

I'm not sure where Eren and I stand anymore, and I'm terrified of finding out.

Soren and Delphine stand with their four children; Valen, Chantelle, Fintan, and Lore. Unlike House Noctis, I'm well acquainted with their faces. Chantelle is the first daughter, second-oldest to Valen. She holds her chin high beside her brother, her sun-rich skin practically glowing like a goddess while she stares down her nose at the rest of us. I see the younger siblings further in the back. Fintan and Lore. Fintan appears to be a younger, lankier version of Valen, with amber eyes and russet brown skin. He's only missing the scars and height to match. Lore is the youngest, observing our party with an inquisitive tilt of her head, the elegant twists of her hair shifting with the gesture.

Dahlia and I flank Jocelyn, keeping close as we approach the steps. Their manor looms overhead, full of pillars and desert plants crawling along the exterior.

"Welcome, Miss Ember." Soren takes Jocelyn's hand, placing a kiss on top of it.

Jocelyn schools her face well. She lets her lips slide into a seductive smile, a far cry from the terrified girl I'd seen at breakfast yesterday. "The pleasure is all mine."

Soren's eyes skim over Dahlia and I, greeting us with a smirk. "Welcome, Ladies. Please, come take refuge from Vulcan's wrath. Valen, greet your betrothed."

Valen steps forward, scar deepening with his scowl. He murmurs a greeting before offering his arm to Jocelyn. She takes hold of it, allowing the Dysis family to lead us inside.

High ceilings and granite floors comprise their manor. Servants are kept busy, flitting past us with baskets of laundry or messages to be delivered. Our footfalls echo through the interior as we're escorted, alerting those within to our arrival. I count the guards stationed at each archway we step through, taking note of their weapons.

*We're guests. Allies. They have no reason to turn on us.* I remind myself, but it doesn't ease my nerves.

I glance at Dahlia with her arms folded behind her back, a nonchalant tilt of her head as she takes in the gilded decor. Two daggers are sheathed at her hips, swaying with her movement. I try to picture her using them on someone other than me and fail miserably.

"Valen, why don't you give Miss Ember a private tour?" Valen's mother suggests when we come to a stop in what seems to be their entertainment lounge.

Plush carpets fill the middle of the room along with soft

chaises, finger-foods, and drinks on a low round table. Guards stand watch in the four corners of the room, stoic and alert. I turn my head to Jocelyn, catching a slight nod of her chin to let her go. They disappear through the threshold, leaving Dahlia and I with the Dysis children and their parents.

"If you'll excuse us." Soren takes Delphine's hand, his lips curving. "My wife and I have meetings to attend to. Don't hesitate to let our children know if you need anything."

Their fading steps click along the tiles, leaving behind a tension-thick silence. Chantelle, the oldest sister, studies Dahlia and I. Winged kohl as sharp as talons slash over lovely olive eyes. Her mouth twists in a saccharine smile, so much like her father's that I bet she doesn't even notice.

"Dahlia and Sage Galvan," she breathes, tasting our names like she's sampling wine. "I'm surprised to see you both in the same room."

"Why's that?" I counter, holding back the bitter edge of my tone.

She smirks just like her father and gestures to the chairs. "Please, sit. My mother would wring my neck if she saw us standing."

I take a deep breath, settling into a chair with Dahlia beside me. She crosses her legs, appearing bored with the whole affair.

"You didn't answer my question," I prod, eyeing the other two siblings who study us with equal suspicion.

She plucks a glass of water from the table. "Your rivalry is practically legendary."

"What did you hear?" Dahlia snaps.

Chantelle hides the twist of her lips behind her drink, taking a small sip. "People whisper of it–the death of the Lavender Flame. Houses tend to remember dragons that fall."

Dahlia's face slides into a frigid mask. She reaches for a glass of wine, taking a long gulp.

"It's not like it matters." Chantelle shrugs. "We're allies now."

"So it seems." I let the threat linger in my words.

Lore watches us with silent intent, like she wants to ask a question, but doesn't know how. Fintan levels us with a cool gaze, not missing a single movement. His tense shoulders tell me he's ready to defend his sisters at a moment's notice.

A pang of sadness twists in my chest.

*What would it be like to have someone to love you like that?*

Not like Ash, who always balks in the face of duty, but someone who has no qualms about protecting their own. I twist the ring on my finger as Eren's face flashes in my mind. I feel the whisper of his lips, his hands cataloging every dip and curve of my body.

"I never dreamed I'd be entertaining Darling Death in my living room." Chantelle flicks a stray hair from her face.

"Excuse me?" My eyes narrow.

"What? You've never heard what they call you?" Her brow lifts with mild fascination. "It's the way you fight skyborn. You tend to fly in and out. One moment you're there and the next you're not. Then you return when your opponent least expects it, delivering the final blow on that gorgeous dragon of yours. You're quick about it. Your enemies never suffer–at least not that I've heard. It's so sweet it's almost... *darling*."

Dodge and evade, a tactic Ash taught me. With Halcyon still considered an adolescent, she's nowhere near the size of Heartfyre. It's why I avoid the larger dragons and try to provide support rather than take on opponents like Valen.

"Not what you were expecting?" She gives me a wry grin.

I deflect. "What do they call Eren?"

A darkness sweeps over her features. Fintan and Lore stiffen, their faces suddenly ashen at the mere mention of Esmeray's Dragon Lord. Chantelle's hand curls around her glass, talons digging in so tight I'm shocked it hasn't shattered.

"The Butcher."

"The Butcher?"

"The Butcher of Esmeray," Lore leans in, braver than her siblings. "Riders say together your Houses can burn the desert to a crisp by sundown."

"*Lore,*" Chantelle snaps.

"Well, it wouldn't burn to a crisp," I say, reaching for the wine.

Chantelle quirks a finely arched brow at me.

I smile back, bringing the drink to my lips and letting her see the Darling Death they whisper about. "Sand melts into glass."

Her mouth presses into a thin line.

I feign a stretch and rise to my feet. "Where's your bathroom?"

"A guard will show you," she waves her hand to the soldier posted at the entrance of the room.

Leather-clad boots pound against the tiles as the guard leads me down three turns before stopping at a wooden door with an iron handle. I watch as he pivots, taking his stance with his back to the wall where he intends to wait. With a roll of my eyes, I push the door open, locking it shut behind me. I take a few steps in, checking my reflection in the mirror. My mouth is taut, cheekbones singed pink, and the skin beneath my eyes bruised. Is this sun-burnt face the last thing my enemies see?

*Darling Death.* I huff and lean over the counter, my nails tapping the stone. I should snoop around, find something of value to give to Eren for our next meeting, but to do that, I have to ditch the guard, and my options are severely limited. There's no windows. No back door. One way in and one way out. I kneel, prying open the small cabinets beneath the sink. Women's sanitary pads line a woven basket next to several vials of pain tonics.

My gaze darts to the door. *I wonder...*

I crack the door open, peeking out at the guard. His stern face turns to me, eyes narrowing. Part of me wants to grin, but I feign a bewildered face and look between him and the empty hall. "Excuse me, um, it seems I… started my cycle." I bite my lip as his eyes go blank. "I checked the cabinets, but there aren't any sanitary pads in here. Do you think you can ask the Lady of the House for more?"

"Er, yes, my Lady. But I must–"

"And perhaps more undergarments too? I'd go with you, but it's quite a mess in here. I can't leave." I whisper, chewing at my lip again.

Color drains from his cheeks as his shoulders go rigid. He clears his throat. "I understand. I'll send for a replacement to wait with you and gather what's needed."

I beam. "Thank you."

He gives a terse nod and bolts down the hall. In a few quick steps, he's gone.

I laugh, opening the door wider. I make a couple of turns for good measure, listening for any trailing steps. When the hall remains quiet, I keep moving. Each knob I turn meets my hand with resistance, *locked* to keep lurkers like me out.

I click my tongue when an ornate door shudders at my attempt to get in, but the carvings on the wood are too similar to my father's study, giving me little reason to walk away and dismiss it. I pull two hairpins from the back of my head and squat in front of the lock. With one hand, I slip the first pin inside and bend it until it forms an L-shape. Using it as a lever, I twist, turning it at an angle to apply tension. With the other hairpin, I insert it over the first, wiggling it up and down to search for the seized pin keeping the lock closed.

A soft *click* emits from the lock and the door creaks open.

Parchments and pens line a polished desk set in front of a fireplace. Bookshelves rest on each side of the room, filled with dust-laden tomes. I cross the distance, peering over papers with Soren's handwriting. Dates, times, and locations are written, but nothing with context. I frown, shuffling through the stack. At the bottom, a brown ledger rests beneath the last piece of paper. I brush it aside, opening the cover.

*Dysis Filtration* is written at the top of the page, along with dates and shipment costs. My eyes scan right to the bottom, landing on a date marked four nights from now. I study the materials listed and the realization dawns on me. *Maintenance costs.* Their water filtration plant will be receiving maintenance soon.

I tuck that nugget of information away and turn to the next page. Orders for weapons, their scheduled deliveries, as well as armor costs for his soldiers line the space.

A dragon screech rips through the sky, shaking the walls and raising the hairs on the back of my neck. My head snaps to the window, heart thundering as I peer through it. A flash of labradorite scales flies up, sweeping past the window so hard the panel shakes. I gasp and stumble back, dropping to the floor as the warmth leaches from my bones.

*Gannon groans, arm lifting to touch the spot. His fingers pull back, shining dark red. I throw my whole weight forward, pressing both hands over the wound.*

Blood. So much blood smears my hands. Thick and hot, spilling out over my fingers.

"*Gannon? Gannon, tell me what to do!*"

My throat constricts as the dragon roars outside, lungs straining for air.

"*Oddica!*" *I scream across the dunes.*

*My fault. My fault. My fault.*

"Sage?"

My eyes blink open to where Dahlia stands, one hand gripping the door to the study. She shuts it behind her and I flinch as the dragon makes another sweep, spotting a jade-scaled dragon giving chase.

Playing. They're only *playing*.

Dahlia's gaze bounces between me and the window. "What are you doing?"

I wipe the sweat from my brow with a shaky hand. "Nothing. What are you doing?"

"Looking for you. Chantelle's pissed you ditched her." She crosses her arms. "What are you really doing?"

"Nothing."

I push off the floor, but she's already made herself comfortable in Soren's chair, combing through the papers. Her gaze snags on the ledger, lifting it closer for further inspection.

My head swims as I take a step, a bitter nausea rising to the surface. "We should go."

Dahlia continues reading, her eyes flicking to me at last. "We should take this to your father."

"No." I start forward. "They'll know it's missing."

Dahlia sighs, thinking for a moment. "Fine," she says, snatching a blank piece of paper and smacking it on the desk in front of me. "Then write."

I glare at the pen she holds up, attempting to hand it to me.

Her own gaze hardens. "Is there a problem?"

"They're our allies."

"So what?" She gestures to the rest of the room. "It's clear you don't trust them either. Any information could be critical in wartime. What do you think happens when we crush Valour and his rebellion? You really think we're going to hold hands and keep the peace with each other?"

I lean back, hands balling into fists at my sides. "That's what the marriage pacts are for."

Dahlia laughs bitterly. "You're a fool if you think that'll stop anyone. Didn't you hear Chantelle? They already fear our House aligning with your fiancé's. How long do you think it'll take the others to rise against us?"

"Is that what Uncle Deon thinks?" I fire back at her.

Her lip curls. "Don't act like your father is better than mine. He only had the advantage of being born *first*."

"Thank Gods for that."

Our eyes lock, neither one daring to back down.

Dahlia lifts the pen. "If your loyalty lies with our House, take the pen and *write*."

I rip it from her grasp, half-tempted to plunge it into her eye. Slowly, I lean over the desk, glowering at her until she reads off notes from the page. When we're done, Dahlia closes the ledger, hiding it under the stack of papers where we found it. She reaches for the parchment–a moment too slow.

I snatch it from the desk, fold it into fours and slide it into my back pocket. "I'll hold onto that."

She rolls her eyes at me, cracking open the door to scan the hallway. I move back toward the window, surveying the gardens below. Movement catches my attention as I spot two figures walking along a gravel path. *Jocelyn*. I follow Dahlia out into the hall, breaking off to the opposite wing.

"Where are you going?" She calls.

"To find Jocelyn."

There's a scoff, but Dahlia tags along. The guards we pass don't pay us much attention, like word hasn't quite gotten out that two guests are unaccounted for.

*Please let Chantelle be stubborn.* I plead with the Gods, hoping no one attempts to stop us from collecting our cousin.

Two glass doors are left open, allowing a small breeze to trickle in. We tread down the steps leading out onto the path. Creosote bushes line the gravel, blocking most of our field of vision. Harsh voices clash with the rocks crunching beneath our feet and I quicken my pace, straining my neck to peer around the corner when we find them.

Jocelyn bares her teeth, hand curled in a fist. Valen's nose is inches away from hers, tendrils of scar tissue crawling up from his throat to his jaw, flexing as he seethes hateful words I cannot hear. Jocelyn jerks back, held in place by Valen's hand crushing the base of her wrist.

"Get your hands off her!" I yell, hand flying to the hilt of my gun.

Valen straightens, releasing his grip. Jocelyn steps back, eyes molten with fury as she creates distance between them.

"Careful now," Valen chuckles, holding my stare. His lips quirk when he finds my hand on my weapon and just how close I am to drawing it. "You wouldn't want to break that precious alliance your daddy worked so hard for."

My sight snaps to Jocelyn. "We're leaving."

She tears from his side, her face fuming.

"I look forward to doing this again, Wife!" He calls after her.

"She's not your wife," I spit. "Not yet."

Amusement dances in his eyes like he's all but won.

I only move when Jocelyn is safely behind me, guarding the rear as we stalk back into the manor. Chantelle and her guards spring from the hall, the ladder red-faced and out of breath.

"Where–"

"We're leaving," I growl, pushing past her. "Send your parents our regards."

We don't wait for an escort, even as the guards trail us out the door. Halcyon and Xantha stir where they wait, wings fluttering with anxious energy. I reach for the bond as I climb into my saddle, letting her golden warmth steady me, but a nagging sensation pricks the back of my head, causing me to turn.

Soren and Valen watch from a window of what I'm sure is the Study. Halcyon growls at the glass panel as I level them with a scathing glare. With a snap of wings, we're airborne, the Dysis manor disappearing into a speck on the ground.

# CHAPTER 19

*I* make a beeline for Jocelyn. "Has this happened before? How long has this been going on?"

Her eyes grow wide as she dismounts from her saddle, but then her expression tightens, her fire and fury returning in one fell swoop. "I didn't need your help! I can handle Valen!"

"Yeah, *clearly*." I gesture to the bruise blooming around her wrist. "That's handling it? Gods, Joce, you should've told me!"

She laughs, reeling back like I'm the one who's struck her. "Wow, you've got some nerve, you know that? For someone keeping secrets, you seem to think you're entitled to everyone else's."

I flinch. "That's... What are you talking about?"

She rubs her wrist. "I don't know what's going on with you lately, but at the rate you're going–you're about to get yourself killed."

A lump rises in my throat. "I just wanted to help."

"I didn't need your help."

"I know," I amend, hoping she'll meet me halfway. "Believe me, *I know*, but I won't stand by and watch someone hurt you."

"Why?" She says, staring straight through me. "We did it when it was you."

My chest cleaves open, bleeding right onto the fire scorching within me. It takes everything I am not to turn over my palms and find the memories woven into the scar tissue. "That's... different."

"Why? Because it's our family? It's okay when we hurt each other, but not when other people do?" She scoffs, blinking in a rapid attempt to hold back the silver lining her eyes.

"Joce," my voice cracks.

She shakes her head, lifting a hand. "Don't. I have my duty, Cousin. And you have yours."

Sand shifts under her feet, leaving a trail of footprints in her wake. I stand there with Halcyon, silent as we watch my cousin flee into the manor. No matter how much love she pours into the bond, I can't feel anything but regret.

*How did I get here?*

I reach into my back pocket, folding open the intelligence stolen from Soren's ledger. I might lose Jocelyn forever, but I won't lose her to a monster.

"Let's go." I jerk my chin, not waiting to see if Dahlia will follow.

I don't give a damn enough to knock on the door, but throw it open with the last shreds of my restraint. Ash and my father's faces rise from where they're bent over the desk in the study, examining a map of our continent.

"I need a word. Now."

My father's eyes narrow, but he nods to Ash who is glued in place, watching me like I've grown two heads. He registers the command after a second, making a swift exit for the door, never breaking my gaze until the moment he passes my shoulder. When it clicks shut, only Dahlia, my father, and myself remain.

"Come back for more?" My father drawls, swirling his whiskey.

I lock eyes with him, not caring if I meet his hand again. "Jocelyn's engagement is off."

My father leans back in his chair. "On whose authority?"

"*Mine.*" I spread my hands over his desk, leaning closer so he can hear the steel in my voice and not mistake it for anything less. "I caught Valen today, man-handling her in the garden. There are bruises on her wrist where he grabbed her. She's not safe. If he can't honor her in their engagement, he won't honor her through marriage either."

My father's stare slides from me to Dahlia. His eyes flick back to me, but I'm not the one he speaks to. "Dahlia, it appears I need a moment alone with my daughter. Thank you for accompanying her today."

Dahlia gives a curt nod. "Of course, Uncle."

Her footsteps thud against the floor until the door shuts again.

My father straightens in his seat. His reptilian gaze slithers over my face, examining me like prey that's grown too bold, too quickly. "What you're asking jeopardizes everything I've worked for."

"And what if it were me?" I counter. "Or Lux? You would feed us to a beast like Valen?"

"Yes!" He slams his fist on the desk, temper bursting from the carefully crafted mask he's worn in front of me all these years. "I would do it a thousand times to save our legacy! Jocelyn can slit his throat in his sleep for all I care, so long as we secure our victory in this war!"

I step back, not believing what I'm hearing. But the truth is right in front of me, my father—a man who would do anything, sacrifice *anyone* in the name of his House. There is no mercy, no room for sympathy in the cold-cut violence reflecting back at me.

*He will never yield, and neither should you.*

I straighten my spine and master my expression, shedding

my skin like scales that have grown too small to contain me. "I will invoke the Ignis Mortem if he kills her, as is my right as the Lady of my House."

My father chuckles like a man who's looked death in the face and won. "You are the Lady of *nothing*. You might wear a ring around your finger, but you wear no crown. I alone stand on the ashes of those who came before me and I will not yield the power of our name for the whims of a little girl! Until you say *'I do'* you are the property of House Galvan! Your loyalty lies with your family *first!*"

My hands shake, not from fear, but from the restraint it takes not to scream. Not to yell. Not to rip the sword from my back and slay the monster before me.

"I see appealing to your mercy solves nothing." I unfold the paper in my hand and slap it on the desk, pushing it across the wood. "Perhaps you'll be willing to make a deal with your daughter instead."

My father scrutinizes the paper like it's a firedrake about to spit flames. "What is this?"

"Intel from the personal ledger of Soren Dysis."

He sketches a brow, plucking the paper from the desk and studying it. "You've been busy."

"It comes with a price," I say, folding my hands behind my back and lifting my chin. "End the engagement. I am a daughter of House Galvan, but I will wed Eren Noctis one day soon unless you intend to incur his wrath. When we are wed, our family will come second in my list of priorities. You'll find I am much more useful as an ally than an enemy."

"Are you threatening me, Daughter?"

"I'm giving you a choice. Don't break the engagement and Sage Galvan will have no choice but to understand." I shrug. "But Lady Noctis will not forget it. I encourage you to choose wisely."

I can't tell if my father is breathing. There is only the sound of him tapping his finger on the desk as if contemplating what to do with me. Between the minutes, I wonder if these are the last few that I'll draw air.

"I'll break the engagement," his voice cuts through the room. "On one condition."

I clench my teeth, waiting.

"You will lead the next mission with a team of your choosing. Prove yourself competent, and I'll rescind the alliance."

My shoulders tense. "That's it?"

Cyrus smirks, a sight that twists my stomach into knots. "Fail, and you will break the engagement with Eren and wed Valen yourself."

My lungs seize for a fraction of a second, the order to breathe not quite registering in my mind. Father leans back with a satisfied smirk. He knows he's caught me in his web and I won't be able to cut free. If I walk away, Jocelyn will be forced to marry a monster. For her, there is no alternative.

*'I have my duty, Cousin. And you have yours.'*

I stare, and suddenly, it is no longer him and I alone in this room. The ghosts of the Galvan women who came before me stand at my side, my ancestors whose dragonsong was also silenced, their wings shredded by the claws of men like just my father.

*No more.*

I will the corners of my mouth to rise, taking joy in the way his face falls.

"Deal. I'll return when I recruit my team." I pivot on my heels, slamming the door on my way out.

Dahlia stands across from the study, arms folded tight over her chest. I shoot her a glare, daring her to comment, but half of her mouth quirks in the whisper of a grin. I shake my head, darting through the corridor.

It doesn't take long for Ash to find me.

"Sage." From the urgency in his voice, I know he's been waiting.

I spin, noting the wrinkle of worry on his forehead.

"What was that?" He skids to a stop, but there's no aggression. It's panic I hear behind his words. "Bursting in? He could have–"

"Could have what? Does it matter?" I cut him off, not giving him time to recover. "I struck a bargain. If you really want to help, meet me in the library."

I start toward the right wing of the compound. A familiar door with whorls of fire waits for me. Gathering my nerves, I bring myself to knock.

Jocelyn's face appears, brows narrowed in suspicion. "What do you want?"

"I need to talk to you. Please. Can you meet me in the library?"

Her lips purse. "Okay."

My heart quickens. "Okay?"

She nods and shuts the door.

My knees almost buckle with relief, but my work isn't done. I turn back the way I came and wait amongst the tomes, wondering who will appear first. I spend my time fidgeting, peeling back frayed cuticles until the first set of footsteps causes me to lift my head.

Ash approaches me slowly, Jocelyn not far behind him. They pass a questioning glance to each other before they look at me. I pop my knuckles, waiting for them to get closer. Everything that happens next depends on their help and I can't afford to lose either of them.

"I'm going to be leading the next mission with a team of my choosing and I wanted to ask you both for your help."

Ash's shoulders go rigid.

"What kind of mission?" Jocelyn asks.

"I don't know yet."

"I do." Ash shifts his weight from one side to the other, a flicker of doubt flashing on his face. "He's planning an assault on the rebels. If he's trying to test you, this is the perfect opportunity."

*And enough room for error.*

I will myself not to react, to regain control of my thumping heart. I have to stick to the facts. *I need them to agree, or this all falls apart.*

"I know this isn't going to work without trust, but there's no one else I'd rather have on my side than you two. I know I haven't been forthcoming lately, and it's no one's fault but mine." I meet Jocelyn's stare. "I'm engaged to one of the most dangerous Riders on the continent and it hasn't made sharing things easy. I'm torn between loyalty to my House and joining another."

"You're becoming reckless," Jocelyn points out. "At a time when you need to be careful."

"I know. I've let my heart rule my head and I'm sorry for worrying you both."

Ash and Joce look at each other, then back at me.

Jocelyn sighs. "Okay. I'll help you."

"What's your plan?" Ash lifts a brow.

"We're going to make one right now," I say, moving toward the nearest shelf and plucking a scroll. I roll it out over a table, unraveling a map of Celosia before I look Ash in his eyes. "Tell me what you know."

Ash points his finger on the lower right portion of the map, at House Tesar's patron city, Narelle. "He's found a safehouse just on the outskirts of Narelle."

"When does he plan to attack?" Jocelyn hovers over my shoulder to see.

Ash's face pinches, like he's not quite certain. "The intent was to move within the week, but it could be any time now."

"Probably sooner than we think," I mutter, the lavender stone winking on my left hand. I have to get word to Eren. I roll up the scroll and pass it to Ash. "Get ready to move at a moment's notice. I'll check back with you guys when I report to Father."

I hurry back to my room, locking the door before I can breathe. But it turns out that not even my room is safe. A wax-sealed envelope rests on my bed, the stamp of my father's signet ring shining clear in the light. I rip it from the blanket, tearing open the seal. My father's intricate writing lines the page.

*Sage,*
*I entrust to you the task of liberating the city of Narelle from rebel occupation. We've located a safe house in the outer district. Below, you'll find coordinates to the location. Riders from House Tesar will be there to assist. Any survivors are to be restrained for questioning. Leave tonight and do not disappoint me.*
*-Cyrus Galvan*

I crush the letter in my fist and hurl it at the wall. I pace the room. House Tesar joining the raid complicates it even further. Which Riders will they choose? How many dragons? How can I get word to Eren? I chew my lip between my teeth.

The bond.

But I've never reached out first before. Eren has always opened the connection. I've never asked him how to do it on my own. I rifle through the snippets of what he's told me.

*A bridge. He said it's like a bridge.*

I suck in a breath and close my eyes, picturing a bridge cut from moonstone with Eren on the other side.

*Eren?* I wait, holding my breath as I listen.

'*Miss me already?*' Comes his teasing reply.

Relief floods my body, washing away the regret of how we left things. His voice is clear as day, whispering in my head like the softest caress.

*I have to tell you something.*

'*What is it?*' Amusement vanishes from his tone, taking on a more serious intent.

*There's going to be a raid on your safehouse in Narelle. Galvan and Tesar Riders will be attacking tonight.*

There's a pause.

'*Which riders from your family?*'

*My brother. My cousin.* I hesitate. *And me.*

'*You'll be there?*' His voice tenses.

*I'm leading the attack. My father is testing me.* I confess, squeezing my eyes shut. *Eren, if we don't find anything he'll know you were warned.*

'*He can't know for sure,*' Eren says at first, but seems to think better of it. '*I'll get out the sick and injured and then we'll fight as long as we can.*'

*You're going to be there?* Fear laces through my words, echoing down the link between us.

'*Wherever you go, I go.*'

*You can't fight Riders with only one dragon!*

Noxainia is huge, but one dragon against Heartfyre, Halcyon, Xantha, and however many dragons House Tesar intends to bring will be a slaughter. He has to know that.

'*I'll see you tonight.*'

I feel our connection snap like he's left the space we share within our minds.

*Eren?*

Nothing.

*Eren!*

The silence of my room is the only answer. I growl, kicking the edge of my bedframe. I need a plan, one that's convincing enough not to blow my cover. I shake my head at the absurdity, running both hands through the thick, knotted tendrils of my hair.

*I have to get this right, or I'll get everyone killed.*

# CHAPTER 20

*S*unbreaker shines through the blanket of night, a silver cluster of stars shining with a crescent moon overhead. It's better cover than we could have hoped for–if this were any other mission, but it leaves the rebels at a severe disadvantage.

It leaves *Eren* at a severe disadvantage.

I try not to bite my lip, glancing between Ash and Jocelyn flying beside me. *'We go in quick, hit hard and fast before they can recover,'* I recall the plan. They were the words of a Rider ready to decimate the enemy, not an informant trying to keep her mask from slipping. *'With any luck, we'll be done with it before House Tesar shows up.'*

*'And if they're already there?'* Ash thought to ask.

*'Then we clean up their mess.'*

My knuckles tighten, clutching the saddle so hard they begin to pale at the strain. If House Tesar gets there first, I don't know how much of my plan I can salvage.

*I don't know who I can save.*

I reach through the infinite dark, carving the bridge from scratch. *Eren?*

*'A little early for our date, isn't it?'*

I hold in the laugh of relief at his coy response. The fact that he can answer means the Tesars haven't arrived. *We're almost there. I don't know how much I can hold back. I have to be convincing.*

*'Do your worst, Killer.'* I envision his smile with the seductive lilt in his voice. *'I can take it.'*

I shiver. *You're insane.*

Narelle's first villages come into focus. I scan the adobe houses below, searching for the mansion of a rich merchant Ash spoke of on the flight here.

"Down there!" Ash points from the back of Heartfyre.

A manor built with high pillars and a stone exterior stands higher than any of the meager homes surrounding it. There's no sign of the rebels, or any villagers below. It's as if they knew to take cover, to flee their homes in the dead of night. It sends my heart pumping, waiting for the moment my team begins to question it.

*Trust Eren.* A small, inner voice nudges me.

I pray to the Gods nobody's in there. "Light her up!"

All three dragons inhale, reeling their necks back. I watch the fire glow through Halcyon's scales, a ball of light rising to her jaws where they part, unleashing a whirling inferno of death. A flush of heat blows back against my face as the manor erupts in flames, wood and rock exploding across the yard.

We watch from the sky, the soft beat of dragon wings feeding fresh air into the hungry flames. When no movement stirs, no sight of retaliation, Jocelyn and Ash look at me. I swallow hard, boring into the flames. *Eren's smart, he must have pulled his people and the villagers.* But if that's the case, where are the soldiers hiding? If they won't move while we're in the air, it means they know one thing; their advantage lies on the ground.

Ours is in the sky.

I shove down the panic slithering in, gnawing through my chest like a parasite. "Let's check it out. Be on guard."

Jocelyn and Ash drop down with me in a rolling sweep. I unsheath my gun, switching off the safety and keeping it clutched between both hands. We move as a unit with my brother and cousin guarding my back. Flames crackle from the mansion, casting a bronze glow upon the abandoned houses. Curtains are drawn, interior dark, leaving us with no way to guess if anyone's inside. Blood rushes in my ears, eyes straining in the firelight. Smoke from the fire hangs heavy in the air, twirling between structures. I scan the windows for movement, waiting for the inevitable.

Several shots ring out, forcing us to dodge for cover. We duck behind a pile of rock blown off from the mansion, exchanging fire with the rebels hidden in the nearest house. I peek around the side of the boulder, firing three rounds into the second-story window where I spot shadows moving.

Two distinctive shrieks rain from the skies as serpentine figures soar down, spitting a wall of flames between us and the rebels.

House Tesar.

"Cover me!" Ash shouts, swinging around from the rocks and sprinting toward the house.

The blanket of fire dissipates as two dragons soar higher into the air, preparing for another attack. Ash runs across the scorched earth, shooting the rebels who run out to meet him. Jocelyn aims for the enemies closing in on us, creeping from their foxholes within the wreckage, but my eyes never leave Ash.

I fire at a lunging rebel's hand, sweat dripping from my brow as the gun flies from his grip, allowing my brother to make quick work of him. Ash kicks open the front door, disappearing through the frame.

"Sage!"

I spin around right as a black-clothed figure swings on Jocelyn. I lift my gun, about to fire when another rebel shoots, the bullet narrowly missing my head. I drop low, firing into their leg and turning back to my cousin. In those precious seconds, Jocelyn has disarmed her opponent, aiming right into the middle of his skull. Blood sprays back, a fine mist of it splattering on the side of Jocelyn's face.

She twists to me, grabbing my wrist. "Come on!"

We break into a run, weaving between bullets and rubble. A dragon roars above us, deep and guttural. Chills crackle over my skin, a spark of lighting jolting my heart into overdrive. I gulp in rapid breaths, pumping my arms faster, and stretching my legs further.

Jocelyn and I burst through the entrance of an empty house, collapsing to the ground. She scrambles to lock the door, hunching down to gasp for breath. A sheen of sweat and a layer of soot covers her face. I try not to look at the blood drying over her cheek and shut my eyes, focusing on breathing.

"Where's Ash?" I rasp, pushing myself up.

Jocelyn shakes her head. "I don't know. He went into that house. I didn't see him come out."

"We have to find him."

Jocelyn peeks out the window, spying the Tesar reinforcements moving in. A company of ground soldiers dressed in gold and blue uniforms search the houses. Shots thunder from where they make contact, causing us both to flinch.

"I thought this was a safehouse." Jocelyn settles back to the floor, chest rising and falling with labored breaths. "It's like they knew we were coming."

"It doesn't matter." I change the subject. "We need to find Ash. Then we can get back in the sky."

"And burn them all to Hell," she swears.

I give her a nod, because it's the only thing I can think to do.

We take a back door in the kitchen, circling around to the house where we last spotted my brother. I keep my weapon close, inching across the sand. Shadows dance along the walls, threatening to jump forward at any moment.

I exhale, steadying my grip on the gun. If I have to kill Eren's people to protect mine, I'll do it, but there's a writhing pit in my stomach, an intense feeling of *wrongness* that causes my fingers to shake.

The back door to the house flings open, but it's Ash standing in the doorway. My knees wobble, ready to buckle when I notice the grim look on my brother's blood-stained face. He waves us inside, shutting the door behind us.

"Ash, what is it?" I say as he leads us up the stairs.

"*This.*" He opens the door at the top, leading to an empty room full of bodies.

I wrench my eyes from the carnage, holding back the gag in my throat from the coppery scent of blood pooling on the floor and spot the hulking contraption pointed to the opening of the window. A ballista armed with a dragon scale-tipped spear winks in the crackle of flames outside.

My jaw drops. "Is that... *dragonscale?*"

Ash nods. "From the Nightstalker."

I spy the scale, not just any color, but the obsidian black shade of Noxainia's scales. It can only mean Eren sanctioned this weapon... and intended to use it tonight.

*Do your worst, Killer.* The smug memory of his voice echoes through my head.

"But... nothing's stronger than dragonscale," Jocelyn insists, terror lacing her voice.

"Exactly," Ash mutters, gesturing to the ballista. "One precise hit to their eyes or wings—hell—even down their throats would be enough to bring them down."

"We should go," I whisper, staring numbly at the ballista. "We'll burn it down and be done with it."

Ash nods his head. "We'll tell Father when we get back."

Sharp whistles cut through the air. The three of us run to the window in time to witness the spears flying through the air. A red and blue-speckled dragon banks a hard right, barely missing the spear aiming for its wing. Two other spears miss, one soaring past a gold dragon entirely and the other bouncing off the edge of the blue dragon's scales. Our heads snap down, spotting the ballistas peeking out of separate houses as rebels reload the spears.

Ash curses. "We need to stop those ballistas."

"We should split up," I tell them, betting on Eren's protection even though it's the last thing I want to do. "We'll each disarm one and get back in the sky. Then burn this place to the ground."

"Fine by me." Jocelyn reloads, storming down the stairs.

Ash and I part ways at the bottom.

"Be careful," he says, ducking out the door.

I take a deep breath and try to do the same.

Outside, bodies of soldiers and rebels alike lay bleeding on the ground. I step over them, avoiding as much contact as I can, but my boots collect grains of bloody sand. I creep along the edge of the house, spying the rebels on the second level of a home across from me. I'm about to make a run for it when an arm yanks me back, a large hand smacking over my mouth and muffling my scream.

"It's me!" Eren hisses, dragging me into the darkness of a house before he lets me go.

I stumble back, hands shaking. "What the *hell?*"

His brows furrow. Only his eyes are visible with the mask on, but they're all he needs to understand that something isn't right. "What's wrong?"

I laugh, exhausted and unhinged. "What's wrong? I'm trying not to kill anyone while also trying not to get my own family killed! And the ballistas? Are you kidding me? You didn't think I should know about something that can kill my dragon?"

He sighs. "You saw them."

"Yeah, I saw them," I mock, crossing my arms. "You know we can't leave here without destroying them."

"I figured as much."

I stare at him, gaze hardening.

"Don't give me those eyes. My people know what you look like. They know you, your family, and your dragons are off limits."

"And what if they forget? What if they stop caring? Dragonriders are all the same to you, right?"

"You're different."

"Are you sure?" I step closer, craning my neck to keep looking into his eyes. "My family killed a lot of rebels tonight and I let them. I might have to kill more if they get too close to my team."

"They've been warned," Eren growls, palming my throat and backing me into the wall. "They know not to touch you." His voice drops dangerously low. "They know the consequences."

I take a sharp inhale, intoxicated by the cloying scent of leather and cypress.

"And what would you do if they did?" I say, more breathless than I mean to as his thumb traces over my pulse in soothing sweeps. I'm ashamed to admit I missed it, that his hand around my throat ignites a fire within me that I can't control.

I'm not His, and he's not mine, but damn if I don't want to forget all of that at this very moment.

His thumb drifts to my chin, pausing beneath my bottom lip. He leans closer, bringing that decadent scent with him. "I would hunt them down, every last one of them. I don't care who I have to kill, but know they'll die screaming." He releases me, quickly increasing the space between us.

I shudder, raking in a breath and watch him as he peeks through the curtains before he faces me again. "What do you need from me?"

"I need to win." I square my shoulders, collecting myself. "I can't go home without a victory."

Eren's mouth seems to twitch under the mask, but I can't be sure. "I'll give the order to retreat."

"Eren–"

"Go," he says, backing out of the room. "Before they find us."

When Eren fades into the shadows, I pry open the back door. Gunfire booms across the desert, the fire of the manor raging on in the chaos of battle. I sprint into the night, unnoticed by the soldiers and rebels locked in fights near the mansion. I'm able to creep up to the house with the ballista and slide open a window unseen.

*"Sage,"* I hear Jocelyn whisper.

I turn as she jogs up to me, joining my side. Relief courses through me at the sight of her unharmed, but if she's done, that means this house and Ash's are the last ones we need to hit.

"Did you see Ash?"

"He's already done. He's summoning Heartfyre as we speak."

"Okay, let's finish this."

Jocelyn follows me through the window.

Voices stir from the second level, heavy boots stomping across the floorboards. I keep my gun close, ascending the stairs with careful steps. Pausing at the shut door, I listen to the voices arguing within, muffled through the wood. Jocelyn gives me a nod, waiting for my signal.

*Now or never.*

I kick open the door.

Jocelyn fires the first round and I hear the sound of a body drop, but I freeze, gun aimed at the person in front of me. Azara stands near the ballista, eyes wide. Behind me, Jocelyn shouts and I turn my head as a gun clatters to the ground. Oddica's there, trapping Jocelyn in a chokehold where she struggles to stay upright. Her shocked eyes are glued to mine. I snap my neck back to Azara who's lifted her palms in surrender.

"Go on," she threatens. "Show us who you really are, *Rider*."

I lock eyes with her, lift my gun a fraction of an inch, and fire.

The bullet grazes her ear. Azara feints, only to rise with a swing of her fist. I let the blow come, ears ringing when it connects with my jaw. I hear a struggle behind me and footsteps running out. Jocelyn wheezes near the stairs, shooting rounds after them. I groan, holding a hand to my pounding jaw. Jocelyn squeezes the doorframe, bowing her forehead on the wood.

Rising to my feet, head still reeling, I dust off my pants. "We should–"

The click of a revolver cuts me off.

Slowly, I lift my gaze.

Jocelyn's tear-stained face glares back, one hand aiming her gun directly at me. "Start talking."

I lift my palms. "Joce, what are you doing?"

"Don't do that. Don't play dumb. You're a lot of things, but you're not a lousy shot." She flicks off the safety. "Why did you let them get away?"

My head spins, the world too fast for me to keep up. *She knows.* How do I tell her with this curse? How can I convince her I'm not her enemy? *How do I avoid a bullet in my chest?*

"You're a sympathizer," she spits.

"No, I–" The mark flares, burning a hole in my throat. *Find a way around, tell her anything!* "I made a–" It burns hotter than ever, ripping a strangled cry from my throat and bringing me to my knees.

Jocelyn pauses, mouth parting, but she doesn't lower the gun.

I pant on the floor, gaze catching on the sleeve that hides my mark. *This is it. You have to choose.* I squeeze my eyes shut, willing the thought to reach across to the stars to wherever Eren is hiding.

*I'm sorry.*

I yank my sleeve up and tear off the bandage. The Nightstalker glows white with power, an iridescent light that fills the room.

Jocelyn gasps. "You're one of them!"

"No!" I shout, clapping a hand over my throat as tears race down my face. I hold her stare, pleading for her to piece it together.

I see the wheels turn in her mind, her eyes widening. The gun drops to the floor. Jocelyn kneels in front of me, taking my wrist to examine the mark. "Who did this?"

I shake my head, locking my eyes with hers then trailing the path to the Nightstalker tattoo.

"Valour," she breathes. "You found him, didn't you?"

A shuddering breath escapes me as I hang my head.

"We have to tell your Father. We'll get the High Mage to–"

"No." I grip her hand tight. "Please."

She stills. "Don't tell me the High Mage–"

"It doesn't matter! You can't say anything because... this is *wrong*."

Her face blanches. "I don't understand."

"Joce." I take both of her hands in mine. "I've seen things that give me nightmares. Our people suffer under our rule. What we're doing to them is *wrong*."

She rips her hands from me like I'm contagious, snatching the gun as she rises to her feet.

"I've tried to forget it. I've tried to push it aside, but I can't forget the things I've seen."

"So what then? You want to hand them the war?"

"No! But something has to change! We can't keep going this way."

"And that mark?" She points an accusatory finger. "What is it exactly? Does it make you his puppet?"

I open my mouth, but the fire returns, the mark glowing in answer.

She drops her finger. "You can't even tell me."

The dam breaks and the tears slide down my face, dripping to the floor.

She swears. "All this time! You knew where he was hiding!"

I shake my head, because that is the only thing the magic will allow.

"You're a gods-damned traitor."

"No." I step forward. Jocelyn lifts the gun again, warning me to stay back, but I don't falter. "You weren't there when me and Dahlia sat with the Dysis heirs. You didn't hear the things we talked about. The moment we crush the rebellion, it's back to fighting each other. Too many people fear our family and Eren's. It's going to start all over, more and more death until there's nobody left. Is that what you want, Joce? How many of us have to die in the name of a House our people fear?"

"No!" She shouts, angry tears slipping from her eyes. I can see the gears turning in her head, the doubt planted and growing. "But why would you side with our enemies? What makes you think they won't kill us too?"

"I give you my word!"

"And that's supposed to be enough?"

"It used to be."

Jocelyn's tears stop. She lowers her gun and shakes her head. "Your word is worthless."

My heart breaks open, pieces shattering with the bond I've irrevocably broken. "Joce."

She holds up her hand, unable to look at me. "I need to think."

I watch her leave down the steps, further and further until she's a shadow in the night.

Once again, I'm alone.

# CHAPTER 21

*T*he entire village in Narelle is incinerated, leaving their people with no home to return to. *Is Eren ready to take this on? Can he handle the influx of refugees?* Jocelyn's tear-stained face flashes in my mind. *Is this the night I meet my execution?*

In my father's study, I deliver the report. His expression doesn't budge at the mention of the ballistas, not even a twitch. An uneasiness settles in my gut, because I know that vacant stare to be something far more deliberate. He's thinking, and that's never a good thing for anyone else.

At his dismissal, Ash and Jocelyn leave the room. I force myself not to turn my head and watch my cousin leave. *That's a good sign, isn't it?* If she intends to turn me in, wouldn't she do it upon our return?

"Well," my father uncaps the decanter on his desk, pouring a drink. "It appears your mission was a stunning success. You must be pleased."

I can hear the pettiness in his tone, a trap he's waiting for me to fall into. I won't give him the satisfaction. "I fulfilled my end of the bargain."

"Yes, you did." He takes a sip, sharp eyes studying me beyond the glass. "I'll break the engagement, but know the consequences that follow will be your own doing."

"I can live with that."

"Can you? Given that Soren's reaction is still unknown, it would only be fair to gather collateral to share in good faith, wouldn't you agree?"

My spine stiffens. "What kind of collateral?"

Cyrus traces the patterns of his glass as he speaks, as though this is no more important than the weather. "Find me something to use against House Noctis. You're a Dragon Lord's fiancée now. It shouldn't be too difficult."

Warmth drains from my face. "What in the Gods' names could I give you that he wouldn't be able to link back to me?"

"You're a smart girl." My father rises with a smirk. "I'm sure you'll figure it out. Bed him before the wedding if you must, but I want something valuable enough to appease Soren when he receives such heartbreaking news."

I nearly wince at the callousness, but the thought that my father would ruin me to further his agenda is no longer surprising. With a nod I leave the room, increasing the distance before I break my composure. Each day I spend in our home seems to dissolve my world even further, the walls and furniture warping into a space I no longer recognize.

*Why do you cling to it?* A part of me asks.

A fearful, desperate part of me answers. *Because I don't know who I am without them.*

Heels click along the tiles, breaking me from my thoughts. Aunt Natalya strolls through the corridor with a book in her hands, browsing over the pages. The utter nonchalance reignites the spark of fury within me, fueling my steps forward.

"How could you do it?" I snarl, jabbing a finger when I'm upon her. "How could you let her marry a monster?"

She startles, head snapping up from the book. "What?"

"Valen! How could you let your own daughter marry him?"

"I–" My Aunt falters, lost for words.

"Forget it," I wave her off, disgusted. "I broke the engagement–no thanks to *you*. Just know it came at a great cost."

I start to turn when lithe fingers wrap around my wrist.

"Did my brother know?"

*Did he know Valen was a monster?*

I nod.

She sucks in a breath, releasing her grip. "It seems you have saved both of my children. I am indebted to you."

"A lot of good that does me," I mutter, turning again.

"A bit of advice, Niece."

I halt, keeping my back to her.

"My brother is not untouchable. He only wants us to believe it."

"Is that treason I hear, Aunt?"

"Only an observation, Darling." Her heels echo as she saunters past me, pausing at my side. "Powerful men often have something to hide."

She exits out the other end of the corridor, right on time for another door to open. I move back, hiding in the cover of an alcove. Around the corner, my father leaves his office, heading down the opposite end of the hall.

An idea unfurls, stretching its roots across my mind. Before I have time to think better of it, my feet are already carrying me to the study. I brace myself with one deep breath and slip past the doors. Being alone in my father's office feels like treason of the highest caliber.

I approach the desk first, dragging my fingertips over the smooth mahogany. He hasn't left any papers out, leading me to wander into the first drawer. Maintenance expenses, guard salaries, and trade calculations lie in the loose parchments. I stack them on top of the desk until I reach the bottom of the drawer. When I discover absolutely nothing, I huff, piling them back in with a little more force than necessary.

A light *click* emits from the bottom when I shove the stack down, the panel bouncing against my palm and the papers between. I pause. Slowly, I take the papers back out, finding the bottom of the drawer now loose and slightly lifted.

*A false bottom.*

Beneath it rests my father's ledger with our insignia on the cover. I flip through the pages, finding that they're not much different than the things written on the parchments I'd seen, but a page titled *Galvan Filtrations* brings me to a halt.

Gallons of water per month are recorded from the beginning of the year until... they begin to dwindle. I read the shrinking numbers, measurements broken down from month-to-month to week-by-week, each scribble written more aggressively than the last. And this month... This month is the lowest amount of water we've gathered in the entire year. I flip on, discovering loose papers tucked in the ledger from the previous year, a completely opposite record to the numbers I'm seeing. I scan my father's notes in the margins, suggestions of decreasing rations and drilling for new wells.

I collapse in his chair, setting the ledger down. Our water collections are decreasing, and no one in our family seems concerned. I recall each interaction, every fragile word exchanged between myself and my family, but nothing remotely hints that they knew.

But Aunt Natalya did. She practically sent me here, didn't she? And my mother probably does. What about Ash? Is this why he holds such a steadfast loyalty to our House? Does he think Father will lead us out of this? Suddenly, it clicks together—all the times he told me to trust him, to fall in line and maintain order. It becomes clear why our father bit his tongue at the Conclave, why he didn't argue my engagement to Eren so long as two of his children managed to unite with a wealthy House. It adds up—why he doesn't care about anything other than survival, because our family is damn near *extinction.*

Without water, our trade goods barely matter. Should these numbers reach the other Houses, our alliances will be cut or renegotiated altogether. We'll be at the mercy of the other families because we are no longer worth the gold my family spends. I breathe out, holding my head in my hands.

*This can't be real.*

And the riot... it's a direct result of my father cutting rations. The people were right to protest. They're right to curse our name in the streets. They've always been *right*.

We are not guardians of peace. We are brutal oppressors.

I place everything back where I found it, wandering out to the corridor in a haze of numbness.

"Sage."

I jolt.

Ash appears with an expectant look. "Are you ready to fly to Esmeray?"

"Yeah," I answer, voice hollow. "Ready."

Eren's waiting for me when we land. Kamari and I trade places once again, his sister leaving with Ash and Rune while I stay behind.

His brow creases when he sees me walking up the steps, bag in tow. He takes it from me, leaning down in an attempt to get me to look at him. "What's wrong?"

I glance at the dragons as if they might hear me miles away

in the clouds. "My father wants me to find blackmail on your House."

Eren's eyes narrow. "Why now? I thought the mission was a success."

"It was but... I made a deal with him to break my cousin's engagement to Valen Dysis. He's a monster and I couldn't let her marry him. He said if the raid was a success he'd break it, but now he wants a peace-offering he can give to Soren."

"He wants to cover his own ass," Eren amends, looking none too pleased about it.

"I think he's testing my loyalty, first with the raid and now this."

A slow smile soften's Eren's face, his cool eyes beaming. "You stood up to him."

I lose my train of thought entirely. "Yeah I... guess I did."

I'd been so wrapped up in the bombshell I uncovered, I hadn't really thought much about the gravity of challenging my father—only that I had to succeed.

"We should celebrate." He turns, leading the way up to the manor.

"Celebrate?"

"I'll fly you into Esmeray," he carries on, opening the door. "There's a gala being thrown by the High Mage. We'll attend."

"A gala?" I stop dead in my tracks. "Don't we have... *other things* to do tonight?"

Eren faces me with a devious grin. "Oh Killer," he purrs, stepping closer. "I can think of endless *other things* I can do with you tonight. You're going to have to be much more specific, lest we have an unfortunate misunderstanding."

My heart quickens. "I–" I blink, lowering my voice for only him to hear me. "I meant rebel things."

He chuckles and I damn myself for the heat that stirs within me at the sound. "Plenty of time for that, but this evening is ours. Or do I need to resort to *other things* to persuade you into joining me?"

"No," I mutter, face flushing. "I'll go with you."

"So good for me," he murmurs, pushing open my bedroom door.

I scowl and snatch the bag from him. His laughter trails from the hall as I lock myself inside. I toss my bag on the bed and pause. Newly mounted shelves line the walls filled with... books. For a heartbeat, I stare, noticing that these shelves aren't the only new additions to the room. Beneath the books, the surface of the dresser gleams. Crystals now line the polished wood, each consisting of various shapes and colors. Amongst them lie rougher stones with unique patterns rising from the rock. *Fossils.*

A collection.

I reach a hesitant hand to the shelves, dragging my fingertips over the spines. Grasping one in my hand, I pull it down and flip through the pages, allowing the scent of parchment to flutter up to my nose. The corners of my mouth rise on their own volition. I place the book back and pluck a polished lapis lazuli from the dresser, turning it over in my hands as I move to the armoire.

Several new gowns fill the space within; beaded, jeweled, and embroidered. Most of the gowns are silver or black, matching the Noctis family's colors, but there are a few that honor my house—weaved with the softest, most vibrant fabrics in shades of red, black, and gold.

A silver and black gown glints off the light, catching my attention. I push the other dresses aside, revealing sharp white gems stitched along the V-shaped neckline and one sleeve of silver dragon scales glittering back at me. I snatch the hanger, lifting the dress from the wardrobe with a smile.

I draw a bath in the meantime, sinking into the steaming

water filled with bubbles and a hint of aloe and bergamot soap. I rattle my mind, searching for any trace of the High Mage of Esmeray, but my list of names comes up short. Melantha was the first High Mage I've met and I'm not so sure I'm eager to meet another. I roll the lapis lazuli in my grasp, watching the gold flecks shimmer, but it doesn't bring me much comfort. I set it aside on the edge of the tub and suck in a breath, ducking under the bubbles. Beneath the water, I can almost lose myself to the darkness. It's warm, cradling me in a lovely embrace. It's so sweet it's almost promising—the oblivion that might come with it.

*How much quieter would it be to forget everything altogether?*

When my lungs reach a burning point, I break through the surface, gasping for air.

"I was worried I'd have to pull you up."

I jump, spotting Eren leaning on the sink. He flashes me a crooked grin, though it doesn't quite reach his eyes. There's a strain behind it, like the smile is more for my benefit than his. My gaze rakes over the onyx suit he wears. His polished black shoes gleam as he saunters forward, each footstep thundering off the bathroom tiles.

I shiver, keeping my chest buried under the cover of the bubbles. Eren's eyes don't leave mine for a moment, locking me captive. He prowls around the tub, dragging a wooden stool to sit behind me. I twist my neck, watching as he removes his coat in one swift movement and folds it over a towel rack on the wall.

His eyes darken as he unbuttons the ends of his sleeves, rolling them up to his elbows. "Turn around."

"Why?" I challenge, ignoring the rapid pulse in my chest.

"Because I told you to."

"You think I care?"

"You were such a good girl earlier. Do you want me to beg, Killer?"

The thought intrigues me, Eren on his knees, Celosia's

greatest threat brought to heel at my feet. Begging. For *me*. I bite my inner cheek, fighting to keep a straight face even though I can hear my blood rushing in my ears. "You don't seem like a man who would beg for anything."

His mouth tilts in an almost smile at my defiance. Then it falls. "Please?"

A hint of weariness lingers in his voice. I frown, finding it so unlike the unshakable rebel I've known him to be. I don't think I've ever heard him say the word 'please' before, and certainly never as soft as he makes it sound for me. Despite my better judgment, I turn.

Eren's hands reach to the left, grabbing one of the containers of shampoo from the edge of the tub. I hear him pump a dollop of it in his palm before a set of strong fingers thread through my hair. A breath escapes me as he sinks his fingers in, gripping the back of my hair and giving it a tug. I'm yanked back, flush against the tub with his fist clutching a handful of my hair. My eyes flutter, blinking up past the sparks tingling down from my head to my spine, right where I find Eren smirking above me.

"Relax," he says, like it's the easiest thing in the world.

My heart skips a beat. I have left myself completely at his mercy.

Eren brings his other hand to my head, smoothing the shampoo over my scalp. His other hand loosens, working to lather the soap into my hair. I close my eyes as his fingers dig in, massaging my head in heavenly circles. The muscles in my back begin to ease, my limbs falling pliant under his ministrations. I can't break myself from picturing those strong hands on my bare skin, knuckles scarred and palms calloused from years of riding. As he continues gripping and pulling my hair in lovely strokes, a flame crackles within me, burning lower and lower as I recall those same hands gripping me in other places.

*Think of something else.*

My eyes snap open. "Thank you for the... collection."

"Did you like it?" His hands keep moving, massaging the tension from my head.

"I did."

*I also liked our kiss.* It was over too fast. I replay the night in the manor, how his mouth ravenously claimed mine. *You ran from it–for good reason.* I remind myself, but as that little flame burns brighter, I can't seem to remember those reasons.

A moan slips past my lips and his hands freeze for a moment. I open my eyes again, finding his already on me. I notice his throat bob, his hands continuing those glorious circles. I shut my eyes, biting my lip to hold back the next noise that threatens to escape.

"Gods, Eren," I breathe when he reaches the top of my scalp.

He stops, his voice huskier than I remember. "I pictured you saying that under much different circumstances."

A teasing smile works its way to my lips. "Were those circumstances among *other things* you mentioned?"

One of Eren's hands leaves my head entirely, clutching the bottom of my jaw and tilting my face to him. "Don't play with me, Sage," he whispers, inches from my mouth, his eyes darkening with an unmistakable shadow of desire. "Not unless you want me as bad as I want you."

His lips are so close I can taste his breath on mine. Sirens wail in the back of my head at the confession, warning me that this is spiraling out of control, but the thought of kissing him begins to feel less like a betrayal and more like an oath. The flame in my core pulses, aching with need, beckoning me to take what I want and not be sorry for it. But I know if I lean forward, none of it will be an act anymore, it will become something destructively *real*.

Eren's hand slips from my hair, his other releasing me. He clears his throat, rising. "I'll meet you in the foyer when you're done." He snags his jacket off the rack, vanishing from the room.

I shudder, glancing at my reflection over the sink. A crimson flush blooms over my face, grazing over my chest. I shut my eyes, turning from the mirror and banishing the image. *Gods, what am I doing?* I hold my nose and sink under the water.

Out in the bedroom, I snatch the dress from the bed and slip it on, arming myself with daggers under my skirt and a small gun for my thigh holster. I'm not about to leave the entire night in Eren's hands.

*Annoying, calloused, hard*– I shake myself from that train of thought. I tread down the steps into the foyer where Eren stands by a crackling fireplace.

He rakes me in for a moment before his gaze pulls to mine. "Shall we?"

I take his outstretched hand, his rough skin instantly warming my fingers. He walks me to the front of the manor where Cantorix and Halcyon wait. Cantorix's silver eyes graze over the two of us with a passive lack of interest. Halcyon purrs under my touch when I pet her, allowing me to climb up on her back.

Within minutes, we land on a stretch of gravel and stone in front of the dome-shaped Capitol building set aglow with sunstone lights. Esmeray's towering levels shimmer from around and above, glowing brighter as the sun sets below the horizon. Few people wander the streets, mostly couples arm-in-arm taking an evening stroll. A group of children play in a courtyard a few yards from us. Some of them pause, watching Eren and I dismount with gaping mouths. Their surprise strikes me in an instant, their *wonder*. Not fear. They don't run as fast as they can, but creep closer to watch.

My eyes sting at the sight of them.

"Sage?"

"They don't... they're not scared of us." I gesture to the kids, taking Eren's arm as Halcyon and Cantorix lift off, flapping gusts of air as they return to the sky.

"No. They're not," he answers, turning us to the steps of the

Capitol building. "Veronique and I share a vested interest in keeping most of the carnage out of the city. When I know of an attack, I try to send word as soon as possible, and in turn, she works with my family to evacuate the city below ground."

"Veronique. The High Mage?"

He smiles. "Yes. She's quite a force to be reckoned with."

"Does she know who you are?"

Each High Mage shares a unique connection with their Dragon Lord. Taking a Blood Oath is supposed to ensure their loyalty, but as I've seen with Melantha, there are ways to work around the magic. Still, if Eren has a second High Mage on his side, it would strengthen his cause.

"She has her suspicions. Hard to confirm without proof."

"And if she had any?"

Eren's mouth curves. "I don't imagine much would change."

"Does that mean she supports the rebellion?"

"She supports change," he says as two servants pull apart a pair of elegant glass doors for us to enter. "For now, that's all I need."

A chandelier of glass and sunstone twinkles overhead, casting a golden atmosphere upon the ballroom. Circular tables are spread throughout each side like a crescent moon, leaving the center open for dancing and a stage between two sets of sweeping staircases.

Eren guides me in, right as guests part for a woman in a glimmering blue dress with intricate braids woven around her head, flawless dark skin, and crimson lips pulled into a tight grin. "Eren Noctis in the flesh," her honey-rich voice greets us.

My heart skips a beat. Then another.

"Veronique," Eren takes her hand, placing a kiss atop it. "It was my pleasure to receive your invitation."

"Well, what's a Gala without Esmeray's patron?" She smirks, her gaze sliding to me. "You must be Sage. Or shall I call you Lady Galvan?"

It hits me like a punch to the throat. I *know* that voice.

The acolyte.

"Call me Sage." I shake Veronique's hand.

Her eyes glitter with devilish delight. "Ah, what an honor to meet Eren's betrothed. I never thought I'd see the day our Dragon Lord would settle down."

"What can I say, V?" Eren slides a hand around my hip, tugging me closer and causing my heart to stutter. "It appears I've met my match."

She laughs through her nose. "I pity the fools who stand against your union. Please, enjoy the party." Veronique steps aside, waving a hand to the dance floor.

We walk together, his touch like a brand leaving me painfully aware that only the thin slip of my dress separates our skin. I try to focus on the faces of the room, the servants running trays of food and champagne, though none of it can distract me enough to peel my stare from Veronique making her rounds with the guests.

*The acolyte is Esmeray's High Mage!* Is that why she was so confident in offering to remove my mark? If anyone had the power to get around a spell, of course it would be a High Mage. But even as I watch her I can't quite pinpoint why she'd have such a vested interest in an old heirloom. She doesn't strike me as an antique collector. So what does that necklace mean to her? And moreover, did Melantha know who was lurking in her library?

We take an empty table with candles and a grazing board in the middle. A servant drops two glasses of champagne in front of us with a bob of their head before flitting off to the next table.

"How long has Veronique been in your employ?" I pick a grape off the board, chewing thoughtfully.

Eren tilts his head. "She was my father's High Mage–rose to power during his reign."

"Does she like antiques?"

He quirks a brow. "Why?"

I shrug, feigning nonchalance. "Perhaps I should get her a gift once we're married."

His lips pull into a smile. "That so?"

"What? It'd be a kind thing to do."

"You're a terrible liar."

"I hope not, otherwise we're doomed."

"Then I suppose I'm spending my last moments in fine company."

I can't help but laugh and take a glance around the room. "You know, I've been wondering…"

"What's that, Killer?"

"How did you do it?"

"Do what?" He sips his glass, amused.

"Get your people to love you? I know you said you keep the carnage away, but there has to be more to it."

He sets down his drink, thinking. "I take care of those who are loyal to me. I let the Mages practice freely, I donate generously toward public education, and I regulate water more freely than in most cities."

I look down, picking at my cuticles.

"It isn't difficult to not be a tyrant," he adds after a beat. "Our people just want to survive. To earn their love, all you need is a shred of humanity, and a willingness to consider more than yourself."

"Your well never runs dry?" I ask, because I can grasp the rest of it. Don't be a piece of human garbage. Have a soul. That isn't hard, but I think of the lies I've been told—the ledger in my father's desk. Our House is dying. We're going to die of thirst and we damn well deserve it, but our people don't.

"It isn't easy, but we've taken responsibility. My family isn't wasteful. We ration like everyone else and in turn, it allows us to share a bit more than most Houses would dare."

"What happens to our families when this is over?" I lean forward, lowering my voice. "Do you have a plan if you win?"

"*When* we win, our families will be protected. My focus will be on ushering in a new era."

"Where Riders no longer rule," I note, gauging his reaction.

He leans forward, stunning me into silence when his breath caresses the shell of my ear. "Riders shouldn't decide who lives or dies. Just because we possess great power, doesn't mean we should use it."

I swallow thickly. "I always thought we used our dragons to protect each other. To defend our homes."

Eren leans back, studying me. "And now?"

My face crumbles.

*Now I think power doesn't make someone fit to rule.*

I begrudgingly take hold of my drink. "Now I know I'm wrong."

"Forgive my intrusion," Veronique purrs from behind my chair. "But I was wondering if I could borrow your lovely fiancée for a moment?"

I see Eren's eyes flick up at her, his face easing into a neutral mask. "She's all yours."

I rise from my chair, twisting to meet Veronique. She hooks her elbow with mine and leads me to the dance floor. A throng of guests part as we move between bodies, many nodding or smiling at Veronique who returns their acknowledgements with a grin of her own. She's entirely made for this, wearing power as easily as jewels.

"It's such a pleasure to have young blood ruling a prestigious House," Veronique praises, casting her coppery eyes on me. "To have such an open-minded Dragon Lord is a thing most High Mages dream about."

"A Dragon Lord you intend to stab in the back?"

She smirks. "You seemed in need of a helping hand. My deal still stands... assuming you've found what I need."

"Let's say I have," I bluff, willing her not to see right through me. "Why should I give it to you?"

"Aside from the obvious?" She casts a pointed gaze on my sleeved arm.

"Maybe I've come to terms with my fate. Maybe I don't believe you. But that necklace sounds pretty damn important for you to betray your Lord."

"I've done no such thing," she hisses. "Do you think as a High Mage I have no knowledge of my Lord's movements? I've held my silence. I've maintained my *Oath*. I do not care for the whims of men and their wars. I only want what belongs to my family."

At this, I raise a brow. "Are you... *related* to Solasta?"

Veronique laughs. "No, Child. My family came to this wasteland long ago. We served Solasta faithfully with our magic, protecting her and guiding our young Queen. We crafted that necklace ourselves as a *gift*. When the Dragon Lords betrayed her, that necklace was stolen and lost to time. It's taken generations of searching, but now I know it's near." She comes closer, lowering her voice for only me to hear it. "Should you find it, I would be in your debt. Maybe you have come to terms with your bond to Lord Noctis, but I can think of a hundred wicked ways a High Mage can be useful when you're in need of one." She passes me, stopping at my shoulder. "A bit of advice, from one woman to another–take care not to cross your future husband."

"Only when it benefits you?"

She tsks. "I'll tell you one thing about that man. He'll snap your neck, and look damn good doing it."

"You think I should be afraid?"

"I think you should be terrified."

Veronique makes her exit, disappearing within the churning crowd. A dull ache thrums behind my skull at the thought of these choices laid at my feet. Guests begin to part, making way for Eren's dark figure. He looms over me, lips pulled in a fiendish smile. Even with heels on, I barely reach his neck, leaving me with the annoying burden of tilting my own if I want to hold his pale gaze.

He offers me his hand. "Dance with me."

I blink, staring like he might bite. Still, I take his hand with a hesitant grasp. His long fingers wrap around mine, leading me into the fray of couples spinning on the dance floor. Beneath the chandelier, his dark hair shines, shadows cutting the sharp planes of his face. He pulls me closer, a warm hand resting on the small of my back. We ease into a gentle sway.

"You're beautiful," he murmurs, matter-of-factly. Not that I *look* beautiful tonight of all nights, but that I am, simply, and without rebuttal.

"You clean up nicely yourself," I offer, earning a low chuckle that sets my blood on fire.

"I've never seen Veronique walk away so heated. I suppose the honor belongs to you?"

I scan the room for the High Mage, finding her in the arms of a taller woman with garnet hair and sun-bronzed skin. They sway along to the music, sharing laughter and whispers only they can hear. "I guess I just have that effect on people."

"Look at you, already making friends."

A laugh bubbles up, surprising me, and yet I can't help but grin at the delight sparking on his face at the sound. This close, I can appreciate the finer details of him, from the slope of his nose to the square of his jaw and the fullness of his lips where I spy a fine slash of a scar just beneath his bottom lip. It's there my gaze snags.

"Sage," he says, voice thick.

I drag my eyes from his lips to find his face closer than I remember. I'm suddenly too aware of the pale green of his eyes, the muscle of his bicep resting beneath my hand, and the hardness of his chest nearly flush with mine. His hand moves, fingers tracing the curve of my spine. I suck in a breath, back arching. His eyes darken, darting to my mouth. I'm paralyzed in his arms, any rational thoughts left now fleeing. I can't remember why I shouldn't let him kiss me, only that I want him to do it again, so very, *very* much.

"Don't go home."

"What?"

"Stay with me."

At any other moment, I think I would have mistaken it for a command—battled against it—but I hear the rawness in his words. There's a promise there, but of what I'm not sure. If I stayed now, what would it mean? What insanity could possess him to throw away our cover, and how thoughtless am I to consider it? An answer begins to form on my lips, one I'm almost certain I will regret.

A shot rings out, evoking a clamor of screams.

Eren shields me with his body as we race for cover behind a pillar in the room. We peer around the structure, searching for the threat. A group of masked assailants storm the front entrance. Dressed in black with guns in hand, they fire into the crowd.

Eren reaches back, pulling a six-barrel pistol marked with a black dragon across the grip. "What are the odds you'll listen if I tell you to stay put?"

I rip my own gun free. "Zero."

Eren raises a brow, eyes flicking between the folds of my skirts and the gun in my hand. "Alright then," he says with a grin. "Show me how vicious you are."

We move as one. Eren fires the first shot, his bullet landing between the eyes of a gunman. I point my gun at another sprinting toward us, firing. My bullet meets its mark, exploding through the gunman's chest in a spray of crimson. One of them swings his fist at Eren—a second too late. He leans back, grabbing the man's exposed arm and swinging him around before firing into the back of his head. When he faces me, a mist of blood covers his face. I open my mouth, but I don't have time to speak. A shadow moves behind Eren. My hand shoots out, fingers squeezing the trigger on reflex. The shooter falls, my bullet tearing right through the middle of his heart.

A blast of viridescent light fills the room.

We turn, spotting Veronique with her feet apart, both hands splayed as she holds a shield of light blocking the assailants from coming any closer as survivors flee. Bullets bounce off the shield, ricocheting back the way they came. A few more gunmen fall from the bullets, leaving the rest of them scrambling. I'm too wrapped up in the powerful display of magic to notice anything else.

A metallic *click* echoes behind my skull.

It raises goosebumps along my skin, plunging my heart into the deepest pit of my stomach. I stop seeing what's in front of me, slowly lifting my hands.

"Drop it," a gruff voice commands.

I drop my weapon without question.

"Turn around."

It seems to happen in slow motion, my feet barely obeying the order as blood rushes in my ears, muting everything but the man pointing the gun.

*Is this it? This is how I die?*

And then my eyes deceive me.

A ring of blue fire bursts around the man's throat, not burning but–*squeezing*. A living flame. He gasps, clasping the collar of fire with one hand.

"Touch her and you burn."

Eren's words slice through the chaos. The remaining gunmen shout, consumed by the same blue fire. Their screams of agony ring out as they fall to their knees, burning alive. A ring of flames appears around the man in front of me and the collar around his throat grows, tendrils of fire encircling his outstretched arm. The man starts to sweat, beads of it rolling down his face as the heat of the flames seems to increase. He drops the gun with a yelp, his hand red and blistering.

Eren's at my side, stepping in front of me. I move back with a gasp, watching as the man falls to his knees screaming.

"Apologize." Cold fury rages behind his words.

"I'm sor–*I'm sorry!*" The man screeches as the flames churn around his body like a cocoon.

"Who sent you?"

"You're going to have to kill me," the man seethes.

Eren smirks. "I will." He stalks closer. "Shall I burn you from the inside out? Should I start with your blood? Your bones? A certain level of heat is needed before the human body turns to ash. I can play with fire as long as I need to and considering what you've done tonight–I think I'll take my time."

His blood-curdling scream twists my stomach, but it's not enough to make me feel sorry for him. Innocent lives were lost tonight. Someone has to pay for that. Even if I don't understand what's happening–*how it's fucking possible*–there was never an option for this man to walk away unscathed.

I'm not sure if that makes me a monster.

"Who sent you? I promise to give you a clean death," Eren says calmly over the man's cries. "Who was the target?"

"*Her!*" The gunman yells, pupils blown, eyes frenzied as he looks directly at me.

My back stiffens.

"Who. Sent. You," Eren growls, but the gunman shakes his head, cursing us both.

One thing becomes instantly clear–he'll take this secret to the grave.

Eren bores into the man's eyes. "Lucky for you, I like to watch things burn."

Blue fire bursts through the man's eyes and mouth, incinerating him from within. He falls to his side in a charred heap, smoke billowing from the holes of his body. Eren kneels at his side, reaching into a pocket where he lifts a leather pouch. He pulls open the strings, shaking free a couple of gold coins into his palm. Eren's face lifts, eyes finding mine as the realization dawns on the two of us.

A two-headed dragon is stamped over the metal.

The insignia of my House.

# CHAPTER 22

*E*ren stands, bringing the coins to me for a closer look, but I don't need to see them to understand the implication. "Someone in your family wants you dead."

The words sink in, but there's a disconnection. They're a distant idea, flying on the wind, blown away like sand. Instead, something tightens in my chest, crackling to the surface as I consider which one of my dear relatives could *possibly*...

I burst with laughter, echoing off the walls of the empty building. Tears prick my eyes. Eren watches me, his face blank and unblinking. It makes me more hysterical, the twist between shock and concern on his features that are usually so well hidden.

"O–oh, i–is that all?" I gasp between fits, ribs aching.

"You're... laughing."

I giggle, wiping a tear. My mouth hurts from grinning and a part of me knows this is insanely *not* funny, but so many people want me dead that I simply cannot narrow it down and Eren's face is doing little to ground me. I suck in a breath, trying to calm myself–*explain* myself.

"My entire family wants me dead. Dahlia, Uncle Deon, Rune

—hell, probably my own mother! And I wouldn't put it past my father at this point."

"You're too valuable."

"I'm too out of control," I say, sobering. "A liability. He's made it abundantly clear that he hates it."

Eren's jaw flexes, his stare hardening.

I rip my eyes away, glancing at the slaughter around us. Bullet holes riddle the walls. The bodies of guests and gunmen lay scattered on the floor. Veronique is long gone, probably tending to the wounded. I shake my head at the meaningless destruction. *All of this to kill me?*

The guilt creeps in, a shadow slithering from the darkness.

"We should go," he says, lifting his hand like he might touch me, and I take a retreating step from it.

"Don't." I glance between the burnt body and Eren. "What are you?"

"Human."

"No. I saw what you did. You controlled fire with your *mind*."

Eren reaches out his hand to me once more, letting an ounce of the emotion slip through his eyes—pleading with me like he did for our dance. "Come with me and I'll explain everything."

Staring at his outstretched hand, I think of the reasons why I should run. I watched Eren burn a man from the inside out and somehow, there isn't a single part of me that fears him. My own family wants me dead and the safest place I feel is at his side. Even with his secrets.

So I cross the final border between duty and dishonor and slide my palm into the traitor's hand.

MY HAIR IS STILL DRIPPING when I leave the bathroom. Eren sits on my bed, his chin resting on folded fingers. I sink into the mattress beside him, too tired to voice the questions in my head. I've washed off the blood, but there's a part of me that doesn't feel clean. I feel as if I'm wearing an invisible stain. A brand meant for my eyes alone.

*Someone in your family wants you dead.*

"My power comes from Noxainia," he starts, his voice like gravel. "Our bond enables her magic to flow through me, allowing me to use her same fire."

"How? There are no records of Riders ever controlling their dragon's fire."

He folds his hands in his lap, staring down. "When I found Nox, she shared a memory with me when we bonded. It's blood magic, an ancient spell I don't fully understand. If anyone knew, the Houses would use it to exploit their dragons and make themselves more powerful. Do you understand what I'm saying?"

Tell no one. Never breathe a word of it. I should laugh at the notion. I don't think I could if I wanted to thanks to the mark.

I close my eyes. *This has gone too far.*

Whatever spark lies between us, I snuff it out, burying it until there are only cinders. If I don't detangle myself from Eren, I will lose myself in him. No good will come of this alliance. I cannot change who I am any more than I can change the fact that he is a rebel.

"You shouldn't marry me, even for appearances." There's a dry spot in my throat, making the words sound hollow.

"Why?"

"My family is facing a drought. Our wells are nearly dry."

For a few moments, Eren is silent. "That's why your father needed the alliance."

Yes. It's why he was *desperate*.

"Our deal is off," I say, rising. "I want nothing from you and I don't need a magic gag to keep quiet. Riders don't need any more power than we have. Look at what we've done with it."

"And the engagement?" He stands, treading on fragile ground.

"It's over," I whisper. "We don't have to pretend anymore."

"I'm not pretending." His words cut through my façade. "I meant it when I asked you to stay."

"And why would I do that?" I let my tone grow hard, sharpening it into a serrated edge. "Because we shared a kiss?"

"It was more than one *kiss*."

"It didn't mean anything!"

The fire sputters in his eyes. It makes my chest twist. I want to gather the words, snatch them back like paper in the wind, but they're gone–spiraling into a world they can't be withdrawn from. And the worst thing is, they seem to meet their mark.

Eren straightens with a ragged exhale. "Okay. I'll take you to Oddica. She'll break the bond and then we'll never have to see each other again."

"Fine."

But it's not fine. Nothing has ever truly been *fine*.

Eren leaves the room composed, not even slamming the door on his way out. I want to scream. I want him to slam the door and shout back in my face. It's the toxic part of me that wants to brawl because I've never known anything else. But I hold myself back.

He's giving me exactly what I want.

A clean break.

In the foyer, I hear a fireplace crackling from the drawing room. I pause near the archway leading into it, adjusting the strap of the bag on my shoulder. Syrinthia turns her head at the movement, peering at me from a plush chair near the fire.

"Sage. Come sit."

It's the last thing I want to do, but I might as well say

goodbye to the woman who was almost my mother-in-law. I take the open chair across from her, setting my bag on the floor.

Syrinthia gestures to the silver tray in the middle of us. "Care for tea?"

"No, thank you."

She shrugs, refilling her cup. "My son came home covered in blood tonight, though it isn't the first time. I only wonder how you fit into the equation."

"There was an attempt on my life at Veronique's Gala."

"I see." Her silver gaze looks me up and down, searching for what I'm made of. "I know my son, and I know him better than he thinks. He does not swear vows lightly. He will do everything in his power to protect you, but as a mother, I have to wonder, who protects him?"

"He handles himself pretty well."

"As who? Eren or Damon?"

My lungs seize.

Syrinthia stares back at me with a knowing smirk. She sets her cup on the table. "Did you think I didn't know where my son goes at odd hours of the night? Rest assured, our family supports his cause. Eren is my son and the Head of this House. He will have our loyalty no matter what path he chooses, and when the time comes for us to fight, know that I will ride into battle alongside my family. I only ask one thing of you: protect him while he's busy trying to protect everyone else."

"Mother."

I twist my head, finding Eren leaning on the threshold.

"Sage," he regards me, eyes glaring back at his mother.

I rise to my feet. "Thank you for having me, Lady Noctis. I should be going now."

Eren follows me back to the foyer and out the door to the veranda where I stop, spinning on my heels. "Your family *knows?*"

He stills for a moment, then heaves a sigh. "She shouldn't have cornered you like that."

"That's not the point, Eren." I take another step. "I've been bending over backwards doing everything I can to hide this secret, meanwhile, your entire family knows? Is that why you told me not to worry about them?"

"Yes, because they can be *trusted*. Can you say the same about yours?"

I bite my tongue, hating him for being right. "You know what? Fine. No, I can't say the same. Unlike you, I can't sleep soundly at night knowing none of my relatives will cut my throat in my sleep!"

"Then why go back?" He presses, coming closer. "Why do you continue to give them your loyalty when they don't deserve it?"

"Because I can't walk away!" I shout. "Jocelyn knows! And I can't leave her behind without knowing what she'll do! And contrary to your belief–there are *good* people in my family!"

Aunt Nat, Uncle Bruno, Jasper, and Jocelyn all flash through my mind. Even Ash and Lux make the list, because despite our differences, I'd never wish them dead.

He freezes. "Jocelyn knows?"

I pinch the bridge of my nose and huff. "She doesn't know who you are. But she knows I found Damon Valour and she knows I'm tied to the rebellion. Eren, I *had* to show her the mark. She almost shot me in Narelle when I let Oddica and Azara go."

Eren swears, pivoting on his heels and folding his hands behind his head as he paces. "Okay," he finally says. "Okay. There's nothing we can do about it now, but I need you to *think*. Could Jocelyn have been behind the shooting?"

"No. If she was going to kill me, she would do it herself. She was ready to…" I trail off, not wanting to revisit that night. Eren isn't the only one wondering what's waiting for me when I get home. The possibilities haven't left my mind.

"I trust you." He looks out to the cliff beyond before setting his eyes on me. "If I had more time, I'd convince you to stay."

"There's nothing for me here."

I'm not foolish enough to let myself believe we could be something more. If there's anything here at all, it's like the breath between sentences. An almost. A maybe. An idea.

"Now who's lying?" He turns away with a dejected smile.

I watch Eren speak to his soldiers when we arrive, mask on and identity switched. I try to separate the two; Eren Noctis and Damon Valour. Eren is the leader of a great House, a man willing to do anything to protect his family and his people. Damon is the leader of a movement, with thousands of lives affected by each choice he makes. I cannot untangle the two any more than I can untangle the parts of me at war with one another—the girl who wants to stay, and the girl who knows she can't.

Oddica grins when she sees me—Gannon, Draven, and Azara in tow. My breathing stops when I see Gannon, whole and healed. I draw a sharp breath and start forward, locking eyes with Gannon as my bottom lip trembles. His brows furrow, head of messy hair titling until I engulf him in the fiercest hug of my life. Images of his pale face burst to the surface, the feeling of his blood, warm and thick between my fingers as I tried to hold it inside him and *failed*.

"You're alive," I breathe.

Oddica told me he would be okay, but I hadn't realized how much his near-death stayed with me. *Haunted* me.

Gannon is stiff at first, frozen into silence, but slowly his arms wrap around me and squeeze me in a gentle embrace. "Please don't cry for me, Lady Galvan."

I blink, vision now blurred. I pull back, wiping my eyes. "I'm so sorry. I almost got you killed."

His honeyed gaze softens. "It wasn't your fault."

I shake my head because it's not enough, but Gannon only squeezes my shoulder before moving on.

Oddica hugs me next. "Thanks for not killing us."

I huff a half-hearted laugh. "Well, who else would break the bond?"

She releases me, eyes flitting between me and Eren. He jerks his head for her to follow him. Oddica frowns, leaving me to talk.

Draven squeezes my shoulder as he passes. "You're one brave girl."

Azara lingers behind them, arms crossed, but without the tension that normally lines her face. We stand across from each other and I prepare myself to ask the question I should have asked a long time ago.

"What happened to your family?"

Her shoulders become rigid, but she pauses, taking me in. "I worked as a soldier for House Dysis. My family grew crops just outside the city." An iron weight sinks in my stomach as her tale grows familiar. "One summer, I was part of the reinforcements that answered an attack by your House. I was supposed to be fighting, but I deserted to try to find my family. I was almost there, I just had to make it over the top of a hill," her voice cracks and she clears her throat, refusing to show emotion, refusing to let the tears welling in her eyes fall.

"And then I did. I made it to the top where I could see my mother's house. I saw her running with my sisters, their tiny legs trying to keep up. I ran toward them, but then... a giant shadow blocked out the light and I looked up. A pale dragon with moonstone scales soared over us. I thought it would keep going. But it didn't. It dived and opened its jaws, setting fire to everything in its path. I screamed out and reached for them, but fire swallowed the field. When I opened my eyes the skies were black, cinders rained down and there was nothing left where they were standing."

Tears spill from my face, a wave of shock and horror crashing over me. The caverns are silent, every person in the room listening to Azara's story of a loss that may not be so different from their own.

She blinks rapidly, finding comfort in the ceiling. "I swore to myself and the Gods I would hunt the Rider of that dragon down. I spied and searched and discovered who the dragon belonged to. Imagine my surprise when you showed up here as an ally."

"I'm so sorry," I whisper.

"I don't need your apology. I need the world to be different."

Azara moves around me, joining the others who have come to stand around Eren. A shadow falls over his face and in those fragile seconds, we find each other.

He walks over with a grim expression. "We can't remove your mark tonight."

"Why not?"

"We're attacking the Dysis treatment plant," he answers, watching the rebels move around us as they carry supplies. "We'll save a lot of lives if we're successful, and a lot of people will die if we're not."

"Their treatment plant?" I echo, absorbing the gravity of it. "What are you going to do?"

"Blow it to hell."

With the treatment plant gone, House Dysis will have no way to disperse clean water to their people. I think of the riot in Solera caused by lowering their rations. No water at all would create complete and utter anarchy in Aruna.

*Exactly what my family warned of.*

"But their people…"

"We'll siphon as much of it as we can and get it back to Base, but we're ready to take in more refugees. I've made arrangements to send as many as I can to Esmeray."

"You've been planning this."

He nods once. "This is the turn of the war we've been waiting for."

My breath shudders. I look at Oddica, Draven, Gannon, and Azara. Each of them is ready to fight to reshape a world unwilling to evolve on its own. How can I go home knowing what they're about to do and pretend I played no part in it? If this is the move that will force my family to change, how can I stand aside?

"I have to go, but I could arrange for you to–"

"Take me with you."

He pauses, searching my face.

"I want to help."

Eren doesn't try to talk me out of it.

We pile into the trucks, forming a convoy with the others. I'm not certain how much time passes, but I close my eyes, inhaling the comforting scent of cypress and amber. Eren's body heat radiates through the small space of the backseat, scalding the length of my arm where our shoulders touch. His fingers brush mine, sending my heart leaping against my ribcage. I don't rip my hand away, but curl my fingers, threading them with his.

"Gannon." Eren leans forward, not breaking the contact between our hands. "Let's make camp for the night."

"We're stopping?" I perk up, searching the dunes outside of the window. Nothing but a dark and desolate world of sand awaits.

"We'll sleep for a few hours and hit the plant right before dawn." Eren breaks our contact when the truck comes to a stop and a twinge of sadness aches in my chest at the loss. "Come on." He opens the door, holding it for me and reaching out his hand. "I know you're tired."

Our fingers meet once more, sparking an electric current between our skin. I squeeze his hand so tight at that moment, like he's a lifeline tethering me to the earth.

A small fire is erected in the center of our camp where the tents are pitched. Up above, the moon casts a silvery glow over the expanse of sand. I should forget about the dunes surrounding us, but shadows seem to move in the distance. I rub my eyes, certain my mind must be playing tricks on me. When I look again, the desert is the same.

Empty. Unchanging.

Draven jumps down from the bed of the truck, grinning with a corked bottle raised in his hand. "I brought the good stuff."

Eren laughs, his smile on full display as he takes the bottle from his friend. He takes a swig, passing the bottle to me. "Damn, D. You've been aging that."

I sniff the bottle, nose wrinkling as a sour smell pricks my nostrils. "What is this?"

Their voices fall quiet, the flames crackling.

Draven's eyes widen with intrigue. "Don't tell me the Lady's never had barrel juice."

My lips form a small 'o' of understanding. In all the time I'd spent with Ash spying in the cantinas, I would never partake, much preferring to keep my mind sharp. "I never had the pleasure."

"Well," Draven chuckles, waving me on. "Bottoms up, m'lady. Tonight you drink like a peasant."

Not about to face this night sober, I lift the bottle to my lips. The cactus juice stings my nose and throat, throwing me into a fit of coughs as I pass along the bottle to Oddica. Heat blooms in my gut, easing the tension from my body. My thoughts move slower as the bottle comes and goes, like I'm moving through quicksand. I hug my knees to my chest and sigh, wishing this feeling would last forever.

"I wish we could leave this terrible desert behind," Oddica mumbles, a soft blush tinting her cheeks.

Azara hums the same sentiment. Gannon seems to ponder it, one arm propped on his knee to hold his head.

Draven takes another drink. "The Gods have a sense of humor, placing us in a world to scrabble over the one thing that keeps us alive."

"I bet they think it's funny," Azara groans, laying on her back with her arms spread. "I don't know why you Riders stay. I'd fly away and leave it all behind."

Eren stares into the fire, small flames dancing in his irises. Shadows spread across the planes of his face. "There was a time when Riders ventured past the Wastes."

Azara lifts her head and Draven and Gannon straighten. Oddica watches quietly with me, waiting.

"They never came back."

Even the flames appear to hush, spitting a few last embers that twirl into the night to die.

"Search parties flew out, trying to track the lost Riders, only to never be heard from again. Anyone who went too far was said to have disappeared, lost to the desert. Rather than risk losing more dragons, the Houses banned expeditions to the Wastes. Instead, they focused on building their territories, cultivating their crops and water supplies until the world became what it is now."

The fire pops, causing us all to flinch.

I recall the maps I've seen, how our territories are surrounded by dunes–the same ones Queen Solasta supposedly led her people across.

"So no one knows what's out there?" Azara asks, her voice not more than a whisper.

Eren's eyes flick up from the flames, a darkness settled within them. "Death."

Silence fills our camp as the last embers gutter out. The warm, fuzzy feeling in my stomach fades, leaving something cold in its place. For a while, there's only silence and I close my eyes again to bask in it.

Sand shifts behind me.

I twist, finding only shadows and moonlight. The others lift their heads, squinting into the dark. I hold my breath, ears straining, blood thrumming. Did I imagine it?

When nothing happens, I turn back to the others. "Did you hear that?"

It shifts again, a sigh of a phantom wind. Hairs rise off my neck and arms. Everyone reaches for a weapon, scanning the dark. A malignant tension takes root, feasting on our fear. As the seconds tick on, I see shoulders begin to ease, guns slowly lowering.

A wail shatters the night.

Azara flies back screaming. Above her stands a towering shadow in a tattered cloak, sand pouring off the faceless creature within. Several more burst from the dunes surrounding our camp, shrieking at the top of their lungs.

"*Sandwraiths!*" Draven yells, firing at the creature lifting long, ivory claws above Azara.

Bullets pop, echoing like thunder throughout the desert. I fire my weapon at the nearest wraith, hissing as it glides toward me. Spectral eyes glow from the shadows swirling within the cloak, the only hint that a conscious being occupies the rags it wears. My bullets do nothing to slow the creature. They're sucked into oblivion within the tatters of the cloak.

Clouds roll in, blocking out the moon and stars that have been replaced by veins of lighting. The sand whirls beneath our feet as the wraiths close in. A scream echoes while I back away. My attention snaps to the source and I witness Oddica being thrown into the side of the truck. Eren holds his own, weaving between the creatures, slicing wherever he can. His blades do nothing, useless to the beings circling those of us left standing. The wall of sand grows thicker, blocking out the desert and locking us in a ring with the wraiths.

Whispers fester inside my brain as the creatures close in, intensifying as their numbers grow.

Draven grabs the last burning log, the flames sputtering in the torrent of wind. He waves it back and forth, making the three wraiths hiss. I squint my eyes, fighting to keep track of the ones in front of me. Two of them flank my sides, snarling when I fire a warning shot. One of them lunges, its talons carving a path through the flesh of my thigh. I scream, stumbling until my back hits a hard, warm surface. I spin, coming face-to-face with Eren. His gaze darts to my thigh where blood seeps through the fabric, running down my leg. I wince, whimpering as I press a hand to hold it in.

*"Eren!"* Oddica shrieks.

I can't see her, only the luminescent eyes of the wraiths.

*"Eren, what do we do?"* I shout over the wind.

I'm so focused on my fear that I don't notice the presence creeping up behind me. Claws wrap around my ankle, dragging me back. I yelp, slamming into the sand face-first. Gasping, I twist–fighting for purchase. The wraith latches on despite my kicks. It straightens to full height, lifting its talons above its head. I raise my gun and shoot. Again and again, the bullets disappear. My revolver clicks. *Empty.* I toss it to the side, yanking the knives from my belt as the wraith's claws come down to deliver my end.

Blue fire shreds the darkness, a wavering blast slicing the wraith in half. With a hideous wail, the flames consume the wraith, burning it to ashes. I lift my head, flipping onto my stomach in time to watch as a vortex of that fire swirls around Eren in a protective ring, both of his fists encased in flames. He lifts his hand toward his friends, conjuring a burst of fire that rises from the sand around the pack of wraiths surrounding Draven, engulfing their bodies.

Eren twists his hand upward, summoning a wall of fire between the wraiths bent over Oddica and Azara. The creatures shriek, backing away from it. The fire curls in on itself, crashing down before the wraiths can escape.

Any surviving wraiths retreat, burrowing into the sand as if they'd never been here at all. Lightning flashes, clouds roiling with thunder. The sand churns in every direction, spinning, flying, and blinding us. I hold out my arm, hoping to block the brunt of the sandstorm. Reptilian cries pierce the skies overhead, shadows in the shape of dragons flashing in the clouds with each clap of lighting.

A hot grip folds over my hand.

"We need to run!" Eren shouts.

"But the others–" I turn, the sand so thick I'm unable to make out any sight of our team.

A ring of blue flames reappears, tendrils of fire reaching above us. The blue light severs the sand, paving a path to one of the vehicles. Oddica and Draven run toward us. Azara and Gannon slam into the car, fumbling for the doors.

We pile inside, sandwraiths hissing in the shadows of the storm. Draven starts the truck, slamming his foot on the pedal. The truck lurches forward, speeding through the sand. Cries of dragonsong grow distant, lost to the wind.

A copper scent taints the air, biting my nose as I follow the scent down to the claw marks on my leg, still pulsing with pain. Azara sports a gash in the side of her temple that Oddica works at, her fingers flickering white light from the passenger seat.

"There!" Eren calls out, pointing to a vague shadow in the distance.

I try to squint, eyes burning from the fine grains of sand embedded in my lashes. At closer inspection, I can make out a stone structure with a slanted roof, the dilapidated ruins of some long-forgotten building.

Our truck screeches to a stop.

Eren helps me out of the car and I bite my lip, holding in a scream at the flash of pain shooting through my leg. We stumble over sand, slamming through a wooden door that nearly breaks off its hinges. Broken statues of the Gods surround the foyer where an iron chandelier filled with the wax remnants of forgotten candles hangs over us.

Wind howls outside, the ruins shuddering from its wrath. It must be what's left of a forgotten temple, an old tribute to the Gods lost to time, but tonight it serves as our salvation.

Draven pulls his weapon, taking the first step forward. "Let's check it out."

Gannon and Azara come to his side, weapons drawn and aimed. Eren's arms scoop me up like I weigh nothing. I'm too tired to protest and let him carry me through the temple. I'm able to watch Oddica while we explore and find the strain embedded in her brow. She looks paler than usual, but I don't point it out.

We pass a hall of rooms checked by the others, finding nothing except dust-covered relics. They clear the next few rooms; an old lounge area, a kitchen, and a shared living space. Eren sets me on the table in the kitchen, stepping aside for Oddica to come near. I glance at the fine film of sweat on her skin as she examines my leg.

She places her hand over the wound where a dim glimmer of her healing light flares. Her brow pinches in concentration and I feel the stitch of her magic begin to seal my wounds. But the sensation stops. Her light gutters and Oddica sways. Eren steadies her by the shoulders, catching her as she grips the table for support.

"I'm sorry," she gasps. "I was working in the infirmary before you guys came. The deepest layer is healed but I... I *can't*."

"It's okay, we'll manage." He waves Draven over, passing Oddica into his friend's arms. "Get some rest, O."

Eren rummages through the cabinets, turning back to me with a tin box and a green corked bottle in his hands. "Come on." He lifts my arm over his shoulders, helping me limp back to the corridor.

"Where are we going?"

"Somewhere private."

His fire bursts from the sconces bolted to the walls, lighting the hall. He opens one of the rooms, lowering me to the edge of a bed. Eren shuts the door, lighting the other sconces within. His flames flicker, casting shadows along the abandoned room.

"Take off your pants."

It takes a second for the words to register. "Excuse me?"

Eren gives me a flat look, staring at the spot where my thigh burns. "You're still wounded. We need to patch you up until Oddica recovers."

My face flushes. "I think I can manage it with my pants on."

"There's too much sand in it and the fabric is in the way."

"It's not like we have any water." I roll my eyes, ignoring the way it makes my head spin. The bleeding has stopped, but he's right about the sand. It's an infection waiting to happen.

"Actually," with an amused smirk, he pats a small canteen on his belt. "If you need help I can–"

"I've got it," I snap, avoiding his gaze as I stand up. I unbutton the top of my pants and draw a breath, holding it in as I pull them down. I bite the side of my mouth, tasting a bitter, metallic substance when the fabric slides over my shredded skin. I grimace, hands shaking as I muster the strength to push them the rest of the way off.

Eren's there, down on his knees with deft fingers undoing the laces of my boots. "There's liquor in the bottle if you want something for the pain."

"I'll manage," I croak, voice betraying me.

He slips my boots off, one after the other, pausing when he's done. Our gazes meet, and it's not the pain that steals my breath when he rests his hands on my knees.

"Are you going to let me help you, Killer?" He purrs. "Or are you going to suffer in silence?"

"I'm more of the suffer-in-silence type," I say, more breathless than I mean to.

His knuckles brush my knee. A wave of goosebumps pricks across my skin as he gently tugs the fabric off my ankles, discarding the pants in a pile nearby. He takes both of my hands, helping me stand. It's then I notice the ripped pieces of his shirt where blood seeps through.

"You're hurt."

"I'll manage." He ignores my concern, uncapping the canteen and pouring water over the three gashes on my thigh.

I hiss. With the sand gone, I can tell the wound is as superficial as I hoped, but *Gods* if it doesn't feel like lightning.

Eren kneels, popping open the tin where miscellaneous first-aid supplies are preserved in near-perfect condition. He plucks a roll of bandages from the tin and holds one end on the side of the first scratch. He uses his other hand to wrap the bandage around my leg. I suck in a breath as his fingers pass between my inner thighs. He stops, eyes cutting to me. They're three shades darker than they should be, but I tell myself it's a trick of the fire, and pray he thinks I'm just really shitty at breathing. He rips his gaze away, continuing to wrap, but I notice his throat bob. My stomach flutters the next time his fingers brush between my legs, sparking a liquid fire that begins to pool in my center.

I try to be good, try to keep my thoughts from wandering down the beckoning path where his fingers linger, from the thoughts that wonder what would happen if he slid them ever so slightly up and slipped them past the thin fabric between my legs. Eren pinches the bandage with both hands, stopping when his gaze snags on my center directly across from his face.

He rips the bandage with more force than necessary, staring at me again. "You like me on my knees, don't you, Killer?" His voice drops, low and husky.

I ball my fists, fighting the rapid beat of my heart. "So what if I do?"

Eren rises to his feet in an instant, but I grab the end of his shirt. "Take this off."

I watch his mouth curve in a roguish grin. He lifts the ends of his shirt over his head and it takes every brain cell not to let my jaw drop. Broad shoulders packed with muscle shine in a coat of blood and sweat. His left pectoral is slashed with scratches and below the sharp V of his waist, off to the left, rests the wound I originally noticed—three long slashes deeper than the ones I received. My eyes sweep the expanse of his skin, catching on the warped scars along his waist on the opposite side, traveling up to his ribs.

Burn scars.

"Keep looking at me like that and our clothes won't stay on for long," he teases, but part of me hears the promise beneath the words.

I blink and step aside, gesturing to the bed. "You should sit down."

He crosses the space between us, pausing in front of me to lean so close I think he's going to kiss me, but he smirks, reaching further to snatch the bottle from the floor before he settles on the edge of the bed. He pulls the cork free with his teeth while I grab the first-aid tin from the ground and scowl.

Eren spits the cork on the floor and pats his lap. "Don't be shy now, Killer. I've already seen you without clothes."

My face heats at the memory of the bath. "That was different."

He shrugs and takes a sip. "If you're scared just say it."

I glare, taking a step forward before I can think better of it. I stifle a yelp when I lift my injured thigh over his lap and brace my hand on his shoulder, straddling his legs. I steal the bottle from his hand and lift it to my lips.

"Ugh." I hand it back, struggling through the taste.

Eren lifts a brow, a crooked grin on his face.

I shake my head, avoiding his eyes as I set to work pouring water over the scratches and washing away the sand, but as I dab at the wounds, my mind churns with the events of the night.

"What's the plan after you destroy the plant?"

He casts an uneasy look at me as I keep my hands busy. "With any luck, they'll struggle to maintain order and their focus will be on Aruna, not their home."

I pause, looking him in the eyes. There's a wariness there, hidden in the shadows, but they're also glossed, pupils blown. I eye the bottle, how the liquid is lower than it'd been minutes ago.

"And what then?" I ask, hoping he's drunk enough to give me an answer.

He looks away, somewhere distant within the room. "We hold them hostage, take the city, and demand the surrender of the other Houses."

"You can't honestly believe they'll give up when they see what you've done."

He takes a long drink from the bottle. "No, but it should scare them, and then the real war begins."

My eyes land on the burn scars on his side. I touch a hand to it, feeling him shudder under my touch. "What happened here?"

"A battle with House Althea. I never want to meet Idalia in the sky again," he mutters.

"Why didn't you get it healed?"

He gives a wry grin, shaking his head. "It's a dumb tradition in my family. We keep the burns we earn in battle.

For each scar we collect, it shows other Riders we're harder to kill."

His skin is hot beneath my hand, but not unpleasant. I slide it down, fingers grazing over the rise and fall of his abs. He groans softly, his head falling back as his eyes close.

"Why did you ask me to stay?"

I need to hear his reasons. I need to know this is all in my head, that he's a master of deception and I'm just another pawn for him to use.

His eyes open, glazed and unfocused. A soft flush colors his face as he looks at me.

"Because you're angry like me." My heart pounds as he brushes his knuckles over my cheek. "Because I've wanted to kiss you from the moment you dropped from the sky. I've never seen anyone as beautifully dangerous as you."

I shake my head, even as he runs his fingers through my hair. "Eren, you're drunk."

He grips the back of my hair, tilting my head back. "That doesn't make me want you any less." He lets my hair go, cupping the front of my neck possessively. "Do you have any idea–the power you hold over me? I'd make you a Queen if you let me. I'd give you anything, you only need to ask."

"And if I want you?" I breathe, dizzy from what I'm about to do.

His eyes darken as he leans closer. "I'm already yours."

I close the distance, crashing my mouth to his. His arm wraps around my waist and drags me closer, his lips moving in tandem with mine. He kisses me, greedy and starved. I gasp when he breaks the kiss, moving down the column of my neck where he nips the skin above my pulse. A soft whimper escapes my lips, but I bury it in his shoulder, running my hands over the planes of his chest and through the silky strands of his hair. He sucks over his bite, soothing the hurt. I almost don't know where to touch, only that it's not enough. I find myself plunging down this final cliff, sinking to the bottom of a pit where my self-control implodes. At least for the moment, I don't care who Eren is or what he's done, or why I shouldn't feed the writhing hunger inside me.

I want him, and I'm tired of fighting it.

His mouth returns to mine, tongue sliding over my bottom lip. I let him in with a bite of my own, catching his lower lip between my teeth and eliciting a groan that sets my skin on fire. I pull him closer, pressing my body to his. Eren drags my hips forward, where I feel a hard length pressing against me. My core tightens and I find myself grinding against him, desperate for that friction.

He cups the back of my thighs and lifts me without breaking the kiss, walking us somewhere I can't be bothered to look. He places me over the smooth surface of what feels like a table. His hands reach the end of my shirt, pausing. Asking permission. When I nod he lifts it over my head, tossing it aside. I moan into his mouth as our skin touches, his hard torso sending sparks through my skin. He cups my jaw, lips trailing down my neck, dragging his tongue over the most sensitive spots. He makes his way to my chest where he unclasps my bra, running his tongue over each nipple. I shiver as he sucks, biting and marking the soft flesh as *his*.

Eren uses his other hand to lower me down and continues to kiss along my stomach. It's there he waits, thumb grazing the line of my underwear.

I lock eyes with him. *Yes.*

He rips them down, kneeling. He braces my legs over his shoulders, parting my inner thighs. I draw a sharp breath when he kisses everywhere but my center, teasing me with his warm breath, biting and sucking the skin on each side. He wets the pad of his thumb with his tongue, brushing it over my clit in slow, agonizing circles.

"Say you're mine."

I whimper. "I'm yours."

His mouth pulls into a cruel smirk. "Now be a good girl and cum on my tongue."

My hips roll instinctively at the first glide of his tongue. He drags the tip of it over my clit, circling and prodding at the sensitive bundle of nerves. A tightness coils in my gut, building. He pushes my thighs apart, pinning them down when my hips rock. He sucks my clit between his teeth, teasing, just on the edge of pain. I cry out, hands digging into his hair. I drag my nails over his scalp, earning a growl of approval. His tongue eases inside, lapping at the wetness pouring out of me. My breath hitches as my entire core throbs, the tension twisting so sharp I think I might die.

*"Eren,"* I sob, begging. For what, I'm not sure.

He hums deep, pulling back to replace his mouth with his fingers. He works one finger in, stretching me open. "What is it, Killer? Use your words."

But I can't. My breath catches, hips twitching as he slides a second finger in. My hips roll shamelessly into his touch as his fingers plunge in and out of me. Biting pleasure lances through me, heating my blood to a boiling point. My back arches off the table as I cry out, tears pricking at my eyes. Tighter and tighter it builds, the promise of release so fucking close.

"Such a good girl, riding my hand," he purrs. "Look at me."

I didn't realize I closed my eyes, but when I open them, Eren pierces me with his sage-colored gaze, his warm breath caressing my entrance. I can't look away from them as his tongue slides over my clit, sucking, claiming it as his own, watching me come apart under his tongue, and it takes me right over the edge.

My entire body spasms as I shatter. He holds my legs still over his shoulders while I scream, continuing to work my clit with his tongue. The sensation of falling consumes me, stars dancing in my vision as I fight for breath, my body limp and weightless.

Eren slides his fingers out, rising to stand.

I rise on my elbows, still reeling. "What about—"

He lifts his wet fingers to my lips. "Suck."

I do it without question, holding his stare as I lick the taste of myself from his fingers. He slides his thumb over my bottom lip, his eyes burning with desire.

"When I take you," Eren whispers, drawing his fingers back to cup my throat. "It won't be in some ruins in the middle of the desert. I want you writhing in my bed under silk sheets, my hand around your throat, and tears in your eyes as you scream my name. I want to ruin you in every way possible, and then let you ruin me."

I shiver.

He takes his hand away, gathering my clothes for me. I pull my shirt back on and lay across from him on the other side of the bed.

He faces me, gaze roaming my face. "You should get some rest."

He's right. My eyes are half-lidded, struggling to stay open. I rest my head in the crook of my arm. He traces the side of my shoulder. Steady. Smooth. Endearing. I've never had anyone look at me like this before. Like I'm precious. A gift.

His caresses start to lull me to sleep, but I stubbornly fight it, grasping his hand. "I'm sorry I didn't trust you."

He glances at me for a moment and turns my hand over, brushing his thumb over my mutilated palm. "Don't apologize for your scars."

My heart swells in my chest, a soft warmth flooding my being. I don't know what this feeling is, but I know as I lay here with Eren I feel... whole. It feels right in a world where so many things in my life are wrong.

"Sleep, Sage."

I close my eyes and let his touch soothe me to sleep.

# CHAPTER 23

"*S*age," I hear Eren's voice within the fog.

I blink, rubbing my eyes.

Eren leans over me, brushing my hair from my face. "We have to move. Oddica's going to finish healing you."

I mumble a curse, sitting up and tugging on the last of my clothes. I'm tying the laces of my boots when a knock taps at the door. Eren tugs it open once I'm dressed.

Oddica offers me a small smile, kneeling over my thigh. "I'm sorry about before. I'm better now." Her hands glow over the scratches on my thigh, a stitching sensation following.

When she's done, I flex my leg, testing for pain. When nothing happens, she helps me stand.

"Thank you," I say, meaning every word.

"Don't mention it."

We reunite with the others outside, piling into the back of the truck. My heart pounds the entire ride to Aruna, especially when we abandon the car and continue the last mile on foot.

We mark the patrols, slipping through the gates when the city watch changes guards. Aruna is exactly what I expect from House Dysis: dominated and controlled. No citizens wander in the streets. Each of the buildings are dark with windows shut and no life in sight.

The water filtration plant resides in the heart of the city, a steel warehouse rising higher than any of the surrounding structures. A single reservoir rises above the rooftop, pumping water into the facility below. Street by street, we dodge patrols, waiting for the soldiers to turn corners before bolting to the next alley.

We make it to the end of a chain-link fence where Draven crouches, pulling a pair of bolt-cutters from his bag. One by one, we sprint to the back of the warehouse. Most of the guards appear to be at the front of the building overseeing a maintenance crew, and it allows us to move unnoticed.

*That's the thing with most of these families.* I think to myself as Eren breaks through a window. *We're all too arrogant to think anyone would try something this bold.* It's the most brilliant part of Eren's plan. While each family's water reserves are heavily guarded and kept close to their residences, the treatment plants are not. They're overlooked, not because they're unimportant, but because it seems like an unfathomable target.

With no clean water, everyone suffers.

I try to ignore the twinge in my gut, reminding myself that this is a necessary–*temporary* consequence to bring House Dysis down. *We'll get their people out, even if I have to oversee it myself.*

Cool air fans our faces as we move through the warehouse, the temperature far more bearable in here than the outdoors thanks to the moisture. Rows of steel tanks fill the warehouse, shining beneath dim lights. We keep to the shadows, Gannon and Draven planting explosives in each row. I check over my shoulder as I keep watch, taking note of the brass bomb full of wires and gears in Gannon's hands. Sweat clings to his brow as he ties it to the pipe feeding water from one tank to the next.

They continue to the following row where each step of the filtration process connects one tank to the other. I'm not an expert, but I know the basics. Water must pass from a single reservoir like the one on the rooftop, which is only refilled from water shipments. Once it trickles down from the reservoir, the water is pumped from one tank to another. First, in a settling basin, then through a gravel filter, then a sand filter, and then one last tank where it's boiled, repeating the process until it's deemed drinkable by the plant specialists.

"Alright, it's rigged," Gannon announces, setting his watch as he rises to his feet. "Let's go."

"What about the maintenance crew?" Oddica beats me to the question.

Eren's gaze sweeps the room, landing on the far end of the wall beyond the water tanks. "There." He points. "Pull the fire alarm. They'll evacuate."

I make a beeline for it, my hand inches from the lever when a gunshot booms through the warehouse. Metal sparks above the lever, the bullet ricocheting off the wall. I wrench my hand back and whirl.

Ash stands several feet away, dressed in a maintenance jumpsuit and his gun pointed at me. My heart skips a beat, lungs frozen as my palms lift in surrender. Movement shifts behind him. Rune is there at his side in a matching uniform, his weapon trained on me too.

"Well, what do we have here?" Rune croons.

"Easy," Ash orders when I start to take a step back. "No one has to get hurt."

I catch shadows stirring behind them, moving between tanks, but keep my mouth shut and my eyes locked on the brother who's moments away from killing his little sister. My one consolation is that my face is covered. He'll never know who I am, but if I dare to speak, this is all over.

He tracks me with lethal precision, each breath I take is measured and cataloged. I never thought I'd be on the opposite end of my brother's gun, but this is the second time my two worlds collide.

*How long before one of us doesn't make it home?*

I wait, pleading with the Gods for Eren to warn the others of who these people are to me.

*Don't shoot them. Please don't shoot. Maybe Rune, but–*

I can't decide which is worse, watching my brother die, Ash killing me, or dying in a fiery explosion.

"Where are the others?" Ash presses, inching closer. "You didn't come here alone."

Maybe the Gods are on my side, because when Ash takes a step, someone else takes their shot. Ash and Rune duck at the sound, granting me time to pull the lever and run. Sirens blare, red lights flashing in the signal to evacuate. I make it a few feet before a hand swings me around by the arm.

I jerk from Ash's grip, slamming my elbow over his forearm to break his hold. His hand slips, giving me room to slip free, but Ash counters, throwing a punch that connects with my cheek. I stumble, barely blocking the blows he follows me with. If this were any other enemy, I would search for a weakness, but this is my brother, the boy I've been sparring with my entire life. I know all of his weaknesses, and he knows mine.

I hurl a kick to his left knee, hearing the air leave his lungs as his whole leg buckles. I don't stay to watch the effect, darting behind the nearest tank to avoid the shower of bullets bouncing off the warehouse. Gannon and Draven exchange fire with Rune across the room, keeping my cousin occupied to buy my escape. I rise from my crouch, about to make my way over when a hand covers my shoulder. I throw my elbow back on instinct, only for it to be blocked by Eren. Relief floods my body as his hand falls to the middle of my back, guiding me to safety.

"My brother–" I turn when we make it to the window we entered from.

"Gannon and D are leading them out," Eren assures, holding out his hand for support.

I swallow my fear and nod, taking his hand to boost myself up. We clamber out the window, dodging the city patrols screeching to a halt in the front of the building. I spot Oddica and Azara across the street, waving at us from an alley. We break into a run, halfway to our friends when a bullet *cracks*.

An electrical shock pierces my body, stealing the breath from my lungs and the ground sweeps out from under me.

*"NO!"*

Sound drifts, low and muffled like I'm underwater. I blink through blurred vision, desperately turning for the source of the ringing in my ears. Rune stands mere yards from us, clutching his gun.

Eren hovers above me, raising his revolver when the warehouse explodes. He shields me with his body as fire and glass erupt from the building. The blast throws Rune off his feet, shaking the earth beneath us.

*"Oddica!"*

Oddica's slanted face appears, fading in and out of existence. White light reflects off her face, accompanied by a faint stitching sensation below my stomach. Oddica's features clear back into focus, including the droplet of blood oozing from her nose. As my senses sharpen, I notice the cold pallor of her usually warm skin and the coat of sweat drenching her hair. Her healing light flickers–once–twice–before guttering to a stop. Her name begins to form on my lips, but her eyes roll to the back of her head. I don't even have the strength to reach out before she collapses.

Darkness eats the edges of my sight as the others crowd the Healer twitching uncontrollably. In the distance, Rune is gone.

And so am I.

# CHAPTER 24

*A* trail of cypress leads me out of the dark. My eyes flutter open to a pastel ceiling. My fingers twitch, finding soft cotton sheets beneath them. A warm waft of air fans the side of my face and I turn.

Eren lays beside me, dark bags bruising the skin beneath his eyes. His mouth falls in a deep pout, brows half-furrowed in his sleep. I fight the urge to smooth them, to caress the laxed plains of his face. I twist my head the opposite way, discovering a dusk sky through the window of my room. Pushing myself up, I wince at a tenderness in my waist. I clutch my stomach, carefully rising from the bed so as not to disturb Eren.

I switch on the light in the bathroom and ease the door closed. I turn to the mirror, almost staggering at what I see. A layer of fine sand dusts my body, sticking to every crevice of my skin and hair. My lips are cracked, drier than my throat, and the bags beneath my eyes speak to the exhaustion I feel in my bones. I shudder and fill the tub with water, peeling my clothes off when I glance down. My hands freeze.

A dried, rusted splotch stains the fabric over my waist where a coin-sized rip hangs in the center. I finger the tear, tracing the outline until memory slams into my head like a freight train. The warehouse. The bombs. Ash and Rune. The ground falling out from under me. The *explosion*.

I sway, reaching for the counter to steady myself. Taking a sharp breath, I pull my shirt over my head. Black stars dot my vision at the sight unfolding in the mirror. A crude scar rests below my navel, marring the flesh to the right of my waist. I press my fingers to it, flinching when it hurts. I twist in the mirror, finding a wider exit wound scarring my back as well.

Hands shaking, I shut off the water to the tub and peel off the rest of my clothes before settling in. I'm not sure how long I spend scrubbing blood and dirt from my body, but when I emerge from the bathroom, Eren is still asleep and a cascade of stars has speckled the horizon.

Dragonsong chimes in the night, leading me out to the balcony. Halcyon and the brown dragon circle each other in another game of tag. I smile, taking a seat on the stone banister. Wisps of white petals snag my attention as they waver in the night-kissed wind. Moonflowers bloom along the trellis up the walls and encircle the lower half of the balcony. I lift my hand, tracing their silky petals.

"You're awake."

Eren's shoulders sag with visible relief as he takes me in. Unlike me, he must have already bathed while I slept, but his hair is mussed and clothes disheveled like he'd thrown them on in a hurry, only to knock out right after.

He comes to my side now, eyes soft and assessing every inch of me. Once he's satisfied, he reaches over my head, plucking a moonflower from the trellis and offering it to me. I gently pinch the stem between my fingers and bring it to my nose. A sweet, subtle cross between jasmine and vanilla lingers within the petals.

"I think this might be my favorite flower," I muse, twirling it between my thumb and forefinger. I didn't think anything so delicate could thrive in the harshness of this land, but if this little flower can survive, then so can I.

Eren tracks the hand that settles over my stomach, right where the scar lies. "Sage, I'm so sorry."

I keep my eyes on the flower. "What for?"

He runs a hand through his hair, bags deepening. "I let you get shot. I should have protected you. I should have–"

"Eren."

He sighs.

I force the lump in my throat down. "There wasn't anything you could have done. They're my family. I didn't want you guys to kill them. This isn't on anyone but me."

"But if it weren't for Oddica you would be dead. Gods, Oddica–"

"Oddica." My eyes widen. "What happened? Is she okay?"

I watch the guilt pile high on his shoulders, weighing down his face. "She had a seizure, but she's recovering. That's my fault too." He shakes his head. "I should have paid attention. I should have known better. We almost lost both of you. What sort of leader am I?" He scoffs. "People keep getting hurt on my watch."

I take his arm, squeezing. "Eren, none of that is your fault. You're at war with hundreds of people to look after, not just your team. People get hurt. It happens."

"It shouldn't." He withdraws from my touch and I try to set the twinge of hurt to the side because I know it's not me he can't stand. It's the kindness I offer, the forgiveness in my words when he's not ready to forgive himself. I've carried guilt like that for years. I should know the wound is too fresh.

"So... does that happen to Oddica a lot?"

"She's a talented mage," he says quietly, peering at the stars. "But she has limits. It's difficult to get her to slow down. She always insists she's fine, that she wants to help. She could make a comfortable living as a Healer, working at her own pace. Hell, she could become a High Mage if she wanted, but she says her calling is with us."

"I get it. If I had a gift like that I'd want to use it as often as possible."

Eren doesn't answer, though he faces me, his expression taut. "This is only going to get more dangerous."

"I know."

"Sage."

"Eren."

He gives me a pained look. His lips part, but a familiar and yet ancient shriek engulfs the night. Noxainia rises from the canyons, joining in the game of chase with Halcyon and the brown dragon. I gape at them, watching in wonder.

"The hatchlings keep her young," Eren chuckles to himself.

"Halcyon's not a hatchling!" I draw my knees up to my chest, lifting my chin.

Eren's eyes seem to spark. "To Nox, anything smaller than her wingspan is considered a hatchling."

I cross my arms. "Now that's just unfair."

He grins, watching them with me for a moment.

"You know," I say after a while, as the emptiness settles in. "She chose me over my sister."

He tilts his head. "Dragons decide who's worthy."

I recall Uncle Deon's cryptic tirade. *Dragons are fickle creatures with minds of their own, picking and choosing Riders at their whim.*

"Halcyon was the last dragon in our family to bond. Everyone thought Lux would claim her, but every time she tried to approach, Halcyon would turn and fly away." I pause, gathering the memories in my mind like a fractured collage.

"They'd never seen it before, a dragon refusing to bond. I was only eight years old, but they let me try since everyone else was bonded. When she allowed me to get close, I thought my heart was going to burst right out of my chest. I touched her nose and slid my hand to the middle of her forehead. We couldn't take our eyes off of each other. I felt the bond snap into place and everyone watching knew. My whole world changed after that. Lux was crushed. She tried to put on a brave face, but I could tell she was heartbroken."

"With a family like yours, it's difficult for me to understand your loyalty." Eren casts a sidelong glance. "But not impossible."

"I just…" I hug my knees closer, hating how small my voice sounds. "Wanted to belong."

Silence stretches between us until Eren breaks it, softly, and with care. "You never have to see them again if you don't want to. You would be safe here."

*'Stay with me.'* His earlier plea from the gala whispers in my mind.

"What would that make us?" I ask and my face instantly heats at all that's passed.

He smiles knowingly. "Anything you want, though to the rest of the world, we're still engaged."

I wouldn't call us lovers. It's too formal with too much meaning, but the desire to kill him has long fled, replaced with hesitant desire. I can't pretend I've forgotten the temple in the dunes, but I can't fathom losing control like that again.

"I suppose we could be… friends." I dare a glance at him.

His mouth curves, positively feline as he leans in. "Tell me, Killer, do all your friends spread you open and worship you with their tongue?"

I shiver, glaring as he pulls back and laughs. "No, they most certainly *don't*, but I decided you're not my enemy anymore, and you're not an ally I'd stab in the back at the soonest convenience."

"Ah, yes. We both know your affinity for sharp objects."

I roll my eyes. "This might be too weird, not secretly plotting to kill you."

He shrugs. "I can always chase you on the back of Nox while you try to shoot me, just to keep things familiar."

I laugh, unrestrained and without warning. It trickles up to the stars, dancing with dragonsong. Eren falls quiet, staring at me with rapt attention.

I stare back at him, suddenly breathless. "What?"

"Nothing." He takes a step back, his voice hoarse, turning away with some difficulty. "Goodnight, Sage."

I watch him return to the room and hear the distinct sound of my bedroom door shutting. As I sit alone on the balcony, I rest my chin on my knees and listen to the playful screeches bouncing off the canyons. Halcyon sounds... happy.

I brush a mental hand down the bond, making my presence known. Halcyon instantly answers, her joy brighter than the stars. I tuck it straight into my heart and hold it there, cradling it. Thankful for it.

At least one of us has found a place to belong.

It's a brief exchange at the handoff of family. Kamari no longer looks at me with cold indifference, but a probing curiosity as we cross the sands. Her frost-scaled dragon lands with a shriek next to Cantorix, stirring the old man who lets out a gruff protest at the lithe one's spirit.

'Be careful,' Eren's voice whispers in my mind.

I fight the urge to turn and keep my stare trained on Ash. There's no sign of any wounds on his face. No singed hair or shadow of a bruise blemishing his stone-like features. His eyes only soften upon seeing me.

Ash throws his arms around me in a fierce hug. I gasp, pain

flashing through my torso, but pat him on the back regardless. "Did you miss me or something?"

He pulls away, scanning my face with a pinched brow. "Are you okay? I heard about the attack on the Gala."

My shoulders slacken and I try not to make my relief too obvious. Ash doesn't suspect a thing. "I'm fine."

"I kept her safe," Eren drawls, surveying my brother with palpable distaste. He cocks his head, flashing a close-lipped smile. "Do try to accomplish the same while she's in your care."

"I don't need a lesson in protecting my sister," Ash snaps.

Eren gives a nonchalant shrug, brushing a bit of dust off his shoulder. "Interesting. Her scars say otherwise."

Ash stiffens. Even my spine goes ramrod straight, eyes widening.

"Forgive my brother," Kamari purrs from Eren's side. "He can be a bit possessive with things he perceives as his."

"I perceive nothing. She is *mine*. Don't forget it."

Ash returns Eren's glare tenfold, saying nothing, not even a goodbye to Kamari as they mount up. It isn't until they're in the sky that he walks with me back to our family's home.

"There's much for us to discuss, Little Sister."

"What do you mean?"

"Aunt Natalya and Father are not speaking."

My brows furrow. "Why not?"

"When word came of the attack on the Gala, Natalya was in an uproar on your behalf, insisting how an attack on one of us is an attack on all and we should investigate further. When he and Mother dismissed her concerns, she called them heartless fools."

I blink. "All this at dinner?"

Ash's lips quirk. "Yes. It seems our beloved Aunt stole the show last night."

"Must run in the family," I mutter, but my gut twists. For Mother and Father to have such little interest... it only fans the flames of my suspicion. I reach into my pocket, pluck the gold coin stained with blood, and flip it in the air toward Ash.

He catches it, turning it over in his hand. "What's this?"

"Gold from Solera. Eren pulled it off one of the assassins."

Ash tenses. "Do you think it's the rebels?"

I shake my head. "You should have seen it, Ash. This wasn't some rag-tag group playing at war. It was coordinated. One of them confirmed I was the target."

Ash loses his footing for a second, eyes widening, but my stare lands on the leg in question. "Your knee."

He walks with a slight limp, grimacing. "Rebels, which brings me to our next topic–House Dysis lost their filtration center."

I halt in my tracks, shoving guilt aside and making room for feigned shock. "What?"

"Their facility was blown to rubble. We're expecting them to call for aid, but House Dysis is proud. We'll have to wait and see what they do."

"I can't believe this." I glance at the dunes like I can see the path to Aruna from here.

"The rebels are getting more reckless. Father increased the guards around the manor and the reserves. On top of that, we're rotating patrols on the filtration center ourselves. Joce and Jasper are in Solera right now as we speak."

I nod along, but my heart isn't in it, and he notices. "What's wrong?"

I look at my brother and let him see my profound disappointment. "Who's trying to kill me?"

"I don't know, but we're going to figure it out."

"*How?*" I demand. "Our own parents aren't even concerned!" My voice carries on the open sands for anyone to hear, but I don't care. I can't bring myself to be quiet. I'm so fucking tired of being *quiet*. "Gods, open your eyes, Ash! It doesn't matter what I do! I'm still expendable in their eyes!"

"Sage, keep your voice down." Ash's head makes a sharp turn, checking our surroundings.

"No! I'm tired! All of my loyalty, all of that work trying to win back their trust–trying to prove that I *belong* and where did it get me? I'm still nothing to this family and nothing is all I'll ever be to them." I start forward.

Ash catches my arm. "That's not true, and if I had to guess, I'd start looking at that fiancé of yours."

I shake him off. "You know, I'm wondering what you said at dinner."

Ash's face falls.

"Did you say anything, Brother? Did you defend me like Aunt Nat? Did you say *anything* when I was gone?"

His silence is answer enough.

I scoff. "I didn't think so. Eren has shown me more kindness than this family ever has. Someone here wants me dead and you're an idiot if you don't believe it."

I leave Ash behind and storm past the door to the compound. I dump my bag in the foyer, stalking toward the first person on my list for a conversation that is *long* overdue.

Across the courtyard, I throw open the doors to the temple of the Gods. A tall woman in red robes turns her head from a trembling servant.

I take a step inside, offering a smile. "Hello, Mother."

Aurora Galvan's sharp brows pinch, her vulture eyes narrowing in on me like I'm already carrion. She remains silent as I take slow, measured steps down the carpeted pathway between the pews of the temple. The silence is a weapon in itself, a fine-cut blade my mother can use to gut anyone without uttering a word.

"To what do I owe this visit?" Comes her frigid greeting.

"Does a daughter need permission to see her mother?" I give her an equally terse reply.

She clasps her hands together. "Make it quick, Sage. I don't have time for children's games."

I take another step, coming around her to take in the statue of Vulcan. My eyes trail off to the dais, right upon the rust-colored spot that hasn't entirely lifted from the floorboards.

"You might recall there was an attempt on my life this past weekend."

"News was delivered," she confirms, her tone as desolate as her heart.

"What does Father intend to do about it?"

"What would you have us do? Waste precious resources hunting for assassins who have more than likely disappeared?" She scoffs. "*Please*. I thought you'd grown smarter than that. How wrong I was."

I take the hits without flinching, plastering on a honeyed smile. "You see, Mother, I found it interesting that while the attack was made to appear politically motivated, one of the assassins confessed. The target wasn't Eren, nor the High Mage, or any of the influential guests in attendance. It was me. Who has more reason to want me dead than my own family?"

Cold, fiery wrath fills her eyes and her lip curls. "You *vile* girl. Throwing around baseless accusations! You are a Galvan! That's reason enough for anyone to want you dead. You've aligned yourself as a political figure. Little do you know there are *consequences* that come with reaching for power."

"Is that so?" I tilt my head. "They were paid with Solera gold. Something tells me those consequences have names. Shall I list them?" I hold up my fist, opening a finger for each name. "There's Uncle Deon, can't say he's my biggest fan. Cousin Dahlia, who intends to collect a life debt. Rune, who would happily burn my body the moment Ash stops looking. Oh, and let's not forget–*you*."

Every ounce of emotion, even fury, slithers from my

mother's face. She strides forward, one echoing step at a time. I stand still, weathering the maelstrom she brings with her.

"If I desired a bullet in your heart, Child," she whispers, piercing my stare with her own. "I would not miss."

"Perhaps Father then. Maybe he's grown tired of me ruining his plans."

She barks a mirthless laugh. "You might be an inconvenience, but your father is not wasteful. You still fit into his plans whether you realize it or not."

I clench my jaw. "So that's it? Someone tries to kill me and you can't be bothered with it? Would you even *grieve me* if I were dead?"

My mother's eyes roll. "You're alive. Count it as a blessing and be done with it. While you were out twirling in a dress for your fiancé, the rebels made their move. House Dysis lost their filtration plant. Their city is in shambles while you whine about your feelings."

I take a step back, not to retreat, but to breathe air that isn't tainted by someone so cruel. I shake my head and make a start for the exit, but my feet don't carry me further than a few steps before they lock.

*I don't run anymore.*

I spin around and face my mother who looks at me with true disdain. "Can I just ask you something?"

Her brow arches, but I don't wait for permission.

"When did it happen? When did I finally disappoint you so much that you decided you couldn't love me anymore?"

Her eyes rake over me and I wonder if she takes a moment to consider it. I wonder if she's doing the same thing I am–desperately searching for the last kind word we exchanged. Searching for the last time that she held me. The last memory of when she looked at me with love.

I can't remember.

Our eyes meet.

I see a crack in her exterior, and the resignation bleeding through. "When you became everything I warned you not to be."

"Which is?"

"Weak."

Her words knock the breath from me, but I only have myself to blame.

"How can you say that to me? I'm your *daughter*."

She casts a dubious look, giving me a once-over. "You're no daughter of mine."

I laugh, blinking tears from my eyes. I don't know why it hurts. It shouldn't anymore. I know who my mother is, and she's everything I never hope to be.

"You wanna know something funny? Our family is big. So *great* and yet… I never felt more alone than the day I grew a mind of my own." I wipe my face and raise my chin. "I guess it's a good thing I don't need you anymore. I never did."

I turn my back on my mother, on the Gods staring down at me from the stained glass windows and leave them behind.

# CHAPTER 25

*M*y heart is still racing when I return to the manor.

"Lady Galvan," a small voice calls.

I pivot, finding a servant boy bowing at the waist. "Your Father requests you in his Study."

"Of course he does," I mutter, trudging past him.

Two guards part the doors for me. My father rests in the chair behind his desk, peering over a handful of papers. "Take a seat."

"What's this about?" I snap, my mood already ruined for the evening.

His eyes flick up from the documents in his grasp, unamused. "Sit."

I exhale deeply, making my displeasure known as I sink into the chair.

"You're in a mood," he notes.

"I spoke with Mother."

"Ah," he says, setting the papers on the desk. "I see."

"What's this about?" I ask again, crossing my arms.

"What did you gather from your visit?"

I pause. As we stare at each other it dawns on me. I was supposed to spy on Eren's family.

"No."

"No?"

I rise from my seat. "No. I will not spy on my fiancé. If you want information, get it yourself."

"You insolent girl," my father snarls, matching Mother for insults today. "Just what do you think you're playing at?"

I pluck another bloodied coin from my pocket and flip it in the air. It clatters onto the mahogany desk, spinning on its axis until Father slams a hand over it. He removes his palm, eyeing the insignia of our House.

"I'm done playing this family's game. You all want me dead so badly? Fine. Come and get me. I'm not hiding anymore." I turn on my heels, slamming the door on my way out.

Blood boiling, heart thumping, I command myself to *breathe*. One breath in. One breath out. I hear the front door open and boots thumping up the veranda to the foyer. Jocelyn and Jasper step through the threshold. Jocelyn stills, flight goggles in hand. Her brother mumbles something, continuing on with a quick nod to me.

I stand there, heart in my throat until Jocelyn moves forward. Her steps are slow, hesitant, but when she's close enough she surges forward and wraps her arms around me. I squeeze her back just as tight, unable to choke back the soft sob that's been building my chest since I left the temple.

"I haven't forgiven you yet," she mutters, though there is no anger to it. "But I'm glad you're not dead."

"I'll take it," I laugh, reluctant to let her go. "Can we talk?"

Her lips part as she removes her gloves, about to answer when footsteps march down the hall. We turn, finding Ash and my father with equally grim expressions.

I cut off their path. "What's happened?"

Annoyance flashes in my father's eyes, but Ash answers me. "House Dysis has called an emergency Conclave."

"They're going to ask for aid," I say aloud, wondering how my Father will pull it off with our reserves so low.

"We'll see what exactly they ask for," Father drawls, peridot eyes flashing from me to Ash. "Let's go."

"We'll be back by dinner." Ash leans forth, pulling me in for a hug and whispering. "It appears your fiancé had a gift delivered to your room this morning. It's put Father in a sour mood."

I doubt it was the gift in question that put our father in a mood, but nevertheless, I wonder what it could be. "A gift?"

Ash pulls away, jerking his chin. "See for yourself." He carries on, nodding to Jocelyn as he passes.

My cousin sketches a brow at me.

I smile, jabbing my thumb in the direction of my room. "Wanna come see?"

"I'd like that."

In a few turns, I throw open my bedroom door to a burst of jasmine and vanilla. Trumpet-shaped flowers with white petals stretch over each surface of my room. My desk, dressers, and bed are covered in moonflowers. Snipped at the base, they stare up at me like small stars. A warmth blooms within my chest, unfurling like these flowers of the night.

"What are these?" Jocelyn picks one up, examining it in her hand.

"Moonflowers," I whisper, shutting the door.

She twirls the flower with a frown. "At least your fiancé knows what you like." Our eyes meet. "Your father broke my engagement to Valen."

"Did he?" I shift my weight from one to the other. "Good."

"You did that?"

I bite my lip, nodding.

Her bottom lip trembles. "You didn't have to."

"Yes, I did."

Jocelyn sighs, crossing her arms. "I don't believe you meant to hurt us, but I can't understand why you would side with..." she trails off.

I sit down on the bed, wringing my hands between my knees. "It wasn't... *intentional*. I wanted to kill him, but the more time that passed I started to understand. I've seen the wounded. Families and children are being displaced because of our fighting. We're careless with dragonfire. We bring destruction and don't stop to question it. We don't look down at the people below. They hate us, Joce, and it's our fault. They have every reason to rebel."

She doesn't say anything for a moment, but sinks onto the bed beside me. "Okay... I think I can wrap my head around that. But what happens if they win?"

I hang my head, knowing the bond will never let me speak of it. "I can't tell you."

"Gods, Sage!" Jocelyn shoots to her feet, whirling on me. "Don't you think that's important? What do they want? A Council? Representatives? We need to know these things!"

I pause. "We?"

Jocelyn huffs, red in the face. "Yes. *We*."

My heart swells. "You're on our side?"

"I'm on *your* side," she corrects. "But I want to meet him."

I chew the inside of my mouth. "I'll see if that's possible."

"Do you... know who he is?"

I don't try to tempt the magic, but hold her gaze. *Yes.*

Jocelyn purses her lips, but doesn't push. Instead, she sits back down. "You know... I can get behind helping people less fortunate. I'm not a monster. But I'm not going to bring harm to our family."

"I understand. I don't want that either."

She sighs. "I have to go." Jocelyn stands, heading for the door. "You should talk to my mother, by the way. She's been asking about you."

"I'll look for her."

"She's out in the courtyard."

I gather a moonflower in my hand when she leaves and bring it to my nose.

True to her word, Aunt Nat sits alone in the courtyard. Seated on a plush patio set under a wide umbrella, Aunt Natalya basks in the open air with a flock of firedrakes at her feet. The glorified red lizards flap their wings, squawking and snapping at each other over the bits of jerky she scatters, exchanging tufts of fire in the fray.

"Ah, if it isn't my little Firedrake." Aunt Natalya grins as I settle into an open seat. "Would you like any water? Wine, perhaps?"

I shake my head. "I'm fine. I heard you wanted to see me?"

"Oh, I hope you didn't rush over, but yes. You may have heard your parents and I had a little row."

"I did. Thank you for standing up for me."

Her ruby lips curve. "It was nothing."

"It was everything."

Her smile fades. "It's come to my attention that your parents are unconcerned about your safety. I'd like to offer you a bit of advice."

"Such as?"

She glances around the courtyard, leaning in. "I see two options for you. Marry quickly and leave this place. Your fiancé will protect you in a way this family won't. Or... convince Ash to challenge your father to an Ignis Mortem for the House seat."

The breath leaves my chest. "What?"

"You heard me."

"Ash isn't... he would *never*."

"He will inherit it one way or another. My brother is becoming blinded by power. I should have seen it sooner, but the gross misalliance with my daughter and his behavior at dinner has shown me the brother I knew is no longer there.

Children are not expendable, no matter what path they choose for themselves."

I frown, thinking. "Did you know about the drought?"

She nods.

"Even if Ash did that—and I'm not saying he *would*—Uncle Deon would never stand for it. Don't you think he'd challenge Ash's claim?"

Aunt Natalya rolls her eyes. "My younger brother is all bark and no bite. Deon is no leader. He may carry big dreams but that is all they are. His threats have no merit."

"You sure about that?"

Aunt Natalya considers it. "At any rate, Ash being in power would benefit you more than your father grasping onto it. He holds sway with the Houses, but refuses to make peace with the rebels. So what if they want more water? Find a solution to the drought and make things right. Let the people voice their grievances, make them feel *heard*. Can we not coexist? I believe Ash is more malleable to these suggestions, able to be swayed to end this bloody war."

*I'm so tired of scheming.* I think, but bob my head all the same. In a way, it's a relief to know that Aunt Natalya believes in peace. I'm just not sure about the lengths she's willing to go. If Ash is anything, he is loyal to a fault.

"Give it some thought. You don't have to heed my advice, but take it from someone who's watched this family from the sidelines far longer than you. It's better to be proactive than to allow yourself to be strung along in someone else's plans."

I rise, stepping over the firedrakes. "I'll think about it."

"Don't think too long, Darling. The wind is shifting."

As I make my way to the front of the property, I stare at the dregs of sunlight beating over the courtyard. How long has it been since Ash and Father left for the Conclave? An hour? Two? Only the Gods know what's going on there. The Gods and... Eren.

I reach for our bond in my mind, sending my thoughts into the void. *Having fun?*

'Did you find your gift?' A sensual voice replies.

*Yes. Thank you.* I try not to smile like an idiot as I walk across the sand to the dragon caves. *How's the Conclave going?*

'Politics as usual. House Dysis can barely hold order in their city. They're asking for assistance, but without clean water I don't imagine more dragons will quell the riots.'

*Are they asking for water?*

'Yes and equipment for repairs to their filtration plant. Their allies are sparing what they can, but it won't be enough.' There's a smugness to his thoughts, like we've already won.

*When will you make your move?*

'Soon.'

My stomach tightens into knots as I follow the sunstone path. Damp earth invades my nose the further I get. The underground spring rushes within, echoing off the cavern walls.

*Eren... Jocelyn wants to meet you.*

There's a pause in our connection. 'Does she?'

*She's on my side, but she wants answers I'm not able to give her.*

Another pause.

*We could use more Riders. She knows I'm a traitor and hasn't given me up. I trust her.*

'Alright. We'll plan it.'

I leave him alone, wandering through the caverns until I find the curled heap of iridescent scales.

*Halcyon.*

A heap of exhaustion trickles down the bond to me. I frown and quicken my pace, approaching her curled form in the middle of the cave.

*Halcyon? What's wrong?*

Halcyon groans, untwisting her limbs. Her emerald eyes blink lazily at me as she cocks her head, sniffing.

I pet her nose, tracing the scales over her forehead. "What is it, Love? Are you sick?"

Her long neck pulls back. I search her body, scanning for an injury or clue to her behavior when a glint of light catches my eye. My heart stutters, blood quickening.

*No. It can't be. It's too soon. There hasn't been time*–except that's not true. I recall each moment I heard dragonsong on the balcony. Where did they go when they rested after play? Which dragon? When did–

My blood chills. *How long until the others find out?*

Because there, in the middle of Halcyon's nest, lies three shimmering eggs.

*EREN, we have a problem*– I don't get to finish my thought.

Heartfyre lands in the front of the compound, blowing a fine cloud of dust across our property. I shield my eyes with my hand as the dust hits, sand grains bouncing off my body and scattering in the wind.

"Ash!"

He lingers near Heartfyre. My father doesn't spare me a glance, continuing inside where guards flank him the rest of the way.

"Ash, I need your help," I pant, desperate for him to not just listen, but *hear* me. "It's Halcyon."

Ash tenses, eyes darting to the caverns. "What is it? What happened?"

"She–" I lower my voice. "She's laid a clutch of eggs."

Ash's face falls blank. I wonder if he's come to the same conclusion, but the hope is dashed when he breaks into a grin and scoops me up, spinning me around with a laugh.

"That's amazing! Congrat–"

"No!" I shove back, stumbling from his grasp. "You don't get it. They're going to fight over them like *vultures*."

"That's not true. It's already been agreed that Lux and Dahlia–"

I scoff. "Do you really want to see *Dahlia* back on a dragon?"

"That's not for us to decide. This is our duty to our family. If Kamari's dragon laid eggs, I would expect her House to take their pick and share the rest of them. Now, three eggs is a smaller clutch so your fiancé should only receive one."

"Stop! Stop talking like it's already done!"

"Because it *is*, Sage. These were the terms built into our marriage contracts. Be reasonable."

"It's not right. None of this is right."

"What are you saying?"

I shake my head, struggling to find the words, but there's no way to put this delicately. "Does it have to be this way? Do we have to keep fighting? Why doesn't Father make peace?"

"Make peace?" Ash echoes, leaning back like I've struck him. "The rebels want us dead."

"Do they?" I challenge. "Or do they just want a little more water? Maybe they don't want to burn while we battle each other trying to figure it out!"

"Sage," Ash lowers his voice. "What you're saying is dangerous."

"It's about to get a whole lot more dangerous! Why would I give up my dragon's eggs to people who want to kill me?"

My brother shakes his head, rubbing a hand over his face. "We don't have a choice."

I lurch forward, grabbing his arm and squeezing. "There's always a choice. I used to think that there wasn't, but that was a lie. We don't have to be the people we were raised to be. You could do better."

"What do you mean? What is it you want from me?"

"It means you could do a better job. If you unseated Father—"

"Stop!" Ash breaks my hold, turning away. "I can't hear this."

*Fight for me.* I draw a ragged breath as he stops in his tracks. "Fight for me like I fight for you!"

"Tell them about the eggs," he says, hollow and unfeeling. "Or I will."

My hopes are dashed, chewed and spat on the ground like a bad taste. Ash walks away.

And when the sun sets across the shifting dunes, dinner begins.

My father settles into his chair at the head of the table, unfolding his napkin over his lap. Everyone is pretending not to be interested. They sip at their wine, stare blankly at the wallpaper, or find their utensils suddenly interesting, but there is a tension electrifying the air. Uncertainty lingers in the spaces between us like an unfinished question.

What. Comes. Next?

Father clears his throat, a signal that dinner may begin. As the chefs bring out the first course, he casts his imperious gaze over our family. "House Dysis is significantly weakened. Their people are in an uproar over the lack of water being issued. Their ground forces are being used to keep the mobs at bay while their riders guard the new construction."

"How unfortunate to only have one plant," Rune snickers, making my skin crawl.

"House Dysis isn't known for strategy," Uncle Deon stirs his bourbon. "Why don't they use their dragons to restore order? A show of force, lest the people forget who's in charge."

My tongue is quicker than my restraint. "People with no hope have nothing to lose. Incinerate them at a whim and you'll give them a greater reason to fight."

"Indeed," Father agrees dryly, startling me with his reply. "It may prove difficult to rule over ash and bones, wouldn't you agree, Brother?"

"Bones are quieter than uprisings," Deon glowers, sipping his drink.

"Nevertheless, their weakness may be in our favor. We've spared them a few soldiers and gold for their restorations. Water rations have come from House Althea, but they will remain in our debt long after this is over."

My mother hums in agreement and it takes a certain amount of self-restraint for my gaze not to linger. She catches me, however, piercing me with those sharp eyes. I break her stare, glancing at Rune. I've taken special care not to look at him until now. Each time he speaks, a phantom pain shudders through my abdomen. To his left, Dahlia chews quietly, eyes flicking from my father to me. The corner of her mouth lifts in one smooth motion, a smirk that chills my body to the core.

"It seems a celebration is in order," Father continues, raising his glass to me with a heartless grin. "To Sage, for Halcyon has laid a clutch of three eggs."

Delighted gasps erupt around the table, but my heart stops. My arms become lead. I'm so numb I'm not sure that I'm breathing anymore. Somehow, I manage to turn my head to the one person in the room who knew.

Ash is waiting for me, shoulders square and jaw tight. I understood duty once. I admired my brother for his loyalty–his ability to fight for our family, no matter the cost. But now I have learned there is a teetering line between duty and honor, and it is a ledge I cannot pull my brother from, no matter how hard I try.

*He is lost.*

My father cuts into his meal. "Lux and Dahlia shall have the first pick of the eggs. A shame there's only three. The last one will have to return with you to Esmeray."

I throw my napkin down. Heads snap around the table, but I offer a cool smile. "Excuse me."

I fight to control my breathing, but the more distance I put between myself and the dining room increases my heart rate as the realization settles in. *Everyone knows.*

"Sage."

I halt, hands curling into fists. "Get away from me, Ash."

"They had to know. They would have found out sooner or–"

I spin, jabbing my finger into his chest. "You and me? We're done! You're a back-stabbing traitor and you're just like the rest of them!"

I leave Ash in the hall, throwing open the front doors. Dry, night-kissed air fans my flushed face as I carve a path through the sands, straight into the dragon caves. Halcyon is where I left her, curled around the pile of eggs. Her eyes flutter open, steam trailing from her nose as she perks up at me. I fall to my knees, palms digging into the dirt. Her nose nudges me, soft and gentle. It's more than I deserve, and it breaks me apart.

"I'm sorry," I cry, placing my palm atop her nose. "I'm sorry I can't protect them."

*I can't protect you. I can't protect anyone.*

Whether she understands me or not, her gaze is unchanging. She stares at me, head tilted, like she knows I'm upset, but can't fathom why. She chitters, a quiet and soothing sound, nudging me.

*Don't cry. It'll be okay,* her jeweled eyes seem to tell me.

I wipe my eyes. "Can I see them?"

Her body unravels, making room for me to get closer. I hold the nearest egg with both hands. It's warm to the touch with a white exterior and a scaled shell as hard as a rock. Flecks of iridescent blue shimmer over the shell like Halcyon.

Was it the brown dragon that mated with her? *I don't even know its name.* I set the egg aside and study the others, each of them the same size and color. Will the hatchlings look like her, or a mix of the two? I imagine a white dragon with brown spots, or a brown dragon with white splotches. Will they have her eyes? What color will their fire be?

Halcyon settles her head back on the ground and shuts her eyes, huffing. I run my palm over her head to her neck. With each stroke, my hand trembles. A rage unlike anything I've ever experienced consumes me, a fire licking at my veins.

*They've taken too much from me. I will not let them take this from you.*

I turn my head to the eggs. Not a single person in my family is fit for these hatchlings... but I can think of others who are. And with that thought forms a plan.

The winds are shifting, and so are the flames.

# CHAPTER 26

*E*ren sits at the desk in his study with his hands folded, soaking in what I've told him.

"Three eggs," he murmurs to himself.

"I know Halcyon and the brown dragon got on very well." I fold my arms over my abdomen, hugging myself. "It might be him. It's 'him,' right?"

"Nevian." Eren nods. "He's Neith's dragon, but I didn't think he was old enough to..." He shakes his head, sighing. "The others don't play with him much. He's the youngest. Smaller, like Halcyon."

"Eren." I swallow hard. "They can't take her eggs."

He mulls over it, not disagreeing. "To your family, it is their right."

"Screw that," I spit, placing my hands over the desk. "There's still time to make a move. Halcyon won't let anyone close except me. We can take the eggs for ourselves. Let the rebels become Riders. I'd choose Azara over Dahlia any day knowing she's loyal to you and the cause."

Eren's eyes darken, shadows falling across his face as he considers it. "You're proposing we use dragons in the war?"

"Why not? I trust our team more than my family. Why should they become more powerful? You already ride Nox. Imagine what three more Riders on your side can do."

"I have imagined it," Eren says a bit too sharply.

I lean back, attempting to mask my surprise.

He deflates and I spot a flash of remorse as he rubs a hand over his face. "Believe me, it's crossed my mind before, but dragons are how we got here. The Houses became greedy. People are fighting for a world without their terror. How can we guarantee we won't repeat the cycle by creating more Riders? Once someone is bonded to their dragon there's no undoing it. Only through death are we released."

"You don't trust your team?"

"I do, but power like that changes people. Especially those who are not accustomed to it."

"So what then? Let them keep the hatchlings? Why don't you hand them the whole war while you're at it?"

"*Enough.*" Eren stands, towering over me like the warlord I've forgotten he is. "Dragon eggs are a miracle in itself. No one understands how they breed, what conditions must be right. Each new clutch is a surprise. Each egg is *power*. Your family will come for them—obliterate both sides in the effort to retrieve them. We can do *nothing*."

I don't shrink, but glower back, showing him the rage burning within me. How could he not see reason? Do the benefits not outweigh the risks?

"They won't reach riding size for a year," he assures, lowering his tone into a fraction of understanding. "We have time."

I round the desk, coming to stand in front of him. "What if you're wrong? What if we're out of time?"

He lifts his hand, brushing his knuckles over my cheek. "I could wipe everyone from the board right now, but it has to mean something. We can't become the monsters we're trying to overthrow. If you want to win, Sage, you have to hit them where it hurts."

"You're a coward," I seethe, jerking from his touch.

Eren snatches my arm, tugging me back until I hit the hard plane of his chest, his eyes blazing. "You're angry, I can see that. Believe me when I say I understand that anger, but taking their dragons won't do anything except make them more angry. I will not bring their wrath upon us, because if we take their eggs, I must take you too. Do you understand the implication of that? You will officially be a traitor to your House and because I am *selfish*, I will guard you with my life. I would endanger my mother, my sisters, and this entire war to shield you. I would leave them all to burn and turn my back on the ashes because that is only a *fraction* of the lengths I'm willing to go for you."

I draw in a breath, unable to escape from those eyes. They tear me open, making me bleed where I stand.

Eren's grip loosens, his voice lowering. "You know I would give you anything, but not this. Do not ask me to choose between them and you." He cups my face, his gaze a desperate, fragile thing. "Don't you see? I am not strong enough to do the right thing. There is only you."

He pins me to the desk, stunning me with the heat of his body against mine. I can hear my heart thrumming in my ears. His breath fans my lips, so dangerously close I can practically taste him.

"Eren."

"I don't want to be your friend. I want to be your undoing." He lifts my jaw, guiding my mouth to his.

He kisses me, possessive and unyielding. I'm breathless trying to keep up. My hands grip the front of his shirt, dragging him closer. Eren grips the swell of my ass, setting me on top of the desk. As his tongue sweeps over my bottom lip, I forget I'm supposed to be angry. A different fire ignites within me, a liquid flame pooling in my center when his mouth moves to my neck.

He bites at the skin between my neck and shoulder, dragging a small squeak from me. Eren's mouth returns to mine, his thumb pulling my bottom lip down, parting my mouth for his tongue to slip inside. I moan at the taste of him, needing more of it. How could I forget his mouth felt like this?

Eren's hand falls to my neck as he pulls back, resting his forehead on mine. He keeps his eyes closed, breathing hard. When he opens them, his hungry gaze pierces my own. "I need you to understand that I'm not a good man. I will do awful things to protect what's mine and I won't think twice about it. If that's not something you want then we should stop. You should go to your room and lock your door until it's time to leave."

"I'm tired of locking my doors." I move my hand to the back of his head, gripping the thick strands of his hair and pushing him back to me.

A knock pounds at the door.

Eren growls, breaking away from me. "Someone better be dead or they will be!" He moves to answer, taking his body heat with him. I shiver as he swings it open.

Blythe stands in the doorway, a sour look on her face and an envelope in hand. She extends it to her brother. "Word has arrived for you."

"Oh, why didn't you say so?" He gives her a cheeky grin, prompting his sister to roll her eyes as he shuts the door. Eren turns back to me and breaks the red seal on the envelope. His eyes scan the page, amusement dimming from his features.

"What is it?"

He crumbles the paper, setting it aflame in the palm of his hand. "We're going back to Aruna."

SWELTERING, stale air fills the narrow tunnels beneath the city. There's too many bodies breathing, sucking in precious oxygen. Beads of sweat roll from my neck down my spine, forming a sticky film over my skin.

Leather boots thump through the tunnel in steady succession, rebel soldiers marching for the assault on the Dragon Lords of the west. It's impressive, watching them move under the pale light of sunstones strategically placed by Gannon's engineers in the passages. Their shadows twist along the walls that barely allow for two adult-sized bodies to walk shoulder-to-shoulder.

*Breathe.* I remind myself as the air begins to feel thin. Part of it is the mask concealing my face. Draven, Gannon, Azara, and Oddica all wear them like the soldiers, but most importantly, Eren does too. He slips on the persona of Damon Valour like a second-skin, shedding it at will when it's only the two of us, and growing it again to command this legion. He speaks with Draven a few feet ahead, along with other soldiers, confirming their orders for the attack.

Rocks tumble in my stomach, grinding against my intestines. It's not like I've never participated in an attack before. This fear is familiar. On a dragon, I'm nearly untouchable, but on the ground, I've learned how mortal I am—including the people around me. My gaze trails to Gannon, his curls half-hidden by the scarf wrapped around his head. With the mask, only his eyes are visible, and they're focused on the backpack in his arms as he counts his supplies, particularly the brass bombs glinting in the light.

My eyes slide to Oddica next, who's watching Azara laugh with a girl I haven't met.

I step closer, weaving between two soldiers to get to her. "Hey."

Oddica jumps, whirling to me with a blink of realization.

"Sage!" Her arms fling around me in a tight embrace. "Gods, I'm so sorry!"

"Sorry? What are you sorry for?"

She pulls back, keeping her hands on my shoulders. I can hear the tremble in her voice as she speaks. "I wasn't strong enough. I only got to the scar tissue before I seized. You didn't have any tenderness, did you? Gods, everything went wrong!"

"Oddica, I'm okay!" I squeeze her arms, removing them from my shoulders. "I'm alive because of you. No one else."

She blinks away tears. "But you have a scar now."

"Yeah, a really cool one." I hope she can see the smile in my eyes and take a small bit of comfort in it.

We keep walking, not about to fall behind in the throng of rebels.

"How many do we have?" I lost count a long time ago.

"Three thousand. Damon hasn't told you?"

"He's been a little busy." I flick my gaze back to where I'd last seen him.

"You should talk to him. Ask questions."

I drag my stare away. "Maybe later.

"How are you feeling about everything?"

"Scared," I admit. "I'm helping overthrow an entire House. It's… a big deal."

I can't even bring myself to take satisfaction in the idea of Valen's face stripped of its arrogance. An entire dynasty will fall from power if this plan succeeds. Every family of Riders holds a legacy of their own, spanning nearly a thousand years. Overthrowing one of us is no small feat. It will change everything, exactly as Eren planned.

"I'm scared too," Oddica says softly, readjusting her backpack.

There are no affirmations of safety, and for that I'm grateful. I don't want to be lied to, even if it's for my own sanity.

Movement ahead snags my attention. Eren parts from his group, weaving through soldiers to join us.

"See you in the field." Oddica grins, stepping back to give us time alone.

"Hey."

I can't see his mouth, but I detect the playful lilt of a smile in his voice.

"Busy day?" I joke.

We fall into step with each other, carrying on over the beat of footfalls echoing through the tunnel.

"You have no idea," he says bitterly, scanning our neighbors before taking my hand in his and leaning into me. "I want you to stay close. There's going to be charges going off in the city to get their attention. We'll have to dodge the brunt of it as we move through the streets. When enough riders leave the estate, we'll go in."

"Their family will notice." I frown. "They'll come back for them."

"That's why we take them hostage. We'll use them to ensure our retreat if we have to, but I don't intend to lose today." He smirks, though I wonder if this bravado is only for the benefit of the team, a show to keep spirits high.

"What about the dragons? You know how ruthless these families can be. They might not care who you take hostage, or they'll burn the city trying to snuff us out."

"There's a plan for that." I clock the mad glint in his eye. "Have you seen Gannon's bombs?"

I give him a flat look. "Bombs won't do anything against dragon scales."

"These are different, but now that I think about it, I don't want to ruin the surprise." Eren winks. "We also have the advantage of spies within the walls. I had them smuggle supplies in to build ballistas in strategic points around the city. Come what may, we'll be ready."

"Come what may," I repeat, squeezing his hand.

"We're here!" A shout comes from the front of the line.

A set of stairs carved from the ground lead up to pale moonlight. We surface to an enclosed building with shattered windows. Sand-dusted papers scatter the hardwood floors, along with rusted printing presses abandoned throughout the room.

A dozen soldiers join us, rifles slung around their shoulders. I note a new patch resting on their biceps, a symbol I've only seen hidden beneath my clothes. A blue flame is stitched to their uniform with a Nightstalker silhouette in the middle. Just like the mark Eren and I share.

"Enter from the next checkpoint," Eren commands from the top of the door hidden in the flooring. "Get the charges in place and wait for my signal."

The soldier at the bottom of the steps shuts the door while the ones who surfaced with us start their ascent up the stairs in a shadowed corner.

"Where are they going?" I ask, watching them leave.

"There's a ballista on the top level of this building," Eren answers, checking the bullets in his revolver for good measure. "The rest of our legion will enter through different checkpoints within the city where other ballistas are hidden. Once the charges go off, they'll keep the riders busy until we do our part."

I chew my lip as we take the back exit into an alley. Moonlight cloaks us in a pale shimmer. Smoke coats the night in a putrid scent, lingering off recently scorched buildings. Glass and debris line the streets where officers march, patrolling for curfew. Glass crunches beneath their feet, giving us a slight advantage in detecting their whereabouts as we move.

I spot the ivory manor on the highest point of the city, watching over its people like the silver eyes of a wraith. I shudder, brushing my hand over the thigh that was shredded. The wound may be healed, but not the memory.

Several explosions shake the city in succession. I grapple for the nearest wall, gritting my teeth as the earth trembles. Shouting erupts from the streets. Vehicles screech and sirens wail as Aruna's soldiers mobilize, charging back the way we came.

"Let's move!" Eren shouts over the noise, breaking into a sprint.

My lungs ache as we zig-zag through the alleys, arms frantically pumping to keep the pace of our group. Eren doesn't let me fall behind, staying close despite the others being faster. Dragonsong shatters through the chaos, booming like a death knell. Three dragons sweep the sky, the furious beats of their wings sending shockwaves of wind through the streets. Their force shatters windows, blowing debris as they soar toward the explosions. The lash of wind nearly knocks me from my feet, but Eren's arm shoots out for support. I try not to look behind me, not even when screams of terror fill the night, echoed by the crackling shower of fire that swallows them whole.

It's only when the blood-curdling shriek of a dragon pierces my eardrums that I allow myself a glance behind me. A sapphire-scaled dragon barrels from the sky, breaking through a thick layer of smoke to crash into the street. The impact blows us off our feet this time. Brick and stone fling from buildings as the dragon collides with the ground.

Coughing, I push myself to my elbows, eyes widening at the scene just yards down the hill beneath us. The dragon lays limp, wings torn and one long spear protruding from its violet eye. Its rider is nowhere to be found.

"Are you okay?" Eren pulls me up, helping me to my feet even when I can't tear my eyes away from the carnage.

From higher ground, veins of amber scorch the city. Dysis dragons glide over the wreckage, dodging spears fired from hidden ballistas in the tallest buildings. I watch, helpless as a smoky gray shadow dives from the sky. In a single swing, its tail smacks into the middle of one of the rebel-occupied buildings, shaking its entirety. Ballistas continue to fire out of the windows, halting when the foundation crumbles. A scream lodges in my throat as the building collapses. The dragon soars higher, twirling to unleash a torrent of flames as the structure goes down.

Gunfire pops, snapping me back around. Draven and Azara fire at the guards descending from the gates of the Dysis estate, but where they fall, more soldiers take their place. Cyan flames erupt from the ground, rising to create a shield between the guards and us. My gaze shifts, finding Eren at the center of it. Light so blue it's almost silver reflects off his face, conjuring shadows that sharpen and slice at anything remotely soft.

His flames shoot forward, wrapping each soldier in a cage of fire. Hot as dragonflame, they burn to a crisp, falling to piles of ash. With the path clear, we run past the perimeter gates. We're halfway to the mansion when a shrill roar cuts from above.

Jade scales shines over Eren's fire and from the top of the beast sits Chantelle Dysis. Her face is upturned in a snarl, feminine fury plummeting down on us. The dragon's jaws unlock, a scarlet light crawling from its throat.

"Gannon, get the charges!" Eren shouts, sprinting ahead of us to meet the fiery end.

*No!* I want to cry out, but Gannon shoves a cylinder-shaped tube in my hands with a pin at the top. His wild eyes appear in front of me. "Pull it when it gets close! Don't breathe it in!"

*Breathe what in?* I don't have time to ask.

As flames unfurl from the dragon's throat, Eren meets them with a blast. Blue fire clashes against the scarlet flames, the force of the impact shoving the dragon in the opposite direction. Chantelle's dragon screeches, flapping its wings and swerving around the fire.

*"Pull it now!"* Gannon yells.

We pull the pins in sync. Turquoise smoke hisses out of both ends of the bronze cylinder. A cloud of smoke envelopes us, growing larger from the others ripping their pins. I catch the dull shimmer of the smoke glittering in the air, the same noxious, cloying scent I know as *Dragon's Bane*.

Massive jaws snap for us, missing by inches as the smoke creates a screen. It clings to the dragon, drifting up its nostrils. Chantelle's dragon groans, whipping its head from side to side as if to shake off the smoke. It crashes to the ground on all fours, throwing its head back with a deep-throated roar before sinking to its belly.

*"No! Get up!"* Chantelle shrieks from the saddle.

Azara and Draven trap her on each side, pointing their weapons. Chantelle's dragon rests its head on its front legs, eyes drooping unnaturally in the haze of smoke. I've never seen Dragon's Bane work this fast. It's only meant to calm dragons, not act as a sedative. It has to be a more concentrated version—something the rebels cooked up in secret.

Chantelle slides off of her saddle, dropping to her feet with her hands raised. Azara moves in behind her, kicking out the back of her leg. Chantelle falls to her knees with a grimace as Draven hands a pair of silver shackles to Azara. She takes the shackles from him, yanking each of Chantelle's wrists behind her back and snaps the manacles in place. The two of them lift her up by the crook of her elbows and walk her to Eren.

"Please." Her bottom lip wobbles. "Don't hurt them. Just take me."

My heart wrenches as Eren's gaze slides from her face to the cuffs around her wrists. "I don't believe you're in a position to make demands." The cruel words leave his lips, his voice dropping to a lethal tone. "Bring her."

Azara and Draven haul her along in the back of our unit. Eren kicks open the door with a fiery blast, leaving it in a heap of splinters and flames. Three guards rush forward. Eren points his revolver, realizing at the first *click* that it's empty. Shrugging, he rips a dagger from his belt. With a flip of his blade, he launches it at the first guard, nailing them right in the eye. Blue fire encircles the other two, leaving nothing but cinders in their place.

In the living room, Lore and Delphine cling to each other. Delphine pushes her youngest daughter behind her.

"Lore, Run!" Chantelle shouts.

Delphine retreats with her daughter another step until a ring of blue flames rises from tiles around them.

Eren tsks, shaking his head. "I wouldn't if I were you."

# CHAPTER 27

*E*ren takes Chantelle by the arm, jerking her to his side. "Everyone play nice and no one gets hurt." He lifts his palm a few inches from her chin, summoning flames in his hand.

*"You,"* Delphine sneers.

"Me," he agrees with a smirk in his voice. "I won't waste my time with introductions then. My demands are simple. Convince your husband to pledge his loyalty and stand down."

"Soren will never yield this city to you!"

"He doesn't have to." Draven steps forward, clutching a hand-held radio. "We've captured the others."

Eren's eyes spark as he turns his gaze back to Delphine and Lore. "Take them."

His fire dissipates, leaving the tiles singed in a circle around their feet. The others round up Delphine and Lore, locking matching handcuffs to their wrists. Lore's eyes sweep the room, snagging on me as she's led out the door. I hold my breath, unable to breathe, but her stare keeps moving, committing each of us to memory.

I catch Eren next, standing in the wreckage like an avenging

God. My pulse quickens under that stare, but I don't move when he approaches.

"Are you afraid?"

I shake my head, holding fast to those pale eyes. "No."

His fingers brush mine, giving me the faintest squeeze. "You won't like who I am in the next few moments."

"I know who you are." I squeeze back. "And I know who you have to be."

He doesn't say anything more, but steps around me. I'm the last one to leave the wreckage of the Dysis manor and the last to arrive when their family is brought to the steps of Aruna's Capitol building. Soren, Delphine, Fintan, Chantelle, and Lore are lined in a row, shoulder-to-shoulder at the top of the steps, overlooking a crowd of citizens who have wandered from the safety of their homes. Their dragons are nowhere to be found, either gone or collapsed somewhere, I'm not sure. I scan the Dysis family, searching and coming up short.

Valen is missing.

My eyes flick to the sky tainted gray in the haze of smoke. When I find it empty, I turn back to the family and soldiers surrounding them. *Did he get away?* My heart pounds at the thought, but I try to calm my breathing as the soldiers part for Eren. He comes to stand in front of House Dysis, shoulders back and voice carrying over the destruction.

"People of Aruna, you have been liberated!"

There's a stunned silence that ensues, followed by whispers.

"I see your hesitation," Eren goes on. "And I understand your fear. My name is Damon Valour and I am here to bring justice. You need not fear the wrath of Riders, for their time has come to an *end*." He steps aside, gesturing to the Dysis family. "You need not fear your oppressors. They are only human, not Gods."

The soldiers push the Dysis family to their knees. All except the Head of their House. Eren saunters toward Soren who stares defiantly in his eyes.

"Each House will have a chance to pledge their loyalty to our cause," he announces, never breaking Soren's hate-filled stare. "Kneel and swear fealty."

Soren's face twists in rage. *"Never."*

I hear Eren chuckle, nodding to himself like he expected this. His fist collides with Soren's gut while the other clamps around the back of his neck, shoving him to his knees as he gasps for air. "Then I have no use for you in this new world. For their sake, I hope your family is smarter." Eren places his hand on top of Soren's head where blue fire consumes him.

His family screams. Shouts and gasps echo from the crowd, but none as haunting as Soren's blood-curdling end.

"No!" Delphine screams, thrashing against the soldiers.

Tears stream from Chantelle and Lore's faces, but Fintan watches horrified. There's nothing left but shards of bone and dust where their father once kneeled.

Eren's voice booms across the square. "When their spies flock to this city, tell them what you've seen. Tell them the age of Riders has passed. Tell them they are *next*."

A chorus of cheers breaks from the crowd. I crane my neck, looking past the smoldering structures to the stars above.

There are no dragons.

UNDERGROUND, dragons cannot reach their riders and it serves as the perfect prison. My footfalls echo in these silent tunnels dug so deep that I didn't even know they existed. Sunstone lights the caverns, casting an eerie glow upon the rocks. Shadows dance over the top half of Eren's face, making his eyes appear far darker than they actually are.

It's a contest between who will break the silence first, but I can't bring myself to rupture this quiet. I keep replaying Soren's death, knowing word will spread faster than stray embers. Eren has never revealed his powers to the world outside of his team. Now each House will know and I have no doubt they will come in full force.

I think that's exactly what he wants.

I take a deep breath, preparing myself for the task at hand, but as I walk through a hall of cells with iron bars, I feel like a fraud.

"They're just down there." Eren jerks his chin. "Call if you need anything. D and Gannon are just outside."

"What about you?"

He pulls down his mask, revealing a ghost of a smile. "They might not be as chatty with me in the room. 'Sides, I need to finalize a few things with some officers on the occupation of Aruna."

I nod, watching him as he goes. When he's no more than a silhouette, I creep through the hall of cells. Whispers drift, ceasing when my footfalls crunch in the dirt. In the first cell to my left, I find Fintan glaring at me. I don't try to speak to him, moving on when I realize there's no one in the cell across. The Dysis family has been strategically spread apart, with empty cells in between them and no neighbor to shout to on the other side.

Further down sits Lore, hugging her knees to her chest with her head down. I keep moving, ignoring the narrowed slits of Delphine. Chantelle rests with her back to the wall, one knee up and a leg stretched out. She lifts her head, a heap of rumpled, ash-ridden locks falling around her face. Her sharp eyes lock onto me and I can see the hundred ways she plans to carve me up reflected in them. I remove my mask without a word and watch her eyes widen.

Chantelle stumbles to her feet, lunging against the bars. I don't flinch, waiting as she presses her face against the cell.

"I don't believe it. House Galvan has a rat," she spits.

"Whatever insults you're thinking of–save it. You can't call me anything I haven't called myself. I'm here to get you out of this cell. Are you going to listen, or not?"

"I want to see my family," she hisses, shaking the bars.

"I can make that happen if you cooperate."

Her chest rises and falls, slowing once she's calm enough. She squeezes her eyes shut and opens them, giving a single nod.

"Fight for us."

It takes a heartbeat of seconds, her face blank. Then she laughs. It's a maniacal sound bouncing off the cavern walls. "You've taken everything." Her knuckles turn white, her face twisting. "You murdered my father, killed my brother's dragon, imprisoned my family, and took our city. You really expect me to fight for you?"

"*I* didn't do those things. I'm here to offer you a deal." I step closer, careful not to be within her arm's reach. "I want to save your family. If the rebels win, do you expect there to be a place for Riders when this ends? You'll never live as you once did, but you can earn a place. Fight for the people. Be one of the protectors we should have been. Fight to make their lives better and you won't have to live yours in a cell."

"Loyalty isn't bought with promises," she snarls. "Riders will never yield to the weak. Fire reigns in our blood and we will fight until the last dragon falls."

"Don't be stubborn. You can have a life after this. Convince your family to pledge fealty to Damon and join his army."

She laughs and this time isn't laced with insanity. "We'll never follow anyone who isn't one of us. You should know this."

"Damon rides a Nightstalker. He has no intention to rid the world of dragons. He just wants to balance the scales."

She shakes her head, moving back from the bars. "He's damned us all."

"Fine." I ball my fists. "Don't fight for us. At least tell me where Valen is hiding. I can arrange a visit with one of your siblings or your mother, but you have to give me *something*."

"Tell the Gods I said hello." She settles back against the wall of her cell, leveling me with a glare. "If my brother is still out there, you'll meet them soon enough."

I shake my head and turn away from Chantelle.

Outside the prison block, Draven waits for me. I tilt my head. "No Gannon?"

"Duty called." Draven shrugs, walking me back to the main caverns where the others will be.

Sharp pin-pricks burrow into my skull and I sigh, pinching the bridge of my nose.

"You okay? Need any water?" He places a hand on his canteen.

"No, it's a different kind of headache." I rub at my scalp. "I don't see how this war will end well for either side if Riders aren't willing to compromise."

"They'll have to, or they'll lose everything."

I frown. "That's the thing, D. They're willing to die for it."

He makes a low whistle. There are no words between us at first, but I can tell the gears are turning in the General's head. I think he's mulling over the same question I am: how does one defeat an enemy who welcomes death over defeat?

"You need to find something they can agree on," Draven says, breaking the silence. "Something they respect. Make them think it's their choice to yield instead of the other way around."

I chew the side of my mouth. "I'll let you know if I figure that out."

He chuckles. "You do that."

In the main caverns of the base, it's a mix of celebration and commotion. Cheers rattle the stalactite hanging from the ceiling. Refugees drink and dance while soldiers proceed to move crates labeled as ammunition to the cavern that holds our fleet of vehicles. I know I should be celebrating with them, but I can't think past the rock of dread in my stomach.

"Any luck?" Eren appears behind us.

I shake my head. "No."

He nods. "Forget about it for now. We need to get back, my mother sent word that your family has demanded your presence."

"What? Why?"

"I imagine it's due to yours truly."

"Right," I mutter, trying to reel in my racing heart. Of course they would demand my presence. Everything's changed. They'll want to reassess, call in favors, and form a plan.

*I can do this.* I tell myself on the flight to Esmeray. *I'll hold my nerve and I will not falter.*

HOUSE GALVAN IS alight with chaos when I cross the threshold. Shouting blazes from the drawing room, bouncing off the corridor as I approach.

"It appears that not a single person from my family could tear themselves from this debate to greet me at the door," I announce, temporarily claiming their attention for the moment.

"Sorry, Sister." Ash rubs a hand over his face.

Lux rolls her eyes, arms crossed where she sits on the couch near the fireplace. How shocking–the entire family is gathered in one room outside of dinner. My father and Uncle Deon stand, drinks in their grasps. Aunt Natalya lounges on the opposite couch with Jocelyn, Jasper, and her husband, clutching an open bottle of wine like she's given up hope for this family.

I can't say I blame her.

Dahlia and Rune stand side by side, leaning against a table

near the bookshelves. Aunt Zaria sits quietly, picking at her cuticles. My mother joins her, one leg crossed over the other with her mouth pressed in a thin line.

"Now, is there a reason I was summoned from my fiancé so soon?" I cross my arms and lift a brow directly at my father.

"There's been a new development." His jaw clenches. "Aruna has fallen to rebel occupation. If rumors are to be believed, it appears that Valour has the mystical ability to wield fire and has executed Soren with it."

I say nothing, but allow my face to slacken in a show of surprise.

"*As I was saying*," Uncle Deon points a finger to the door, "We must interrogate the mages! There's no telling–"

"Oh, shut it, Deon!" Aunt Natalya snaps in an unusual display of irritation. "We don't need to give the mages a reason to flock into the arms of rebels! We need every ally we can get our hands on!"

"Who's to say they're not in league with them already?" Rune speaks up, defending his father. "How else would a rebel get their hands on that sort of magic?"

"It's a power we don't understand," Lux runs her palms over her thighs, smoothing her skirts. "Perhaps it relates to the Nightstalker. We all read the report. His fire was blue, just like the dragon's."

"I don't give a damn what color it is," my father growls, knocking his whiskey back. "We will tear them apart before they even deign to set their sites on Solera! Ash, summon the other Houses for a Conclave. Natalya, sober up and call a damn meeting with the High Mage. Deon, take the children and scour the library for anything on Nightstalkers and pyromancy. *Now!*" He shouts, storming from the room.

My mother rises, folding her hands. "You have your assignments. I suggest you do as he says."

Aunt Natalya grumbles something under her breath and

slams the bottle down on the table by the couch, taking her husband's arm. Uncle Deon throws back the last of his whiskey and clears the burn in his throat, leading the way to the library. My mother and Aunt Zaria remain perched in the sitting room. I don't bother looking at my mother and instead fall in line with Jocelyn. We stray behind our cousins and siblings. Once we're far enough for our voices not to carry, she spins to me.

"What the *hell*, Sage?"

"What?" I hiss back.

Her dark eyes pierce mine as she drops her voice to a level that's barely audible. "What happened to the Dysis family?"

"They're safe."

"But their father is dead. Care to explain that?"

"He wouldn't yield."

She catches my arm, pulling me to a stop. "Do you hear yourself?"

I jerk my arm from her. "Don't do this. Don't act like we haven't been slaughtering each other for the past year. Does the bloodshed only matter to you when it's one of us?"

She flinches. "That's not... that's not what–"

"It doesn't matter. The kids and Delphine are safe. Nothing is going to happen to them or their dragons, but anyone willing to fight to the death better get comfortable with meeting their end."

"I... don't know what to say to that."

"Say nothing. If you're not going to help then keep quiet."

"I want to help," she refutes. "But I don't know how. You won't let me in."

"I can't arrange a meeting right now, Joce. There's too much going on. Just give it time."

"You've changed."

I nearly come to a halt right there, but force myself to keep walking. "And you haven't."

*I grew teeth and shed my skin because I was tired of being bitten. What did you expect? Of course I changed.*

Jocelyn quickens her pace, joining her brother in the middle of our line. I spy Ash looking from her to me with a questioning brow. I break his stare and keep my eyes anywhere but him. I don't need to give anyone answers, least of all Ash.

We spend an hour in the library, pouring over dusty tomes before my brother is summoned to join Father for the Conclave. Dahlia and Rune work together on the furthest end of the library with their father. Jocelyn and Jasper sift through the opposite side, leaving Lux to search by herself. I grit my teeth, not about to talk to a single one of them when a hand closes on my shoulder.

Ash gives me a squeeze. "Come with me."

I face him, unable to hide my surprise. "To the Conclave?"

"No, to a brothel." He rolls his eyes. "Yes, the Conclave."

"Father won't like it."

"He doesn't have to."

I lower the book in my grasp, facing him with a hard look. "This doesn't mean I forgive you."

"I know, but maybe take it as my apology?"

It's hard to fight with Ash. You can understand a person's intentions and still not see eye-to-eye with them, but it's worse when it's family.

I scan over the room, noting the others who pretend not to listen, and meet Ash's pleading stare. "I'll go, but this doesn't change anything."

An odd smell taints the air, one I do not recognize. Fresh and yet... earthy. If Ash does, he does not comment, though he peers at the sky in wonder. Gone is the blue horizon, replaced with a gray overcast that shields the sun and leeches the color from the canyons.

"What is this?" Father demands as he waits for Ash on the porch.

Ash glances at our father with no answer before offering me his hand. "My sister."

I watch my brother for a moment and clasp my hand in his. He walks me to Heartfyre, snoozing in a heap of red scales outside of the manor. Ash releases my hand and drops to one knee, offering a boost to the bottom of the saddle where I climb above Heartfyre. I can feel my father's gaze burning holes through the back of my head, but I keep my chin up and scan the plains of the desert beyond us.

Three other dragons stand guard around the summer manor when we arrive. I spot Cantorix in an instant, towering over a bronze and malachite dragon. Heartfyre lands near them, sinking to his belly for us to dismount. In the meeting room, the remaining Houses have already gathered.

"Let's commence this meeting." My father sinks into a chair, leaving one that remains glaringly empty.

Ash and I claim a pair of seats at the bottom of the stage. I haven't attended a Conclave since that fateful night I made a deal with Eren. Now he rests at the mahogany table, shoulders back and one leg propped across his knee. His cool gaze flickers over me once and returns to the other Dragon Lords within the same heartbeat.

"We need to strike quickly in a coordinated attack." Kieran Tesar cracks his knuckles.

"I agree," Father states, gaze slithering over the map laid out on the table's surface.

Idalia huffs. "Aruna is lost. Why don't we allow the rebels to voice their demands? We can negotiate for the Dysis family's freedom."

"We do not negotiate with traitors!" My father slams his fist on the table.

Idahlia's lip curls. "And look where it's gotten us."

A pause sharp enough to cut throats rises between my father and his former flame.

"Perhaps she's right," Eren mediates, cocking his head as though there's much to consider. "A temporary ceasefire could work in our favor. They won't expect a counterattack during negotiations."

It's a miracle I don't break out laughing. That's exactly what we would expect, and Eren will likely strike before the Houses can.

"I second this plan." Kieran nods more to himself than the others. "It gives us time to gather our resources."

Our father's face twists in a scowl.

"Let's plan it then, shall we?" Eren smirks, leaning forward. "I propose we strike in the Capitol–"

"It's not enough to strike in the Capitol," Father sneers. "We need to cut the head of this operation. I want Damon Valour. We need to know who he is and what he cares for."

Eren goes still, taut like an arrow waiting to launch. "What do you propose?"

Our father holds his stare. "I want to find what he cares for and rip it to shreds. Break a man's spirit and his resolve will follow."

"You might just make him angry." Eren's lips twitch. "Are you sure he won't return the gesture tenfold?"

"By then he'll be broken. A broken man is no threat."

"I disagree." Eren leans back and I swear his eyes darken. "A broken man is dangerous. A broken man won't stop at something you care for. There is no strategy. No endgame. There is only a debt to be claimed in blood."

His face remains stone, unflinching. "You seem certain."

"Take it from someone who knows." Eren flashes his teeth.

Kieran coughs. "Perhaps we should draw up terms for the negotiation."

"Ah, yes." Idahlia shifts in her chair. "Will someone pass the parchment?"

Ideas are written, plans set in motion, and when the meeting is adjourned I walk with Ash back to Heartfyre. We shove the front doors open and step into the sweltering air. Ash squints at the dark clouds rolling in as we walk back to the dragons. The earthy scent is stronger now, more incessant as I breathe in.

"What's that smell?" It's almost fresh, but thick and hazy with moisture.

"Beats me," Ash says with a shrug, patting a hand on Heartfyre.

I open my mouth, but a shattering *boom* shakes the ground.

The blast sends me barreling into Ash who swings me around, blocking me from the impact. The dragons screech, flapping their wings. Over Ash's shoulder, I see flames reaching to the sky with claws of black smoke.

# CHAPTER 28

The Conclave burns before my eyes. Idahlia and Kieran's dragons whip their heads, shrieking into the sky. Their song of mourning breaks through the crackle of fire, rattling my bones and everything I am.

*"Eren!"* I scream, pushing Ash off me. *"Eren!"*

*Fear*, thick and slimy tendrils of it shoot through my heart like lightning as I race for the smoking ruins. A strong arm catches me by the waist, dragging me back. "Sage, no!"

I whirl, gripping Ash by the collar of his shirt. "Did you see him? Did you see him leave? Tell me you saw him!"

His face crumbles. "No, I didn't–"

I push off, screaming into the bond. *Eren!*

But there's no answer. The connection is empty, void of any living presence. Something cleaves within my chest, a hole so deep I think I might be swallowed by it. His smile flashes, cocky and arrogant and as warm as the flames swallowing the manor.

*"Get off me!"* I scream, the sobs rising as I struggle in Ash's arms. *"Eren!"*

*'I will never leave you again,'* the memory of his voice whispers. *'From this point forward, I will never leave your side. I am*

*bound to you as you are to me. I intend to honor that, now and always.'*

"He can't be dead," I sob, curling into Ash's shoulder. "He's not dead!"

*You told me **always.***

A crack of thunder booms from the clouds.

*'Come what may,'* his voice rumbles.

I gasp, jerking from Ash's arms. Eren stands over us, clothes singed and covered in dust, but *alive.* I stand half-frozen, caught between one reality and another. I can't bring myself to reach out and touch him–to shatter the miracle of this illusion.

A faint smile crests his features. *'Hello, Killer.'*

I sob, throwing my arms around him. "You're alive." His arms wrap over my back, squeezing me just as fiercely. His scent rushes my senses, summoning another sob caught in my throat.

"I'm alive," he murmurs.

"How?" Ash stares, wide-eyed like he can't believe it either.

Eren tenses in my arms and I get the sense that not everything is right. I quickly unlink myself from him, dusting off my clothes and wiping my face.

"I was on my way out when the explosion went off," he answers.

"Our father?" Ash asks quietly.

None of us say a word, but we hear the pop and sizzle of flames lapping at the manor.

"You two should be with your family." Eren attempts to smooth the tangled locks of his hair. "I can send word to the other Houses while you grieve."

"No," I say, gazing at the burning manor. I pry my eyes from it, searching Eren's. "I'm going with you."

"Sage," Ash draws closer, pleading with me. "Our father is dead. We should–"

"I can't, Ash!" I shout. "He may have been a father to you, but he wasn't to me. I can't be there right now. I just *can't*."

Ash steps back. I watch the light dimming in his eyes and find the grief pooling there instead. "Okay."

My breath catches in my throat, but Ash turns, walking away in silence. Thunder cracks through the sky.

"We should go."

I don't need to see Eren's face, the concern is threaded in his voice. In the moments that pass between the manor and Esmeray, I remain quiet. There are no words to convey the spiral of thoughts my mind sinks into.

I thought Eren was dead.

The idea shouldn't have affected me so deeply. I shouldn't have cried. I shouldn't have felt as if I were missing a limb. I was never supposed to care. Caring gets you killed. It makes you weak, because when you care about something–*someone*–you give your enemies something to take from you.

Eren dismounts first, sliding off Cantorix. He catches me by the waist when I jump down, setting me on my feet. My breath catches. His eyes bore into me. I only notice now there's a cut over his cheekbone, the blood sticky on the side of his temple. He's both a living miracle and my worst nightmare.

*I can't do this.* I push him back and move around him, marching toward the Noctis estate.

"Sage," he calls, already at my heels in a few long strides.

I pivot. "I thought you were dead!"

Eren stops, having the nerve to appear shocked by my outburst.

"What happened? Was this some scheme? Did you blow up the Conclave? Did you kill my father?"

"No." His stare widens. "I swear."

"How can I trust you? You just killed the head of one House. How do I know you're not behind this too?"

He keeps his expression blank, his body stoic. "Do you think

I'm capable of causing you that much pain?" He says, taking a step forward when I step back. "To go back on my word?"

I shake my head, fighting the tears pricking at my eyes. "I don't know what to think. I thought you were dead and it–" my voice cracks. "It *terrified* me, Eren. I wasn't supposed to care for you! I *hated* you. I was supposed to kill you and never look back and now..."

*Now I think I'm in love with you.* But I don't send it down the bond. I keep the realization locked in my head, chaining it to the walls of my mind.

He stills. "You care for me?"

"Yes," I laugh, furious and heartsick and none of the things I want to be. "How are you even alive?"

"Luck," he whispers, utterly hollow. "The Gods. Whatever magic binds me to Nox. I was caught in the blast, but the rubble didn't hit me. Even if her magic repels fire I doubt I would have walked away unscathed if I hadn't left when I did."

I close the distance until there's only inches of space between us. "I can't care for you. I can't be two people trapped in two worlds. I don't–"

He cups the side of my face and runs his thumb over my cheek. "I'm in love with you."

A heartbeat.

A breath.

And silence.

Thunder rumbles over us.

Eren swallows once, ripping a blade from his belt and pushing it into my hand. "I want you to take this dagger," he wraps my fingers around the hilt and forces me to point the tip above his heart. "And drive it through my chest if that is what you still desire. You can claim the blood debt for Khione. But know that I will die with no regrets, because I would rather you hate me and be alive than love me and be dead."

A drop of wetness hits my cheek and I jump, blinking at the

sky. I yank my wrist from Eren's hand, slicing his palm in the process. He hisses, clutching the wound while I toss the wretched blade. Another drop hits my chin and I move to wipe it, coming back with what is unmistakably water.

*Rain.*

The droplets begin to trickle, accompanied by a crack of lightning across the sky. I gape at the downpour. In my twenty-two years of living, I've never seen rain. Not like this. I've been told stories about it. Ash had been a child when he last saw it and I hadn't even been born yet. Now it's here, cold on my skin and flooding the sand around my boots.

My mouth breaks into a grin. And I laugh. I reach out my hand, watching the water pelt my skin. Grinning, I look at Eren who's already watching me. He's absolutely haunting in the rain, full of shadows, sharp angles, and every sinful desire.

"What?" I ask a little too breathless.

"You're beautiful."

I drift toward him. "Lie to me."

"What?"

"Tell me this is all in my head. Tell me this is a dream."

He stares, tracking the droplets gliding down my face and landing on my lips. His eyes snap back to mine, darkening. "I'd rather burn than lie to you." He lifts my jaw and kisses me.

It's different from any other kiss we've shared. It's not hungry or possessive, but tender and desperate in a way I'm not prepared for. I lock my arms around his neck, dragging him close and crushing any space left. At this moment there is only him. I'm not the daughter of anyone and he's not leading a war. We're two people, locked in this dream of teeth and tongue and I never want to wake from it.

He reaches down, cupping the back of my thighs to lift me around his waist and carry me up the steps. We crash into a wall in the corridor, never breaking our kiss. Both our hands move, prying open buttons and pushing aside wet clothes. Eren reaches around me, flinging open a door and kicking it closed behind him. I feel him lower us down, my back hitting a plush surface. We break apart long enough for me to see our surroundings.

Midnight blue walls and black furniture make up the room. Black marble covers the floor and above us a glass kaleidoscope dome rules the ceiling, inviting the golden light peeking between the downpour. Every inch of it smells exactly like Eren.

He stands over me, breathing hard. "Are you sure?"

I take him in, mesmerized by the thin shirt sticking to the hard planes of his body. I sit up, gripping the bottom of it. "I don't care that he's dead. Maybe I should. Maybe the fact that I don't makes me an awful person. But I already grieved my parents. I grieved the people I thought they were. So yes, I'm sure. I want this. I want *you*."

He exhales, smoothing wet strands of my hair from my forehead. I take his wrist and pull him down with me. Eren doesn't waste any more time unbuttoning the front of my pants. I kick off my boots, hands flying to his shirt to pull it from his shoulders. Warm, richly tanned skin rests below my palm. I take my time, running my hand down his pectoral over the rows of muscle and right over the sharp V where three slashes of scars rest. I push his shoulder, rising on my elbows until he falls onto the bed with me. I straddle his waist, reveling in the way his eyes darken. I lower my face to his body, placing a kiss over the first set of scars near his shoulder. I feel him shudder under me as I make my way down, tracing each scar with my tongue, especially the burns.

His fist knots in my hair while my fingers unbuckle his belt, tugging down his pants until his length is freed. It springs forward, hard and ready. I suck in a breath at the size, heat rushing to my face. I'm not a virgin, but now I find myself questioning what little I know, if any of it will be enough.

I bite my lip and look at him. "You'll tell me what you like?"

He reaches down to brush my cheek. "I'll like anything you give me."

My nerves say otherwise, but when he settles back down I wrap my hand around the base of his cock, stroking it once to test if this is right. Eren shivers under my touch, solidifying my decision. I bring my mouth to the tip and move my tongue in slow circles, flicking it against the ridge where the skin curves. Eren groans and I fight the urge to smirk. I'm the one making him feel like this. No one else. Clinging to that bit of confidence, I dip my mouth further, bobbing my head, pressing my tongue to his length.

"Fuck," he moans, guiding the back of my head to a steady rhythm.

I stroke the base of his cock harder as I bob my head, watching him unravel under my tongue the same way he watched me. His breathing comes more ragged, his head back as he curses. I flick my tongue against the slit of his broad tip, wanting to hear more. His grip tightens, nudging me further down until a gag escapes me. His eyes fly open, pulling me off to pin me to the bed.

He's over me in seconds, deft hands undoing the buttons of my shirt and the clasp of my bra. I drag my hands through his hair, raking my nails down his back as he kisses a trail from my neck to my collarbone, nipping as he goes. He finds a spot he particularly likes, right above my collarbone where the skin is soft and sensitive. I gasp as he sucks, teeth pressing into the skin, and I whimper.

"Shhh." He cups my neck. "Be good."

I nod, half-dizzy from his touch. He continues to my breasts, palming each one before his teasing licks undo me. I shiver, arching closer. My body presses flush to his bare chest, skin so warm it almost burns. His hands move to my pants where he quickly rips them off, lifting my legs over his shoulders, his face between my thighs.

His thumb brushes over my center, coming away slick. "Look at you, already wet for me." He runs the pad of his thumb over his tongue, humming in approval. Then both hands dig into my thighs as he lowers his mouth, gliding his tongue over my core.

I hiss, back arching. He grips my legs tighter, holding me still as he kisses my clit, teasing me with the tip of his tongue. My legs shake, liquid heat pooling in my veins so much quicker than before. I don't stand a chance, my hips rocking, begging for purchase. He spears me with his tongue, bringing me right to the edge. I cry out, nails stabbing into his shoulders.

I hear him groan as I cum. "That's it, Baby. I've got you."

Limbs shaking, I blink away the haze. Eren moves over me, fingers sliding through the mess he's created. I shudder, feeling a new tightness build where he teases. Right when I think I can't take it, he removes his hand and settles between my legs. He strokes his length, bracing his cock at my entrance. Dark strands of hair tumble over his eyes as he watches me, waiting for me to change my mind.

I'd rather die than stop now, and with one look, I know he understands. He thrusts into me in one long slide and pauses. I suck in a sharp breath, squeezing my thighs against his hips. A stinging pleasure meets my walls, but I know it will pass. And Gods, do I want to feel him move again.

"It's okay." I lift my hips, inviting him to keep going.

He draws back, sliding further this time with the utmost care. Eren holds my stare, the intensity heating my skin as his hips roll, stretching me open to the hilt. He leans down, taking both my wrists and holding them over my head with one hand. I wrap my legs tightly around him, meeting each thrust. He sets a punishing pace, shaking the bed frame with each stroke. Our mouths meet, ravenous for each other. I moan into his kiss, breaking free of his hand to glide my own over the dips of his back. A maddening pleasure begins to build, the ache of that first thrust long forgotten.

As if sensing the tension coiling in my gut, his hand reaches for my clit. My hips rock against him, twitching off the bed as a blinding, pulsing fire bursts within me.

"So beautiful," he murmurs, brushing the hair from my face.

He plunges harder into me, but I can see the strain on his face, the last shred of control he's still hanging onto. I don't want him in control. I want him undone.

"Let go," I whisper into his mouth. "I want you to let go."

That seems to do the trick. He growls, tugging my thigh up, lifting my hips higher to hit the deepest spot within me. I cry out, writhing as he pounds into me. His hand tangles in my hair, drawing my head back to bare my neck. I submit to his mouth, seeing blue stars spark along the drapes of the bed as he marks me with his teeth. But those blue stars unfurl into claws of flames climbing up the curtains. With a shout his hips stutter and in one hard thrust his cock pulses, spilling inside me.

Fire crackles over a table in the bedroom, bookshelves going up in flames.

"Eren!" I gasp, limbs too weak to move.

He pushes himself up, eyes glazed as they take in the fire around the room, and widening. As if the oxygen were sucked from the space, the flames blink out in an instant, leaving singed furniture behind.

"I'm sorry," he pants, head collapsing into the crook of my shoulder. "I'm sorry."

"It's okay." I brush a hand through his hair, my heart still pounding from what we've done. I've never been laid this bare, stripped and lit aflame. Over and over. The fear of letting go is gone, because I know at the end of the fall, Eren is waiting there to catch me.

I want to tell him that. I want him to know what this means for me, but the words stick in my throat, too thick to surface.

Eren stirs, hissing softly as he pulls out of me. The ends of his hair curl in tangled, wavy strands where sweat beads along his neck and brow, his eyes half-lidded as he takes me in. His fingers fall to my neck, tracing the spot he marked with a tenderness I've only ever seen appear for me.

"You're mine," he says with a fierceness to his voice.

"I'm yours." I take his hand, squeezing it.

He casts a wary glance around the room. "I think you're going to be the death of me."

I laugh softly, placing a kiss on his shoulder. Eren's mouth lifts and he brings my hand to his lips, kissing my fingers and giving a teasing lick to my thumb. I shiver, but as much as I want to stay in this bed and listen to the rain beating against the glass above, I know I can't. Nothing good ever comes without a price.

"What is it?"

I sigh, letting my hand slip from his. "I have to go home."

I have to make sure Ash ascends. Our family is only as loyal as our strongest link, and Ash... Ash is not strong. He's going to need help. If there's any hope left for our family, I need to be there. This time, it will be no one's choice but mine to show up, and part of me marvels at the beauty of it. I will be there because I want to be, not because I have to.

Eren nods. "I'd tell you to be careful, but they're the ones who should be."

I smile, moving to gather my clothes. "Do you know what your next move is with the Dragon Lords gone?"

He rolls his neck, popping a few bones in place with a groan. "Each House will need to mourn, but they'll think they can't afford to for long. The Heirs' ascensions will happen quickly. I'll send terms for peace to each House and work from there."

"Do you think it's really an option?"

"Hm?"

"Peace." I fidget with my clothes.

Eren's gaze roams my face. "I want it to be."

I fall quiet. "Who do you think did it?"

"I don't know, but whoever it is has plans of their own."

I nod to myself, trying not to let fear take root. I may have something to lose now, but I also have something to fight for.

# CHAPTER 29

$\mathcal{I}$ 've never heard the compound this quiet. It's different when our family is gone on outings away from home, but this is a new type of silence. Not even servants stir in the halls. It's as if time has ceased, sucked out like a stolen breath.

I find them in the drawing room, each member of our family dressed in obsidian black. Ash speaks in hushed tones with our mother near the fireplace while Lux dabs at her tear-stained cheeks. Dahlia and Rune sit together with their mother, rolling their eyes at my sister and appearing as if they'd prefer to be anywhere else. Aunt Natalya holds a glass of red wine in her hand, but the glass has not been stained by her lipstick. It sits in her grasp untouched. Her husband rubs a comforting hand up and down her arm. Jocelyn and Jasper lift their bowed heads, hearing my footfalls and caring enough to search for the owner of the sound.

Only Uncle Deon is missing from the function.

I enter the room wearing Noctis black, a tight velvet dress that clings to my hips and sways at my ankles. "Well, this is a pathetic scene."

"Have some respect for your father," Mother bites through her teeth.

"Why? The dead don't need it," I snap back at her. "Why hasn't Ash been anointed?"

My brother pales, gripping a crystal glass of what's clearly our father's whiskey. "There's plenty of time for that."

I share a look with my mother whose jaw clenches. She shares the same sentiment, but dares not voice it to her mourning son. Maybe she already has. Either way, it's not enough.

"I disagree."

"What's the rush?" Dahlia picks at her nails. "Mourning has no time limit."

*She's stalling for her father.* I grit my teeth. "We're at war. We don't have time to honor the dead."

"It's not like this family is going anywhere," Rune drones beside her, kicking up his feet on the low table and swirling the liquid in his glass. "Might as well pour one for the old man."

"Ash." I pivot to my brother. "A word?"

Ash sighs, knocking his whiskey back and placing the glass on the mantle. He follows me to the adjacent room, sliding the door shut and placing his hands on the wood where he bows his head.

"Ash, what the hell are you doing?"

I watch his shoulders rise and fall before he removes his hands and turns to face me. In a matter of hours, his face has aged. Sharp lines dig into the hollows of his cheeks, darkened by the fading sun leaking through the window. Crescent-shaped bruises droop beneath his eyes, like he hasn't slept in days instead of hours.

"You don't know what you're asking me."

"The hell I don't! You've been preparing for this your whole life so what is your deal?"

*"I can't fill his shoes!"* His breath shudders, hands shaking as he runs them through his hair.

He's afraid.

"Ash." I inch closer. "You don't have to. I know you loved him, but our father was cruel. He was ruthless and not in the right ways. He would do anything to keep the Galvan name alive, even if it meant hurting us. I don't want that to be our legacy and I don't think you do either. You can change things for our family. You can help guide the other Houses toward peace. But none of it is going to happen if you sit by and let Deon take over."

"Maybe he should." Ash draws a hand down his face, like he can wipe away the tension. It doesn't work. "He has more experience. He knew our father's plays. He might be—"

I shake him. "Get a hold of yourself! You're going to doom us all if you don't act!"

"He'll challenge me to an Ignis Mortem," Ash whispers. "What if I don't win? If he kills me, who's going to look out for you and Lux?"

I pause. "You don't think you'll win?"

"I don't want to find out."

"So you're stalling."

He hunches over the back of a plush chair in the room, knuckles digging into the cushion. "He wasn't supposed to die yet. I was supposed to have more time. What if I win and I make the wrong choices?" He lifts his head, his face a wreck. "What if I'm the one who ruins our House?"

"That's not possible." I cross the room, forcing Ash to look at me. "The only thing worse than making the wrong choice is not making one at all. Right now you're not doing anything. You're standing still. Life doesn't care. War doesn't care. Our Uncle doesn't care, hell—I bet he's loving how you're not doing anything. But you need to snap out of it, because if you don't step up he'll come for you. It's only a matter of when."

"I know," he says, but I don't think he hears me.

I sigh, moving for the door. I rest my palm on the handle. "Don't wait too long."

Out in the sitting room, no one's moved. I track their bored faces, stopping on my mother. As if sensing me watching, her eyes shift to me. Her jaw ticks, a subtle movement, but it's out of place—a crack in her exterior. Part of me wonders if she's holding back, if maybe she's as upset about Ash stalling as I am. I nearly take a step forward when heavy footfalls echo off the tile from the corridor.

Uncle Deon struts through the doorway. "Ah, Sage," he greets, far too chipper for someone who's lost their brother. "There you are. I've been meaning to speak with you."

The heads of our family turn, their interests finally piqued.

For now, my best play is a friendly one. I can't be here to help Ash if Deon suspects my meddling. "How can I be of service, Uncle?"

"That dragon of yours, the white one—"

"Halcyon." A hint of my annoyance slips out.

"It would seem she's still guarding her nest. That's a problem. With my brother gone, we're going to need those hatchlings to bond quickly. Would you be a dear and see if you could collect those eggs yourself? Bring them back to the study when you're done."

"Absolutely not."

Silence devours the room.

Uncle Deon's shoulders shift. They roll back, his spine straightening as he walks forward. I stand tall, clenching my jaw as he draws near. He pauses in front of me, offering a terse smile. In a quick flip of his hand, a hard *smack* fills the room.

Ash shouts, lunging toward us, but Deon is quicker, pointing a gun to his head.

Everyone freezes.

"There's going to be some changes around here," Deon

announces. "My brother is gone, and I will be taking his place." He turns his arm, facing the barrel of the gun to me. "Starting with *you*."

"Me?"

"Your disobedience has run unchecked for far too long. It would have been so much easier if you'd just died at that damn Gala like you were supposed to!"

The world tilts on its axis as the breath leaves my lungs. "It was *you*."

Deon grins. "Surprised, Niece?"

"You fucking *craven*."

"Sage," Ash warns, shifting.

Dahlia is on her feet in an instant, a revolver in her hand and aimed for my brother. "Oh, how I've *waited* for this."

"Hey!" I shout at her. "It's not him you want. It's me."

She turns, a flash of fury crossing her features.

I stare at them both, Uncle Deon and Dahlia. "You want me dead so badly? Fine. Now's your chance." I look Dahlia in the eyes, banking on the moment we've been waiting for. "I challenge you to the Ignis Mortem."

"Gods help us," Natalya whispers.

Uncle Deon lowers the gun, a slow smile curling on his face. "What do you say, Daughter? Shall you have your revenge?"

Dahlia lowers her gun, holding my stare. "I accept your challenge."

We're escorted to the ballroom in the center of the manor, our family made to gather and watch as Dahlia and I take to a makeshift ring. Guards come forward with a set of ceremonial swords I've never seen before, almost decorative in craftsmanship. Each hilt is fashioned in the shape of a dragon, the steel polished and shining as they're handed to us.

"You fight until one of you spills enough blood to gain satisfaction," Uncle Deon declares.

What he neglects to say is that there isn't enough blood in

the world for Dahlia. I see it in her eyes as she swings her sword in practice, twirling it at her side.

"Begin." He smirks from his seat.

Dahlia charges me with a yell.

I parry her strike, side-stepping her attack and trading places with her. She growls, whirling on me with a series of swipes. Our swords scrape with each blow, metal clashing against metal. Sweat breaks across my brow as I take each of her attacks. One thing is clear. She's been training far longer than I have. I exhale when we break apart, clearing my mind. I can't waste time being in my own head. It doesn't matter how hard she's trained. I will not fall to my cousin.

I make the next strike, slashing at her blade first before swinging low at her legs. Dahlia barely blocks my swipe, jumping back. I come at her, harder and faster, feinting when she moves to block my blow and I spin—slicing across her thigh. Dahlia shouts, clutching her leg and spinning, not about to have her back to me.

"I learned that from a friend." I grin.

*"You're dead,"* she snarls, swinging.

I surge forward, countering the blade with my own. *Think. What's her weakness?*

She's angry. I feel it in the weight of every swing. I can use that. Anger is hasty. Emotions are sloppy. She wants nothing more than my end, so I invite her to it.

"Your dragon is dead because you were sloppy," I shout, baiting her. "You blame me because it's easy. Because you don't have to blame *yourself.*"

She screeches, slicing the air between us.

I dodge, throwing more arrogance into my words. "It must drive you crazy, knowing Halcyon survived and Khione didn't."

*"Don't say her name!"*

I watch her come undone at my words and smile wide,

driving the spear home. "If you'd been a better Rider, Khione would still be alive."

I leave my left flank open and watch as her eyes slide over. I wait the extra seconds as she springs toward it, adjusting her grip to change the angle of her strike. And then I move. I block the blow, gliding past her and cutting a gash along her back.

Dahlia screams, stumbling to the floor.

I'm on her in an instant, kicking her shoulder to push her onto her back. I lift the sword over my head, ready to plunge it into her heart when I hear a strangled cry. I find the eyes of her mother, Aunt Zaria, with her hands clapped over her mouth, tears streaking down her face. I find Rune, fists shaking at his sides. Uncle Deon remains unmoved, watching me.

I lower the sword to Dahlia's chin, holding her stare. "This is *over*." I step back, casting my sword to the side.

Deon rises, lifting his gun once more. "No, I'm afraid it's not."

Ash roars, shoving Deon's arm up where he fires a round into the ceiling. *"Run, Sage!"*

I break into a sprint, hearing the exchange of gunfire as I run through the halls and out the front door.

Vulcan blinks from the heavens above, stretching his wings clear and bright across the sky. As my shoes crunch the sand, I see the goddess Linette shining through the dark as I run. Sunbreaker, Dragon of the North, also lurks above. Elion watches too, the Phoenix God of war, and with him is Anvi, the goddess of water. Nyra, the Maiden of Death. Oryn, the God of justice. I've never seen so many of them in the sky at once, though did I ever pay much attention? All the Gods I told myself I didn't care to know and their children's children—present on this night, holding their breath and peeking in on a human girl fleeing for her life.

Halcyon nests in the deepest part of the caverns. Hot mist clings to my skin as steaming pools of water gurgle in the distance. Halcyon lifts her head with a growl until her eyes zero in on me. I pant, lifting my palms. "Hey, Girl. It's just me."

Her emerald eyes appear to soften, her head tilting with a greeting chitter. I risk a few slow steps, pausing in front of her. I let her decide how close she wants me to be, but my heart pounds in my chest.

*We have to go.*

Through the bond, a warm glow radiates from her mind. No aggression. No suspicion. My heart swells at the fact that she trusts me wholeheartedly. I place my palm over her nose and receive a delighted bump in response.

"We have to leave. We have to get your babies out of here."

Her head moves back, body uncurling to reveal the three ivory eggs. A sob, heavy and thick builds in the back of my throat.

*This war has to end.*

I stare at Halcyon's eggs. They should be a miracle, but now, picturing Dahlia and Lux as Riders in Uncle Deon's army makes them feel more like a death sentence. I'm boxed in on all sides, the family I fought to protect now at war with itself. Every carefully drawn line has become blurred, blown away in the sand. I can't continue to lie to myself.

I can no longer be loyal to this family.

Because a loyal daughter would not pick up the eggs and slip them into her bag.

A loyal daughter would not climb atop her dragon and flee in the night.

A loyal daughter would stand and fight.

But loyalty has only ever paid me with scars, and I no longer desire to add to the collection.

# CHAPTER 30

*T*here isn't a cloud in the sky when I land in Esmeray.

Eren waits stone-faced on the veranda. He pries his eyes from Halcyon's settling figure, his gaze roaming over my face as I cross the distance. Somehow his features are harder, more devastating in the shadows between stars.

"What's in the bag?"

I hold my nerve and stand my ground, placing a hand over the bulge of my pack. "If you truly love me, I need you to trust me."

Eren cranes his neck, peering into the audience of stars. For the longest of heartbeats, he doesn't say anything. Then he lowers his pale eyes to my face and allows a slow, roguish smile to slip. "It's a beautiful night to die."

Nothing is mocking about the way he says it. Eren doesn't use his words with resignation. I hear it for the promise it is.

Live or die, he will fight at my side.

I RETURN to the cells alone. A dull ache pulses in my shoulder from the weight of the eggs, but I adjust my hold on the bag and keep my chin raised. *This has to work, or I've doomed us for nothing.*

Chantelle lifts her head, glowering through the bars.

I reach into the bag and lift an egg without saying a word. Chantelle's eyes bulge. She staggers forward, a shade paler.

"For Fintan. To replace what was lost."

She grips the bars, her mouth twisting. "As long as we fight for that traitor?"

"No." I tuck the egg back into the safety of my bag. "Don't fight for him. Fight for *me.*"

It's a bold notion, but if Riders like Chantelle won't bow to Eren, maybe I can offer a different option. My family name is right. I've earned my place in battle. *Darling Death* has to mean something.

Her eyes narrow, reflecting nothing but suspicion.

"Would you do it?" I prod. "Would you follow me if I swear to protect your family? Would you fight in my own personal squad?"

Her eyes stray as though searching for her siblings in the dark.

"Come on, Chantelle. With Valen gone, you're next in line to lead your family."

"My brother will come for us."

"And if he doesn't?" I raise a brow. "What if he's dead? Or abandoned you? Are you really going to let your family rot down here?"

She chews her lip, her gaze darting between empty cells once more.

"I know you love them too much for that," I whisper, taking a dagger from my waist. "If you agree, I can't live in fear of your betrayal. I need your oath in blood, and then I'll swear one too."

Her face snaps to me. She looks at my outstretched hand holding the hilt of the dagger, but I note her hesitation and take a leap of faith. I flip the end of my blade and swipe it across my palm. I ball my hand into a fist and hold it out in her direction, allowing the drops of crimson to paint the ground beneath our feet.

"I, Sage Galvan of House Galvan, swear to you, Chantelle Dysis, that I will do everything in my power to protect your family if you swear fealty to me." I offer the dagger again.

This time the blade is taken.

She drags it over her palm and squeezes a fist through the bars, staring me in the eyes. "I, Chantelle Dysis, swear fealty to you, Sage Galvan. I shall bring you no harm nor dishonor. Your enemies will be my enemies. I vow to be your sworn sword in exchange for the protection of my family."

We clasp hands, exchanging one vow for another and allowing the Blood Oath to take root. Whatever magic the Gods have left us, I feel it stir. A current moves between us, the sensation a whisper of what the dragonbond is. We are Bloodsworn, the highest oath of fealty one Rider can swear to another. It is the price Eren demanded that Soren Dysis refused.

The ground quivers.

Dust and fine grains of rock rattle from the ceiling. Then a louder, unmistakable *boom* shakes the caverns. Her wide eyes meet my own.

I shout down the tunnel. *"Get them out!"*

Eren and Draven appear, masked and rushing to slam their hands on the walls beside the cells. Their touch causes the doors to slide open, an enchantment tailored specifically to them.

Chantelle runs out, sprinting to Fintan and Lore who are the first ones to venture from their cells. As she collides with them, holding her family close, I spy Delphine watching her children with a wary expression.

"What have you done?" Her voice rasps.

"Everyone move!" Draven shouts.

Rock crumbles above us. Stalactite crashes to the ground while more explosions reverberate through the caves. I hear screams echoing from the northern side of the base.

"What's happening?" Chantelle yells at me.

"I don't know!"

I pump my arms harder, willing my legs to carry me faster. Eren and Draven take the lead, breaking a path through sprinting soldiers and screaming refugees. We make a hard left, sprinting toward what everyone else is running from. The main cavern ceiling is broken open to a night full of stars and a gunmetal dragon breathing fire into the base.

"Get back!" Eren pulls me just in time as more rocks come tumbling down. "We'll take the east exit!" With his hand in mine, we rush past the flames, leaping over rocks and debris. Dragonfire sets the tunnels aglow and from the broken ceiling, I hear the shrieks of more than one dragon.

*This is an attack.*

"Call your dragons!" I yell to Chantelle as I reach across the bond for Halcyon. A protective cry of fury answers back.

"You killed my dragon!" Fintan shouts. "We should be running toward Valen, not away from him!"

"I am Bloodsworn!" Chantelle jerks her brother by the arm. "I decided what's best for this family and it's not our brother! You wanna ride again? Then *fight!*"

We reach a set of stone stairs leading up to the surface. Eren slams his hand on the wall, causing the door above the steps to blow away in a cloud of dust. Outside, blasts of kaleidoscopic flames set the night aglow. Valen's dragon hovers above the largest hole in the earth, unleashing a torrent of flames. I spy more dragons flying in the air, wearing the sigil of House Tesar, but nothing chills me more than the black banner with a gold, two-headed dragon.

Kallix circles, blowing white-hot flames into the ballistas popping up from the ground. Jasper flies on Tanith, delivering with a blast of his own. Following behind her brother, Jocelyn glides on the wind like a golden arrow on Xantha, diving to unleash a shower of flames.

*How?* The question sits in the most horrified part of me. *How did they find us?*

Halcyon's shriek pierces the air. I snap my head, spying her incoming from the opposite direction. Noxainia's screech sounds after her, a black bullet tailing my dragon.

"Meet us in the sky!" I order Chantelle, darting for Halcyon.

My thighs scream in protest, but this fight is far from over and I don't intend to die on the ground. Halcyon makes the lowest sweep we've ever practiced, tilting her body to the side. I make a running jump, hurtling for the saddle. My fingers meet hard leather as she lifts up. I grip the horn, swinging my leg over to sit upright as the ground disappears. I look around us at the sheer chaos unfolding.

Eren sweeps up behind me, pausing in place.

"There's too many," I tell him.

Even with Chantelle and Lore, four dragons against seven is no match, not even with Nox's speed and size.

Eren's jaw flexes, but he sets his sights upon Valen raining the most destruction below. "We'll fight until we can't anymore. I'll take Valen."

"Eren—"

But he's gone, careening toward the beast.

Chantelle appears beside me with Lore, her sister riding a dragon with sleek silver scales. "Where do you want us?"

I peer out into the night, staring past the dunes toward

Esmeray. We'll never survive this battle, not on our own, and if Eren won't make the call–I have to. I just hope he forgives me.

"Send Lore away."

"What?" She pipes up behind her older sister.

I turn to Chantelle. "You are Bloodsworn and I order you and your own to hold this secret even in death. Have Lore fly to Esmeray and tell Syrinthia Noctis it's time to make good on her vows."

Chantelle's face slackens. Lore's eyes grow wide, coming to the same realization as her sister. Chantelle's throat bobs, her head turning. "You heard her."

Lore sucks in a breath, nodding once. In a flap of wings, she darts toward the darkness, disappearing into shadows and moonlight.

Chantelle continues to stare. "What a pair you two make."

"Judge me while you fight."

Not waiting to hear her retort, I make a dash for Xantha.

Halcyon blows a teasing whorl of fire at Xantha's face, catching the dragon and rider off guard. I see Jocelyn's head snap as we fly by and Xantha gives chase just as expected. Halcyon spins in mid-air, twirling higher before turning to face her. Jocelyn pauses, hovering in the air with me.

"How?" I demand.

Her expression sours. "Our uncle would go to the ends of the earth for power, did you expect anything less for those eggs?" I watch her spot the bag at my hip, her face tightening. "He hired a mage to track you."

A sickness spreads from the pit of my stomach, calcifying in my bloodstream. *I led them right here.* "Did you come to take them from me?"

Her gaze flicks to mine. "No." The relief is instant, but short-lived. "Ash challenged Deon to the Ignis Mortem."

I can't breathe. "Where is he?" I notice now that I haven't seen Heartfyre in this attack.

"Laying in a pool of his own blood."

An invisible knife twists in my chest.

Jocelyn must see it on my face. "He was alive before I left. Your mother and sister begged for his life."

Dragonsong shatters the world below us. I spy Chantelle's dragon colliding with another that flies the banner of House Tesar. Further away, Valen and Eren are locked in a battle of talons and teeth.

I look my cousin in the eyes. "You don't have to fight for him. Fight for me. Trust that I know what I'm doing, even if nothing else makes sense."

Jocelyn sighs, rolling her neck. "I guess it's a good thing I didn't plan on going back." And then she grins.

I can't decide whether I should laugh or cry at the glorious sight. But I don't have time to decide. Fire shoots from the mouth of a garnet dragon soaring straight toward us. Jocelyn and I break apart, returning to the fray of battle. Jocelyn flies after the dragon with Jasper, who instantly changes sides, trailing after his sister.

Taking the revolver from my belt, I switch off the safety and allow Halcyon to bring us down. I fire my gun at one of the Tesar brothers, redirecting their attention. Their golden dragon spins, snapping at Halcyon's tail, but she moves quicker than he can. She counters, shifting around to dig her teeth into one of his wings and tearing off shreds of flesh and sinew.

The dragon screams, flailing with a torn wing. I turn and shoot at its Rider, forcing him to retreat. I squint at the darkness, tracking the blasts through smoke and shadows. Eren and Valen have disappeared. I crane my neck, searching the stars.

The moment of stillness costs me.

A blink of movement stirs in my peripheral vision. Halcyon flaps her wings a second too late. A red dragon of similar size snatches Halcyon's leg by the teeth, pulling a guttural roar from her throat. I whip my head around, finding Agni Tesar in the saddle, the youngest daughter of her family. I fire back at her, but she only ducks, and despite Halcyon's best efforts to shake her loose, the dragon does not let go.

I tighten the strap of my bag and push off the saddle, running down Halcyon's back and diving into Agni's saddle. I rip my blade free as I fall, slicing at the girl. She struggles to hold on, blocking my advances while trying to stay put in her seat. I manage to cut her arm, sending her reeling, but the distance only allows her to wrench her knee back and shove her boot into my chest. I tumble off the saddle, grappling for purchase. I take my dagger and stab into the hide between scales. Her dragon unclenches its mouth to shriek.

That's all I need.

I rip my dagger out and let go, spending three seconds of freefall through the air until Halcyon catches me. I land in the saddle with a grunt, clutching the horn to pull myself in from the side. I sit up with a grin, laughing to myself as Angi retreats.

I reach for a different bond. *Eren, where are you?*

A bullet pops behind me and I turn.

It happens in a blink.

Gray jaws clamp around Halcyon's neck.

*"NO!"* I scream as spurts of blood spring from the teeth digging into her flesh.

I look up to the saddle of the dragon yanking us from our flight path and see Valen grinning. I'm forced to hold on tighter as his dragon swings its neck, jerking Halcyon along. She flaps her wings, kicking her legs and screeching. My heart shatters at the sound while I scramble to lift my gun, firing countless shots at Valen, but his dragon's movement is too rapid. Each bullet is a near-miss, his dragon weaving and diving as it steals us away.

*"Let her go!"* I howl, unable to climb, unable to do anything but wait for an opening.

Valen takes us higher, further from the ground than anyone

else in the battle. His dragon releases its hold, letting Halcyon break free temporarily, only for its heap of razor teeth to strike again. It rips at her wing, tearing it to ribbons.

I can't tell Halcyon's screams from my own and fire blindly at the dragon's face. I try to stand, but Halcyon is shaking too hard, desperate in her attempts to escape, but the attack doesn't end. He aims for her other wing, his long neck reaching around to shred that one too. I take that moment and pounce. I land on all fours, stabbing my dagger into the dragon's neck. It doesn't respond, continuing to bite and tear at Halcyon. I grit my teeth, forcing myself not to look back at the screams and crawl forward.

*Hang on! Please, please, hang on!*

Valen spots me, shooting several bullets, but even he has a hard time aiming. I push up and run once I'm close enough and aim for Valen's throat, but his dragon moves again, throwing my arm into his shoulder. He yells, knocking me off with his fist. I gasp, mouth pulsing, and a metallic taste on my tongue. Valen lunges, throwing me back with another punch. My vision blurs as I block the next one. I reel my hand back, about to throw my own punch when a flash of searing pain lances through my body.

I feel Halcyon's wings, now nubs of bone struggling to fly as if they're my own. I feel her terror, her neck gushing with blood as she struggles to breathe and I wheeze as if I'm the one choking.

Valen hits me again, right in the nose where it stuns my senses. The knife clatters from my grasp as I lay there, shaking with pain. I feel teeth stab into my abdomen, my left ankle and calf pulsing. All of her injuries are mirrored and though I barely bleed, I feel as if I'm the one who's dying.

*No!* I push past it, lifting my head.

Valen's hands lock around my throat, squeezing. "I'm going

to gut your pretty little dragon, and then I'm going to kill you too."

He lifts me by the neck and whips me around, showing me the view of Halcyon's shredded body.

*"No!"* I sob, tears spilling. *"Please! Let her go!"*

Valen's dragon holds her by the neck once more, but I can see the slashes, the ribbons of flesh hanging where she's been gutted and ripped apart. Her wings are no more, just strands of sinew clinging to ivory bone. Her emerald eye searches, landing upon me. Through the bond, I see the image of myself reflected in her eyes. I watch her blink, the edges of her sight blackening until that beautiful eye closes and our bond flickers.

Valen's dragon releases its jaws and lets her body slip from its teeth.

Halcyon falls.

*"No!"* I wail, kicking and screaming. *"You monster!"*

"Don't worry!" Valen chuckles. "We'll make sure she lands safely!"

His dragon dives. We race after Halcyon, her limp body plummeting. There's nothing I can do to stop it, but I still reach. I reach for the bond in my mind, but her side is quiet. I reach out my hand, fighting Valen's hold to no avail. Even though I cannot catch her, I reach.

*Save her! Someone save her!* I plead to the Gods. I plead to anyone who will hear me. I hope that Eren will appear. I hope that Nox will catch her. I hope that she will rip Valen to shreds. But nobody comes.

I reach and I reach and I reach.

And I watch her hit the ground.

*Boom.*

The sound rattles my teeth. A cloud of dust blows up at us. Valen's dragon lands smoothly in the newly-formed crater where Halcyon's broken body lies in the sand.

"Let me go!" I sob, clawing and scratching at his hand.

He swings me around, backhanding me. My head swims through the shock of pain. I barely register him dragging me off his dragon. He brings me toward the body, but not too close, only enough to observe. Halcyon's eye blinks open, half-lidded. Valen forces me to my knees, holding me by the back of my hair. Halcyon tries to lift her head, barely an inch from the ground before collapsing again.

"I'm sorry," I sob uncontrollably. "I'm sorry, I'm sorry, *I'm sorry!*"

Valen's dragon crushes her neck under its foot, digging its talons in.

*"Stop!"* I scream. *"Leave her alone! I'll do anything! Just stop!"*

Valen's voice snickers beside my ear. "Anything, huh? Tell her how worthless you are. Tell her what a pathetic excuse of a Rider you are. Tell her this is all your fault."

"It's my fault! It's all my fault! Please, have mercy!"

"Mercy? Was there *mercy* shown when I was scarred?"

I can feel her dying. Each shallow breath pierces my lungs and slows my own heart.

"Astaroth," Valen commands. "Finish her."

The dragon lifts its head and roars. Its neck dives like a snake, ripping a chunk of flesh from the base of Halcyon's throat as I scream. I scream until my throat is raw. Until no air is left and no sound comes out.

Her emerald eye does not close. Her eyeball rolls to the back of her skull, leaving the white exposed.

Unseeing.

No more.

I gasp as a new pain sears me from within. I feel the bond stripped from my bones and scattered to the Gods in pieces.

A gleam of gold blinks past us.

Xantha lands, Jocelyn sliding down her wing as Astaroth growls.

*Jocelyn!*

"Ah, my betrothed. What a lovely surprise." Valen yanks me to my feet by the hair, using me as a shield.

Jocelyn's eyes widen as she draws her dagger, spotting Halcyon's corpse. "What have you done?"

"Joce," I sob. "Run. Get the others."

She grips the knife tighter, her resolve hardening. My stomach sinks. She's going to fight him with impossible odds.

"Joce, run! Get help!" I plead.

She can't fight by herself. What is she thinking? Jocelyn inches closer, her hand shaking. A sharp slice sighs through the night. Warmth blooms over my stomach. I look down.

The hilt of Jocelyn's dagger protrudes from my gut.

"I'm sorry," she whispers. "I didn't want to do this, but... you've left us no choice. Your friendship–" her voice breaks. "Your friendship meant a lot to me though."

Valen lets me drop to my knees as she turns away, walking back to Xantha.

"Now you can die with her," he spits, shoving me to the ground.

I land on my back, gasping at the stars.

I watch their dragons return to the sky. Wings flap, fluttering like heartbeats. Then nothing. I gape, black dots dancing at the edges of my vision. I start to hallucinate, thinking I see more dragons passing through the stars. In the back of my mind, I try to count them as they pass. Three. Five. Nine. No, ten. But that's impossible.

A dream. A beautiful dream to die with.

'Sage! Where are you?' Eren shouts through our bond, but even his voice is distant. I'm not even sure it's real.

I turn my head and study Halcyon's body. A tear slides down my temple and I look away. In one last attempt, I wrap my hand around the hilt of the dagger and pull. I scream, barely lifting it out, and drop my hand. With a shudder, I peer into the vast constellations. I find Sunbreaker instantly, and the other Gods still watching.

Another tear slides out. *I'm going to die out here.*

Alone. Forgotten. Sage Galvan, traitor to her people. Savior of no one. Hero of nothing. Who did I think I was, daring to fight an uphill battle? Who was I, aligning with the rebellion? How foolish I was to think I could make a difference.

*I'm nothing.*

I stare back at the Gods, letting my fury boil to the surface. The pain begins to cease, replaced with a more familiar friend. My fists shake, not with fear, but rage.

I'm dying. There's nothing left to be afraid of.

*Except me... they should be afraid of me.*

I scream, throwing all of my pain and wrath into the ragged sound ripping from my throat, shredding the mercy left in my soul apart. My head falls back, my body growing limp. I take a shallow breath.

*Let me live... Let me live so I can **end them all.***

A single, soft *crack* pops a few feet away. I muster the last of my strength and lift my head. My bag is no longer around my waist, but forgotten in the sand near my feet where Valen made me kneel. The flap of the bag is open.

One egg peeks out in front of the others with a single crack split down the middle.

# CHAPTER 31

*T*hey say when you lose enough blood, you'll lose consciousness. If this is a dream, it's the only plausible explanation. Or maybe this is one last nightmare to carry me into the afterlife. Perhaps there is no mercy here.

Another *crack* and the shell splits apart. Tiny limbs flail in the sand, paper-thin wings flapping. The stray pieces of shell fall from the hatchling and I question if I've already taken my last breath. I must be dead. I must be, because how is it possible for the hatchling's scales to be black?

It blinks its eyes open. Two pairs of irises the color of pink tourmaline stare back at me, its head tilting. The hatchling slithers forward, chittering like a small bird. It crawls on top of my chest, its weight practically nothing. As it watches me, slit pupils dilating, I don't bother to stop the next tear that spills.

"I'm so sorry." I carefully lift my numb fingers, caressing a trail of ivory scales from the top of its head to its neck. The hatchling doesn't bite me, but leans into my touch like an old friend. "No one's coming for us."

*We're both going to die out here.*

It tilts its head, assessing my words. It flicks its small tail, slicing it across the edge of the blade protruding from my gut.

I suck in a breath. "Careful!"

But it does not seem to bother the dragon. Traces of its blood slide off the blade into my wound and I grimace. Taking one deep breath, I clutch the blade, ripping it free with a scream and toss it to the side. I lay my head back on the sand, panting as my vision grows hazy. The stars fade in and out, but clear or not, they are just as spectacular. I start to understand Eren's earlier sentiment.

"At least it's a beautiful night to die."

The hatchling's face blocks the stars from me, its odd eyes peer into my own. Like the snap of a whip, I feel a new bond lock into place and gasp. It locks around my heart like a cage, merging one life with my own.

"Why?" I squeak as the pain grows more incessant. "Why would you do that? I'm dying."

The hatchling turns its head, looking at my wound. I don't have time to breathe when magenta flames spew from its mouth, setting my abdomen on fire.

I thought my throat was too raw to scream, but I stop hearing sounds altogether. The fire courses through my veins, lighting up my capillaries from within. My body glows, each vein on the surface lighting with the hatchling's flames. Then the heat cuts off. I pant, sweating, shaking and unable to move.

The hatchling reappears in front of me, chirping.

I squeeze my eyes shut and reopen them. Slowly, I move my fingers. Then my feet. I lift my head, finding the shirt over my waist burned away and smooth skin left in its place. I raise a trembling hand, prodding my stomach for the wound. It's gone. Not even a scar. I push up to my elbows, sitting in the dirt. Halcyon's body continues to lay still. The rest of her eggs remain abandoned in my bag.

The hatchling hops out of my lap, watching me stumble to

my feet. I lift the bag and sling the strap across my chest before turning back to the hatchling. I kneel before it, offering my hand. "I don't know what you did, but thank you."

The hatchling surges forward, crawling up my arm and settling around my shoulders. A few feet away lays Jocelyn's dagger, tinted red with my blood. I grab the hilt, examining it in the moonlight. A sun rests where the hilt meets metal and an intricate dragon's head rises from the pommel. I wipe the blood on my pants and rise, tucking it into my belt. *One day I'll drive it through their throats, and they too will know what it's like to choke on their blood.*

I move toward Halcyon, placing a hand on her nose and holding back the tears. Crying will do her no good now. "Forgive me."

There's no spark of an answer. Her skin is cold and her eyes are vacant, so I take a step back. And another. Another. Until my back is turned and I leave my girl behind.

For a while there is no sound but my feet trudging through the sand. I swallow, my throat drier than the air I breathe. I press on as the hatchling sleeps along my shoulders. In a way, her soft breathing soothes me. It's a constant sound keeping me from the brink of madness.

*'Sage.'*

I spin, searching for the voice. It takes me half a second to recognize it.

*Eren?*

*'Sage.'* Relief floods our connection. *Tell me where you are.*

I lift my chin, searching the stars. I've been following Sunbreaker, hoping I can reach Esmeray before someone else finds me.

*I don't know. There's nothing but sand.*

There are no rocks. No rotting structures of a bygone era. No landmarks to identify my location. I have to hope he'll see me, a wandering spec in the vastness of dunes.

Sand shifts behind me and I whirl.

No tracks stand out. The sands are still. Did I imagine it? Even the hatchling stirs from its sleep, peering into the darkness with me. My heart pounds. I take Jocelyn's blade, gripping it tight as I take a step back. My mind might be playing tricks on me, but I'll be damned if we die out here.

The sands shift again, closer this time.

I spin around, slicing at open air. A chorus of hisses erupts around us, sandwraiths rising from the dunes. *No.* Fear prickles my skin, sending a shiver right down my spine. *No. No. No.* Six of them stalk forward, their white eyes glowing with hunger. I gulp, meeting the gaze of my hatchling. We've come too far to die like this.

*I'm sorry, Eren.*

*'Sage?'* I can sense his fear. *'What's happening? Sage!'*

I set my feet apart, lifting the blade, and gripping it tighter until my hand stops shaking. I won't run. I will make my last stand here.

"You should go," I murmur to the hatchling. "If you can fly, get far away from here."

But the hatchling only winds itself tighter around my shoulders, unleashing a furious wail at the wraiths.

One of them springs forward, slashing with its talons. I swipe back, leaving my right side exposed. Claws rake down the side of my back, ripping a shout of agony from me. My hatchling shrieks, blowing a small gust of fire at the wraith but it does no good. They lunge at once.

I grab the hatchling, holding it to my chest and shielding it with my body. *"No!"*

A surge of magenta flames explodes from me in a powerful burst. The wraiths scream, burning into cinders. I lift my head as the last wisps of tourmaline flames wink out. For a breath, the night is silent again.

Dragonsong screeches above.

Nox glides to a stop across from us, kneeling low for Eren to jump. He dashes through the sand, skidding to a stop. His eyes land on the hatchling, hissing and snapping at his approach.

"Halcyon?"

My throat tightens. "Gone."

He studies the hatchling. "How?"

"Valen and... Jocelyn," my voice cracks at her name.

Eren cups the side of my face, bringing my forehead to his. "I'm sorry. I tried to get away. I couldn't leave fast enough. And then my family–"

"I know," I sob. "I called them. I had to–"

"No," he kisses my forehead, wrapping his arms around me. "You did the right thing. My mother sent word to House Althea. They joined our cause and it turned the tide. They called a retreat."

I recall the shadows of dragons in the sky, the hallucinations I'd been so sure of.

"What can I do?" He pulls away, holding both sides of my face with his hands and wiping my tears with his thumbs.

My knees buckle. I want to bury myself in the warmth of his arms and never open my eyes again. But a hot, blinding flash of rage stirs within me.

No more dead dragons.

No more death.

I pull back from his arms, exhaling. "Take me home."

SOLERA BLAZES with the light of dawn. The mountains bleed like pomegranate juice along the horizon, soaking in the early rays of the rising sun. Lavender wisps dance over the canyons, washing the land in a dusty haze.

"I hope you have a plan."

Eren offers his hand, helping me slide off Nox. I've never seen his dragon washed in the light of day. Onyx scales shimmer like glass along her hide, her sapphire eyes large and beaming. Her presence marks a shift in the score. There is no point in hiding. House Noctis came to the aid of rebels. Eren is now a known traitor.

I stare at the compound, watching the guards flee from their watch towers to deliver the news that a Nightstalker has landed. "Before you found me... we were surrounded by wraiths and I... did something."

Eren nods. "I saw the blast."

"I'm like you, aren't I?"

"Yes."

I steel my nerves, strap armor to my heart, and brace myself. "Tell me how to summon it."

"In the beginning, my emotions controlled it." He eyes the running guards. "For a while, I was angry and burning everything in my path, but anger isn't control. It's an illusion. There's not enough time to teach you before you go in there, but hold onto that rage. Let it collect like a well within you and when you're on the brink of bursting, visualize what you want to happen and unleash it tenfold."

I nod as we walk together, side by side.

Eren kicks open the front door. The manor is silent. I can hear my own heartbeat in my ears. The hatchling purrs, clinging closer as we stalk through the corridors. They know we're here and I know where they're waiting.

In the ballroom chamber, Deon waits at the head of our family. His wife and children stand beside him while my mother and sister wait on the set of stairs, halfway up like they're prepared to flee. Aunt Natalya and Uncle Bruno sit on a chaise a few feet back, watching the scene unfold. Guards examine us from the walls, but do not interfere. They will not move until my uncle commands them. I sincerely hope he does.

As we get closer my Aunt gasps. Lux cups a hand over her mouth. Dahlia and Rune lean closer, enamored by the sight of Nightstalker around my shoulders. The hatchling hisses.

"I always knew you were a worthless traitor," Uncle Deon sneers.

"Where is my brother?"

He smirks. "Dying like the coward he is."

My hands ball into fists. "I've come to challenge you to the Ignis Mortem."

"Your dragon is dead." Dahlia smiles smugly. "You're no Rider."

Funny, that didn't stop her from accepting my challenge.

My hatchling shrieks, blowing magenta-tinged fire at my cousin. It travels no more than two feet from where I stand, but the point is made. "Does my dragon look dead to you?"

Deon growls, prying the sword from his belt.

I take Jocelyn's knife, pointing it at him as I find her horrified gaze behind my aunt. *I'll deal with you later.*

I flick my eyes back to Deon. "Show me your craven heart, Uncle, so I might carve it out with the blade you sent to kill me."

"I accept your challenge." He unbuttons the front of his coat, tossing it into his wife's arms.

I gently take the hatchling, handing the creature to Eren. "I need you to stay here, Little One."

The hatchling tilts its head and I take that as its understanding.

Uncle Deon rolls up his sleeves, flipping the blade around in his hand as he circles me. "Unlike your brother, I will not hesitate. Your father's line of cowards will end with you."

I summon the surge of fire roiling within me and let it break through the surface. Jocelyn's dagger erupts in pink fire, lengthening the blade into a sword of flames. Aunt Natalya and

Uncle Bruno stand, my aunt clutching her husband's arm. I find Lux gripping the banister, my mother's facade of calm wrecked by the sting of shock. Jocelyn has paled to a sickly color.

I hope she dies like that.

Uncle Deon lunges.

I counter his first swing, knocking his blade to the side with my own. I side-step his following swipe, slashing at his waist as I move. Uncle Deon jumps back, but the fire of my blade singes his clothes.

With a roar, he swings again, slashing down. "I'll enjoy killing you. You're just as weak as your father!"

I knock the blade with my dagger, whirling as metal scrapes along metal. "How does it feel, Uncle? To sit in my father's chair? I bet you dreamed of this day."

He grunts, blocking my next blow. "I spent *years* having to stomach the sight of Cyrus leading this House to ruin. You think you can do a better job? *You*? A *child*?" He laughs, half-mad with power. "You don't know the price this House cost me, but I'd pay it again. I'd sign away my soul before I let you take it from me!"

My eyes narrow as our steel knocks again. "It was you, wasn't it? You wanted my father's seat so badly that *you* blew up the Conclave!"

He bares his teeth, pushing harder against my blade. "Did you think I would let this family die in this Gods-forsaken desert? Cyrus was prolonging the inevitable! He was going to drain us until the very last drop—and then where would we be? Without water, we are *nothing*. I had to do something. What good are dragons if they never venture beyond the Wastes?"

I suck in a sharp breath. *Beyond the Wastes?*

Deon maneuvers around my dagger, catching me along my arm as I reel back.

"You're insane!" I dodge his attack, countering with my fist to his face. "There's nothing beyond the Wastes!"

He stumbles back, wiping the blood from his mouth. "Your ignorance will be your undoing."

He charges for me, swinging his sword. Faster than he can parry, I duck beneath it, slicing my blade along his stomach for the killing blow.

Our family gasps.

Rune and Dahlia start forward, but a wall of cyan flames flares from the tiles encircling my uncle and I in a ring of fire. Eren only smirks at their faces.

In the ring, Uncle Deon wheezes, clutching his abdomen. A red blistering slice blemishes his skin, his clothes burned clean off wherever the blade has struck.

I shove my sword forward, up between the left side of his ribs, and twist. Aunt Zaria screams. I lean close to my uncle's shocked face. "The only traitor in this family was you."

I rip the blade free.

My uncle's body hits the tile with a *thump.*

"Congratulations," he rasps. "You've inherited a graveyard."

His body stills, the light dimming from his eyes.

Eren's fire dissipates into smoke as I turn to my family. Tears stream down Dahlia's face, but her mouth curls with fury. Rune's throat bobs as he holds his sister back. Unlike her, he knows a threat when he sees one.

I keep my dagger burning, staring each of them in the eyes. "By the rules of the Gods, I have won. I alone rule this family. If anyone disagrees, then *go.* I'll grant you the mercy of a long life if I never see your face again. For those who think you can beat me, step forward now. Let the Gods hear your screams."

No one moves.

"Except... *you.*" I point my blade.

Everyone's head turns to Jocelyn.

"What is this?" Aunt Natalya's face darts between the two of us. "I don't understand."

"Would you like to tell her, or should I?"

Jocelyn exhales, lifting her chin. "I drove a blade through your gut, but I should have picked your heart."

Her mother gasps. *"Jocelyn, your own kin?"*

Her jaw flexes. "Someone had to stop her."

I start forward, but Aunt Natalya throws herself in front of me, falling to her knees.

"Please," she clutches my wrist. "I know what she's done, but I beg of you as a mother–do not make me grieve my child this night. I can live with her in exile, but not if she's dead."

I pull my wrist from her, glaring into Jocelyn's hateful gaze. I shouldn't do it. I shouldn't spare her, but Aunt Natalya sobs at my feet and I cannot hear anything else.

"Leave," I command. "And never return."

A shuddering breath escapes from my Aunt as Jocelyn marches out of the compound. Jasper stares after her, shifting his weight like he might go too, but he glances at their mother and goes to her side.

Uncle Bruno kneels with Aunt Nat and Jasper. Then Lux. My mother meets my gaze. Slowly, she too sinks to her knees. Rune kneels before me next, leaving his sister and mother to decide. Aunt Zaria, still shaking, kneels. Dahlia doesn't break my stare as her body lowers, both knees hitting the floor.

I cross the distance, lifting Dahlia's chin, and forcing her dark eyes to peer into mine. "Why stay?"

Dahlia's lip curls, but she regains her composure, eyes traveling to her mother's shaking frame. "She won't survive without me."

I glance at Aunt Zaria who keeps her head lowered, avoiding my gaze.

I catch Eren's stare. *What do you think I should do?*

*'Sending her into exile would be giving Jocelyn an ally.'*

And cutting Dahlia off from her mother would give her a new reason to hate me.

*'You could ensure her loyalty with the Blood Oath,'* he suggests. *'See what her love for her mother is worth.'*

I take a moment, watching each of them bow their heads. I flip the dagger in my hand, extinguish the flames, and offer Dahlia the hilt. "I want your word in blood."

Dahlia snatches the blade from my grasp, ripping it across her palm and balling it into a fist before me. As the first drops of blood hit the floor, she speaks with no hesitation. "I, Dahlia Galvan, swear fealty to you, Sage Galvan. I will raise no blade nor hand against you. My sword is yours. My life is yours. From this day, until my last."

She speaks the words with conviction, but to what end?

With the Blood Oath sealed, I tuck the dagger back into its sheath. "Now, someone take me to my brother."

"Up here," Lux's voice trembles as she rises.

I follow her up the stairs, winding through the west wing of the compound where she stops at a carved door. "Will he live?"

"I don't know," she whispers, pale as a wraith. "He needs a Healer."

"Talk to Eren. We have someone."

Lux nods, leaving me to it.

I push open the door. Ash's room is filled with paintings and stone dragon figurines. Each painting depicts a scene more beautiful than the last, images of the five great cities and a dream beyond it—a lush green world only an artist would think of.

I follow the sounds of labored breathing to the bed. I brush dark curtains aside to find Ash under the blankets, beaten and bruised. Both eyes are swollen in shades of red and purple. A gash bleeds from his temple, staining the bandages placed over it. His chest is wrapped in bandages too, but the blankets hide the trails of larger bruises from my sight.

"Sage," he groans, his lip split.

I take his hand. "I'm here."

Ash tries to grin, but it's more of a grimace than he probably intends. "What is it?"

I shake my head. "Nothing. Are you okay?"

"You've lost something."

It takes everything within me not to shatter. I shake my head again, attempting a smile. "As long as you're here, I'm whole." I cradle Ash's hand to my face in the placement of a hug.

"Deon?"

"He's dead," I whisper, gauging the swollen plains of Ash's face for a reaction. "I killed him."

"Then that makes you…" Ash falls silent. Then a low rumble of laughter shakes his chest, turning into a fit of coughs and gasps as he winces. He chuckles softly. "You are amazing, Little Sister."

I laugh, even as tears fall. "I'm glad you finally think so."

"I've always thought so." He turns his head. "I'm sorry I wasn't a good brother to you. I thought I was protecting you, but… I smothered you. You needed a hand, not a shield." Ash watches the ceiling for a minute. "When he pointed the gun at you, I… I saw red. Once you got away, I challenged him without thinking, but I was winning. It came time to deliver the final blow and I hesitated. All I could think was that he was someone's father. *Rune's* father. I know you two never really got along, but he's my friend. The same way Jocelyn is your friend." I wince, hoping he doesn't notice. "I didn't want to kill him. I didn't want to kill anyone, but he wanted to kill me."

"He said Mom and Lux begged for your life."

Ash blinks at the ceiling. "I wouldn't know. I blacked out." He faces me once more. "Sage, you can change things now."

"We both will."

"No. It has to be *you*. Send word to the other Houses. Show them who you are."

"Ash," I start to stand, dropping his hand. "You need rest."

He reaches out, squeezing my hand with a force that doesn't match his broken body. "Send word."

I settle for a nod. Ash finally lets me go. I take a deep breath, exhaling once I'm out the door. I shut it behind me, resting my forehead on the wood.

"How did it go?" Eren leans against the wall with the hatchling snoozing on his shoulder, studying me.

I offer a tired half-smile, walking toward them. "He needs a Healer, but I think he'll live."

"I've already sent for Oddica."

I pet the hatchling with the pad of my finger. I'd forgotten about the other Houses. How will they take the news when it reaches them? How many are dead after the fight in the dunes? What chaos will unfold without any treaties in place? Are we meant to return to the war we started with?

Eren lifts my chin. "What is it?"

I sigh. "Ash thinks I should call the other Houses and show them who I really am."

A smile twitches at his lips. "Are you sure it wasn't the poppy juice talking?"

"I'm sure it was exactly that."

Eren brushes a stray hair from my face, seeming to consider the thought. "Why not?"

"Hmm?"

"Chantelle followed you. She gave you her Blood Oath freely."

I frown. "I'm not sure I would say freely. It was either that or rot in a dungeon with her family."

"Riders are stubborn. She would have rather spent her whole life down there than swear fealty to me. But she did it for you. Think about it."

I pause. *'Riders will never yield to the weak.'* Chantelle once told me. *'We'll never follow anyone who isn't one of us,'* she'd sworn, and her words rang true. It took a powerful, cunning leader like my father to get each House to agree to the treaty forged in the first Conclave. Even Uncle Deon sliding into his place did not make the Houses falter. He seized power for himself and they still followed him to attack a common enemy.

Chantelle refused to follow Eren for starting the rebellion. But Eren became a nightmare for Riders to fear. He had a dragon and power we'd never seen before. For the first time in centuries, Riders were scared.

A veil of madness drapes over my thoughts, quieting them all. There is one more debt to be paid, and I will not leave it unclaimed. "I have an awful idea."

"I love awful ideas."

"You," I snap my head to the guard on watch in the corridor. "Bring me my father's signet ring. You can cut it off my craven uncle's finger."

The guard nods, scurrying from the hall.

A sly grin slides onto Eren's face. "What has that devious little mind of yours thought of, Killer?"

"No one outside of this House knows my uncle is dead." I drift toward the window, watching the dawn rise. "We're going to hold one last Conclave."

# CHAPTER 32

## ~ EREN ~

*a*ll three heirs answer the summons.

Xavier Tesar and his brother Ronan are the first to arrive. Idahlia Althea, having barely escaped the blast, arrives with her daughter, Davina, following close behind them, exchanging tense glares.

"Traitor," Xavier spits. "Who invited scum like you?"

Idahlia keeps her cool, casting a withering look upon them. "This is a Conclave. All Riders attend."

"She's right." I step out from the shadows with a smirk. "Welcome."

Their eyes begin to search the chamber, landing on the waste of space named Deon Galvan staining the tiles red. My sweet Killer has a sense of humor, leaving his body as a warning to the others.

"What is this?" Xavier snarls, his brother's hand already reaching for his gun.

I chuckle. "We just want to talk."

"Then *talk*," a new voice enters. Valen Dysis darkens the room, his clothes still stained with Halcyon's blood. With *Sage's* blood. I lock eyes with him, the fire within me crackling to life, itching to incinerate him, but it's not my life to take. It's Sage's.

"Eren Noctis... or should I say, *Damon Valour.*"

I grin, taking a bow at the waist. I haven't changed from my leather uniform. If the Tesar brothers haven't made the connection, Valen just did it for them. "In the flesh."

Idahlia is the only one unsurprised, waiting patiently with her daughter.

"I have a proposition for you," Sage's voice echoes from the top of the stairs.

She starts to descend, rays of golden light leaking through the windows to wash her in their fiery glow. Chantelle and Lore guard each side of her, their faces cold. She's never looked more beautiful, or more deadly. The hatchling clings to her shoulders, its eyes scanning each being in the room. Fintan, Delphine, and Sage's family watch from the top of the stairs, holding their breath.

Valen's eyes narrow. "That's impossible. You should be dead."

"I'm not." She smirks. "But you will be." She turns her merciless gaze upon the room. "I challenge the Head of each House to the Ignis Mortem. You can swear fealty to me now instead, but do not refuse me. I will hunt you to the ends of the earth and kill you for the craven you are before I lay waste to your House."

She lets them stew in her words and I catch her stare with mine. She speaks like a Queen—Solasta reborn—and my chest swells with pride. The girl once overshadowed by her family now stands tall, brimming with power she's barely scratched the surface of. All will know her name and they will grow to fear it. Worship it as I do.

I take the first step, dropping to one knee and swiping my dagger over my palm, making a fist and squeezing. "I, Eren Noctis, swear fealty to you, Sage Galvan."

My life has been nothing more than one dark night, but now

the brightest star shines before them all, lighting the way out. There is no one better suited or more deserving of the Blood Oath than her. I'd carve my own heart out and lay it at her feet if she wished it.

Idahlia hesitates. She's a smart woman, a strategist, but to forfeit the autonomy of your House is a gamble even the wisest ruler would take time to consider. It's a shame she doesn't have any.

"I accept your challenge." Xavier steps forward, taking a dagger from his brother.

Sage gives him a lethal smile and whispers to her hatchling. The creature flaps its wings, flying from her shoulder to mine. She unsheathes the sword on her back. Magenta flames spurt from the blade, causing everyone to jump back in surprise.

*Bloodfire.* A magic so old it's been forgotten. A power so great, Sage hasn't begun to fathom what she can do with it.

Only Valen remains still, watching in malicious fascination.

Xavier holds his ground. He cuts at her blade, metal upon metal singing a sharp tune. Sage follows the momentum, countering his blow with one of her own. He leans back to avoid the slice of her flames, but he leaves himself open. She hooks her ankle behind his and shoves him back, forcing him to stumble, and advances, but Xavier regains his balance, parrying the smack of her blade. For a brief second, he gains the upper hand, forcing Sage back one step after another. But Sage is smarter than she allows anyone to see.

She lunges to the right, leading Xavier on. Rather than strike with her blade she swings her foot at his leg, kicking his knee with an audible *crunch*. Xavier screams and Sage pounces, swiping for the wrist holding his sword.

*Slice.*

Xavier's hand thumps to the tile. She grabs a fistful of his hair, dragging his head back to look at her. She holds her flaming dagger to his neck. "Yield!"

Xavier bares his teeth, mad with pain. "Never!"

She relieves his head from his shoulders.

The blade cuts through his neck like paper, searing the stump right off of his body. As his torso drops, Sage swings the head to the others, her face half-splattered in blood like the Maiden of Death. *"Stand against me and die!"*

Idahlia and her daughter sink to their knees, swiping their daggers across their palms. "We swear fealty to you, Sage Galvan. From this day, until our last."

Sage drops the head, kicking it to Valen where it rolls to a stop in front of his boots. She points her weapon. "You're next."

Valen grins, stepping into the ring of Bloodfire that surges. He stalks toward her, freeing the sword from his belt. Sage readies her stance, gripping her dagger tight. If there's any hesitation left, it dies on the sigh of the first swing.

Valen swings his sword, meeting her blade with a heavy smack of steel. She swipes his blade to the side with hers, countering with a swing to his neck. He parries her blow, striking back with double the force. She blocks a jab at her thigh, aiming for his torso in return. Valen reels back, swiping at her feet instead. She sidesteps the attack, twirling with her blade. Despite Valen's effort to dodge, it swipes across his bicep, cauterizing his flesh.

He roars and rushes her, swinging his sword from left to right, forcing her to retreat. Her thigh is slashed in the process, but she does not falter. Sage deflects the next blow, spinning into his orbit. While he tries to lean back, putting distance between them, she uses his momentum against him. Sage reaches out, slamming the pommel of her sword into his face. His nose gushes red, pouring with blood. It's enough to stun him, but she does it again, this time with her fist. Valen stumbles back, but Sage latches onto his arm and drives her blade through his throat.

He gasps, a choking, garbled sound. She banishes the flames, twisting the steel in his windpipe as he stares, wide-eyed.

"I'll see you in Hell," she whispers, pushing him off.

Valen collapses, gurgling as his body twitches. He stills, dead at last.

Sage breathes, craning her neck to the ceiling, popping the bones within it. She sets her gaze upon Ronan Tesar, the last Heir. Ronan swallows once, lowering his knees to the floor. He takes the blade offered by Idahlia and slices his palm. "I swear fealty to you, Sage Galvan. From this day, until my last."

But it's not enough. Their words are sealed in blood, but why stop there? The Dragon Lords will always vie for more power. If left unchecked, they will seek ways to break their oaths, slithering between loopholes. Dominion must be established, lest they forget their vows, and the time has never been more right.

I step forward into the power vacuum left in Sage's wake. "Hail the Dragon Queen of the Celosia Desert! Long live Sage Galvan, the one true Heir!"

*My Maiden of Death.*

# EPILOGUE

## ~SAGE~

*I* want to believe there is a world in which I am the hero, but I don't think heroes are as wicked as I am. I stare at my palms, tracing the scars that line them. It's been weeks since I washed away the blood, but they feel no cleaner.

Seraphine stretches from her perch on the railing of the balcony. She's grown to the size of a large cat, shedding black scales left and right in favor of larger ones. I look up at the full-length mirror, studying those tiny scales stitched to the bodice of my dress. Halcyon's scales have been carved by dragon-tooth drills, shaving them down into chest and shoulder plates. The strongest armor known to the Celosia desert, now worn by its Queen.

*Queen.* The word still feels foreign on my tongue.

There hasn't been a monarch since the Age of Conquest when our ancestors discovered this land and built a home. Until they betrayed Queen Solasta, slaying her and splitting into the Houses we know today.

*The Houses you took by force.*

I grimace at the sunset, finding no comfort in it. I have no doubt they will find ways around the Blood Oath to defy me, and why wouldn't they? I changed everything.

Along with forming a new monarchy, a Council has been established. Representatives from each city have a seat on the Council, non-Riders voted in by the people of their territories. The Heads of each House do not keep a seat on this Council. It's now my job to represent their interests. But the High Mages of each city do.

I watch members of the Council arrive through the streets of Solera, parking in front of Solera's Capitol building where I observe from above.

A knock taps at the door.

"Come in."

Eren slinks to my side, leaning against the wall. "What's on your mind, Killer?"

I shake my head, coming away from the balcony. On the dresser near the mirror, a silver crown of diamonds and rubies sits untouched. Two dragons fold into each other, rubies planted into their eye sockets, a beautiful homage to Seraphine.

"Did you come to check on me?"

Eren hesitates. I turn, finding his eyes already on me.

"I have something to tell you."

"Okay," I say slowly, unsure of what brought this on.

"You are my Queen." He steps closer with a new fierceness in his eyes. "And I love you. From this day, until my last, I will love you. Because of that, I need to tell you a secret my family has carried with us from the age of Solasta."

My heart stutters. "What kind of secret?"

"There was never a conquest." He looks into my eyes with a grim expression. "Look around you. There was nothing here to conquer. It was an exodus."

"Eren, what are you saying?"

"There is a lush, green world beyond the Wastelands. It's a place where magic thrives. It's a world our ancestors fled."

I shake my head. "No. No one survives beyond the Wastes. You said it yourself, no one is ever seen again."

"Queen Solasta had her High Mage place a curse on the borders beyond the Wastes. Anyone who dares to cross it will die, that's why they're never seen again. That's why it is forbidden."

I laugh in disbelief. "That's impossible. What you're saying doesn't make sense. Why the hell would we abandon a world like that for this one?"

"Bloodfire."

I blink and he closes the distance, taking my hands in his own. "The fire you wield isn't like mine. It's a power I can't begin to explain. It nearly wiped our ancestors out. But if knowing this isn't enough–if you want to find that world and take it for yourself, I will follow you. I will not leave your side, not unless you command it."

I yank my hands from him, stepping back. "Why are you telling me this now?"

"Because," he pulls a velvet box from his coat, opening it. A gold sun with a fiery opal center winks at me. "You are Solasta's one true heir and this belongs to you."

*The necklace.* A breath escapes my lips. This is the amulet Veronique searched for, the necklace her ancestors crafted for Solasta.

"Solasta shared your same gift, it's why her people killed her, but upon her death, my family took her amulet–the key to escaping the Wastes–and hid it until her Bloodfire heir returned. That power is dormant right now, Sage, but as Seraphine grows it will only get stronger."

I glance at my dragon nestled on the railing. *Bloodfire.* If what Eren says is true, not only have I shattered the world of Riders, but I might be the thing that incinerates it. I look out to the world beyond, gripping the railing with both hands. The metal glows, warping under my touch.

I sense the Bloodfire within me, a writhing beast crackling below the surface. In truth, I don't think there are any heroes or villains in a story, but if you ask me where I think I stand between the two, I can only think of one answer.

I hear him close the box, his footfalls approaching my side.

"Come, Sage." Eren offers his arm. "We have a coronation to attend."

*Neither.*

I am something much worse.

# ACKNOWLEDGMENTS

First, to Jake, the love of my life, my husband, and my best friend. Thank you for providing me with endless snacks, encouraging me to drink water, and for reminding me that I'm a human who needs real sustenance and not just coffee to properly function. Your patience knows no bounds and I am forever thankful to call you my other half. I love you. Always and Forever.

To Chantz and Kay, for always listening to the initial pitches and ramblings of newly formed ideas. For being nothing short of family. For years of friendship, misadventure, and endless more to come.

To my Book Club full of brilliant young women: Sav, Em, Zae, and Kait. Meeting you girls will forever be the most wonderful happenstance I have ever been a part of. Writing can be a very lonely journey, but you girls changed that part of my life for the better. You all championed this book before ever reading it, gave me invaluable feedback, and provided excellent recommendations for my TBR list. Thank you all for beta-reading the dumpster-fire versions, keeping me sane during imposter syndrome, cheering me on, and crushing it at bookish events. I love you ladies so much.

To my Mom for reading bedtime stories when I was little—even when I tried to rewrite the words. To my Dad, for working so hard to provide for our family. For smiling so big every time I come home. To my baby sister, Kendra, for being the smartest, strongest little girl I know. I love you all so much.

To my friends and extended family, for showing me endless love and support. Thank you for your kindness and for making me feel so loved.

To Mrs. Brams, my fifth grade teacher who took me by my hands and told me, "Never stop writing." I heard your voice for years, and I still do.

"Thanks to Gage for being built different, not sweating on my book, not dying in a trailer, not losing his toe, and actually finishing the drafts I sent." Gage, my friend, thank you for being my first beta-reader. No, I have not downloaded Warframe.

To Tony, for listening to my story ideas over the years and for building the PC that most of this book was written on. I hope your life is filled with an endless supply of Dr. Pepper and Nacho Cheese Doritos.

To my cats: Luna, Calvin, Tina, and MooMoo for always keeping my lap warm, for keeping me company in a quiet home, and for reminding me of the little things. And to Cuddles, for being the cutest sidekick and Book Club mascot.

To Skippy and Cinder who are no longer with us, but were there for all of the stories that led me to this one. I miss you so much.

And to you, Dear Reader, because I always save the best for last. Thank you, for picking up my book and giving it a chance. As a debut author, I am terrified in the most wonderful way. Thank you, sincerely, for embarking on this journey with me. I hope to see you again soon for Book 2 and for many other stories I have yet to tell.

# ABOUT THE AUTHOR

Iris Quinn is based in the Mojave Desert. When she isn't day-dreaming of faraway worlds and steamy love-interests on company time, she can likely be found cuddled up with a cat and a warm cup of coffee. Dynasty is her debut novel, and she hopes to have the privilege of writing for the rest of her life.

Follow her journey on irisquinnauthor.com
or TikTok, Instagram, and all other platforms.
(@irisquinnauthor)